D1178686

DEATH SENTENCE

Also by B.M. Allsopp

Death of a Hero - How it all began

Death on Paradise Island

Death by Tradition

Death Beyond the Limit

B.M.ALLSOPP

DEATH
SENTENCE

FIJI ISLANDS MYSTERIES 4

Coconut Press

First published in Australia in 2021 by Coconut Press

Copyright © B.M. Allsopp 2021

www.bmallsopp.com

Contact the author by email at bernadette@bmallsopp.com

Print book ISBN 978-0-648891I-4-7

E-book ISBN 978-0-648891I-3-0

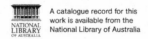 A catalogue record for this work is available from the National Library of Australia

Exclusive to Fiji Fan Club members

One of the things I've learned about my readers is that they are just as fascinated by the lovely islands of Fiji as I am. If you enjoy this book, I invite you to join my *Fiji Fan Club*. I'll welcome you with something new to read that you won't find in any book store. I'll tell you more after you've finished this mystery.

THE PRINCIPAL ISLANDS OF FIJI

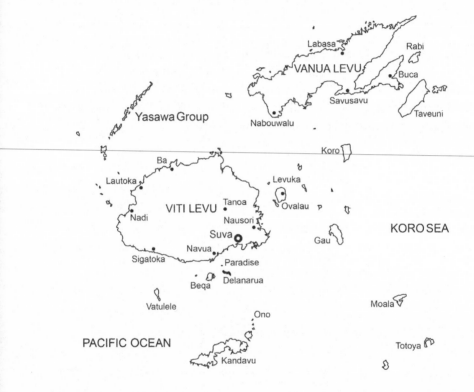

Labasa
Rabi
VANUA LEVU
Buca
Savusavu
Taveuni
Yasawa Group
Nabouwalu
Koro
Ba
Levuka
Lautoka
Tanoa
Ovalau
VITI LEVU
KORO SEA
Nadi
Nausori
Suva
Gau
Navua
Sigatoka
Paradise
Delanarua
Beqa
Vatulele
Moala
Ono
PACIFIC OCEAN
Totoya
Kandavu

AUTHOR'S NOTE: The village of Tanoa is fictitious, as are Paradise and Delanarua islands.
Other places on this map are real, but nearly 300 exquisite small islands
are omitted.

PROLOGUE

The two constables didn't see the child at first. As they entered the fowl yard, squawking hens rushed them—jumping, beating their wings, raking their rivals with their talons. The flurry of feathers and dust died when the birds discovered the strangers did not bring food. In a fury of loud clucks, they stalked off, cruel eyes glaring.

Inside, the shed was dim. The shaft of light from the doorway fell short of the nesting boxes, whose occupants clucked in mild protest. Movement in the straw caught one constable's eye. She stepped closer.

An arm, not a wing, enfolded matted human hair.

'Come, come, what have we here?'

She brushed away the heaped straw. The trembling child kept on cradling his head. His long hair, filthy and studded with debris, cloaked his back. Congealed dirt and faeces coated his skin. He stank.

'Come, come, little one. Let's look at you. Stand up.'

She tried to lift the emaciated child to his feet, but he seemed stuck in his squat. He uttered soft, guttural clucks, his head bobbing. He squawked when the constable patted his back. Could all his little scabs be peck wounds?

Suddenly, his head jerked. Still squatting, he waddled two steps and dipped his head. He pecked up a shred of cabbage, chewed and swallowed.

The other constable switched on his radio. 'Sir, we've found the boy in the farm's chicken shed. He's in a bad way.'

TUESDAY

eleven years later

1

Detective Inspector Josefa Horseman dashed into the cool of the lobby. It was after five o'clock and the bar was busy with most tables taken. He spotted his friends through the glass walls, laughing together out on the shady terrace.

He squeezed around a table blocking the doorway. Detective Sergeant Susila Singh glanced towards the opening and waved. Dr Matthew Young turned around and grinned. Horseman pointed back at the bar and went to place his order. When he joined them, he lowered himself into his chair, sliding his right leg under the table, hoping they wouldn't notice.

'Ordered, mate?' Dr Young asked as a young waiter served him with a Fiji bitter and Susie with a Chapman soda.

'Sure have. Go ahead, don't wait for me.' He eased his knee slowly to an oblique angle under the table.

'What did you do to make your leg stiff?'

Horseman gave up. 'I don't know—probably spent too much time in the station today.'

'Hmm...what have you got to say on the matter, Susie? Has he been sneaking out to jog in the midday sun?'

Singh looked at him, amused. Even in the shade, her green eyes sparkled like the sunlit sea. 'If he has, he's been doing that behind my back. We're flat out getting every file and bit of paperwork in impeccable order for our new superintendent. At least I have been. I can't keep my eye on what my boss does every moment, of course.'

The waiter must have rushed Horseman's order, because he set down the icy Fiji Bitter only moments later on a coaster bearing the national rugby emblem and message: *Holiday Inn Suva proudly supports the Flying Fijians.*

'*Bula,*' they chorused as they raised their drinks. Already their glasses ran with rivulets of condensation.

'Still no word on the appointment?' Dr Young asked.

Horseman shrugged. 'None that's reached me.'

'Isn't that odd?'

'I reckon. I've been thinking the commissioner wants to bring in a super who doesn't want to move to Suva.'

'Why, mate? Suva would be the top of the tree, wouldn't it?'

Horseman drained his glass. After all his years in Fiji, Matt didn't reason like a Fijian.

'Not necessarily. There's the pull of relatives and place, and fear of the city by people who've never lived here.'

'And Suva's so expensive if you don't have relatives here to help you out. Rent for a decent house? School fees?' Singh added.

Horseman nodded. He was still boarding with Matt ten months after his return to Suva, and he needed to get his own place. It wasn't only the rent. Suva's supply of accommodation was in crisis.

'Of course, if the commish intends to promote a chief inspector to the job, those considerations wouldn't apply so much. Only the most contented chief inspector would resist a promotion to stay in his rut. Or her rut.' He smiled at Singh.

'Are there any women chief inspectors?' Dr Young looked doubtful.

'One in Public Relations, and one in Training,' Singh replied. 'None in CID—no inspectors, for that matter.'

The observant waiter served them another round of drinks and small bowls of banana crisps and bhuja.

'Here's to you, Susie. You'll be the first detective inspector in the force!' Singh's irritated frown melted away as she flicked her black hair behind her shoulders and clinked her glass against Dr Young's.

The hubbub of conversation died as Fiji One's six o'clock news fanfare blared from the big TV on the side wall. The newsreader leaned forward to the camera, her eyes wide.

'Just in, the Controller of Prisons has announced the impending release of the notorious child abuser, Mr Dev Reddy, after serving only eleven years of a twenty-year sentence. Every adult in Fiji will remember the 'chicken-boy,' the most appalling and grotesque case of child cruelty ever to occur in Fiji's child-loving islands. From early childhood, Kanan was kept in a fowl yard by his father for eight years before the police took any interest in a neighbour's reports. Naked and alone, the toddler was abandoned to the mercy of chickens, his only source of food, warmth, and comfort.

'The public reacted with outrage.

'Viewers will recall, experts who studied cases of children brought up by animals predicted that Kanan might learn human ways following his rescue. Our investigation indicates that this happened only to a limited extent.'

Dr Young looked grave. Singh and Horseman exchanged horrified looks.

'We'll cross now to the government buildings in Suva, where the Controller of Prisons, Ratu Savenaca Tuilau, has agreed to answer our questions on your behalf.

'Ratu, sir, are you responsible for releasing this convicted child torturer and abuser only halfway through his sentence?'

'As Controller of Prisons, I am responsible for all approvals of parole and remissions of sentences.'

'Eleven years ago, the public disapproved of Dev Reddy's twenty-year sentence. Most people were so outraged by his cruelty, they wanted him put away for life. Do you think the citizens of Fiji have forgotten this unpardonable crime after only eleven years?'

Ratu Tuilau looked at the interviewer with the kindly condescension of his chiefly rank. 'I don't expect many people have forgotten, and any who have will certainly remember now. Quite rightly, the public played no part in Mr Reddy's trial and sentencing, and they played no part in the decision to approve his application for parole.'

'Ratu, representing the public interest, may I...'

'When considering each and every application for parole, my officers do indeed consider the public interest, balancing that with the interest of the prisoner, the interest of any victims of the prisoner's crime, and of their families.'

'With respect, Ratu, how can you put a child abuser's welfare ahead of the safety of the public?'

'Where did you get that idea from? It is not the media's role to whip up public fear. My office will release a statement about Mr Reddy's remission of sentence at ten o'clock tomorrow morning. For now, let me assure your viewers that the public is in no danger whatsoever from his release.'

While Horseman's mind raced, his heart lurched with grim foreboding. Remission of sentence for Reddy? More like a death sentence if Fiji One has anything to do with it.

***

'Didn't you two know about this?' Dr Young looked from Horseman to Singh, who both shook their heads, bewildered.

Horseman shrugged. 'I think the controller wanted to announce this tomorrow. Maybe Security Division knows about it and has plans to protect Reddy. Let's hope so. But it's weird for CID not to be involved in identifying threats to Reddy and his family. At least. Even to Kanan, the chicken-boy himself.'

'Fiji One's identifying the threat to the public—trust them to do that,' Singh waved at the TV.

On the screen, a smug-looking reporter was accosting people in the street, mostly middle-aged women, inviting them to share their outrage at the release of Dev Reddy. Plenty were eager to voice anger, fear, anxiety or whatever the interviewer wished in return for the chance to appear on television.

'She's just across the road, on Victoria Parade. I'll go out and put in my two-cents worth. She's missing the viewpoint of a middle-aged Australian man.' Dr Young hauled himself upright and walked back inside.

Singh's hand flew to her mouth. 'He's not really going to—is he?'

Horseman shrugged. '*Oi lei*, who knows? Let's keep watching.'

They angled their chairs to face the screen, but Dr Young's lanky figure and sandy head didn't appear, not even in the background. Eventually, the street interviews ended. and Dr Young returned with fresh drinks, followed by a waiter with dishes of baked cassava wedges, chilli sauce, and battered fish cocktails.

Dr Young grinned. 'The camera veered away from me no matter which angle I approached from. Lucky I put this order in on my way out. I may have been deprived of my democratic voice, but at least I can eat and bore my friends.'

Horseman doubted whether Matt had really tried to get on the street interviews, but his friend and landlord sometimes surprised him. '*Vinaka*, thanks, Matt. Just what I need.'

Singh pulled in her chair, and Dr Young loaded her plate. They ate with relish. The batter was crisp, the fish morsels moist. The cassava was fluffy inside the salted skin.

Horseman pondered his reaction to the news. Reddy's release announcement had been leaked to the press, which was stirring up a furore. He imagined later news bulletins, revivals of footage of the case from eleven years ago, the headlines in the morning papers, the radio interviews and talk-back programs. The details in the controller's official release at half-past-ten would be completely swamped by hysteria whipped up by the media. All under the guise of 'public interest'.

Had Security Division been warned? He'd better contact the chief superintendent. He hoped he'd be told to mind his own business, that plans were drawn up and ready to go.

Dr Young shoved the bowl with the last two wedges at him. 'Not like you to avoid food, mate. Finish these off.'

He was surprised by the concern on both smiling faces. 'Sorry—just remembering how unpredictable a mob can be. I think I'll go back to the station, see if I can suss out what's happening. We're without a super, so I feel kind of responsible for CID's response.' He ate a wedge. Past its peak fitness, like him.

'I'll come, too. I'd like to help,' Singh said.

'No, you go home. Really, I just need to reassure myself Security is aware of the media coverage.'

'Exactly. I won't be able to sleep not knowing. And I'll never get to be an inspector if you don't let me in on this behind-the-scenes stuff.'

Horseman raised his hands in surrender.

WEDNESDAY

2

Detective Chief Superintendent Tawaga was just as shocked by the news of Reddy's impending release as Horseman.

'You'd better come with me to Security's joint meeting on the matter at eight. Police HQ. Always a good idea to have an outsider along who can talk common sense. And they'll listen to you. Never fathomed why anyone would want to listen to rugby players. In my humble opinion, rugby is for watching. But there it is.'

Just before eight, Horeman and DCS Tawaga joined the assembled officers. After the Security chief listened to complaints about the lack of notice from Prisons and the alarmist media reporting, the meeting settled to planning for the worst case: that public demonstrations would spill into the streets of Suva, become violent, leading to injuries, damage to property and opportunistic looting. At the extreme, lives could be lost. But no one expected that in Fiji.

The police band was touring New Zealand, which meant both the Riot Squad and Traffic were short of officers. Still, a plan evolved that made the best of what they had.

'DCS Tawaga, have you any suggestions to add to the draft plan? From the CID point of view?' the Security chief asked.

'*Io*, yes, sir. Just to let you know, I've authorised DI Horseman to review Reddy's release and any features of the case that may prove pertinent to the public security risk we now face.' DCS Tawaga nodded to Horseman, who sat beside him. 'Of course, Joe Horseman needs no introduction to any of you.'

Horseman wished his superiors wouldn't bring up his rugby fame like this, but he nodded amiably to the table.

Tawaga continued. 'The review needs to be a quick and dirty one—'

'It should be quick, with Joe on the job,' a voice called out.

Chuckles rippled around the table.

The Security chief cut in. 'Detective Inspector, I realise you haven't started on your task yet, but what are your initial questions?'

'I want to identify specific threats to security—names of groups and individuals. Who threatened Reddy during the investigation eleven years ago? I remember he received threats during the trial and the judge cleared the court several times. Who disrupted the trial? Who demonstrated at the sentencing? I'll also find out about threats to Reddy inside prison. Reddy served part of his sentence in St Giles, so I'll find out what I can from the psychiatrists there.'

'Good. Just bear in mind the object of our protection isn't Reddy; it's public order.'

'*Io*, sir. I assumed it was important to keep Reddy safe from anyone who threatened to harm him.'

'The whole country wants to harm him, man!'

Horseman hesitated to contradict his senior officer. 'That's the general mood at the moment. But it seems to me there won't be many individuals who will seek him out to assault him or worse. I hope to identify those few individuals. Or some of them at least.' As he articulated his swirling ideas, his initial confidence drained away.

'The usual problem applies—we can't arrest offenders until they offend. Still, your intelligence will be welcome, Joe,' the Security chief replied.

'Sir, do you agree it could be more effective to provide Reddy with personal protection?' Horseman asked before he caught DCS Tawaga's glare.

The Security chief chuckled. 'I'll need to see the evidence you come up with first, eh?' But your approach is sound. Remember, the emphasis is on evidence. What you'll be hearing from psychiatrists is simply medical opinion.'

'*Io*, sir.'

'*Vinaka*, thank you, for coming this morning and taking this job on.'

A uniform entered and handed a fax to the chief. He skimmed it and looked around the table. 'Prisons has sent through the text of their official announcement. Hardly advance notice—just eighty minutes ahead of the entire world! Well, DI Horseman, you have forty-eight hours before Reddy walks free at ten-hundred hours on Friday. Keep in close touch with DCS Tawaga, who'll liaise with me. Our plans will be fine-tuned before then, but we'll adjust them if your intelligence warrants that.'

'*Vinaka*, sir,' Horseman said. No pressure then. And when would his new super arrive?

***

When Horseman got back to the station, he found the young detective constables crowding around Singh's desk.

'Have you got the notice from Prisons?' Horseman asked.

'Came through here ten minutes ago,' Singh replied.

'Let's see. The security chief just waved it about.'

'It says nothing useful except Reddy's release date.'

'Even so, that's the deadline for CID's intelligence report. That means forty-eight hours for you and me to come up with a list of potential threats to public safety. DC Musudroka, get us a big pot of tea. I'll need to spend the rest of the morning refreshing my memory of the case. I'm sure DS Singh's memory never needs refreshing, but I see she's got hold of the case files.'

'Kau's photocopying the most relevant parts for us,' Singh said. 'I was at teachers' college when they discovered the chicken-boy. I remember the uproar in the media—it was huge and went on for a long time, what with the trial and follow-ups on what happened to the poor little boy. But it was a Suva story. People in the west, including me, didn't feel so involved. So I need to study the file just as much as these DCs who were in primary school then and only interested in rugby.'

DC Apolosi Kau entered and placed piles of collated photocopies on the table, careful to arrange them in sequence. Singh checked each was complete, assembled the components into four bundles, and annotated each title page with initials in purple, yellow, green, and red. Kau placed the bundles into four waiting box files and stuck corresponding coloured stickers on the lids. Singh wrote the initials on the labels. This was her way of making each officer responsible for one copy, and woe betide anyone who mislaid theirs. Horseman smiled to himself.

When Musudroka returned with the loaded tea tray, they each took a large mug and looked expectantly at Horseman.

'I don't know much more than Sergeant Singh. I didn't work on the case, and I was away playing internationals during most of Reddy's trial. Eleven years ago, there was no easy Internet access to Fiji media overseas. I saw newspapers that were airmailed to the team so we wouldn't feel totally cut off. Once Reddy was sentenced, the furore died down, and the media moved on. I need to study the file just as hard as you three.'

Singh scattered pencils, highlighters, and coloured Post-it stickers on the table. 'Apo and Tani, please take notes as you skim. As I always say, it adds to your reading time at first, but it'll become second nature to you and save you tons of time down the track. Helps your memories, too. Mark up your files with questions, highlight main points, any contradictions, any points missed you'd expect to be there. Use the stickers so you can find what you've marked fast.'

Kau nodded, serious, helped himself to highlighters and stickers, and put on his glasses. Musudroka grinned and took his time pondering the choice of colours. '*Oi lei*, what if I get my colours wrong?' He ran his hands through his wavy hair.

Horseman was impatient at Musudroka's mock anxiety. His own anxiety about this case review was all too real. 'Don't waste time, Tani. You don't know how lucky you are to have DS Singh as your sergeant. She's the most methodical detective in the force. She's training you in her secret methods. You're on the inside track already, man! Unless you throw away the chance.'

'*Io*, sir.' Musudroka was shocked. Horseman usually tolerated the young DC's joking.

'We have less than two days to identify risks to public order posed by Reddy's release from custody. While I don't remember any details about the case, a few things puzzled me in the media coverage back then. The first strange thing was that the boy was locked in with the chickens for eight years on a small farm without any neighbours or relatives knowing, or at least reporting this. Is this possible, only ten kilometres from Nausori and Suva airport?'

'Weird, sir.' Musudroka was trying to make up for his frivolity. 'But there are Indian farming families in my district who keep themselves to themselves. Often because the head of the family is a dictator.'

Singh nodded. 'You're right. Such monstrous behaviour couldn't be hidden in a Fijian village. But Indian farmers live on their lease holdings, widely separated. Even so...'

'Good—keep an eye out for any clues to that in the file. The second thing I couldn't work out at the time was why no relatives came forward to look after the abused boy, Kanan. I vaguely remember several of Reddy's children had emigrated to Australia and New Zealand, but some were in Fiji. Kanan was a late child, born many years after the next youngest. Not long after his mother died, the remaining children left their father and Kanan on their own. Kanan ended up in the chicken house.'

'It's incredible,' Kau said, frowning. 'Reddy must be insane.'

'He must,' Horseman said. 'He might have ordered them all off his land. Family disputes are nothing new. But it's very difficult to run a farm single-handed. Whoever worked for Reddy must have known about Kanan. Still, when the case blew up in the media, Kanan's brothers and sisters, uncles, aunts and cousins would eventually have heard the story, even in Australia and New Zealand. Why didn't any of them take him in?'

'Maybe they offered.'

'Look into that.'

'He's profoundly disabled, or so we're led to believe,' Singh said.

'The media also claimed experts would be consulted about Kanan's behaviour and education,' Horseman added. 'Maybe his relatives thought they weren't qualified to educate him.'

'Poor kid. Where is he now?'

'Sunshine Home, somewhere near Namadi. I guess credit's due to the media for not harassing the child. I wonder why? You'd think in a slow-news week, a follow-up human interest story on Kanan would fill a page and attract interest.'

'Apparently, there are no miracles to report.'

'Right—let's start on our files. Two hours of study, then we draw up our investigation plan.'

Horseman tried to model his sergeant's superlative note-taking skills as a demonstration to the young probationers, but her faultless method didn't come easily to him. Rather than display his own fragmentary notes to the boys, after half an hour he took his box file to his own desk and made much better progress doing the job his own way. Months ago, he'd adopted Singh's coloured highlighters and stickers for his files, which sped up retrieving elusive facts. But his own skimpy, scrappy notes made more sense to him when he was thinking things through.

He'd finished the original investigation file and prosecution submission and was starting on the surprisingly slim trial transcript when his phone rang. It was Chief Superintendent Tawaga.

'Joe, the deputy commissioner has just confirmed the appointment of the new acting detective superintendent of Suva Central CID. In other words, you've got a new boss. I'm ringing you and the other inspectors individually before the appointment's gazetted, so each of you can tell your own teams.'

The chief's booming bass voice was a hoarse whisper. Horseman waited a beat. 'Acting superintendent, sir?'

'Ah, excuse me. A messenger was in my office. Now I can speak. *Io*, the appointee's rank has been one holdup in settling this. He's currently chief inspector for the Western Islands, and as such, the most senior CID officer in that—um, shall we say, lightly populated district. Some on the appointments board felt a promotion to head up CID at Suva Central was a step too steep. Others pointed out he is experienced in command, no matter the classification of his position.'

Horseman knew he would never make senior command. Even if he did, the mind-numbing bureaucratic machinations would drive him to drink, or at least to the punching bag in the gym. He couldn't succeed because he'd never last through the long, drawn-out series of skirmishes to win a battle or negotiate a truce. His mind wandered—did he know anyone in the Western Islands district? He could only think of one detective and a uniform sergeant. He'd never even heard of the top cop in CID.

The unforgettable name wrenched his mind back to the chief. Had he heard right?

'Do you know him at all, Joe?'

'Sorry, sir. I didn't catch the name.'

'Saula Ratini. You haven't served under his command, but you might have run into him on a course or something.'

He hadn't thought about Ratini for years. Now, the name dredged up nightmares from long before he'd joined the police. He'd been just eighteen years old, proud to be selected for the university's first-grade rugby team. And incredibly naïve.

'Is this the same Saula Ratini who was a detective sergeant in Suva around twelve or thirteen years ago?' He prayed it was a different man.

'*Io*, that's right. When he was promoted to DI, he took up a vacancy in Western Islands. Been there ever since. Been DCI there for five years now. It's high time he got back to a town again, in my humble opinion. But you would've been just a kid when Ratini was at Suva Central.'

'I was, sir. A first-year student at the University of the South Pacific.'

'I'm curious—how did you run across Ratini?'

'I was unlucky enough to discover the body of USP's rugby captain in the changing shed. DS Ratini interviewed me several times.'

'Rough, eh?'

'DS Ratini?'

'Was he?'

He decided he should be open with Tawaga about that terrifying time. Without complaining, if he could. Clearly, the chief super was sussing out potential problems between Ratini and his DIs. Maybe there were reasons other than seniority why Ratini was only going to be an acting superintendent to begin with.

'Sir, I was completely ignorant of police procedure. I wanted to help my captain's family. I realise now I must have been a nuisance, asking questions. But DS Ratini treated me as the chief suspect in Seru's murder. He seemed to hate university students and enjoyed me squirming on the end of his stick.'

Tawaga's bass chuckle surprised Horseman. Had he said too much?

'Yet you joined the force yourself. Ratini didn't put you off. I hope you didn't join to get your revenge.'

'Not at all, sir. Ratini had moved on when I joined. DI Navala, the SIO on that case, persuaded me to join up.'

'Oh, how did he do that?'

'He said Police would always beat USP at rugby.'

The chief chuckled again. '*Oi lei*, he's a clever man. You must miss Navala.'

'*Io*, it's only during the last three weeks since he's retired that I realise what a great super he was. I've been lucky.' He refrained from saying he thought his luck in superiors had run out.

'DCI Ratini is known for his "tough cop" approach with witnesses, especially potential suspects, so I don't doubt you remember your experience accurately. The man does come on strong. However, he gets results, consistent results. It's his success in closing cases that's got him promoted.'

'I hope I can learn from him, sir.' He heard the insincerity in his own voice.

'I do, too, Joe. You're much too young to be set in your ways.'

'True. Sir, when does DCI Ratini take up the job? Four of us are studying the Reddy files, and I expect to have an enquiry plan ready by early afternoon. Then we can get cracking. That's if you want us to go ahead. But DCI Ratini will want to do things his way.'

'I'll bring him down to the station around eleven o'clock tomorrow. Remember, he'll be acting superintendent by then, and I'm sure he'll expect you to use his correct title.'

'*Io*, sir.'

'And I want you to go full steam ahead on the Reddy enquiry. You need to brief Security by Friday morning at the latest. Preferably end of Thursday. It's good experience for you in inter-divisional teamwork, Joe.'

'Acting Superintendent Ratini may not want me in charge, sir.'

Tawaga's chuckle rumbled through the earpiece again. 'Nonsense, Joe. He will have forgotten you annoyed him years ago. He probably just put on that hostile front, anyway. You'll do a great job on the Reddy report.'

3

As soon as Horseman got a grasp on his own file, he joined the others at Singh's desk. He wasn't surprised she insisted Kau and Musudroka apply her file review system to the letter. But the probationers' frowning faces showed they were struggling.

'Chop, chop, now!' Her tone was brisk but not impatient.

'This is so slow, Sergeant! You finished ages ago, and you've been teaching us at the same time.'

Musudroka thumped his fists on the loose-leaf bundle of trial transcript he was reading, sending several pages fluttering off the edge of the desk. He scraped his chair back, bent forward and retrieved all but one of the pages. Kau leaned over and picked up the last one, handed it to Musudroka with a lift of his brows.

'Tani, you're in training. Of course you'll be slower than Inspector Horseman and me for a time. But believe me, you'll speed up and the system will become second nature to you. Don't you want to be quick? You certainly can't be promoted beyond DC if you can't review a case file. You could even be sent to Traffic or...'

Horseman intervened. Singh was right but he could understand Musudroka's frustration. 'I've finished and I need my lunch. You two do, too. You can eat here while you finish your job. Sergeant Singh and I will clear out. I reckon you can finish off before we get back.'

Musudroka groaned. 'Better make it a long lunch, sir.'

'Just to do you two a favour, I will. I'm feeling generous.'

Singh got the message and grabbed her shoulder bag. He clapped Musudroka on the back.

'You can do this, Tani,' he said. Then he followed Singh's swinging ponytail out of the office and down the stairs. As usual, not a shiny hair was out of place.

They emerged into harsh sunlight and oppressive heat. It took less than a minute to cross the road and gain the shade of the shop awnings opposite them, but Horseman's face was sweaty and his waistband felt damp already. He squinted to protect his eyes from the glare. Singh looked cool in her large sunglasses.

'Tawaga told me our new super's been appointed. I think it could be a disaster. I've got to talk it over with you. How about Arabica?' He shouted over the noise of midday crowded footpaths and traffic.

'Great. I need to get away from these diesel fumes.' She sneezed as if to demonstrate her point.

They ducked off Renwick Road and into a one-way lane edged with old colonial timber buildings, their balconies jutting over the roadway. Not many right angles in evidence here. Two more acute turns in the maze immersed them in therapeutic wafts from roasting coffee beans. The aroma intensified as Horseman pushed open the heavy warehouse door. He liked to patronise Arabica, which processed and exported Fiji's own coffee, grown in the highlands. His patriotic decision was helped by his addiction to strong espresso, acquired when he played professional rugby in Japan, of all places.

Didi, the manager, was determined to remain primarily a coffee merchant and roaster. He'd succumbed to demands from aficionados of Arabica's product to include a few tables in the old warehouse for tasting events. Later, he added a regular coffee menu. Now, he served sandwiches, scones and biscuits made and delivered by his mother daily.

'But this is as far as it goes,' Didi had protested. 'No tea, no food menu. No kitchen. The only thing we cook here is coffee beans!'

They sat at a tiny table in the corner and the waiter brought them coffee. He soon followed with corned beef and cucumber sandwiches.

'*Vinaka*,' Horseman said. 'This and the smell is all I need.'

'I can't wait to hear the news. I'll eat while you talk, sir.'

Singh steadily munched through precisely half the sandwiches while Horseman related his encounters with DS Ratini.

'He hated me. I still have no idea why. If he really was just a bully, what's he going to be like now? Over the last ten months, we've built up a good little team. I can see him wrecking it in a few days. Enjoying it, too.'

Singh pushed the plate of sandwiches towards him. 'Thanks for warning me. He sounds like a bully. But I hope he's become more mature and professional over the last thirteen years.'

'I hope so, too. But I'm not exaggerating, Susie. I shudder when I imagine him lording it in Super Navala's office.'

'Sir, it's okay anticipating the worst if you can prepare for it. But we can't. Let's keep open minds.'

'You see, I put it to Tawaga that he could release me from this Reddy report and give it to Ratini. But he refused. He needs it ready for Security tomorrow night.'

'Well? What could he do?'

'I know. I know Tawaga hasn't much choice. But he's set me up to rattle Ratini's cage before the guy even knows he's going to be my boss.'

Singh looked at him sympathetically, almost indulgently, like she would with the probationers. 'What's the worst that can happen?'

He ate a sandwich while he thought. 'I don't know, but it'll happen to me, not you.' The worst was that Ratini would undermine the trust the team had in him, Horseman. But he couldn't say that to Singh.

He swallowed his last mouthful. 'I'm going to keep on Ratini's good side. Whatever Tawaga says, I'll offer to hand over the Reddy file if that's what he wants. Now let's get back and get that plan together.'

4

'Right, let's begin. Singh, what did you get out of Prisons?'

'Only the bare records. Reddy went to hospital twice in his first year in Suva Prison, because of violent assault. A year later, he was referred to St Giles due to disturbed behaviour. St Giles admitted him as a long-term prison patient and he stayed for five years, then transferred to Naboro prison farm on the recommendation of the St Giles psychiatrist. He stayed there, apparently stable until eighteen months ago, when he suffered multiple injuries in a fight with another prisoner. After hospital treatment, he was sent back to St Giles, where he remains. Until Friday.'

'We need to fill in the gaps, especially about the attacks on him.'

'Yes, I managed to get an appointment with an officer who sounded helpful. I reminded him that public security depends on their cooperation. Three o'clock.'

'That should put the wind up them. Take Musudroka with you. I'm off to meet Dr Krish Acharya, the supervisor of St Giles. I'm not sure how much I'll get out of him—you know what doctors are like about patient confidentiality. I'll see if your emotional blackmail trick will open him up, Singh.'

Singh shrugged, smiling. 'You can only try.'

'Kau, I'd take you with me but I need you to comb through all the media coverage since Monday. Make a list of individuals and groups who are likely to take their protest to the streets, or to Reddy himself. He's likely to be the focus of any violence.'

Kau looked puzzled. 'But nobody cares what happens to him, sir.'

'*Io*, everyone wants to see him dead,' Musudroka agreed.

'Your *everyone* can't include the police, Tani. Apo, your *nobody* can't include us either. We're sworn to uphold the law, no matter what our private opinions are. The Fiji government holds Reddy in safe custody until Friday. After he's released, the police must protect him from threats and assaults. You know your duty, boys.'

'*Io*, sir.' The pair nodded.

***

The bad, the mad and the dead resided on the western fringe of Suva's central business district. The bad - or these days, those on remand - lived behind the decaying concrete wall of century-old Suva Prison, right opposite the Public Works Department jetty. The prison compound took up all the level ground up to the vertical green wall of the escarpment. At the top of the cliff, the mad sheltered in St Giles Hospital, Horseman's destination. As more than half the in-patients were prisoners, the proximity of the two institutions made sense. But Horseman had never visited St Giles before.

He continued on past the prison, past the Royal Suva Yacht Club on the left, and the large compound of St Elizabeth's, the former leprosy hospital, on the right. He turned right into Reservoir Road, which bordered the cemetery. The pandanus mats screening two new Fijian graves made the place look like a home for the dead rather than a disposal site. A group of mourners gathered around one grave, sweeping the mat-covered surface free of leaves and dust with coconut brooms.

Reservoir Road climbed steeply, looping past the Chinese cemetery, then the military cemetery, until it came to the driveway to St Giles. The cluster of modest timber buildings hugged the clifftop directly above the prison. But who would look down on the grey blockhouses when the glittering green of the harbour lured their eyes? He was glad the patients could gaze out to sea.

As soon as he opened the door of the weatherboard reception block, a cheerful office assistant leapt to her feet.

'*Bula vinaka*, Inspector Horseman. My, you're most welcome! I'm Essie. Dr Acharya is in his office. It's in the men's ward. Please come with me.'

He'd heard horror tales about St Giles, involving filth, violence and haunting screams. They walked past long, low blocks edged with deep verandahs that looked clean enough and no more weather-beaten than most hospital buildings intended for the sane. The men's ward was built of corrugated iron. The long side walls of the dining room and dormitory reached only halfway to the roof, but the deep verandahs protected the interiors from rain. No wonder the air smelled fresh. They passed a man sitting on the veranda floor, rocking. Another talked softly to himself while a third stared into space.

'How many male patients are staying here now?'

'Thirty-seven. Some are working in the garden or the kitchen now.'

'How long do they usually stay?'

'*Oi lei*, it varies. A few weeks, for observation and diagnosis. We discharge some when they're stabilised. Mostly, they live with their families and come back as outpatients periodically. It's hard for the ones who live far away and can't return for checkups often enough. Hard for the families, too. We do our best with God's help. Here's Dr Acharya, right at the end of the row.'

Essie knocked at a blue door with a fresh white sign lettered in black. 'One of the patients painted the doctor's door recently. He's a sign writer by trade. Now he's feeling better, he's enjoying doing some jobs about the place. We're all—ah, *bula* Dr Acharya. Here is Inspector Horseman.' Essie beamed and left them.

'Good afternoon, Detective Inspector.' Dr Acharya's greeting was solemn. His dark trousers and grey short-sleeved shirt reinforced his grave face. About Horseman's height but with a leaner build, his stooped shoulders and jutting neck suggested he spent a lot of time in his office.

'Come in, please.'

The office was plain, but a wide louvred window in the end wall looked over Suva Bay. The desk was placed so the doctor could take in the view whenever he looked over the top of his computer monitor. Bookshelves lined another wall and a bank of old grey filing cabinets another.

'Come through to my consulting room, Inspector Horseman.'

An open doorway led through a plywood partition to a space equal in size to the doctor's office. Patterned pandanus mats covered the floor. He took in at a glance the low, narrow metal bedstead covered with a blue spread, two plastic chairs set at a round table and a few stools against a wall. But two pictures hanging side by side brought him to a halt, then drew him closer. Both were underwater scenes peopled by sea creatures and plants.

'Yes, they're powerful, isn't it?' Dr Acharya's use of *isn't it* instead of *aren't they* led Horseman to guess the doctor had grown up in India, not Fiji.

Horseman stared at the seascapes. 'Are they by Semisi Maya? I saw some of his paintings at a Red Cross exhibition. They're striking. I hear some are hanging in Government House, too.'

'Yes, he couldn't hold a brush, but he rubbed the paint on with his hand, elbow and knuckles and then carved into it with sticks and brushes he held in his mouth. They're remarkable. I find they're great talking points with my patients. Excuse me, please sit down.'

Where was he expected to sit? He glanced at the doctor, then pulled out one of the plastic chairs and sat at the table.

Dr Acharya smiled slightly as he took the other chair. 'My apologies, Inspector. I've got into the habit of letting my patients choose where to sit. When I came to this country five years ago, I noticed my Fijian patients got agitated when I directed them to sit on a matching chair. They ducked their heads and slid down in their chairs. In time, I discovered this was because they perceive doctors as high status and feel uncomfortable unless their heads are lower than mine. Now I invite them to sit without indicating where. Some sit on the mats, others on stools, a few on the bed. Except one patient suffering from grandiose delusions who took a chair and wanted me to sit on the floor.' Dr Acharya's smile broadened into a grin.

'I can see you're dedicated to your patients.'

'Well, I'm not doing my job if I introduce a status anxiety into their minds when they are already deeply disturbed. Putting an easy solution in place is not sufficient to demonstrate dedication, isn't it?' He shrugged.

The doctor evidently enjoyed discussing at length, even disputing, or maybe especially disputing. Any other time Horseman would, too. How could he get to the point politely? Maybe the psychiatrist was a mind reader because he spoke first.

'I understand you want to ask about Dev Reddy.'

'Yes, Doctor. I've seen his basic record from Prisons, so I know he was admitted here twice as a long-term patient. How does the coordination between the prison and St Giles work?'

'When prison staff are concerned about an inmate's disturbed behaviour, which typically is unpredictable violence, incoherent speech and irrational acts, the supervisor can apply for a prison removal order from a magistrate. St Giles can't be a dumping ground for difficult prisoners, you know. If this is approved, the prisoner is brought here by warders who guard him or her during the admission process through to placement in a locked room—we have three here in the men's ward and another three in the women's ward. Initial admission is for a fourteen-day period of observation and assessment, which can include emergency drug treatment if we diagnose the prisoner as violently psychotic.'

'How did Reddy end up here for years?'

'If prisoners are acutely disturbed, they cannot live in prison. They certainly won't get better there, but here they have a chance. In time some recover, while others suffer from chronic disorders that can be managed well with a drug regimen administered by prison nursing staff and periodic reviews at St Giles. All patients can be managed to some extent, but some never achieve sufficient stability to return to prison. I can only speak for the last five years of Reddy's sentence. He was one of those who remained stable here at St Giles but on return to prison, he broke down and became acute. His report stated his relapse was triggered by hostility and even violence from other prisoners, even warders. I can't vouch for that, but I've seen him bruised and with a broken rib. On one occasion we admitted him here after an operation up at Crown Memorial Hospital for a ruptured spleen after a beating. That could easily have killed him, but he's proved he has a tough constitution.'

'Do you know who attacked him?'

Dr Acharya shook his head. 'No. I have no way of finding out, and what could I do if I knew who they were?'

'Nothing, I agree. However, it's my job to identify how Reddy's early release threatens public security. To me, that includes risks to Reddy's security. My sergeant is trying to find out the names of his attackers and their whereabouts from Prisons.'

'That's an optimistic ambition.'

'If anyone can find out, it's Sergeant Singh. She has her methods.'

The doctor raised his eyebrows. 'Loyal as well as optimistic. Why are you a police officer, if I may ask?'

'For that very reason, I suppose.' Horseman smiled. 'Most police are optimistic and loyal. So, are you saying you kept Reddy here to protect him?'

Dr Acharya gazed at him. 'We don't express it quite in those terms. You appreciate from what I've told you it's not in anyone's interest, particularly Mr Reddy's, to have him become stable here, return to prison where he's beaten up and reverts to psychosis, then come back up the hill to us again. Rinse and repeat. Rinse and repeat. He's not the only one.'

'He was at the prison farm out at Naboro on the last stretch. I thought that could be a suitable environment for him since he was a farmer.'

'Reddy was stable there for some time—a year, I think. Then another inmate attacked him with a machete. Luckily, he turned around, saw the man about to lunge and jumped away. Still, he suffered a deep cut in the buttock, which took a long time to heal. It's appalling. After that, I certified the only successful treatment plan for him was to serve his sentence here. He's been stable for four years now. He's never been violent. He's flourished, as much as he can here. Our food gardens have flourished under his charge and produce all the greens and tomatoes that the St Giles community needs. Pawpaws and bananas, too.'

'Then why did you recommend his release, Doctor?'

'The rationale of the psychiatric hospital as asylum is over, even in Fiji. Governments all over the world fund hospitals to treat the mentally ill, especially now that effective drugs are available. Providing shelter from the world, except during acute episodes, is not within our scope. Neither is sheltering the world from the mentally ill. As I said, Mr Reddy is stable. He's served eleven years, he's at the age where Prisons don't want the responsibility. He believes he'll be safe if he returns to his farm. A neighbour has been share-farming Mr Reddy's lease, but his house is vacant and that's where he wants to live. A social worker is making his house habitable. He'll be able to come into Suva on the bus to attend outpatient clinics here.'

'Even if he's safe on his secluded farm in the Rewa backblocks, I doubt he'll be safe on the bus after the media campaign since Monday evening.'

Dr Acharya sighed. 'I didn't imagine anything like this would happen.'

'I'll make a case for police protection for Reddy. It may not be approved, though. He's Public Enemy Number 1 for most of the police, as well as the public.'

'Surely...' The doctor raised his hands.

'Doctor Acharya, we need to know about Reddy's mental illness to protect him and to protect the public from him. People believe he's the embodiment of evil, a worshipper of Satan, or possessed by demons, according to their religion. You're the only one who can enlighten us.'

The doctor straightened his back. 'Medical records are private and I am not at liberty to disclose them.'

'I'm not asking for his records. I wouldn't understand them, anyway. To help Reddy, I need a simplified explanation of his diagnosis and the implications for his behaviour. Keeping a little child isolated for years in a fowl yard is extreme. Why did he do it?'

The doctor said nothing. Horseman waited for what seemed like an age. Then Dr Acharya looked at him and spoke. 'Very well. I can see it might help combat the superstitious fears that are stoking the public. Prison staff observed him engaged in long conversations with himself, sometimes arguing, sometimes angry. He cowered in corners when spoken to. When he came here, he was diagnosed with paranoid schizophrenia. A Hindu holy man told him what to do to prevent demons from possessing him—that's what Reddy told the doctor. After some time, about a year I believe, he stabilised on a drug regimen and returned to prison. That's when the cycle I told you about began, and indeed it was a vicious cycle, literally. This was before I took over five years ago. I'd like to tell you about Mr Reddy's current diagnosis.'

'It's not paranoid schizophrenia anymore?' Horseman asked.

The doctor wagged his head from side to side. 'Yes and no, it's hard to be definitive. However, I'll tell you briefly because I can't tolerate the glib labelling of patients who are suffering torments of the mind.'

'Please go on, Doctor.'

'After many hours talking with Mr Reddy, I decided he was suffering from Capgras delusion. It's quite rare. To get back to your question, when I asked him why he kept his child in the chicken house, he insisted that child was not his son. According to him, his own son disappeared when his wife died two years after his birth. He supposed the little boy had decided to go with his mother when she died, but he wasn't certain. However, he was confident his true son, Kanan, would return later. In the meantime, the replacement child could not live in the house, which was Kanan's place and must be kept ready for his return. Mr Reddy believed the imposter child was possessed by a demon who was intent on destroying his home, his farm and his family. He needed to confine the demon child outside his house to protect his property. At the same time, he couldn't bring himself to kill the child, maybe because that would simply release the demon.'

'*Oi lei*! I can get to grips with that mad logic, though.'

'Mad in the loose sense that what's true to the sufferer is false to everyone else, yes. However, there are reports of cases where Capgras delusion was caused by organic changes in the brain. It's possible to have Capgras delusion without being schizophrenic.'

'Is Reddy schizophrenic or not?'

The doctor smiled. 'I wish it were so clear-cut. On balance, I think so, as he responds well to the current drug regimen we use for paranoid schizophrenia.'

'But why didn't his family intervene? I can't understand that. Kanan has brothers and sisters.'

'I can't help you there. I know Kanan's closest sister was fourteen when he was born. That was when Mr Reddy was fifty and his wife was forty-three. There are another four children—let's see.'

He took a while finding what he wanted in the file. 'Yes, when Kanan was born, there were three sons aged twenty-seven, twenty-five, and twenty, and two daughters aged twenty-three and fourteen. The two eldest sons had already migrated to New Zealand. The twenty-year-old son was at USP and staying with a cousin in Suva. The elder daughter married a teacher in Vanua Levu. At the time, the youngest daughter was the only child at home.'

'Still, it's mind-boggling.'

The doctor read further in the case notes. 'Ah yes, I recall that now. When Kanan was a year old, the elder daughter migrated to New Zealand with her husband and children, taking her teenage sister with them.'

'That would have left only the student son. I guess he didn't visit home very often.'

The doctor shrugged. 'I can't speculate, but the remaining son graduated only a few months after his mother died, when Kanan was around two years. His brothers then arranged for him to join them in New Zealand.'

'Such a family story isn't exactly rare, but how could Reddy survive? Just a father in his fifties and a toddler.'

'Grief and isolation can readily tip the predisposed into delusion and psychosis. But I have no way of knowing about Mr Reddy's mental state before this happened. What I'm sure of, because he never wavers on this, is that after his wife's death, he penned Kanan in the chicken run. He avoided contact with him, for fear of the demon polluting him.'

'*Oi lei*, it's an outrage. I can understand why people get so inflamed.'

'Especially when they unconsciously recognise their own darkest impulses. They've got to stub those out on tragic people like Reddy.'

There was something in what the doctor said. Terrified people could turn deadly in an instant.

'It's a miracle the child survived, isn't it?'

'Again, there's no point in me speculating when I don't know. If you need to answer questions about Kanan, talk to the manager of the Sunshine Home, where he lives. You might even visit to get a fuller picture. If you need it, that is.'

'Have you been to visit Kanan, Doctor?'

The doctor nodded. He looked even more grave if that were possible. 'I thought I should check on the child's actual situation, in case the records weren't accurate. As a doctor, it would be inhumane if I allowed an injustice to continue through my own negligence.'

'I agree. And did you discover an injustice there?'

'No, not at the home. I think Kanan lives in the best place for him under the tragic circumstances. People care for him. His injustice began at birth.'

That didn't sound like psychiatrist-talk. What was Dr Acharya implying?

'I would have thought it began when his mother died.'

'Maybe. I encourage you to visit the Sunshine Home. If you need to see me again after that, I'll be happy to talk some more.'

5

Nowadays, Suva Prison housed prisoners on remand waiting to be tried. The conditions here were deemed too grim for convicts, who served their time at one of fifteen correction centres spread around the country. The space vacated by prisoners had been converted for use by prison administrative staff.

A guard radioed their details through and the steel door swung open. Singh and Musudroka followed another guard to a two-storey concrete building.

'Looks like a prison, Sarge,' Musudroka joked.

Singh ignored him. Inside, the building's previous layout had been gutted and converted to decent-sized offices with portable partitions. These were painted the sky-blue of the Fijian flag. Floor-to-ceiling panels of glass louvres were inserted into the walls. The original small square windows high up in the walls remained. Her Majesty Queen Elizabeth, rather faded by years in the tropical light, kept a serene watch over her subjects' industry.

The assistant manager, Jeremaia Domo, greeted them with a broad smile and outstretched hand.

'*Bula, bula*, officers!' He favoured Singh, then Musudroka, with a prolonged handshake. 'Welcome to Suva Correction Centre.' He ushered them into a small conference room and waved at the wooden table and chairs. 'Sit down, sit down. What can I do to help you?'

Two green files lay before Domo.

'As I mentioned on the phone, Mr Domo, my CID unit's job is to identify the threats to public security that Dev Reddy's release presents. By Thursday evening.' She smiled. 'You can see I need your help.'

Domo stopped smiling. 'You've come to the right place. But I don't understand why your job is necessary. If Mr Reddy presented any risk to public security, his parole application would have been rejected. Stands to reason, doesn't it?'

Singh smiled again. 'It does indeed, sir. I'm sure Security Division has the utmost respect for your work. Nevertheless, the media has sensationalised the news of Mr Reddy's early release so Security wants to be prepared for public demonstrations.' She shrugged. 'I'm just a humble detective sergeant. I've got my job to do.'

'*Io*, I understand. Fire away.' Domo laid his hands on top of his files.

'I'm grateful, Mr Domo. Please tell me why you approved Dev Reddy's early release.'

'Good, you come straight to the point, Detective Sergeant. First, the prisoner has served more than half his sentence. Second, he is in his seventies, and so unable to perform manual labour. He has already passed the average life expectancy of Fijians. Third, he presents no danger to the public.'

'I see. Was Mr Reddy ever involved in assaults or fights in prison?'

Domo looked wary. He clenched his fingers around his files. '*Io*, he was, he was. Although it is not possible to prove, his guards believe he was the victim of sustained attacks, both verbal and physical. Reddy defended himself when attacked but always came off worst. His attackers claimed he had assaulted them.'

'Why was he attacked so regularly?'

'It was the nature of his crime, of course. Offenders against children always cop it rough in prison.'

Singh glanced at Musudroka, who needed little encouragement. 'Wouldn't prisoners leave such an old man alone, though?'

'Constable, young thugs spoiling for a fight aren't at any risk from an unarmed old man.'

'Why did you send him to St Giles, Mr Domo?'

'Because he became more and more disturbed, Sergeant Singh. Unpredictable and incomprehensible to prison staff. Chanting, talking to himself, conversing with invisible companions, that sort of thing. Not uncommon in here. The guards recognise the symptoms. No connection with the real world that the rest of us live in.'

Domo leaned forward, his stare intense. 'Now, we can't just send prisoners up to St Giles to get rid of them. Far from it. You should see the protocols for getting a prisoner removal order, which is what we need even to take a prisoner with a broken bone to hospital. It's a book! We sent Mr Reddy up there for diagnosis and treatment, just like everyone else.'

'And he has stayed at St Giles for years at a stretch?'

'*Io*, St Giles was in his best interest.'

'Can you tell me who his attackers were?'

'Well, they're not likely to be in prison anymore.'

'Exactly, Mr Domo. They're probably free civilians. They may have maintained their hatred of Reddy and be rallying others to agitate against him, even to whip up anger in the community. That's the sort of person I mean by a threat to public security. I need to pass on the names of anyone who attacked Reddy in prison to the Security Division chief.'

'Well, I don't know about that. Our files are confidential.'

'I agree, and CID officers can be trusted to keep them that way. The deadline for this report is tomorrow evening. We don't have time for an official requisition. You wouldn't want public disorder to break out because you didn't give Security the information you have on file, would you, Mr Domo?'

'I understand your problem, Ms Singh, believe me. I'll send you a copy of the relevant parts of Mr Reddy's file tomorrow.'

Singh smiled. 'I'm grateful for your cooperation. But please, I'm happy to wait here while you have the relevant parts of the file copied. Or to save you time, just copy the whole file, and the CID team can do all the work of picking out the relevant bits. I promise you, only our four officers will see the file, which will be locked away safely after use.'

She stood and held out her hand. Domo stood and shook it, nodded and left the room with the files.

Musudroka stared. 'How do you do it, Sarge?'

***

Singh and Musudroka passed through the steel door and faced about ten chanting protesters. Two prison guards marked an imaginary barrier three metres from the entrance. Most of the chanters were middle-aged Fijians. Three brandished cardboard placards, lettered in both English and Fijian. In Singh's experience, placards in two languages were made explicitly for television. This gathering was a publicity stunt. Who was behind it?

'What's this?' Musudroka was taken aback.

'The first demonstration against Reddy's release.' The group chanted in Fijian, 'Keep Reddy locked up.'

As they watched, press reporters jumped out of a taxi, cameras held aloft. More ran across the road from the yacht club.

'There's the Fiji One camera crew. I wonder if they're live. We'll edge closer and observe. I'll radio Kau—he can check the TV now.'

'*Oi lei*, we're in the right place at the right time, for once!' Musudroka sparked up.

Two placards were crafted from brown cardboard cartons, the lettering broad-brushed in black. Definitely home-made by different authors. They shouted KEEP EVIL CHAINED UP! and DON'T LET REDDY OUT! The third was a white plastic corrugated board fixed to a piece of bamboo, the red inscription more careful. The single word HOOK filled the top half. Below were the words HANDS OFF OUR KIDS.

'Is that a kids' charity, Sarge?'

'I haven't heard of it, Tani. Could've started up yesterday just to oppose Reddy's parole. An opportunistic charity.'

'Oh, I get it, like opportunistic theft. Look, that big fat guy's moving to the microphone. It's an interview.'

They missed the reporter's introduction but now stood as close to the microphones as the media crew would permit. The group's spokesman was indeed big and fat, a figure common in Fiji. But it was his youth that made him stand out from his fellows. Singh thought early thirties, no older than herself. He was Fijian, clean-shaven, cropped frizzy hair, dressed in a voluminous brown-and-white *bula* shirt and black tailored sulu. He stepped forward confidently, signalled to the others to stop chanting with a downward swipe of his hand. Singh could see him as a preacher.

'What are you doing here today, Mr Nata?' the eager reporter asked.

'My friends and I have come here, to the impregnable prison gates, to petition our respected authorities to stay their hands. They must not unleash an evil-doer who imperils the safety of all our precious children in Fiji.'

He spoke calmly, deliberately. He paused, gazed into the camera lens, and spread his arms wide and smiled. 'We want to protect all our children—children of all races, all creeds.'

He paused again, nodded. His smile disappeared. 'You know the evil-doer I refer to is none other than Dev Reddy, convicted of the most unspeakable, the most unimaginable, the most evil abuse of his own son, his sacred charge, gifted to him by God on high. You all know what he did. You don't need me to tell you. For his crimes, this criminal was sentenced to serve twenty years in prison. Clearly, the intention of the learned and wise judges was that Reddy should die behind bars. But now, after a mere eleven years, this man will be released into society, free to work his evil again. We ask our government to think. Wise leaders, we humbly beg you to keep Dev Reddy, heinous child abuser, behind bars. Wise leaders, we humbly beg you to keep our precious children safe from this monster! Wise leaders, we humbly beg you to do justice!'

Nata clasped his hands together as if in prayer. He was ardent as he looked into the camera. Singh looked at Musudroka, who stared at Nata.

The reporter was quick to fill the pause. 'Mr Nata, tell us about your new charity, HOOK.' The camera panned to the white placard.

'*Io*, gladly. Of course, we have all observed the rising tide of depravity lapping the shores of our islands, God's islands, in these dark times. All of us learn with horror of crimes of cruelty and abuse against little children. Assault, murder, even rape! More and more frequently, crimes against children are prosecuted in our courts. How many more remain secret from the law? I say ten times as many, nay, even ten times tenfold.' He closed the fingers of his right hand, stabbing the air repeatedly.

The camera operator gestured to the woman with the white placard, directing her to move so the TV viewers could see the placard beside Mr Nata's head.

'I have prayed long about this. What did Jesus say about those who sin against children? *It would be better for him if a millstone were hung around his neck and he were cast into the sea.*'

Nata's followers endorsed his words with *Amen*, raised hands and solemn nods.

'God called me last Monday evening. When our watchdog, Fiji One, barked to warn us the abuser Reddy would soon be on the loose, God called me to do something about it. Something about Reddy, and something about the hundreds of other monsters who threaten our innocents, the beloved of Jesus. That night, my wife and I chose the verses I have quoted for our Bible study. Hands Off Our Kids, that's HOOK, came into my mind during our closing prayer. I promised God I would fight those who do evil to children with all the strength He gives me.'

'That was less than two days ago, Mr Nata. How did you gather your supporters so quickly?'

'I'm a lay preacher at God's Gospel Church at Samabula. The elders permitted me to speak at our Christian Outreach meeting last night. The message of Jesus fell on fertile ground. Reddy's parole troubles parents deeply.'

His supporters crowded closer to their leader, thrusting the placards forward. Their insistent murmuring grew in volume until Nata quietened them with a raised hand.

'We decided to waste no time, to pursue our mission without delay. So here we are the very next day, outside this fortress of the law, to urge our righteous cause. More people wanted to join us here, but are faithfully serving their employers. They are with us in spirit.'

'From what you've just said, your mission is rather broader than keeping Reddy in prison. Am I right?'

'Correct. Our demand to repeal Reddy's parole order is urgent and immediate; otherwise, he'll be free on Friday, in just two days. Our first campaign must succeed. However, after our first success, we have much work to do. Much more.'

'Do you intend to campaign against the early release of other prisoners convicted of crimes against children?'

'*Io*, we do indeed—when their parole applications come up. However, I see work of a different kind ahead of us: positive work to educate parents. I envisage our members will work through their own churches, temples, mosques and schools to make the blessed islands of Fiji a better place for all children.'

He beamed into the camera, his face animated by his righteous vision. Surely he was winging it. Singh admired this ability while recognising it was one she'd met in fraudsters several times.

'I know many viewers will want to help HOOK. Where can viewers make their donations?'

Nata's surprise looked genuine. Was that possible? He stared at the reporter for a beat.

'*Io, io*, donations are most welcome. Your viewers will appreciate HOOK is one day old, so we do not even have a bank account.'

Now he had recovered his smooth preacher manner. He turned his head to the camera. 'If you wish to support our campaign to stop Dev Reddy's release, send your donation to HOOK, c/o God's Gospel Church, P.O. Box 73, Samabula, or deliver cash in person to the church during office hours. If you wish to join our rally tomorrow, come to God's Gospel Church at Samabula this evening.'

Nata's supporters broke into song behind him. Could this happen spontaneously? Nata joined in, his fine baritone rising above the more distant voices. Singh knew very few Christian hymns, but this was her favourite: 'Jesus loves the little children.'

Singh noted HOOK's contact details during the singing. She was pleased to see Musudroka doing the same. They would look into Mr Nata's background as soon as she returned to the station.

'What do you reckon about that performance, Tani?'

'Polished, Sarge. A lot of people will agree with them. Whatever their intentions, we'll have to list HOOK as a security threat.'

'Well done, Tani. If you keep thinking clearly like that, you'll make a good detective. One day.'

THURSDAY

6

'Detectives, it is my great pleasure to present your new superintendent to you. After locking up all the criminals operating in Western Islands, Acting Detective Superintendent Ratini has nothing more to do there.'

The assembled Suva Central CID officers chuckled politely at DCS Tawaga's joke. Ratini smiled around the room. His smile froze as his eyes lighted on Horseman, who glanced away immediately. Ratini had not forgotten his prey from all those years ago and wasn't pleased to see him again.

As the formalities continued, Horseman glanced surreptitiously at his new boss. Ratini's face had thinned, his body thickened and his hair greyed. He sported a bristly moustache and modest paunch. He was tidier than before, but only a bit. Few Fijian men wore work clothes that were ill-matched, unironed and even dirty, like Ratini did a dozen years ago.

Today his floral *bula* shirt was rumpled, his jeans clean but frayed around the cuffs as the hems had never been taken up to fit him. He'd given up his baseball cap, but maybe that was a concession to formality. It wasn't every day an officer was promoted by the commissioner at Police HQ, after all. He remembered Superintendent Navala, always formal in a long-sleeved business shirt and tailored sulu, the wrap-around Fijian skirt. For an occasion like this, he would have added a tie and jacket, just like Tawaga had today. Horseman knew which style engendered respect and trust in the public. Did Ratini want to rebel, or was he just oblivious to his appearance?

At Tawaga's invitation, the detectives clapped enthusiastically to welcome Ratini, who stepped forward to address his new subordinates.

'*Vinaka*, Chief Superintendent Tawaga. I'm surprised everyone in Suva hadn't forgotten all about me after all those years in Western Islands, eh. Just goes to show promotion by merit still operates, eh.'

The detectives exchanged glances, unsure if this remark was a joke. In case it wasn't, they smiled rather than laughed. Ratini frowned.

'It's good to see a few familiar faces from the old days. *Oi lei*, I see a favourite rugby star among us. Josefa Horseman. What a surprise—I never knew you were a policeman now! Brains as well as brawn, eh. But that remains to be proved, I guess.' This time, everyone laughed. Ratini's love for a scathing put-down hadn't changed.

Playing to his audience, Ratini went on. 'You lot won't know I met our Rugby-Sevens star when he was a student. He discovered a body at the university rugby field, so he was an important witness, indeed a suspect for a time. What a tangle that case was! I gave young Joe a hard time, but I believe in rattling suspects' cages. I get results, don't I, sir?' He looked at Tawaga, who smiled and nodded.

'Anyway, I sorted that mess out within the week, but I wouldn't have thought young Joe would want to go near a police station again! Turns out I must have inspired him to join up. Though I'm not sure how much time he's actually spent on detective work in the last ten years. I'm amazed he's a DI now.'

The laughter trailed off. Tawaga looked relieved when uniforms carried in the elaborate morning tea customary on such occasions. They set up a trestle with a snowy cloth and arranged the tea urn, crockery and platters laden with sandwiches, hot sausage rolls, curry puffs and scones with jam. No one would need lunch today, but most would probably still have it.

Tawaga clearly felt on safer ground now as a host. He spread his arms to encompass the room. 'I invite each of you to have a chat with Acting Superintendent Ratini while we enjoy our tea. Afterwards, he wishes to meet with each DI and team to review your current cases.'

To show goodwill he did not feel, Horseman approached his new boss for a quick handshake and greeting. Ratini focused on Singh, predictably immaculate in dark trousers, crisp white shirt and yellow jacket, her hair up in a gleaming bun. Ratini held a cup in one hand and a plate piled with food in the other. He glanced at Horseman's proffered hand, shrugged and winked while he chewed.

'*Bula*, Joe. Sorry I can't shake hands now.' He sprayed morsels of puff pastry over Singh as he spoke. Horseman admired her all the more for not stepping back.

Later, they ran into each other getting refills at the tea urn.

'Believe me now?' Horseman asked.

Singh lifted her brows in agreement. 'He didn't get promoted for his diplomatic manners, did he?' she muttered. 'Maybe he *is* a top-notch detective.'

***

Horseman, Singh, Kau and Musudroka sat in front of the desk in what Horseman still thought of as Navala's office. He outlined their current cases to Ratini. The most serious was a string of burglaries and thefts. A colleague, DI Vula, had noticed they bore the same trademark—no fingerprints were left behind. Since then, the two DIs and their teams worked on them together. The thefts included good quality jewellery, cash, household items and tools, so they were initially classified as general domestic break-ins. But when many of the general items were found dumped by quiet roadsides, the detectives twigged that the thieves targeted high-value jewellery.

'I heard Vula's team report on that. Those scum are getting bolder, the break-ins are coming thick and fast now.'

'Either that or their intelligence about the homes of Suva's good quality jewellery is getting better. That's another angle we're looking at.' Horseman kicked himself for claiming more knowledge than Ratini. Maybe that was why Ratini hated him all those years ago.

'Whatever the reason, we need to crack this one quickly. It's bad for public confidence. *The Fiji Times*, *The Sun* and *The Mirror* are scaring the surburbanites, even those that own nothing more than a shell bracelet.'

'*Io*, sir. I agree.' Horseman could be honest about this one. 'However, on Tuesday Chief Super Tawaga asked me to report to Security Division on the risks to security from Dev Reddy's early release. He was convicted —'

'I know, I know who he is! That cruel child abuser. Causing trouble after all this time. What were Prisons thinking of?'

'We've spoken to prison officers and the St Giles doctor already, sir. They're convinced Reddy presents no threat to the public at all. However, the protests that the media are encouraging certainly do. We've also identified three ex-cons who attacked Reddy more than once when they were incarcerated together. Persistent rabble-rousers against Reddy over the years in the media are on our list too. Sir, I'm happy for you to take over direction.'

'*Oi lei*, Joe! The deadline's tomorrow? Don't think you can palm it off on me. Tawaga mentioned it to me. You're stuck with it, my pal. You've no choice but to get it done. It'll be a box-ticking exercise, I'm sure. Just make sure that you deliver the report on time. Then all four of you are back on the jewellery thefts. That's a proper CID case.'

'*Io*, sir. *Vinaka*.'

'Hang on, do you really need DS Singh for this Reddy report? Wouldn't it be better for her to continue to help DI Vula with the jewellery case? Isn't that what you'd prefer, Sergeant?'

'To produce an accurate report, all four of us must give it our undivided attention, sir. We've less than twenty-four hours until the deadline.'

'So you have. All right. On my desk at nine o'clock, Horseman. I'll need to review it before it goes to Security.'

'*Io*, sir.'

'Make sure he doesn't antagonise people with his questions, Singh. That's what he did on his first case. And he was only a witness, then!'

Singh managed a weak smile. 'Thank you, sir.'

The two probationers hung their heads in embarrassment. Horseman could imagine their confusion—he'd been here before. He was sure now Ratini had not changed his ways. Why would he, when they got him what he wanted?

Horseman stood. '*Vinaka*, sir. You'll have the report tomorrow.'

7

'I've got an address for Kirilo Makuluva,' Horseman called out.

'Good. Um, remind me who he is,' Singh replied.

'One of the thug prisoners who got his kicks out of beating up Reddy, regular as clockwork. Never alone, of course. Must have backup to take on a man in his sixties. So, he got a few cronies to help him. Kirilo's a confirmed crook, breaking and entering, robbery with violence. He's in and out of prison, longest sentence two years so far. At the moment he's out but still under supervision and staying with relatives at Lami village.'

'Do you want to talk to him?'

'*Io*, I do indeed. And Singh, as you were the one who charmed Reddy's file out of the prison officials—'

Musudroka snorted. 'More threats than charm, Boss. I was there! Couldn't believe it.'

Singh looked smug. 'You were there to watch and learn the art, Tani.'

The probationer shook his head. 'You scared me, Sarge.'

'When you both stop interrupting me—*Vinaka*. As I was trying to say, Sergeant Singh can come with me to suss out Kirilo Makuluva. I've put him on the list anyway, but I need a sense of the man. He's the only one of these reprobates anywhere near Suva.'

'Wouldn't miss the chance, sir.'

'Kau, how's your media trawl going?'

'I've got a few names who wrote frequent letters to all the newspapers through the investigation and the trial and for a while after Reddy went inside. Interest last rekindled on the tenth anniversary of Reddy's conviction. Two of the stirrers against Reddy crop up each time the media revive the topic.' Kau shoved his glasses up his nose and looked up.

'Good work, Apo. Note them all down and include some press clippings from the two persistent campaigners. Can you finish that and a brief summary before Shiners training this afternoon?'

Kau grinned. '*Io*, sir. I'll make sure I do.'

***

The road wound through the hills, climbing to the ridge of the Suva peninsula. The suburban roads were like a giant unstructured spider web, sprawling untidily from one precarious anchor point to another. And everywhere, the luxuriant growth born of heat and three metres annual rainfall threatened to tear the web apart.

Horseman turned into a short cul-de-sac. There were only six houses. Sure enough, the Sunshine Home for Children sign was at the end. It was a two-storey concrete-block building like the family houses in the street, painted cream.

'We'd better park in the street,' Horseman said.

As they walked down the drive, a second building with a wrap-around verandah appeared behind the first.

'How many children stay here?' Singh asked.

'Twenty at the moment. Kanan is an adult now. Besi, the house-mother, told me when the chicken-boy story reached Australia and New Zealand, offers of funds flooded in—to the Red Cross, to embassies, to churches, to Save the Children. And not just offers—international bank drafts, even foreign currency. It must have been a total mess. But Save the Children stepped in and guided the establishment of the Sunshine Home for Children. They reckon nearly all the money sent from overseas to help Kanan found its way to Sunshine.'

'I hope they got a good auditor to trace it all. I can't understand why people send off good money when they've no idea where it's going,' Singh said.

Singh knocked on the front door.

A bright-eyed teenager opened the door. 'Are you the police?' She sounded excited. 'I'm Noor. Come with me. Aunty Besi is in the kitchen.'

Noor led them along a hallway that ran the full length of the building. Floor-to-ceiling glass louvres made it just as bright as the verandah outside. They passed an office, empty playroom and a nursery with three cots and three sleeping toddlers. The hall ended at an open door through which wafted the appetising smell of baking bread.

'Here are the *ovisas*, Aunty!' Noor grinned at them and sauntered off.

Matron Besi was unexpectedly tall and slender, her grey hair an old-fashioned Afro style. Horseman pulled himself up for expecting her to be overweight and big-bosomed. But then, all the matrons he had met, including his own mother, actually *were* overweight and big-bosomed.

'Come in, Josefa Horseman, you're most welcome. What a thrill it is to shake your hand.'

'*Vinaka vakalevu,* but the honour is all mine, Besi. You're an angel, caring for children who have no home. Let me introduce my colleague, Detective Sergeant Singh.'

'Call me Susie,' Singh said as they shook hands.

'You came at the right time. The little ones are having their afternoon nap and the older ones aren't back from school yet. Petero and I can get on with the dinner and tomorrow's baking in peace. Mainly Petero. He's made tea for you and the scones are just out of the oven.' She suddenly looked anxious. 'You do have time to stay for tea, don't you?'

They didn't, but Horseman couldn't resist fresh scones. 'We'd be delighted,' he said.

Petero was shorter and even leaner than Besi. His moustache and hair were neatly trimmed. He shook hands, too, then covered one end of the central pine table with a blue-and-white check cloth. He set out thick white crockery, milk and sugar, scones, butter and pineapple jam, then poured their tea from a battered aluminium teapot.

'This is wonderful, Petero. I wish we had you at the police station!' Horseman said sincerely. 'Won't you join us?'

'*Vinaka*, but I must keep going. I'll drink mine as I work.'

Horseman washed his mouthful of scone down with scalding tea. 'Besi, you know we're here to check if there are any potential threats to Sunshine Home caused by the early release from prison of Kanan's father, Dev Reddy.'

'Do you think he's going to come looking for Kanan?' Besi was wide-eyed.

'Dr Acharya, the medical director of St Giles, thinks that's very unlikely. Dev Reddy suffers from a delusion. He believes Kanan is not his son, but a devil who replaced his son. That's why he isolated the little boy in the chicken yard, so that his true son could return to his rightful place in his house.'

'Does he still believe that after all this time?'

'*Io*, as I understand it. His medication has made him stable, but he still believes his son was replaced by a demon. He hopes that when he moves back to his farmhouse, his son will also return there.'

'What a tragedy. Mental illness is a terrible waste, I think. Most of all, for innocent Kanan.'

They all nodded in sad agreement. Petero filled the silence by pouring everyone more tea and offering the scones again.

Singh poised her pen above her notebook. 'Besi, has anyone got in touch with you since Reddy's release was announced?'

'*Io*, the papers, the radio and television, but no one else. They all ask for interviews, for pictures of Kanan, they even ask to video Kanan. The cheek! That poor boy wouldn't understand what any of it was about. I've refused all approaches, including cash payments.'

'Can you trust all the staff to do the same?' Singh asked.

Petero turned to the table. His deep-set brown eyes were intense. '*Io*, she can, *ovisa*. None of us can comprehend the torture that Kanan suffered as a child. The life he led was Satan's work. He will never recover. We have promised God we will protect him with our lives and make his life happy. What better purpose could there be for my life? I am blessed to have this chance.'

The lump that rose in Horseman's throat wasn't scone.

'What about neighbours? The media won't give up before Reddy's release.'

'They're really quiet and respectful. Two middle-aged expatriate couples and a large Indian family—all their children have already left school. Do you think I should speak to them?'

'*Io*, you know them. Simply ask them not to speak to the media on the topic and explain why.'

'I noticed you have a perimeter fence but no lock on your gates, no security lights.'

'No, it's so secluded and peaceful here. The fence is to mark our boundary and keep the dog in. She's not aggressive, but she knows how to bark!'

'Good!'

'We shut the gates at night. But it's easier to leave them open during the day, what with deliveries and our minibus.'

'This afternoon, I want you to buy a big, strong chain and a padlock for your driveway gates. High tensile. I know it's inconvenient, but I want you to shut and lock the gates every time a vehicle or person comes or goes. The same for any side or back gates you have—Sergeant Singh and I will walk around your boundary and check. Do you have a caretaker?'

'That's me, sir,' Petero said.

'Good, I'd be grateful if you came with us on our boundary check. Do you ever employ extra security?'

Both Petero and Besi shook their heads, worried.

'I recommend you employ night security immediately. It's just a precaution as the media have already been harassing you. Just until this sensation dies down.'

Petero nodded. 'My cousin works for Eversafe. If he can't come, he'll get us someone.'

'The minibus is in your drive now. Don't you use it to bring the schoolchildren home?'

'No, we want them to be just like the other kids at school. They catch the public bus with their friends. They like that. They'll be on their way home now.'

'I suggest you drive the children to school or anywhere else by your own transport from tomorrow morning. Until this media storm blows over. Reporters could wait for Sunshine children outside school—ask them questions, take photos, video.'

Besi stared. 'I hadn't thought about that. I can see it's possible. The kids would think it was exciting. But would they stoop so low as to trick children?'

'*Io*, they would. With some reporters, the hunting instinct takes over. They're dogs after a cat. Their prey has no rights as far as they're concerned.'

Petero slotted two trays of bread rolls into racks above the workbench. The warm, yeasty aroma was cheering. He seemed energised.

'Well, Besi, we can do everything the *ovisas* have told us right away, can't we? It won't even take long or cost much.'

'*Io, io*, I'm grateful. But what you've said has come as a shock, you know. It hasn't quite sunk in.'

'I'm glad you can easily improve your security.' How could he ask about Kanan without sounding like a nosy reporter himself? He couldn't think of a way.

'Besi, it would help us if we knew more about Kanan's condition.'

The matron sighed. 'He's a twenty-two-year-old man who behaves like a three-year-old. On his best days, a four-year-old. A happy, playful four-year-old. A little boy who can understand a lot but can't speak more than a handful of poorly articulated words. He suffers from cerebral palsy and global delay, probably from being deprived of oxygen during his birth. He has restricted motor control for which he has daily physical therapy. Speech therapy, too.' She was word-perfect on a speech she had repeated many times.

'It's wonderful so many people want to help him.'

'*Io*, everyone who meets him loves him. You may wonder how the Kanan Foundation can fund all this. Well, Kanan funds it. He looks after himself and twenty other neglected and abused children as well. When Kanan's story hit the world, pity, sorrow and money overflowed. When well-off Australians and New Zealanders saw the first video of him perching on a chair, pecking at his food, folding his arms like wings, when they heard his clucks and crows, when they saw his scabbed, hen-pecked skin, they cried and sent cheques to the television stations, to the papers, to their embassies.

'Save the Children here in Suva offered to set up and supervise a foundation. I was caring for Kanan at the government orphanage, trying and failing to educate him, and Save the Children invited me to become a director of the foundation. When we realised there was more than enough money to care for Kanan for the rest of his life, to buy this beautiful house for him, we decided he would want to look after other children who had no one who loved them.

'He enjoys the company of the other children. A dozen have already grown up and left us for promising futures. He will never know it, but he provided those futures for his playmates. However, when we finally accepted that Kanan would never become an adult himself, we agreed we would never exploit his condition or allow the media on our premises.'

'Usually, sponsors want to keep up to date with their charitable projects. Is that not the case with your donors?'

'*Io*. We send newsletters with photos. About five years ago, Save the Children organised a public relations company to make a video about Sunshine Home. It's like a professional movie, with beautiful footage of the children. We sent the CD to all our donors. They loved it and every year some come from overseas to meet Kanan. It's fun for him to have visitors. He charms them. Every week, he gets letters, cards, drawings and photos from overseas. And some even want to volunteer here.'

'Really? Does that work out?'

'*Io*, usually cheerful, energetic young people on their gap years. Some stay for a few weeks, others a few months. Aussies, Kiwis, Americans. Both sides benefit from getting to know each other.'

'Sounds great!' Singh said.

'We benefit even more when someone comes along who's experienced. Right now we have Sachi from Australia. She's wonderful with all the children, but especially with Kanan.'

Besi smiled sweetly to herself for a bit and no one broke the silence.

Then she stood up. 'My goodness, how I rattle on! After all that, I'd better take you to meet our celebrity himself.'

'Are you sure?'

'Didn't I say Kanan loves meeting friendly people? I don't know if he understands anything about rugby, but he often sees it on television when the others are watching. He'll be pleased to meet Joe Horseman. Come along!'

The matron led them the full length of the hallway to the room at the opposite end of the house. The sound of hammering came through the wide-open door. A man squatted on the floor, his hunched back to them. He was pounding something hard, a wooden mallet clutched awkwardly in his fist.

Noor, the girl who'd greeted them, grinned and jumped up. 'Kanan loves his carpentry bench. He hasn't noticed you.'

'*Io*, come and meet him,' Besi said.

Horseman was disconcerted. He glanced at Singh, who looked rooted to the spot. The man before them had thick, wavy hair, as glossy and white as a seagull's feathers. His visible skin, on the back of his neck and his right arm wielding the hammer, was also white—as white as a sheet of paper.

They stepped around to face Kanan, who grinned at them, hammering all the harder, driving a wooden dowel into a hole in his bench.

Besi smiled at the officers. 'You didn't know then?'

They shook their heads.

'He wants to show you how well he can hammer.' She raised her voice above the din. 'Stop now, Kanan. You have visitors.'

Another woman, older than Noor, sat in front of Kanan. The matron introduced her as Sachi. She smiled and nodded to the visitors but quickly switched her attention to Kanan. Indulgent, she reached forward and gently guided his hammering hand to a stop. He jerked his head up and beamed a crooked grin at Horseman and Singh. His face was pale, his eyebrows, lashes and stubble as snowy as his head hair. His irises were the lightest blue Horseman had ever seen.

They joined Kanan on the floor, shook hands and played. Besi was right—Kanan was fun, just like a playful preschooler. He forced Horseman into a wrestle by falling on him. Besi chuckled and nodded her permission. Horseman felt Kanan's surprising strength, but also the torsion of his tendons and joints. That must be painful. He made a show of trying and failing to roll Kanan off him. Again and again. The toddler-man shouted and squealed with glee.

But they had a deadline. Fortunately, a dozen of Kanan's playmates barged in from school and distracted him. By the time the detectives had completed their security inspection, adding more padlocks and a small fence repair to Petero's list, Kanan and all the others were seated at the long narrow table in the dining room eating bread, jam and fruit.

Petero promised to get the security jobs done that afternoon.

'Please, Besi, make sure the gates are locked all the time. Only open them for people you've invited. It's a necessary precaution just for a little while, I hope.'

'Come back and see us again, Detectives. Kanan likes you both.'

***

Singh took the wheel for the return trip to the station. 'I never heard that the chicken-boy was albino. Did you?'

'I don't think so. I wouldn't have forgotten that. I was so startled when I looked through the door and saw his white hair—that must have been obvious to Besi and the carers.'

'They'll be used to it. But maybe most people know Kanan's albino before they meet him. Don't worry, you covered your surprise in an instant. His father isn't albino, is he?'

'No. I've never seen a photo of the mother.'

'I think albinism's one of those genetic quirks that pop up every so often. Believe me, it was no fun at school having light green eyes when everyone else had brown.'

Horseman couldn't help smiling inwardly, but he didn't dare laugh. It wasn't the first time she'd mentioned being teased at school because of her lovely eyes, the colour of the sunlit shallows. He reckoned all the boys had fallen in love and all the girls had been jealous.

'There were two albino brothers at my boarding school. I remember when they arrived. They were shy and kept to themselves at first. No wonder—they must have been teased when the teachers weren't around whatever school they went to. Kids can be cruel when they run in packs.'

'Yes, they can.'

'Anyway, we soon got used to them. One of them was a fantastic singer—a strong, true bass. The choirmaster loved him. The other one was mad for rugby and would have been a strong player. But his skin got so burned, it sort of cracked up into weeping sores that spread. They must have stung like hell, but he still wanted to play. The sun damaged his eyes, too. That was discovered when he was taken to hospital with a fever. His skin sores got infected and poisoned his system. He did recover, but no more outdoor sports after that. It was lucky we had indoor basketball, hardly any schools did, so he took that up. But his passion was rugby.'

'Do you think Kanan's father rejected him because he was albino?'

'Possibly. Do you know if any of Reddy's other children are albinos? But, but, but, we mustn't get distracted. We've got our report to finish tonight.'

'Oh, but you're going off to training, taking the boys with you and leaving it all to me!' She grinned at him.

'Keep your eye on the road. If Apo and Tani have finished their sections when we get back, they can go home after training. I'll be back at the station before six-thirty. We'll soon put it together and polish it up.'

'Ha—I'll remind you of that around half-past ten!'

'Sunshine Home's very comfortable, isn't it? Seems so well-run, too. It's wonderful that Kanan has a home. Unlike me. I told Matt I'd find a place of my own before his kids come back from uni for Christmas. That probably gives me six weeks at most.'

'Still, you don't really have to. Matt enjoys having you share his house.'

That made him think. How did Singh know that? 'He's very easygoing, but it's time I found something for myself.'

8

Apo, Tani and the traffic constables put the Shiners squad through their paces competently now. More than competently. Horseman stood on the sidelines, observing the rugby skills of the shoe-shine boys after nine months' training. Not to mention a season in the Suva Juniors competition just behind them. He allowed himself to be proud. He was proud of his volunteers, too, who turned up faithfully three times a week during the match season, their rosters permitting. At first, Musudroka would set up whatever exercise the boys wanted, even if it meant throwing them into scrummage without warming up first. Now he understood rugby training was about discipline and science. If he was a trainer, he couldn't be one of the boys.

Lemeki from Traffic blew the whistle for halftime. Lemeki had played for Police 1st grade for twelve years some decades ago. He was only five years from retirement now and his experience was second to none. Horseman strolled across the field to chew the fat.

Before he reached Lemeki, a boy raced over and intercepted him. Tevita, the instigator of the Shiners and Horseman's devoted fan.

'Joe, Joe, I got something to tell you, Joe!'

Horseman stopped. 'Sure, Tevita. Go ahead. I've noticed you're more focused this afternoon. Keeping your eye glued to the ball.'

Tevita shrugged and looked away, acting cool. But when he looked up again, his face glowed with pleasure.

'Something you don't know, Joe.'

'*Io*, I'm listening.'

'Interview today, Joe. I had interview with my boss at Police Garage, Sergeant Walo. Tough boss, Joe.'

'Come on, Tevita, why did you have an interview?'

'Sergeant Walo, he say I'm on probation, must have interview after I work one month. I worked one month, Joe!' Tevita couldn't have been more elated if he'd won a gold medal.

'Congratulations, Tevita. That's a solid achievement.'

'Sergeant Walo, he say I do good job washing vehicles. My vehicles are cleanest and shiniest. I got two more months on probation, but boss is gonna give me senior officers' cars to clean right away. Commissioner's, too, Joe! How about that!'

'That's wonderful, Tevita. Sergeant Walo trusts you to do an excellent job. He's already promoted you.'

'He say I'm a good boy.'

'I'm very pleased to hear that. You always did a perfect job shining shoes, so you now do a perfect job shining cars.'

'True, Joe, true! I never thought about that.'

'How do you like living in the apprentices' quarters? Is that going okay?'

'Okay, Joe. All good. I have a bottom bunk in dormitory, we got bathroom next door, laundry. I got a locker to keep my things safe. I get meals in canteen—plenty to eat. I think I like to stay, Joe.'

'Good idea, Tevita. The garage is a good chance for you: a job and a home, too.'

'True, true. I know you pleased, Joe.'

He whooped and ran off. One more Shiner with a home, at least for now. But there were still others squatting underneath the Albert Park grandstand, under market stalls, anywhere with some protection from the torrential Suva rain.

The whistle blew and the boys dashed back to the field for their favourite part of training—the practice game.

It was over two months since Horseman had broken his ankle in the line of duty, on a tuna longliner, of all places. He couldn't risk permanent damage to another joint, so he stayed on the sidelines, observing keenly and taking mental notes. When Dr Pillai, honorary team physician, pulled up near the grandstand, Horseman crossed to greet him and help carry the boxes containing the Shiners' post-training dinner.

'What have we got tonight, Doctor?'

'Nothing special, Joe. tuna sandwiches, corn cobs and cassava. A couple of watermelons as a change from bananas. Not as nutritious, mind, but boys need variety, too, even though they'll eat anything.'

'You've brought wonderful meals, twice a week for nine months now. It's not just the food. They know they can count on you.'

The diminutive doctor ducked his head, avoiding the praise. Horseman marvelled again at the density of Dr Pillai's coarse black hair, which sprouted upright from his scalp. There was no room between the hairs for a parting.

'I've been watching Tevita. He's got more energy and stamina after a month of lodging and canteen meals at the police garage. He's playing better all-round.'

'Yes, good food will do that for teenagers. It's only in cases of extreme deprivation that damage is irreparable.'

They took a box each and headed for the trestle table the boys had set up during the break.

'I met one of those today. Kanan Reddy, kept penned in a chicken yard by his father for eight years. Dev Reddy's being released from prison tomorrow.'

'Tragic, tragic. The father must have been deluded, maybe still so.'

'The St Giles psychiatrist told me he is but insists he presents no danger to the public. He believes his son was replaced by a demon so won't go anywhere near him. Kanan has a mental age of three or four but has a comfortable home, carers and treatment for his cerebral palsy, lots of playmates and toys. He seems happy.'

'My goodness, that's a better outcome than anyone could have expected. I'm pleased to hear it.'

'Did you know the boy was an albino?'

The doctor stopped unpacking the sandwiches. 'If I ever heard that, I forgot it. But I don't think I'd have forgotten that. It explains a lot.'

'Tell me about it.'

They resumed laying out the food. 'In India, albinos suffer discrimination in all areas of life. Some ancient tales feature supernatural white beings, malign ghosts and the like. My goodness, superstitious relatives and neighbours would not welcome an albino child in their midst. Kanan's father would have been susceptible to believing his child was possessed by a devil. Are any other family members albinos?'

'I'm not sure. I want to find out. All the other children have emigrated.'

'See if you can track down family photos, especially large family groups. That would be interesting. It's a rare condition in all races, inherited when both parents carry a certain recessive gene.'

'I haven't heard of any superstition surrounding albinos in Fijian culture. But they're teased by kids who should know better because they look so different.'

'The only difference is that they lack melanin, which protects the skin and eyes from the sun. In the tropics, their suffering is worse than elsewhere. But there is no other difference between them and the rest of us. If their poor vision is aided by glasses and they are allowed to sit close to the board in class, their educational achievements should be normal.'

When the final whistle blew, the boys ran for the grandstand taps, eager for their meal. To be eligible for the free dinner, they had to arrive at training on time. The incentive worked: no one had ever been late. Not once in nine months. Sixty-two training sessions.

'To see the kids at Sunshine was an eye-opener, Doctor. They looked healthy and well-cared for. They're not with their families, but they seemed happy. I think if our neglected Shiners could find safe homes, the same would happen for them. Make sense to you?'

'Security is an important foundation for health, even for teenagers who are eager to try out their wings. My goodness, it's hard to isolate one factor as the most important. But if you don't have to worry about where you're going to sleep, it's easier to go to school, easier to get a job, and you've got more time for leisure.'

The boys were jostling eagerly as they lined up.

'You know, I don't know every boy's situation as well as I should. How about we ask around while they're eating? D'you think that's a good idea or not? Or maybe too intrusive?'

'Let's do it, Joe. These boys lack adult attention. They'll welcome your interest, I'm sure.'

9

Singh had headphones on. She motioned Horseman to join her in front of the TV recording trolley beside her desk. How had she got that? The station's few machines were usually broken or in the chief super's office. He pulled his chair over and put on the earphones she handed him.

News Focus was just starting. Indira Choudhury spoke to the camera, her eyes wide and unblinking, her tone confiding. Did she really think this trick would convince viewers they were about to witness a sensation? She could well be right.

'The controversial release on parole of convicted child torturer Dev Reddy has stirred the parents of Fiji to protest. Yesterday, News at Noon covered a rally outside the gates of Suva Prison—the very portals from which Reddy will emerge, a free man, tomorrow. Our cameras were there again today to bring you a much bigger protest this afternoon. Tonight, our focus is on the leader of those rallies, Mr Ravai Nata.'

The camera panned to reveal the pudgy-faced man sitting beside the presenter, a jug of water and two glasses on a table between them. He had dressed up for the interview in a white shirt, blue tie and dark grey jacket. Nervous, he looked at the camera and said, '*Bula vinaka.*'

'Mr Nata, why did you demonstrate at the prison yesterday?'

Nata cleared his throat. 'Because I am outraged, outraged that a man who is guilty of the most despicable crime is about to rejoin society after only eleven years behind bars. Only half his sentence. A man who has tortured his own child for nine years should be banished from society for life! For life! All the members of God's Gospel Church are of the same opinion. We know we speak for the nation when we demand our government reverse this wrong decision.'

Nata's voice, at first hesitant, strengthened to a resonant bass as he spoke.

'Tell us about your role in your church, Mr Nata.'

'I am a lay preacher. My church recognises God called me to preach the gospel. Jesus proclaimed sins against children could not be forgiven. He said, "It would be better for him if a great millstone were hung around his neck and he were thrown into the sea". God's punishment is worse than that. On Monday night, God moved me to found a group we call Hands Off Our Kids, or HOOK. Our aim is to hook up evildoers and remove them from society. That is what the police and the courts are supposed to do, but they don't. They go easy on the likes of Dev Reddy.'

'The Controller of Prisons stated that Reddy's sentence was reduced because of his good behaviour, his old age and his medical condition. He claims the public is at no risk at all from him. Don't you agree the law should show compassion?' Ms Choudhury's tone was sarcastic.

Nata gazed into the camera. 'I believe the law should show compassion, yes, but not to Reddy, the man who imprisoned his son in a fowl yard for ten years! For ten years! Leaving him an imbecile who pecks his food from the ground! Compassion belongs with the victims, the innocent children.'

'Forty per cent of Fijians are Hindus or Muslims. Is HOOK just for Christians?'

Was Indira interviewing or providing a platform?

Nata smiled a little. It was obvious this was the question he wanted, the chance to show his campaign against Reddy was free of prejudice against the ethnic Indian population, of whom Reddy was one.

'Absolutely not! All three religions in Fiji condemn crimes against children. HOOK urges all parents to help us hook up evil and cast it out.'

'How can they do that, Mr Nata?'

He held up one finger. 'One, by telling us about evildoers who sin against children. By all means, report to the police, but we've just seen how soft the law is these days. These days, we know the police don't bother to do anything about such reports.'

Now he raised two fingers. 'Two, by bringing direct pressure on these criminals: gather around their homes, tell them of God's condemnation every time they enter or leave the house. Eventually, their guilt will force them to scurry away, scurry away.'

Singh looked at him, her face as appalled as Horseman felt.

He showed three fingers to the viewers. 'Three, help by giving us any small donations you can spare to fund our work. You can give in person at God's Gospel Church at Samambula or deposit at any branch of the ANZ Bank, account number 374-872.'

'Thank you very much, Mr Nata. You have given our viewers food for thought.'

Had the presenter delayed just a little before cutting off Nata's bank account details? Would a Fiji One boss rap her over the knuckles for what amounted to soliciting donations?

'He's got a bank account set up since the interview yesterday,' Singh observed.

'He's ramped up the volume, too. Something worries me, though. He stops just short of incitement to violence. Suggests to me he's thought this out carefully for some time, or that he's got an advisor who knows the law. I suspect it's the latter.'

'I agree. Anyway, it just confirms that Nata and HOOK should stay on our list of threats to public order.'

'Certainly does. Let's move them up the list.'

A tap at the door heralded a constable bearing a loaded tin tray. Spicy aromas circulated through the CID floor.

'Your order Detective Sergeant?'

'Yes, thank you. Put it on my desk, please.'

'Raj said he'll be across to collect the tray before they close. So, if you can bring it down to reception when you've finished...'

'*Io, vinaka vakalevu*, Constable. How thoughtful of you, Susie,' Horseman said. 'Are we expecting company?'

'No, I just thought we deserved it. And unlike you, sir, I think we could be in for a late one with this report.'

'You do? I'd better get the tea, then.'

'Let's eat first. I've got a draft structure done. We can fine-tune that while we eat.'

'Sure, then it's just fill in the gaps, eh?' He patted his stomach.

Singh rolled her eyes in mock despair.

FRIDAY

10

Singh woke in terror. But the grinding roar was only a back-hoe moving past the women officers' barracks. Maybe plumbers had come to fix the centimetre of water that had flooded the bathroom two months ago and still not drained away.

What had happened to her six o'clock alarm? She grabbed at her trusty pink plastic alarm clock. It showed eight o'clock. She confirmed the time on her mobile phone. She must have slept through the alarm. As she'd expected, they didn't get the report done until eleven o'clock. She'd fallen into bed as soon as she'd got home, but hadn't slept well.

At least the bathrooms weren't closed for repairs yet. It depressed her to have to paddle through the flooded floor after her shower. She'd rather not consider the trillions of bacteria and worse multiplying in the lukewarm water. When she got back to her room, she wiped her feet with antiseptic and dressed rapidly in her royal blue trouser suit and yellow blouse. No time for a bun, even though she might have to present their report to the security super. She snatched a scrunchy and combed her hair back into a ponytail.

Why did she even stay in barracks? Few women sergeants did. They were either married or lived with relatives. Just five other women were living in the sergeants' apartments. Still, the word *barracks* said it all. Military accommodation, even though in a leafy suburb, close to the centre of Suva. She could never afford private accommodation around here. And she liked to save money. Since she had moved to Suva, her frequent paid overtime swelled her pay packet every month. She was amassing more than she had expected.

However, when she made detective inspector, she would have to find her own accommodation. And she desperately wanted to be the first woman detective inspector in the Fiji Police Force. Her only genuine regret would be leaving Horseman, the best boss she'd ever had. Really, the only superior who'd treated her as an equal in her entire career. The others hadn't treated her badly, but Horseman had shown her what true respect was. And she didn't idolise him like most; she didn't care about rugby. But it would be a miracle if there was an opening for another detective inspector in Suva station.

She dashed out the barracks' gate and across the road to the bus stop. No, she'd be mad to delay applying for promotion to spend longer in cheap housing or clinging to a sympathetic boss. She mustn't be sentimental. In fact, she'd take immediate steps towards her priority goal: promotion. She'd been studying whenever she got the chance, which wasn't often enough. She would get the schedule for DI exams next year and make sure she met all the requirements. She'd need Horseman's support, so she'd have to tell him her plans. She knew she could trust him absolutely, but she hated confiding her dreams to anyone.

The bus pulled up with a grating of gears that set her teeth on edge. She hopped up the steep steps, paid her fare and squeezed down the aisle. Usually she gazed towards the sea, but this morning she examined the houses out the window. Best to start looking for accommodation now. She had no idea of the Suva rental market at all but suspected she was in for a rude awakening. Unless the nonsense sparked by Reddy's release blew up, she'd start on Saturday.

She agreed with Horseman: the major security threats were to Reddy himself. But she had doubts about the wisdom of releasing into the community an old man with no family support. Especially a schizophrenic who believed his son had disappeared twenty years ago, and a demon had replaced him.

11

Acting Superintendent Ratini summoned Horseman and Singh by telephone. Ratini's office was two metres from their CID door. Superintendent Navala would have simply loomed in the CID doorway if he'd wanted him. But Ratini had every right to run his office his way, Horseman reminded himself.

Ratini must have approved of the report because he chose to present it himself to the security chief this morning. That was the highest praise Ratini was ever likely to give him. But he wondered what spin he would put on the document.

'I suppose we're about to find out how our work was received,' he said to Singh as they approached the door.

'Come in, come in!' Ratini's voice was gravelly.

They entered and waited. Ratini frowned at them, open-mouthed as if their action was preposterous.

'*Oi lei, oi lei,* sit down!' he barked.

Ratini looked at Singh. He smiled. 'I'm not annoyed at you, Susie. I'm a bit irritated by Security's attitude. Don't get me wrong, the chief appreciated the quality of our report. But he cross-examined me on every point!'

'That must have been difficult, sir. Quite unfair, as you only joined us on Wednesday.' Singh sounded all sweet sympathy. Ratini looked up, alert, but Singh looked as she sounded.

'Did they accept our findings?' Horseman hoped this question was vague enough not to alarm Ratini.

Ratini wagged his head, judicious. '*Io,* by and large. The chief was pleased to have the list of prison troublemakers—we saved them a lot of work there. And the nutters who didn't give up campaigning for the death penalty for years after the Reddy trial. Of course, Ravai Nata and the other rabble-rousers popping up this week were already on their radar.'

'Are Security's plans finalised, sir?'

'They'd better be, Reddy's released in six hours. I gather the plans are standard for any large gatherings that might spill onto the streets. Extra constables around the parks and major streets, courts, prison—obvious really. Mobile squads on standby and so on.'

'What about protection for Reddy? We pointed out that he's the person at most risk from his release.'

'I don't get your attitude to that mad bastard, Horseman. Do you, Susie? You've got more sympathy for him than for his wretched son.'

'Not at all, sir. I recommended that both Reddy and the Sunshine Home need round-the-clock police protection.'

'They said something about mounting a guard on the Sunshine Home for twenty-four hours. But I don't think they're in the mood to do anything for Reddy beyond escorting him home. Even that's a concession, don't you think? I wouldn't care if someone murdered him outside the prison gates. And the nation's with me.' He smirked.

Ratini would like nothing better than an argument, but he wouldn't get one.

'Do you know the details of Reddy's escort, sir?'

Ratini puffed out his cheeks and slowly released the air as if his patience was being tested. 'No, it's not relevant to Suva Central CID, is it?'

'I'll check on that with Security, for my own peace of mind. Crime prevention and all that, sir.'

Ratini shrugged. 'Those jewellery thieves will love this, eh? Police attention elsewhere. Tomorrow I want your crew back on their trail.'

'*Vinaka*, sir.' Horseman could hardly believe Ratini was allowing him the rest of the day on Reddy. Maybe he knew more than he was letting on and was toying with him.

***

'Susie, get the boys back on the jewellery case. Lend them to Inspector Vula for the rest of the day. They need to be up to speed. I've got a feeling the fallout from Reddy's release is going to be worse than our acting superintendent imagines. Police are responsible for protecting a released prisoner from known threats. If no one else wants to take that on, you and I must.'

Singh grinned. 'I think you're right, sir. Definitely. Don't worry about Tani and Apo. I'll make sure they know their duty!'

'Oh, and please use your prison contact to find out exactly what the arrangements are for Reddy's release. I need to get it from the horse's mouth. Will they process him at the prison or St Giles?'

'Yep, I'm on it.'

***

He called Security Division. To his disappointment, the sergeant confirmed that no resources would be allocated for Reddy's protection after he was driven to his farmhouse in a police vehicle.

'That's far more than any other released prisoner gets,' the sergeant commented.

'It's not enough, considering the risks to the man's safety,' Horseman said.

'You're fair-minded, I'll give you that, sir. But most people hate the man—scared of him, too. A man who could do that to his son—he could do anything to anyone. Heaven only knows what's going on in his mind! He's a mad dog, that one. Good people just want to stay well away from evil like what's in him.'

'Let's hope they do. If people are so scared that they don't go anywhere near him, there'll be no problems. Just a few noisy demonstrations in Suva that you guys can handle easily.'

'*Io*, that's what we're expecting.'

'Are you posting a guard on Sunshine Home?'

'*Io, vinaka* for that tip. A constable's already up there. We hadn't thought of that ourselves. If no one has been sniffing around after twenty-four hours, we might pull him out.'

'I recommend keeping a guard on until Monday morning.'

'*Io, io*, I hear you. People are outraged about crimes against children, but if we can't spare a constable to protect these little ones who have no homes of their own, we're just hypocrites, aren't we? Nothing but hypocrites. I'll tell the chief what you said.'

'*Vinaka vakalevu*, Sergeant. I'll send him an email and mention you've been helpful.'

'Been thinking, sir, I'd like to help you out with your shoe-shine boys' team. If there's something I can do. Third-grade Police team for seven years before I got married and put on weight. Those boys are rascals, but you're doing something for them. Something good.'

'*Vinaka*, Sergeant. You'll be a great asset to me and the boys. Turn up when you can: Mondays and Thursdays at half-past four at Albert Park. The Shiners do as much for me as I do for them, but it's what they're doing for themselves and each other that could make all the difference to their lives.'

The sergeant chuckled. '*Io*, off the streets and out of trouble for two afternoons a week, at least.'

***

'Dr Acharya, I'll get straight to the point. Reddy is due to be released in five hours from Suva Prison. Demonstrators will protest at the gates before and during his release. The media will be in a frenzy, too. We will drive him to Rewa in a police vehicle, which will probably be followed. All this presents some physical risk to Reddy. From what I've learned, mainly from you, his mental state could suffer much more gravely. What's your professional opinion?'

Silence for a few moments, then a sigh. 'I agree with you. Such circumstances would be stressful for anyone, but for Reddy, they could easily trigger a psychotic episode. If I'd foreseen any of this media circus, I wouldn't have signed off the standard release arrangements.'

Another pause. Horseman waited.

'The situation has ramped up quickly. How could you have predicted it? What I'm hoping is that you'll do something about it now. But it would have to be right now. Immediately.'

The psychiatrist must be used to making instant decisions when patients suffered crises, surely.

'Yes, I can try. I'll ring a prison official—one of the few who value my opinion. I'll urge him to authorise Reddy's release from St Giles. But I have a fail-safe Plan B, which I've used just once before.' The doctor's tone was firm now.

'Fail-safe sounds like what I'm looking for, Doctor.'

'Yes, I can refuse to surrender custody of Reddy to the prison officers when they come to pick him up. There's nothing they can do.'

'Sounds good.'

'There's a fair chance the official channel will work, however. Give me your direct number again and I'll let you know how I get on.'

'*Vinaka*, good luck, Doctor.'

Next, he had to get a sense of Ravai Nata's potential for damage. He knew where he'd be. And he wanted Singh with him.

12

God's Gospel Church was a modest timber-framed structure with a red corrugated iron roof. Panels of odd sizes and materials formed the walls, united by sky-blue paint. One of the newer charismatic churches that had popped up in Suva, it benefited more from its congregation's enthusiasm than from their money. Situated in a back street of Samabula along with modest car-repair workshops, a bakery and tailoring businesses, Horseman doubted the congregation had much spare cash.

He parked further down the street and walked up. His leg wasn't cooperating today; he needed to stretch it.

'Looks like the HOOK rally is assembling here, all right.'

A dozen or so people milled around the church door. Colourfully dressed in sulus, they chattered and smiled, in a festive mood.

'*Bula vinaka*, is Mr Nata inside?'

Some of the women exclaimed when they recognised him. A couple of men offered their hands.

'Welcome, Josefa Horseman. *Io*, Ravai is inside.'

About fifty people thronged the space. Many were working on cardboard signs: lettering, trimming, fixing to rough handles. Others clustered in small groups, praying. At the centre of the action was Ravai Nata. He was shorter than Horseman expected, pudgy-faced and overweight for a man in his thirties.

'An unlikely leader, don't you think?' he asked Singh as they watched the bustle.

Singh raised her eyebrows, considering. 'Not sure. He's certainly a leader, though. At Wednesday's rally outside the prison, I noticed how all his people's eyes were on him. Most of them were a bit nervous, but as he spoke, they gained courage from him. You could feel it. He's a rousing speaker.'

'Hmm. That mightn't be so good for us. But I can't really see this lot hurling rocks, can you?'

'I know what you mean. I hope not.'

'Let's introduce ourselves.'

'Josefa Horseman! I never thought I'd meet my idol!' As he pumped his hand, Nata gazed at Horseman as if he was the only person in the church. He had large, wide-spaced eyes, full lips and the warm, rich voice Horseman remembered from the TV interview.

'I'd like to have a chat with you somewhere quiet, Mr Nata.'

'Indeed, indeed. There's a small office back here. Is it about HOOK's protest at the prison gates this afternoon?'

Nata led them to a partitioned room at the back of the church, set up as an office. He graciously gestured to a battered old table with six plastic chairs arranged around it. Nata took the head so Horseman and Singh sat together on one side.

'Mr Nata, you may not have realised the police are treating Reddy's release as a threat to public order in Suva.'

Nata's shoulders straightened. '*Io, io,* of course it's a threat. That's the reason we founded HOOK just last Tuesday. That's the very message we want all Fiji citizens to understand.'

He leaned forward, one hand extended in a gentle, inclusive gesture.

'Releasing a man like Reddy, full of evil, is a deadly threat to the children of Fiji and therefore to everyone. If we can tolerate such evil, what does that tolerance do to us? It means we accept evil, we give up on respecting God's commandments, we stop endeavouring to build a world where mothers and children are free from the fear of evildoers. Such tolerance corrupts us.'

'Believe me, DS Singh and I are committed to building a world like you describe. We do it through enforcing the law, without favour to anyone.'

Nata leaned back a bit. 'I wasn't aware I had broken the law?'

Horseman smiled. 'As far as I know, you haven't. But I want you to understand the police consider there's a risk that could happen. At a crowded rally, people can mill about on the road, causing accidents. People get worked up, angry, throw stones and other missiles. Angry people lash out at others who disagree with them. People get hurt, even in Fiji.'

Nata relaxed. 'Josefa, I understand what you're saying. But the scene you fear will not happen at a HOOK rally. We are Christian parents. We will peacefully express our views, which are the views of the vast majority of Fijians. The idea of us using violence is, well, preposterous.'

'That's good to hear, Mr Nata,' Singh said. 'But it happens. I've experienced it myself, personally, in the aftermath of the rallies about land leases some years ago. Some people get fired up over their grievance, they hardly know what they're doing. They break the law and, yes, hurt people without thinking. And it makes them feel good, powerful. Next, they want to feel that power more, so... I think you get the picture.'

'We're here to ask you, as a law-abiding citizen and Christian family man, to use moderate language to express your viewpoint this afternoon. You clearly have a lot of influence over the others here. Please use it wisely. I urge you to prevent your followers from taking the law into their own hands.'

'Police officers will be there to keep order and protect everyone's safety. But it would be much better if that weren't necessary.' Horseman smiled and stood up.

Nata also stood and offered his hand. 'HOOK members are law-abiding. We will express our views strongly, as is our right. But only in words, Josefa, only in words.'

13

'Reddy for freedom?—No! Reddy for freedom?—No!' The chant got louder with every repetition.

'Reddy to die in prison? Yes! Reddy to die in prison? Yes!' The new chant found favour with the protestors, quickly drowning out the first. The pun on the prisoner's name suggested to Singh they were planned and shared the same author. Ravai Nata didn't strike her as the witty type. But you never knew—a lesson she'd often been taught but hadn't learned.

Dev Reddy was due to walk through the gates of Suva Prison at half-past four.

He was five minutes late and the protestors were getting impatient. They waved their placards with vigour. Some signs proclaimed HOOK —Hands Off Our Kids, others repeated the text of the chants. Yet others, scruffy and scrawled on flattened cardboard cartons, exhorted viewers to Get Rid of Reddy, Keep Evil Behind Bars, Suffer the Little Children, Unforgiven, and more.

Singh estimated around two hundred protesters, all getting restive. They surged against the prison doors. That would get them nowhere, but they couldn't do any harm. Plenty of constables were about.

She skirted around the edge of the crowd, making sure she was not within the scope of TV camera lenses, then joined the footpath beside the high concrete prison wall. About a hundred metres along, the wall turned right, skirting a narrow side street. She half-expected another crowd around the solid steel gates of the vehicle entrance fifty metres on. But no, only a few bored reporters, leaning against the wall and smoking. They'd already given up. She turned. No one had followed her. Too caught up in their own fervour.

Without warning, the gates slid apart and Singh slipped inside. She got in the waiting police vehicle. The instant the gap between the gates was a centimetre wider than the car, the driver gunned the engine and sped away. The reporters were caught napping. They dived on their mobile phones and ran for their cars.

Despite her nerves, she'd enjoyed that. She wondered how Horseman was doing. Why hadn't he called her?

***

Dr Acharya was resolute. He smiled kindly at the prison official who had come to transport Dev Reddy back down the hill to the prison to go through the discharge process.

'Come on, Officer, you've known me for years. I understand perfectly that we don't normally discharge patients from prison here at St Giles. I know better than anyone that St Giles is a hospital, not a prison. However, Mr Reddy's medical condition has changed and I can't allow him to go there right now. You have done nothing wrong. I'm sorry you've had a trip for nothing.'

The prison officer looked unconvinced, but as Dr Acharya had told Horseman, there was nothing he could do. Essie, the ever-cheerful assistant, lifted his mood with a mug of sweet milky tea and a plate of Paradise biscuits. She then served Horseman and the doctor.

'Is your driver waiting in your vehicle? Tell him to come in. I've poured him a mug already. It's waiting for him at the reception counter.'

'*Vinaka*,' the officer smiled and spoke into his radio transmitter. 'He'll be here in a moment.'

It took time to change discharge arrangements. But Singh would get the prison manager moving. If Reddy had to run the gauntlet of the media and protesters at the prison, he would surely flip out, or whatever the medical term was.

Dr Acharya's phone buzzed. He snatched it up. Ten seconds later, he smiled with relief. 'Relax now, Officer, and enjoy your tea. That was your boss, Mr Domo. He will arrive in a few minutes to discharge Mr Reddy himself.'

Horseman downed his tea, then paced outside reception, looking out for the police car. When Singh waved from the back seat as the car pulled into the gravel bay, he wanted to yell, 'Mission accomplished!'

Singh introduced Domo. Horseman shook hands heartily and they went back to Dr Acharya's office.

'I'm grateful to you for coming, Mr Domo. Obviously, you found my updated medical assessment convincing. I'm happy to elaborate further or answer any questions you may have.'

'Not necessary, Doctor. Your opinion is trusted. I understand that patients' conditions change, often suddenly.'

'Indeed, you're right. In this case, Mr Reddy's still fit to be discharged from St Giles. It's the incredible media campaign against him that I didn't foresee. And all these demonstrators with nothing better to do than harass the mentally ill. That's what could trigger his relapse into psychosis.'

'*Oi lei*! Some people! Why can't they mind their own business?'

'Do you want to meet Mr Reddy on the ward? Or shall we bring him up here to reception?'

'Here is good. You can send for him now. You've got the paperwork for me?'

Dr Acharya handed over a bundle of different coloured papers. 'You'll find it's all complete.'

Domo checked through carefully. Then he extracted papers from his satchel, copied some details and ticked some boxes.

A tap on the open door and an orderly ushered Dev Reddy in. The man was around seventy and looked his age. Short, stooped from a lifetime of farm work, he looked up at Horseman. His hooded eyes were ringed by black patches like bruises. His cropped hair was still thick and quite white.

'Aren't I knowing you from the television? You're Joe Horseman, the rugby player.' He glanced at Dr Acharya for confirmation. His eyes were shrewd enough.

'Spot on, Dev. Let me introduce you. Inspector Horseman is a police officer. He's coming with us to your farm, help you settle in.'

Reddy ducked his head and shook Horseman's hand for a long time. 'Thank you, sir.'

The doctor introduced Singh, whom Reddy greeted with suspicion.

Domo asked Reddy for his personal details, which he gave correctly and with no obvious effort. 'Do you understand I'm releasing you from prison today? You'll be a free man as long as you obey the law. Your parole officer will visit you tomorrow and set up a regular weekly meeting with you. You must meet your parole officer every week or you'll have to go back to prison. Can you do that?'

Reddy ducked his head. 'Yes, sir. Thank you.'

'Where are you going to live?'

'In my farmhouse on my block in Rewa.'

'Are your family there?'

'No, sir. My wife is dead and my children are all leaving long ago.'

'Will you be all right?'

'Yes, sir. I am liking farm work. And my youngest son may be coming home. I hope so.'

Domo looked sharply at the doctor, who smiled back.

'We'll miss your work in the gardens, Dev. You've trebled our vegetable production.'

Dev looked behind him, fearful. 'The others are knowing what to do. Just be making them do it. Don't be letting them get lazy.' He frowned in disapproval.

The doctor smiled. 'I'll do my best, Dev.'

Reddy looked doubtful.

'Have you got all your possessions with you?'

Reddy nodded. 'Yes, sir.'

The orderly lifted a black Flying Fijians sports bag.

'Good. Well, sign this form, and you're a free man.'

Reddy signed. Domo countersigned.

'You've served your sentence. Good luck, man.'

'Where is the bus stop, sir?' Reddy asked.

'Dev, have you forgotten? I will drive you to your farmhouse in my car. Inspector Horseman and Sergeant Singh will come, too, and check you're safe.'

Reddy bowed his already stooped back. 'Thank you, sir, but there is no need.'

Horseman and Singh exchanged a glance. He doubted the old man was fit for independent life after eleven years of incarceration.

'Let's get going,' the doctor said, picking up Reddy's bag.

'We'll follow you, Doctor,' Horseman said.

As Singh approached Reservoir Road, Horseman noticed a couple get in a white Mazda parked at the side of the road. The woman had binoculars around her neck. They pulled out about fifty metres behind Doctor Acharya.

'Susie, d'you think they parked there for the spectacular views from the clifftop?' He noted the Mazda's number.

'I hope so, sir. We'll know soon enough.'

Horseman radioed the number through to Traffic for checking and prayed his sudden fear was groundless.

14

An hour later, they crawled across the Rewa bridge and into dusty Nausori.

'Half-past five on Friday—couldn't be a worse time for this trip.'

He was impatient to get out of the peak-hour traffic, where they were so exposed. The surge of adrenalin hadn't completely subsided, either.

'Won't be long now, sir. I haven't spotted the white Mazda for a while. That's good, isn't it?'

'Possibly.' His mobile rang.

'*Bula*, Doctor... good... good.' He ended the call.

'Reddy says they're about ten minutes away.'

Once past the little Suva International Airport, they left the traffic behind. A left turn took them along rutted gravel roads through a landscape of lush intensive horticulture. Dense groves of bananas and pawpaws, plantations of root crops with their leafy tops, intensive patches of tomato bushes, plots of spiky pineapples and endless rice fields.

'A feast for the eyes, isn't it? I feel more optimistic already.'

'Man, these farmers know their stuff! You don't get a patchwork like this in the west. I feel hungry just driving past!'

'Yep. Mind you, it'd be hard to fail on the Rewa alluvial flats. Best horticultural land in the country, my Mum always said. Is it okay with you to turn the air-con off?'

Singh nodded and Horseman flicked the switch. He lowered the window and breathed in the soft, damp, earthy air. Still hot and sticky, but natural.

'I'd better concentrate on the map.'

He spotted the red roof of Dr Acharya's car glinting, parked under the shade of a spreading mango tree. After all this time, the only evidence of a lane or driveway into Reddy's farm was a couple of concrete pipes laid in the deep drainage ditch beside the road. Any planks that may once have bridged the pipes had rotted away. Still, Dr Acharya's sedan had made it. Singh eased the bigger police vehicle across and followed the track of flattened weeds to park behind the other car.

The doctor emerged from behind the mango tree.

'Come in, we're in the house.'

They waded through weeds, past orange, guava and banana trees that provided food and shade in the past. The corrugated iron house sat about a metre off the ground on stumps. A pitched roof defined the original farmhouse in the middle of the building. Like everyone else, over the years the Reddy family had added lean-to rooms on three sides and a verandah across the front. But the Reddys had achieved a superior level of prosperity at some stage in the past: the verandah was closed in with glass louvres rather than wooden shutters. What's more, bamboo gutters edged part of the roof, carrying rainwater to a tank fitted with a tap at the side of the house. This was a rare convenience for smallholders.

But now the house was neglected. The split guttering was choked by flourishing weeds, and the roof and walls showed rusty streaks through the peeling paint.

Horseman felt a surge of dread. 'How can this place be habitable?'

The doctor looked embarrassed. 'The social worker was supposed to make sure it was okay—at least a minimum standard. But Dev is pleased to be here. Let's go in and face the worst.'

They ascended the wooden steps one at a time—Horseman last, as he was the heaviest. Reddy appeared in the doorway. His eyes darted around like he was confused about where he was. But he seemed to recover in a few moments.

'Thank you, *ovisas*. Welcome to my house. It is still here.' The corners of his mouth turned up slightly.

There was no electricity, although Horseman had noticed lights in farmhouses as they drove along this road. Power lines must have reached these farmlands after Reddy went to prison. In the dimness, Horseman could just make out a wooden workbench around two sides of the room, with open shelves underneath. A spirit stove sat at one end of the bench. Someone had stacked basic supplies at the other end. Cooking pots hung from hooks on the wall. A few plastic drums of water stood neatly beside new plastic washing bowls. The floor was swept and a new coconut broom stood in a corner. Someone had made an effort.

'May I open the shutters?' Horseman almost gagged at the heavy, musty air, laced with rodent droppings stirred up by the sweeping.

'Yes, sir,' Reddy replied. He looked behind him, then stepped behind Horseman, peering out of each shutter after Horseman opened it and fitted the prop.

Light flooded in. An old table and chairs filled most of the room. A cupboard stood beside the front door and two tin trunks sat against the opposite wall. Shelves attached to the wall held a few framed photographs, dusty books. In pride of place was a Hindu house shrine with religious statues and brass bowls. Faded pictures of the elephant god, Ganesh, and a goddess hung on a wall, their edges curling.

'Can you show me the rest of your house, Dev?' Dr Acharya asked with a smile.

Reddy straightened his back, revealing just a trace of the proud householder. 'You come, *ovisas*.'

As their eyes adjusted to the near-dark, Horseman considered the low platform beds, the few cupboards and chests. Where were the colourful curtains, hangings and pictures all jostling for space in the typical Indian home, however humble?

'Let me make you your first cup of tea, Mr Reddy.'

'Thank you, Josefa Horseman. Please, call me Dev.'

He poured water into a pan, set it on the stove, then searched for matches.

'Have you got matches, Dev?' Reddy produced them from a pocket and lit the stove. He then lit a hurricane lamp and placed it on the table.

When the water boiled, Horseman threw tea leaves in a small pot, poured on the boiling water and stirred in sugar. He found three chipped enamel mugs, a glass cup and two spoons, put them in a plastic bowl and poured the hot water over them. He let them sit for a minute. The social worker hadn't bought milk but there was a tube of sweetened condensed milk. Singh helped him carry the things to the table.

Reddy looked as proud as if he'd conjured a feast for his guests. He offered condensed milk to everyone, but only he and Singh added it to their tea. The sweet tea aroma worked to reduce the musty, rancid smell of the house. It was almost cosy in the lamp's glow. He still couldn't imagine this situation working out for Reddy. With no family support, how could he survive, let alone manage his illness?

As if he read Horseman's mind, Dr Acharya asked, 'Dev, how do you like it back in your old farmhouse?'

'I hoped my youngest son would be coming back by now. But maybe he sees I am returning, and he will be coming tomorrow.' His mouth curved slightly in a sad smile.

'Doctor, who did the shopping and cleaning?' Singh asked.

'I asked the social worker at St Giles to check on the situation and got a key copied for her. Precisely who did the work, I don't know. I'll ask her tomorrow. But he's got what he needs for a few days if he doesn't feel like going out straight away.'

'Is there a neighbour you can ask for help if you need it?' Horseman asked.

'I won't be needing help. My neighbour, Gopal, will be here soon.'

'Dev, now I've seen how remote your farm is, I doubt you're safe here. You're taking a colossal risk in staying here. As a police officer, I'm not happy about it.' Reddy said nothing; just gazed around the room.

Singh smiled at Reddy. 'Have you got a phone? I don't see one here in the living room.'

Reddy frowned. 'No. Telephones may bring bad news. I don't want one. But there's a public phone back down my road, on the corner. It's only a ten-minute walk.'

Horseman tried one last time. 'Until you get used to life outside St Giles, you would be much safer in lodgings with someone to look after you, Dev. Dr Acharya can get you a place like that, can't you, Doctor?'

The doctor smiled. 'I can and I've already told you about that, Dev? But you turned it down. Do you want to change your mind? You still can.'

'No, I'm not changing my mind. I've had enough of other people. And if I'm here on my own, my son may come home.'

The doctor patted his patient on the shoulder. 'You can decide where you want to live now, Dev. You're no longer a prisoner or a hospital patient.'

Horseman knew the challenge of entering the outside world after an extended spell in hospital. Even for the sane, like himself. He couldn't see Reddy coping at all, even without angry haters who wanted him dead.

He handed Reddy his business card. 'Dev, if you change your mind, please go to the public phone and call me. If you're in any trouble, please call me. I'll help you.'

Reddy examined the card with care, then put it in his pocket.

They were finishing their tea when there was a rap on the wall and a firm voice called out. 'Dev? Are you home now, Dev?'

'Here is Gopal,' Reddy told them. He opened the door.

Gopal hesitated when he saw the people sitting at the table. Reddy waved him in.

Gopal nodded to Dev. '*Namaste.*'

'*Namaste*, Gopal. Come, have tea with us.'

Gopal looked around the room. 'No, no, thank you. I just came to check you were back here, Dev.'

Gopal kicked off his flip flops and came further into the room. He stood by the table, shifting from one foot to the other. Despite his nervousness, he stood erect. He looked about fifty, taller and stronger than Reddy.

They all shook hands and introduced themselves. Gopal's hand was muscular, dry and calloused. He'd clearly washed after his day's farm work and dressed neatly in clean clothes: a checked shirt and grey polyester trousers. Why had he prepared so carefully to visit Reddy?

'I see you have some help, so I'll go. Goodnight to you all.'

Horseman followed him to the door, stepping out to the small landing. He spoke quietly.

'Gopal, it's a relief to me to see Dev has a good neighbour, after all this time. Do you have a telephone?'

Gopal pulled a battered old mobile out of his pocket. He held it out with pride.

'You're more interested in technology than most farmers. I'd be grateful if you could help me,' Horseman said.

'I'll be happy to help, Inspector Horseman. What can I do?'

'You've probably seen the TV or papers. Do you know about the protesters against Reddy's release?'

Gopal nodded. Horseman couldn't read his attitude.

'It's possible they'll come here. I don't expect you to keep watch—not at all. But if you hear any shouting around this house, please call me. Dev's been threatened and he's alone.' He handed Gopal his card.

'My farmhouse is some distance away. But if I notice any disturbance, I'll call you.'

'It worries me that none of Reddy's children communicates with him. Do you know why that is?'

Gopal shook his head. 'That's a long story, Inspector Horseman. And I must be going home now. Goodnight.'

'I'm grateful for your help, Gopal.'

Horseman was reluctant to leave Reddy, but unless he took on the role of night watchman, there wasn't much more he could do. While Dr Acharya took Reddy carefully through his medication regime, the two detectives washed up, then patrolled the overgrown farmyard. Funnily enough, beyond the few sheds and overgrown house orchard, plantations of orderly crops flourished. A cow lowed in the distance. Mynah birds shrieked as they roosted in the mango trees. But there was no sign of human life. It was dark when they drove off, leaving Reddy alone.

SATURDAY

15

'*Yadra*, Mr Horseman. Kiti Samisoni, Paradise Real Estate.' Her eagerness gushed from the phone.

He'd made the appointment days ago and forgotten all about it. He put down his toast. The TV morning news was reassuring: crowds of protesters shouted demands and waved placards, but so far noise was the only problem and that wasn't a crime.

He killed the TV sound. '*Yadra*, Kiti. Am I late?'

'Not at all,' she lied. 'Would it help if I picked you up?'

'*Io*, let me give you the address.'

'Oh, that's close to a flat I'm going to show you. I'll be there in ten minutes.'

'*Vinaka*, I'll be ready.' He felt more positive already; he liked the old area where Matt Young lived. It was central and quiet. But the streets were lined with colonial weatherboard houses which he couldn't afford.

Kiti pulled up outside a large two-storey house built of concrete blocks. External stairs led to an uncovered landing on the first floor. Kiti flashed a dazzling smile. 'This flat may well be the answer to your prayers, Mr Horseman.'

'Call me Joe, please. Is it on the ground floor?'

'No, it's on the first. Beautiful fresh air and views. And there are only two flats upstairs.' Kiti spoke as if to a child at his birthday party.

He thought the louvred windows looked small. 'I can't wait to see inside.'

The railing on the stairs was rusty and loose. The door opened outwards, forcing him to back down the steps, so tiny was the landing. Inside was a spacious lobby smelling of fresh paint, some of which spotted the tiled floor. Three doors led off the lobby. Kiti unlocked one with a gold number 4.

'Didn't you say there were only two flats upstairs?' Horseman asked.

'*Io*, the upstairs flats are very spacious. Come on in, you'll be amazed at this living room.' Kiti smiled brightly.

Horseman wasn't amazed, but the living room was okay. The side windows looked into the house next door, but there was a view of the sky and trees through the back. No porch or verandah.

'And it includes the furniture, too.'

He sat on the low sofa and the wooden base bowed, forcing his right leg into a tight bend. He thrust it out straight and hauled himself upright using the sofa arm. Irritated, he lifted the thin foam cushion and a piece of plywood to reveal broken webbing trailing on the floor.

'If I was interested, I'd require the flat to be unfurnished.'

'That might be a problem for the landlord, but don't worry, Joe, everything's negotiable.'

'Let's see the kitchen, then.'

'The kitchen's off the lobby. Shall we finish up in here first?'

'That's a strange arrangement, isn't it? Going back out your front door every time you want something from the kitchen?'

'Oh, no one complains. These are popular flats.'

The kitchen was small, with a noisy fridge and a simple gas stove. There were padlocks on two full-length cupboards. Weird.

'Why the padlocks?'

'Oh, the other tenants, a nice young couple, like to keep their things exclusively for their own use. You have the same cupboard space on the other side, here.'

'Sorry, Kiti. I didn't understand this flat shared a kitchen. I'm wasting your time to see any more. I must have my own kitchen, inside my own front door.'

Kiti looked incredulous. 'Are you sure, Joe? These are very popular flats—never vacant for more than a week.'

'*Io*, I'm sure, Kiti.'

'In that case, I'll have to scrub the second flat off my list, too. However, my third flat is completely self-contained and may well be what you're looking for.'

'Where is it?'

'Up near Flagstaff.' Kiti's broad smile returned.

Flagstaff was an odd assortment of houses, small blocks of flats, shops and businesses. But there were more schools there than in any other part of Suva. Lots of schools meant the area was quiet at night.

'You'll have magnificent views from up here,' Kiti observed as they climbed higher above the town. She pulled up outside Suva's only residential tower: a building everyone loved to hate. Eight storeys and a lift were unknown in Fiji when it was built a dozen years ago.

'Have you ever visited one of these flats?' Kiti asked.

'No, I've never known anyone who lived here. I thought embassy staff and other foreigners lived here.'

'There are a lot of expatriates, but some Fijians, too.'

'No police officer, I bet.'

Kiti beamed. 'Ah, that's where you're wrong, Joe. There's a flat reserved for the current United Nations Police representative.'

'Hardly comparable to a detective inspector at Suva Central!'

'It's a different lifestyle from what we think is normal, but it has its advantages—security, a lift, a manager, cleaning service, for a start.' She ticked them off her fingers. 'Don't dismiss it without consideration.'

'Is the rent within my budget?'

'Um, well, slightly over. Not much!'

'Okay, I'll take a look, if only out of curiosity.'

There were four flats on the fifth floor. Kiti flung open the door, ushering Horseman through to light and glorious views of trees, the town, sea and sky. A sliding glass door led to a small balcony. He looked down and saw the rally around the courts and crowds filling Ratu Sukuna Park. They looked insignificant from this distance. Maybe this was the correct perspective.

'Wouldn't you feel wonderful waking up to this?' Kiti asked.

He had to admit he would.

'Wander through yourself. Poke your nose into everything,' Kiti invited.

The small flat reminded him of overseas hotels he'd stayed in for rugby tournaments. Compact, functional, efficient, impersonal. Designed so an expatriate single or couple could unpack their suitcases, be safe and comfortable for a year or two, then pack up and leave. Could this flat suit a Fijian, enmeshed in clan, village, church, gardening and gossip? No, it was an alien environment.

But the flat tugged at him. He wanted it, even though he knew he couldn't afford it - Kiti was tricking him. Perhaps he just needed to escape from the pressures of the job at the moment. Be on his own.

The phone vibrated in his pocket. He couldn't make out the caller's voice above the noise of other voices in the background.

'I can't hear! Speak up!'

'Gop—Insp—rseman, I—pal. Pl—co—!'

16

Horseman didn't try to decipher Gopal's precise message. The fear in his voice and the anger of the shouts that masked his words were enough. Standing on the balcony high above the roofs of Suva, he first called Nausori, the nearest police station to Gopal. He convinced the duty sergeant to dispatch as many constables as could be mustered to Reddy's address. Next he contacted Security, but no constables could be spared as the crowds in Suva were building up.

'*Vinaka* for letting me know, Joe. I'll keep in touch with Nausori.'

Next, Ratini, who answered his phone with an impatient growl.

'Why are you bothering me with this on a Saturday morning? I'm looking at houses today. Have you any idea what a hell that is? Just about the most exasperating morning of my life so far! And it's not ten o'clock yet!'

It was the first time he'd ever felt empathy with Ratini. 'I know it's difficult, sir. They tell me it's a simple equation of supply and demand.'

'*Oi lei*! It's got to be rigged, must be. And not by a policeman! I feel like marching right back to the Yasawas. My wife's going to hate Suva, I know. The town's changed a lot in a decade and not for the better.'

'Sir, I wanted to let you know protestors are out at Reddy's farm. I promised him I'd come if there was trouble. I'm heading there now.'

Ratini gave a half-hearted growl. 'Can't Nausori handle that?'

'I don't know, sir. Dispersing the troublemakers shouldn't be a problem. But they won't understand the context. I want to find out who's involved and why, so I can protect Reddy.'

'You don't have much choice, do you? This is what comes of making wild promises to help people instead of sticking to protocols.'

Horseman could tell Ratini's heart wasn't in his grumbling.

'*Vinaka*, sir. Good luck with your house-hunting.'

'Hell, I'd rather be hunting criminals. Better rate of success.'

***

Horseman leaned on the Landcruiser's horn and barged through the fist-wavers and police arguing on the road outside Reddy's house. A police car and paddy-wagon parked on the road enclosed the action. Two constables brandished their batons, a couple of demonstrators grimaced as they rubbed an arm, a shoulder. He'd scored a new vehicle with working air-con, so he couldn't hear what they were yelling.

He turned sharply off the road, glad of his seat belt as he lurched across the concrete pipes, braked and got out. The front yard, last night overgrown with high grass and prickly weeds, was flattened as if a cyclone had swept through. Reddy's visitors had gone beyond words this time. Missiles had smashed the glass louvres enclosing the veranda. Across the front of the house, someone had sprayed the giant words REDDY TO DIE in red.

He showed his ID to the nearest officer. '*Bula*, Constable. What did you find when you got here?'

'Sir, maybe a dozen men shouting their heads off—sounded like fifty! A couple of women, too. But they've gone now, along with their husbands. Strolled off along the road to catch the bus at the corner.'

'When did you get here?'

'Fifteen minutes ago, sir. We told them to stop disturbing the peace and disperse. You should talk to our senior constable, sir.'

He pointed his chin towards a strong-looking man with an outsized, bristly moustache. The senior constable noticed Horseman and approached, his hand outstretched.

'*Bula vinaka*, sir. Constable Maika Toga. I wish we were meeting under different circumstances, but it's still an honour. Your phone call took us by surprise. We heard about the rallies in Suva but never dreamed...' He shook his head. 'This hard core still here—they're so worked up, so angry! I know this man committed a terrible crime because I discovered Kanan eleven years ago and arrested Dev Reddy.' Constable Toga finally let go of Horseman's hand.

'Really? I believe a neighbour tipped you off?'

'*Io*, my colleague and I searched all the farm buildings and we found him. The state of that child! We believed God guided our steps that day.'

'*Vinaka*, Constable. A good day's work.'

'*Io*. But I don't hate Reddy, who was out of his mind. How can you be so filled with hate for someone you don't know personally?'

'I'm wondering that too, Constable. Perhaps one of them does know Reddy. I noticed the side door to the house is hanging off its hinges. Is the house clear?'

'Oh, my word! We raced straight into the crowd throwing rocks at the front. They didn't stop when a constable asked them nicely, believe you me! I'm sorry I didn't even notice a side door. Reddy's not inside, is he?'

'I don't know. He was here last night. Let's skirt the house first. You go that way. We'll meet at the steps.'

Horseman ordered another constable to check the space underneath the house, then met Toga at the side entrance. 'Careful of the rotten steps. I see a few have given way since I was here yesterday. Let's hope the invader broke his ankle.'

He glanced at Toga's ample girth. 'Better still, you wait at the bottom and arrest anyone who falls down the stairs.'

He thought light thoughts, stepping on the ends of the stairs and resting some of his weight on the handrails. Not only was the flimsy door hanging from one hinge, there was a jagged hole where the cheap lock was driven through the hollow core of the door.

'*Bula, bula*! Police. Anyone there?'

He stepped inside. All the wooden shutters were closed but he could make out the scanty furniture upended, the utensils on the kitchen bench swept to the floor. He repeated his call, then paced around two walls of the dim living room. Through to the bedroom, where cupboard doors hung open and the thin mattress tipped off the bed. He stepped out to the closed-in front verandah, littered with glass shards, rocks and pieces of concrete block. A few had pages torn from a notebook taped to them. He unwrapped one. The question REDDY TO DIE? again. He photographed all the damage with his phone and put the paper-wrapped rocks in a plastic supermarket bag he found on the kitchen bench.

He called 'All Clear' to Constable Toga and went back down the steps. The constable checking under the house called All Clear, too. Horseman hoped Reddy was safe with Gopal. Come to think of it, where was Gopal? He'd expected him to be here. But Gopal might want to avoid getting involved in a police matter—most people wanted to avoid that.

'Was Gopal here when you arrived, Constable? Gopal Prakash, Reddy's neighbour? He was the one who called me here.'

'No, no one was here except the vigilantes. Bastards!'

They walked around to the front yard. Horseman scuffed his sneaker through the mess. 'Get a man to go through the debris here. We need to check for any items that might identify individuals, any weapons and so on.'

Toga gave the order to the constable who'd just crawled out from underneath the house. 'I've had a gutful of this lot! What—vigilantes?

Io, that's what they think they are. They're really jumped-up busybodies with a taste of power. Now they've got that, they want more, and then more after that. No one needs them—we've all got the law and the Fiji Police Force and the courts. Y'know, Inspector, I tried to be tolerant of citizens expressing their opinions and I didn't want the hassle of the paperwork, which has never been my thing. So, the half-dozen who stopped screaming abuse when we asked them to—well, we let them go on their merry way.' He stared levelly at Horseman.

'You exercised your judgment appropriately, Constable. Well done.'

'But here we are, after nearly half an hour, five of the bastards are still all fired up and arguing the toss with my boys. I've had enough. I'm arresting them all for disturbing the peace and taking them back to the station. The sergeant can lay additional charges, I'm sure.'

'Go ahead, Constable—you don't need my authority. Here's evidence I collected inside the house. I'll bag and label it in my vehicle and hand it into your safekeeping. Ask your sergeant to store it with extra care. We might need it in a future court case.'

'*Io*, I will indeed. I'll put another man on to searching the yard while I process this rabble.'

'*Vinaka*, I'll try to find Reddy. I hope he's safe with his neighbour. I'll call Gopal Prakash now.'

Gopal said he hadn't seen Reddy since the previous evening. When he heard the ruckus from Reddy's direction in the morning, he approached the farmhouse to confirm what was going on. Alarmed, he'd called Horseman and then gone about his farm work.

Urging Gopal to call him if he saw or heard anything of his neighbour, Horseman searched the back yard. Maybe Reddy had escaped and hid in one of the decrepit sheds. He took one of the constables along. Reddy was a helpless creature, whatever terrible crimes he'd committed under the spell of an unshakeable delusion. Each shed had a rusting corrugated iron panel serving as a door. They got in just by pulling the iron panel open. They called, shone their torches into, under and over everything inside. Two were in better repair: one stored fuel, the other animal feed and fertiliser. Maybe Gopal Prakash used them.

Some distance away was the last shed, which was low, fitted with two rows of fruit boxes and rails.

'This must be the chicken coop where Reddy kept his son,' the constable exclaimed, looking horrified. He ran out, as if chased by a savage dog, across the yard and past the house.

Horseman lingered, noticing trampled wire, broken posts and planks in the undergrowth where the run's tall fence had stood sturdy ten years before. He pictured the tiny toddler, his white skin and silver hair filthy, scrabbling with the birds for food scraps thrown over the fence by his father who believed him to be a demon. Surely, he would have died but for the supply of raw eggs. Here was Kanan's prison, right here. Here was the dirt he'd scratched for grains, here the rail he'd perched on. How old was he when he learned to do that? Had he shared a nesting box with a soft warm hen when he was little? Or had he always been at the bottom of the pecking order, literally?

He made his way back around the other side of the house, where the water tank stood. He looked in the privy—nothing. Few smallholders' houses boasted indoor bathrooms, but an innovator like Reddy who installed a water tank and guttering—well, he may have tried to rig something up for his family.

And he was right. There was a lean-to abutting the tank stand furnished with a pipe that fed water through to a shower head and a tap lower down. A new plastic basin was wet—Reddy must have used it last night or this morning. Below the level of the tank stand platform, there was no internal wall.

Horseman said softly, 'Are you there, Mr Reddy? It's Joe Horseman.'

He heard a groan, then a whimper of fear. 'Are you hurt? I'm here to take you somewhere safe.'

17

The black-and-yellow police barriers toppled as protestors surged from Ratu Sukuna Park onto Victoria Parade. The barriers were symbolic but almost always did the job in laid-back Fiji. Almost. Not now.

The rally turned into a mob. From the security post on the first floor of the Telecom building, Horseman looked down on thrusting fists, placards and strangely, one or two skewered teddy bears. Cars and buses stopped, honking as the mob took over the street as though the traffic wasn't there.

The Security chief ended his radio orders, left the video relay screen and joined Horseman on the balcony.

'No substitute for the bird's-eye view, is there? Not for an old dog like me. Can't do without all the equipment, but you can't get the right perspective.'

'*Io*, sir.'

'*Vinaka* for sorting out the demonstration at Reddy's house, Joe. Good of you to take the sorry wretch to hospital. But I can't approve a police guard on Reddy's ward. Not with this mob kicking off here. Sorry, especially after all you've done for us. We'll be keeping an officer at the Sunshine Home, though.'

Fear stabbed Horseman in the guts. 'Has there been any disturbance there?'

'Just reporters being pests like you predicted. They've come back down here to join the excitement. But we'll keep twenty-four-hour watch until Monday morning.'

'*Vinaka*, sir.'

'I don't like to retreat before a mob, but this is dangerous. Look at those faces—all fired up and off on their power trips—they won't even see a taxi, never mind get out of its way! When the reinforcements get here—any moment now—we'll close Victoria Parade to vehicles and throw up a heavily manned cordon around the court buildings. Uniforms will clear the way for vehicles to exit Victoria with batons if necessary.'

Dozens of constables in blue marched onto the main road from side streets. They put on white gloves and began creating space around the trapped vehicles and directing them away. Despite their fervour, the demonstrators responded automatically to the white gloves. At least for now.

Most protesters turned right out of Ratu Sukuna Park, heading towards the government and court buildings beside Albert Park. But some turned left, in the direction of the market and further on, the prison. Did they intend going home or joining the smaller rally at the prison? It was quite a hike to the prison. Might some enjoy a detour to Suva Police Station along the way?

'*Vinaka*, Chief. I'd better be getting back to the station.'

The chief's eyes continued to scrutinise the action on Victoria Parade. '*Io*. Investigations will take a back seat with this security emergency. If I were you, I'd ask Ratini if your team could perform guard duty for Reddy at the hospital.'

'I'm grateful for the suggestion, sir.' Fat chance.

The chief shot him a shrewd glance. 'You reckon he'll turn you down, eh? If you really believe it's important, you'll put it to him, anyway. But if he says no, remember that the hospital has its own security staff, y'know. Nurses check on injured patients frequently. There's always someone about: cleaners, meal deliverers, orderlies. When I was in for my gallstones, I couldn't sleep because I was never left alone!'

'*Vinaka*, sir. I'll be off now. Call if you need me.'

The crash and ring of breaking glass snapped their heads back to the street as the first shop window smashed. A moment's silence as the mob drew breath, then roared. A man pried a white-painted rock from a garden border, hurled it at another window. He was too excited to be accurate. It pounded into a woman's head and she hit the pavement.

The chief strode back to the control desk. Horseman swung himself down the stairs and hurried out to the street.

***

He was right. About a dozen hesitant protesters stood at the gates of Suva Central Police Station. Normally wide open during the day, the iron railings were locked and uniformed officers questioned visitors before admitting them through a narrow pedestrian gate.

Clearly disappointed, the placard carriers conferred together. Horseman watched as a grey-haired man stepped forward, stabbed the air with his placard and shouted, 'Reddy to die!' His voice was raspy through overuse, but impassioned and still loud. After a few repetitions, the others joined in and the chant strengthened.

Another T-shirt displayed the acronym PACK in letters drawn with a marker pen. Underneath were the words: Parents Against Cruelty to Kids. First HOOK, now PACK. How many more activist groups with snappy names would pop up? Did PACK have a bank account set up, too?

He approached the gate. 'Constable, take down their names and addresses, please. And the details of any others who join them later.'

'*Io*, sir. Move them along?'

'No, not if they stand back like they are now. If they try to crowd you or stop other people from going in, then order them to leave. Vandals are smashing shop windows on the Parade. There are plenty of uniforms there to deal with it. Keep your sergeant updated.'

'*Io*, sir. We'll handle them.' He grinned.

Horseman could do with a roti or two, but the food vendors had all disappeared from the streets. That was a litmus test of public order. Better to earn nothing than to risk your barrow overturned and wares stolen.

He crossed the road to Hare Krishna's to buy a takeaway, but it looked like he was too late. Before he opened the door, two employees came out, carrying wooden storm shutters.

'I'm afraid we're closing, Inspector. Have you heard what's going on a hundred metres away? Not worth the risk. We haven't been witnessing a riot for a good many years now. No, it's been a good many years. It is fortunate we are having the storm shutters, isn't it?'

'Yes, yes, you're wise.'

'Don't you be worrying, sir. So much good food is remaining. I will pack some boxes for you. We will not want to be wasting, my goodness, no.' He leaned the shutters against a window with care and dashed back inside.

Horseman smiled in gratitude and followed him in. Food never went to waste in Fiji. It was one of the things he liked about his islands.

***

He carried two plastic shopping bags loaded with Hare Krishna boxes into the CID room. The probationers, Musudroka and Kau, were sitting with Singh at her desk. Of course, all leave was cancelled, even for CID, just in case. They all had mugs of tea but he couldn't see any food.

'What a shame. You've already finished lunch, I see. Hare Krishna's closed. I got all these great curries, rice, sambals, dhal, pickles, naan, you

name it, for a song. The guys wanted to donate it to the hard-working
police, but I couldn't let them do that. I guess I'll take it downstairs to
the uniforms—they'll polish it off.'

Musudroka was just about drooling at the fragrance escaping the
boxes. Singh caught Horseman's eye and laughed out loud.

Kau looked reproachful. 'Sir, it's nearly two o'clock and we haven't
had lunch yet at all.'

'Really? Well, rustle up some bowls and spoons, Apo. It looks like the
uniforms lose out again. Is our acting super back?'

'*Io*, sir. About half an hour ago.'

'Good. I'll see if he wants to join us for a curry.'

Musudroka and Kau exchanged looks that said *what the hell?*

He tapped on Ratini's door and entered on hearing an irritated '*Io?*'

'*Bula*, sir. Did you have any luck with the estate agent this morning?'

'No, I did not. Too small, too shoddy or too expensive. My wife's in
her village with the children and won't come to Suva until she can move
into the house we're going to stay in.'

Did that explain Ratini's dishevelled appearance and creased shirts?
Not really, wherever the Force was putting him up would have a laundry
service.

'I suppose that's understandable, sir. Have you had lunch? I've
brought back a load of curries and all the trimmings from Hare Krishna.
They closed early because of the demonstrations. The constables are
setting it up for us now. Would you like to join us? You're very
welcome.'

To Horseman's astonishment, Ratini's angry lines smoothed. '*Oi lei*!
Vinaka, I don't mind if I do. *Vinaka*.'

The probationers' faces fell when he returned with Ratini. Of course,
Singh showed courtesy. She gave Ratini a bowl and spoon and invited
him to serve himself from the boxes she'd lined up neatly at one end of
the work table. When she removed the lids, the blend of heavenly
aromas switched Horseman's appetite to extreme. He swallowed the
saliva flooding his mouth.

No one spoke for some time. When their bowls were empty, each
officer leaned back, faces relaxed into contentment.

'Let's finish it off,' Horseman suggested.

Over their second helpings, they shared their mornings' events.
There'd been another house break-in and jewellery theft the night
before. Singh and the DCs were part of the team, following Ratini's
instructions. Their news seemed to satisfy him, perhaps because he'd
just enjoyed a decent meal. He grumbled about his fruitless house hunt,

but in quite an amusing way. Was it possible this mellow boss could agree to a guard for Reddy in hospital? What had he to lose?

The probationers set about clearing the table when everyone had finished. They were learning.

'You've trained them well for kitchen duty, at least,' Ratini said, getting up. '*Vinaka* for lunch. I'm normally a meat-and-fish man myself, but those Hare Krishna flavours are damn good.'

This grudging acknowledgement was his opening.

'Sir, I want to tell you more about the attack on Reddy at his house this morning. And I have a proposal to put to you.'

Ratini's face tensed. 'I'll listen. Come to my office.'

Well aware of Ratini's chronic impatience, Horseman briefly related the events up to when he delivered the unconscious Reddy to Colonial War Memorial Hospital.

'To bring you right up to date, I checked on his condition before I left the Security post. He has a broken jaw, collar bone and fractured skull. He remains unconscious. They're waiting on a brain scan to assess how serious his head injury is.'

'So? You tell me how terrified this poor old man was when you found him hiding under the tank. How much more terrified was that little two-year-old locked in the fowl yard?'

'I agree. Dr Acharya says Reddy was insane and should never have been prosecuted. Anyway, he served eleven years and is now free.'

'And look at the chaos he's created in less than a day!'

'Sir, I told you about Reddy's injuries just to show you how violent and vindictive some of these self-styled activists have been already. They won't give up.'

'*Io*, some of them are off their rockers. Don't they have enough trouble in their own lives?'

'Reddy is completely helpless in hospital. He needs protection. Singh, Kau, Musudroka and I are all willing to do guard duty by his bed. Unless we're all ordered out on the streets, we can do three-hour shifts. That's six hours a day per officer.'

Ratini glared but said nothing. Horseman waited.

'It's quite practical, sir. What do you think?'

Ratini drummed on the desk with a pen for a while, then looked up. 'No. Horseman. I don't approve. The police didn't release the devil from custody, so we're not responsible for his safety.'

'He's a citizen of Fiji, sir.' Even as he spoke the words, he regretted them.

'And one we could well do without. His safety is not a top contender for my officers' time.'

'I'm sorry that's your decision, sir. I should let you know I'll be spending some of my free time at the hospital. The others may choose to do that, too.'

Ratini shrugged, the muscles of his face tensing again.

'Remember, we cancelled all leave until further notice.'

18

At six o'clock, Horseman strolled along Victoria Parade. He'd never seen the main street so empty on a Saturday. The police cordon had held around the government buildings, where the courts were the focus of the protestors. Most of these had long gone, driven out by hunger, thirst and fatigue. Unluckily for the activists, the street vendors had cleared out in the morning, and cafes, takeaway shops and restaurants had put up their storm shutters after the first stone was thrown. So unless people had brought packed lunches with them, their hunger increased throughout the afternoon.

Their voices gave up after hours of enthusiastic shouting. Security predicted this and ordered water supply cut off to taps in parks and streets. This meant public toilets also had no water—just an added incentive to call it a day. Horseman smiled to himself. Safer and so much more effective than a baton charge.

The final mercy was the downpour around five o'clock. It lasted fifteen minutes, long enough to change the minds of those still at the government buildings and prison. Long enough to wash the streets, too. The buses were running and taxis were prowling once more. For a moment, he considered walking up the hill to the hospital for the sake of fitness, then hailed a cab.

Hospitals sparked no fear in Horseman. His mother had worked his entire childhood as a visiting nurse, based in cottage hospitals. Sometimes when he was bored on school holidays, she took him on her rounds, teaching him basic first aid. But it was her prominence in the Fiji Nurses Association that gained Sister Sala Horseman her formidable reputation in medical circles. This opened doors for her son, even at Colonial Crown Memorial. Indeed, the triage nurse on reception greeted him with pleasure.

'Ah, *bula* Josefa Horseman! What brings you here? Not injured in the riots, I hope?'

'Not at all, Sister. Have you had many casualties?'

'Not many at all. Fewer than a dozen, only two admissions. One woman with concussion from a hit on the head and a man with a shoulder fractured by a police baton.' She looked up at him, reproach in her eyes.

'I've come to visit a casualty I brought in myself around midday. Dev Reddy. He lapsed into unconsciousness during our journey from Rewa. How is he?'

The nurse's smile disappeared. 'That was you? Wait while I check with the ward, Inspector.'

She turned away to telephone. When she put the phone down, she said, 'He seems stable but he hasn't regained consciousness yet. You won't gain anything by visiting him.'

'No, you're right, Sister. I hope he'll gain something, though. There are men fired up who want to kill him. He is not safe here, but there are no constables free for guard duty. I will take turns to guard him with some detective colleagues.'

He smiled, trying to reassure her. She looked apprehensive but directed him to Reddy's ward willingly enough. There, the nurse on duty escorted him to Reddy's bed, one of four crowded into a room designed for two. Three were occupied. He showed her his ID.

'This patient is at risk of further attacks, Nurse. Is there any small cubicle where we could place him, out of sight of passers-by?'

The nurse was wide-eyed. 'No, sir. No free space at all. You know what it's like here at CWM.'

'*Io*, I do. I'll be guarding Mr Reddy for the next three hours, then a colleague will take over.'

'I'll try to find a comfortable chair for you, sir.'

'*Vinaka*, that would be great.'

He checked the details on the clipboard hanging at the foot of the bed. He needed to check the patient's name most of all, as the figure lying in the bed could have been anyone.

Two bruised arms lay on top of the white sheet pulled up to the man's chest. The hands were swollen from efforts to ward off blows to his head. Canulas delivering fluid and medication punctured each arm. White bandages wrapped around one shoulder and his head. More bandages hid most of his puffed-up face and an odd metal frame with wing-nuts braced the jaw. His mouth was open enough to allow a tube to pass through. More tubes entered his nose. A blinking monitor, drip stand and cylinder stood beside the bed.

Horseman leaned against the wall beside the monitor to rest his knee. It was going to be a long evening until Musudroka came to relieve him at nine.

When the nurse came back an hour later, he was still propping up the wall but had slid down to the floor, with his legs stretched out in front of them.

'Are you all right, Inspector?' the nurse asked, her hand over her mouth.

'Sure, if Reddy's enemies come, they'll trip over my legs before they can get to him.' But really, he was too weary to stay upright.

She turned and dragged in a swivel office chair on casters. It was padded and had quite a high back. An orderly wheeled in a television on a trolley, complete with a long cord, and set it up. The two fussed a bit while Horseman levered himself slowly upright. His right knee was so stiff, he leaned on the end of Reddy's bed to get into the chair.

'*Vinaka vakalevu*, both of you. You're very kind.'

The nurse looked stern. 'Nonsense. Make sure you massage that knee and take a short walk every twenty minutes. You've been overdoing it today.'

As the nurse went out, the orderly handed him a remote control and headphones. 'King Country's up against West Coast in the New Zealand Heartland competition at eight o'clock. Should be some great rugby! I'll bring you something to eat and drink when I can.'

'*Vinaka*, but don't trouble yourself, please. Your patients need you more.'

'With luck, I might catch some of the game myself. We're predicting a quieter Saturday night than usual, sir. The rallies are over, but people are staying home to be on the safe side. So I hope we won't have any fights or accidents.'

'I hope so, too. You've clearly got your finger on the city's pulse. Let me know any news you hear on the grapevine if it's no trouble.'

'No trouble at all. I miss seeing you up there on the screen, showing us all how rugby should be played.'

'*Vinaka vakalevu*. You flatter me, but I miss playing God's own game. I hope I'm not washed up yet.'

'Can't wait for your comeback, Josefa Horseman. I'll get you a cup of tea and something to eat now.'

Reddy's chest continued to rise and fall regularly, but no other part of his body moved. The waves on his monitor were more or less regular. Horseman didn't know if this was good or not. The flat on the fifth floor sprang into his mind. Suddenly, he longed to be closeted there alone, removed from the mess of the city.

***

The orderly was right; the Heartland game was exciting. The second half had just begun when a patient trolley rammed Horseman's chair. Startled, he scooted out of the way and whipped off the headphones.

'Sorry, sir,' the orderly said. 'We've got a new casualty. An assault at Albert Park.'

'Are the police on it?'

'Not sure, sir. I think an ambulance brought him in. Just a teenager.'

'I'll go out to the corridor and use my radio. It's time to stretch my legs and you can't transfer the patient to his bed with me cluttering up the place.'

The duty sergeant was abrupt. 'Boy mugged while dossing under the grandstand in Albert Park. Constable heard cries. Victim semi-conscious, couldn't answer questions. Ambulance called.'

'*Vinaka*, Sergeant. I'm at the hospital now, in the same ward. If he comes to, I can question him.'

'Good sir. Just let me know if you succeed and I'll get the information to the right place.'

When the orderly wheeled the trolley past him, he returned to Reddy's ward. The same nurse was arranging her new patient neatly, smoothing his sheet.

'He's calling for you, I think, sir. He said, "There's Joe. Can I see him?" Do you know this boy?'

Curious, he went to the bed in the opposite corner from Reddy. There, tucked in with more care than he'd ever received in his life, lay Mosese, foundation Junior Shiner and one of the most promising rugby players. His eyes were closed, not because he was asleep, but because he'd been punched in the face again and again. His swollen nose veered wildly off-course.

'Mosese, it's Joe. Can you hear me?'

The boy's head turned slowly and one eyelid lifted a crack. '*Vinaka*, Joe, you come to help me.' His mouth turned up in a smile.

'What happened, Mosese?'

'I am at rally at government buildings, Joe. Good fun. Then it rains and everyone goes home. I go to the grandstand in Albert Park. I often camp there. I hide my duffle bag under there, my shoeshine box, too. In corner under some planks. When I get to my corner, get out my sleeping bag, big man jumps me. I fight him but he's too strong. Then *ovisa* wake me up, carry me out. I wake up here.'

'You're in hospital, Mosese. You're badly beaten but you're safe now.'

The boy was silent. 'Is he asleep, Nurse?' Horseman asked.

Mosese stirred. 'Where am I?' he asked before drifting off again.

'I can't be sure,' the nurse said. 'He could be suffering from a concussion. He's going for a brain scan as soon as your patient is done.'

'What? Mr Reddy hasn't had his scan yet?'

'No, Inspector. Radiography should send for him sometime this evening.'

'Do you think Radiography may need a reminder, Nurse?'

'It's not my job, but since you're so anxious about it...'

'*Io*, I'm anxious because he's unconscious. Surely, it's urgent to diagnose the extent of his head injury? Couldn't you tell Radiography you're concerned and you're bringing him down now with a police escort? They won't forget him if he's blocking their doorway.'

She looked stunned. 'That's not the way we do it here.'

She picked up the phone.

Horseman switched off his television. Anyway, the game was over. As he helped the orderly push Reddy's trolley to Radiography, he decided to do whatever it took to speed up the action in the hospital.

He was thankful to be there when Mosese was brought in. The boy was rough and tough on the surface but lacked stamina because he didn't get enough good food to eat. Mosese had talent and drive, but his chances in life weren't great. This wasn't the first time he'd been attacked. He was in constant danger because, like so many others in this town, he didn't have a home.

SUNDAY

19

Tina bounded after the stick, splashing through the waves to seize it and drop it proudly at her master's feet. The dog loved nothing more than a long walk along the beach, nosing through seaweed for rotting delicacies, retrieving sticks for Horseman, barking at sea snakes and crabs. Horseman took pleasure in her happiness, her solid body and sleek brindled coat, her transformation from the emaciated creature of just five months ago.

His American girlfriend, Melissa, had insisted on rescuing the homeless mother dog and her four pups from the streets when they encountered her while strolling along Victoria Parade. He'd told her not to touch the disease-ridden animal, but what he first viewed as sentimentality had proved to be a rock-solid kindness at her core. Although their passion had cooled off since then, he felt her presence now, urging him to do something more for the street kids in his Junior Shiners team.

He whistled for Tina. Her attention fixed on him, with a look that said *Do I really have to?* But when he whistled again, she trotted to him, distracted only once by a stranded jellyfish. He snapped on her lead and they went up to the road. It was too early for the cricketers to be at Albert Park, now empty except for a few joggers. The door to the space underneath the grandstand was ajar. He pulled it wide and went in.

The fixed ventilation louvres augmented the light from the door. At the front, where he had to get down on his knees and crawl, he found the planks and trestles Mosese had arranged as his hideout. Now they were scattered, flung about as if in anger. He searched among them and turned up the boy's empty shoeshine box, upended but still intact. He pulled some gloves from his pocket. A few minutes later, he found some rags, which he put in the box, but no brushes or polish. To hell with the bastard! Fuming, he got to his feet and systematically paced the entire space.

He was halfway done when Tina tugged on her lead, nose to the ground. She must have picked up a scent from the box or rags. He unclipped her leash. Tail beating, Tina nosed across the ground to the storage rooms abutting the highest wall. They were all locked. She went on to the end of the row and into a fifteen-centimetre gap between the outside wall and the storeroom partition. She looked up at him, eager for his approval.

'Good girl, Tina! I didn't know you were a sniffer dog! Would you like to work for the police?' He patted her and her tail beat even faster.

'Well, let's see what you've found.'

It was a scruffy Air Pacific sports bag, faded and dirty. Mosese would be proud of possessing it, even so. A sleeping bag was stuffed inside, together with some old clothes that were little better than the shoe-shine rags. At the bottom was a pair of flip flops as thin as cardboard, and the worn rugby boots he'd acquired just two months before.

'Mosese will be grateful to you, Tina. And with any luck, we'll find the bastard who robbed him and put him in hospital. Well done, girl! You can come along with me and deliver your evidence to the station.'

Council workers were raking up litter around the government buildings and sweeping Victoria Parade. Some shopkeepers were already taking down their storm shutters but the majority were playing it safe. It was weird seeing Suva boarded up and not a breath of wind. Ratu Sukuna park was empty. He thought it unlikely the Reddy protesters would give up completely after one day. Some would turn out around midday when they were at leisure after church. The Security chief's mind must be running along the same lines as constables patrolled on foot with batons drawn and stood guard on the pavements at regular intervals.

Shattered glass indicated the protesters had broken four shop windows—not many, but four too many. Had these concerned parents helped themselves to the stock as the shopkeepers hid or fled? As one was a shoe shop and another a camera store, it was likely. He felt nothing but contempt for looters—criminals taking advantage of the anonymity the riot gave them.

By the time they reached the station, his pleasure at finding some of Mosese's possessions had vanished. But the desk sergeant clapped his hands in thanks.

'*Vinaka vakalevu,* sir! If we don't get good prints from this box, I'm a monkey's uncle! I'll bag this lot and get it to the SOCOS right away. The lad's in hospital, eh? Fill in his name and yours and you'll be able to get it back to him. A scum who would stoop so low must have a record, eh? I reckon we'll get him!'

'Is anything kicking off around the prison this morning?'

'Not yet, not yet. I hope they got it out of their systems yesterday.'

'Me, too. I'd better take the dog home. Then I'm off to the hospital to give Mosese the good news. I'll see you later. *Moce mada.*'

***

'Sorry I'm late, Susie.'

Singh's head jerked up from her chest. It took her a moment to realise where she was. Her green eyes were shadowed. She pulled herself upright in the chair. She had a compact pink ring-binder in her lap. The television was off.

'That's quite okay. Thanks for calling me. If you hadn't, I would have worried.'

'Any change in our patients?'

'Mosese's on the mend, sleeping soundly now. The doctor said he's concussed but his confusion has gone and his memory's returning. They want to observe him for another day and straighten his broken nose. There won't be anyone to fix his nose until Monday. After that, they'll discharge him. He's got a cracked rib, too. I suggested they keep him for an extra day or two since he hasn't got a home to go to. He'll benefit from resting in a safe place.'

'You're right. Let me tell you about Tina, my new detective...'

When he finished, Singh frowned. 'So he can't get his clothes back, such as they are.'

'Never mind, I'll pick him up a few things at Garment City if it's business as usual tomorrow. He'll need a sports bag with a decent zip, too. I can give him one of mine.'

'D'you think you can choose clothes he'll like?'

Was she serious? 'Yes, I do, Sergeant Singh. Why—anything wrong with my clothes?'

She grinned, her usual energy returning. 'No. You just always look rather neat, sir. A teenage boy won't go for neat.'

He couldn't believe what he was hearing from the queen of neat herself. 'Well, how's Dev? Any visitors?'

'No visitors for Dev. The staff are rather vague. They look concerned, though. You'll probably have more luck with them. He started tossing his head from side to side two hours ago, getting more agitated, but he didn't answer when I spoke to him. I called the nurse and later a doctor came. She said his head must be still and ordered a sedative. After a while, his head stopped thrashing. He looks like he's sleeping.'

'That's what you should be doing now, Susie. I'll stay until lunchtime. But unless they lift the cancellation of leave, I can't allow any of you to do more hospital guard duty. Not with Ratini's attitude. Technically, he's right. No officer is off duty at the moment. So none of us has any private time to spend visiting the hospital.'

'I don't know, sir. Ratini was quite polite at lunch, wasn't he? Almost human.'

'*Io*, he surprised me.'

'And we're all standing by and can be back at the station in ten minutes if we're called in.'

'The business district's quiet at the moment. If it stays that way for a few more hours, the commissioner could lift the emergency and restore leave. In the meantime, many thanks.'

'No trouble. Call me if you need me.' She got up and slung her backpack over her shoulder.

20

'Joe, wake up, mate! Better come with me to the hospital.'

Horseman opened his eyes, slow to rise from the depths.

'What? Sure. What's happened to you?' It was still dark. His landlord stood by the door, fully dressed. Matt wouldn't ask for help unless he was in a crisis.

'Not me, mate. Just got called in. It's Dev Reddy. A nurse just found him dead.'

Failure and dread flooded Horseman. His personal failure to protect a helpless victim of crime and dread of what his investigation might uncover.

He hauled himself out of bed and stretched. '*Oi lei*, Matt! If I'd done my job properly and supplied a twenty-four-hour guard, he could be alive.'

'Come on, Joe. The man had a head injury and was unconscious—unpredictable outcome. Almost certainly, he died naturally.'

Horseman pulled on black jeans and a short-sleeved shirt. He thought of Singh's accusation and left his shirt outside the jeans.

'Except people bashed him up—that's how his head got injured.'

'Yeah. What I meant was, it's highly likely he died of last Saturday's injuries, and highly unlikely someone murdered him in hospital an hour or so ago.'

'We've still got to find who bashed him at his house. I haven't even followed up with Nausori police yet.'

'Well, I hate to break the news to you, but you're not Superman. You can't bend the space-time continuum.'

'Now, that would be a handy talent.'

Tina sprang up from her bed on the verandah as they shut the door behind them.

'Not this time, girl. Your job's guarding the house.' Horseman ruffled her coat. It was still dark and Tina lay down again.

Horseman's mind slowly surfaced on the drive to the hospital.

'If the staff doctor thinks Reddy died from his injuries, why is it urgent to call the chief pathologist in at five in the morning?'

'That's a better question. One, because the patient's injuries were criminal acts and his death escalates the investigation and any subsequent criminal charges.'

'Yep, got that, Prof.'

'God, spare me from students who think they're funny!'

'Go on. Two?'

'Of course. Two is media interest. There's been nothing else on the news for a week and now the man everyone loves to hate is dead. What with the riots he sparked on the weekend, interest will be hysterical. The hospital is calling in extra security guards right now. The director rightly wants an answer as soon as possible. He doesn't want to issue a statement saying, in effect, "We don't know what happened." Make sense?'

'Absolutely. We can't rush, though. It'd be worse if you gave a definite answer then found out later you were wrong. Then the press could whip up a campaign about the incompetent doctors endangering our lives.'

'Yeah, there'll be pressure, though.' Dr Young pulled up around the back of the hospital, beside the morgue roller shutter discreetly labelled 'Deliveries'.

'Before we get into the stairwell, I'll call Ratini. Then I need Ash Jayaraman and his SOCOs. We need to seal off that ward as a crime scene.'

Dr Young raised his eyebrows. 'Doubt that's possible, mate. You can try, of course.'

'If the manager refuses to move patients, we'll just have to make do with Reddy's quarter of the ward. Having the ward full of police will disturb patients more than being moved.'

'I don't like to call Singh so early after all she's done over the weekend, but I'll have to.'

'She wouldn't forgive you if you left her out, mate. I'll go up. I'll leave the door unlocked. Come up when you've made your calls. I won't move Reddy until you get there.'

***

Before going to Reddy's room, Horseman sought out the nurse who discovered Reddy had died. She was attending to other patients; there was no nurse to take over from her until her shift ended at seven o'clock. Horseman told her he'd find her then.

When he got there, one patient had already moved. Mosese was feeling much better and wanted to help Horseman with the investigation.

'You can help us, Mosese—I'll talk to you later on.'

The boy grinned. 'Unless I die in the night.'

'Your wisecracks are back. You must be better.'

'I want to be an orderly. I never knew this job before. Do you think I could do this, Joe?'

'Why not? Orderlies do important and useful work. You could find out more from the orderly who takes you to your new ward.'

When Mosese and the other patient were wheeled away, Ash's two SOCO assistants started on the crime scene checklist.

'Ash, we need the full treatment here, even though Matt Young thinks Reddy probably died from his beating.'

'You bet, sir.'

Horseman joined Dr Young at Reddy's bed. The contraption around his jaw was knocked to one side. The bandages around his head were loose. Singh's report of Reddy tossing his head around in the early hours of Sunday morning could explain that. Or not. The pathologist turned down the sheet, exposing the dead man's thin legs and horny feet sticking out beneath the scanty white hospital gown. The tubes attached to the cannulas in his arms were cut, the nasal tube was gone.

The pathology assistant cut Reddy's gown up the middle with scissors and peeled it off with care. Dense purple bruises marking the lighter skin of his trunk made him a pitiful sight. He'd suffered a mighty kick in the groin or possibly a blow with a club; his bloated genitals were midnight blue. A catheter was fitted to his penis, but only about eight centimetres of tube remained.

Dr Young pulled his magnifying glass out of his pocket and began his initial examination, dictating his observations to a digital recorder.

Singh rushed in. 'Good morning, gentlemen—although it won't be good, will it? The very thing we predicted and tried to prevent has happened.'

She faced the dead man, brought her hands together and bowed her head for a moment. Horsemen knew she felt as bad as he did.

'Anything yet, Matt?' she asked.

Dr Young gave her a sad smile. 'Good to see you, Susie. I don't want to remove his bandages here. Or turn him. I'll take him down to the lab now, on this bed. Ash, when you've finished here, please come down and process the bed in my lab.'

'Good, that's what I'd prefer, too, Doctor.'

'Mr Reddy will jump the queue. I'll have a cup of tea and start the postmortem right away. Are you two going to witness?'

The two detectives glanced at each other. 'Stay if you want,' Horseman said. 'I'm going to talk to the nurse who found him dead and any other staff who were around—the three patients in the ward, too. I'll call in at the lab before I leave, Matt.'

Singh thought for a few moments. 'I think it's better if I go straight to the station, sir. Get a major case file set up, the board and timeline. Even if Reddy wasn't attacked in his hospital bed, it's still manslaughter and possibly murder.'

'Good. One urgent task is to follow up with the Nausori cops. I don't know what happened with the men arrested at Reddy's house on Saturday morning.'

He turned to Ash. 'I picked up evidence at the house, too—if nothing's happened with that, I'll request the Suva SOCOs take it over. I don't think Nausori station will mind, but I'll play it by ear.'

'Fine by me, sir. We'll get a more satisfactory result if we process all the physical evidence attached to the case in our lab. Maybe if I offered to take in a Nausori officer or two to observe and assist, that would be an incentive for them to agree with no argument.'

'Wonderful idea, thanks, Ash. The sergeant there's a diligent sort— he'll probably jump at that chance.'

'Singh, we still don't know Reddy's family's whereabouts in New Zealand. We need to track them down.'

Singh pulled out her notebook and spent a minute writing a numbered list. 'I'll trawl through the original file we used for our report. Relatives weren't our top priority last week, but there must be some names and addresses somewhere. This will be a good chance to get our probationers up to speed in finding people.'

Her eyes were now alight with anticipation of the hunt. When he looked at the dead man, he noticed there was only one pillow on the bed. He glanced around. A second pillow was wedged behind the bedhead. It must have got dislodged. He pulled it out and placed it on the foot of the bed.

'Here's Reddy's other pillow. You'd better take it with you.'

21

Bimala Bannerjee sat in the staff break room holding a large mug and flipping through the pages of a Bollywood magazine. When Horseman tapped on the open door, she started, then got up quickly and introduced herself. She was short, with a long, thin face. Her bright purple uniform hung loosely on her slim frame. A laminated ID card hung around her neck on an orange lanyard. It didn't surprise him she looked tired; it was one hour before the end of her night shift.

She sounded bright enough. 'Call me Bima, Inspector. Would you like a cup of tea? I've just made a pot.'

He had drunk nothing since nine o'clock on Sunday night. '*Vinaka*, I would if it's not too much trouble.'

He took a chair at Bima's plastic table and sipped the tea gratefully. 'I want to ask about the events of last night. When did you first check on Mr Reddy?'

'Oh, it's all on the chart—you'll get the exact times from that. I came on shift at eleven o'clock and it was probably twenty past when I got to Mr Reddy. Checked his monitor readings, blood pressure, temperature, his drips—everything on the list. There were no significant changes from his readings two hours before.'

'Was he unconscious?'

'Either asleep or unconscious. He didn't respond when I spoke to him.'

'When did you next check on him?'

'As he had a head injury and was unconscious, he was on two-hourly checks. So, sometime around one, then three and again at five o'clock. That was when I found he had died, so I remember the precise time. I glanced at the monitor and the lines were flat. I don't know why the alarm didn't go off. There was no pulse and he wasn't breathing.'

'What about his drip lines and nasal tube? Were they still connected?'

Bima's eyes narrowed a little. 'I'll have to think about that. I don't remember checking them. Once I knew he was dead, it's possible I skipped the other checks. I'm not sure about that. There wouldn't be any point, would there?'

Horseman smiled. 'I suppose not. What did you do?'

'I looked for Matron. I found her at the nursing station—that's like the ward office. She came quickly and took over.'

'Were any of the other three patients awake?'

Bima swallowed more tea in haste. 'Mr Reddy was the only one on two-hour checks overnight. All was quiet and the curtains pulled around each bed, so I can't be sure. I assumed they were asleep. Am I in trouble for something?' Her eyes were anxious.

'No, Bima. I just need to know exactly what happened. Did you stay in the room and help Matron?'

'Yes, there's a routine when a patient dies. Two people are needed. But when Matron confirmed that Mr Reddy was dead, she went back to the station. When she returned, she told me the police would come soon and not to do anything more.'

'Did you cut the drip lines and nasal tube while she was out of the ward?'

Tears welled in the nurse's eyes. She nodded. 'It's part of the procedure. Matron didn't tell me to stop working before she left.'

'Were you surprised that Mr Reddy died?'

Bima pulled a tissue from a box on the table and dabbed her eyes. She sniffed. 'Not really. Old and a head injury—he was at risk. Still, he'd been pretty stable for the last day so we thought he had a fair chance of recovering.'

'Bima, I want you to search your memory. Did you see anyone last night who wasn't a regular staff member on the ward? Anyone at all, maybe asked for directions or just passing through?'

Bima finished her tea and looked up at him. 'No one. I came on at eleven and we permit no visitors after nine.'

'*Vinaka*, Bima. You've been very helpful. Before you go, I'd like you to write down the names of everyone you saw around the ward during your shift. Just the name and what job they do here.' He handed her a pen and notebook turned to a blank page.

The nurse looked worried. 'I can try. I mightn't remember everyone I saw.'

Horseman smiled. 'No need to be anxious, it's not a test. Just do your best. I'll sit here and finish my tea, and you can go home as soon as you're done. It's quarter to seven.'

***

Luckily, the orderly was working an extended shift. After pacing through most of the hospital's corridors, Horseman encountered Naca Colo piloting an empty trolley one-handed, humming "Onward Christian Soldiers" and conducting himself with his free hand. He stopped, grinned and stepped forward, hand outstretched. There was no need for Horseman to introduce himself.

'Josefa Horseman, I heard you were here! A privilege to meet you, sir. My word, there's always a silver lining to these dark clouds, eh? Rallies and riots down below in the town, patients dying up here, and now our star Flying Fijian comes to save us.' After a vigorous shake, Naca continued to grasp Horseman's hand in both of his, pumping it slowly.

'Come now, you exaggerate, Naca. I'm bound to disappoint you if you expect so much of me! I'm a police officer doing a routine job—that's looking into Mr Dev Reddy's death in the early hours of this morning.'

Naca looked to be about fifty, short for a Fijian and sturdy. Energy radiated from his alert face and muscled limbs. He let go of Horseman's hand and grabbed the push-bar of his trolley again.

'Now why is that, Josefa? Patients die here every day but we don't see the police here very often.'

'Naca, you're on the ball and you can guess the reason. Mr Reddy was badly beaten on Friday night and he died this morning. The men who beat him up are guilty of a crime. Now it's an even more serious crime, probably murder. My job's to track them down and bring them to justice.'

Naca's face sobered. 'There are some who reckon whoever beat the devil up was bringing justice. What do you say to that?'

'You know what my answer is, Naca.'

'*Io*, you say everyone can't go meting out justice as they see fit. The law must be the same for everyone.'

'Well said, Naca.'

'But I can see the other side, too. What about God's justice?'

'You know your Bible better than me, I think. Doesn't God say "vengeance is mine?"'

The orderly smiled broadly again, enjoying the debate. 'True, true. And Jesus said, "Judge not, lest you be judged." Where does that leave the courts, eh?'

'We could toss this issue around all day, couldn't we? But I need to ask you a few simple questions. Did you go to Dev Reddy's room last night?'

'No, I started at eleven o'clock. The room was full and there were no patients in or out. It's always quiet on Sunday night—only emergencies are admitted. Just the nurses doing their rounds.'

'Did you see anyone you didn't recognise in the corridors?'

Naca paused. 'No, but I heard the fire door bang at one stage. I remember I thought it strange, as I'd passed Bima leaving that room and going into the next one just a minute before. Then I saw her moving on to the next room a few minutes after that. So it wasn't her.'

'Who could it have been?'

'I wasn't concerned enough to call security. I decided Bima could have called a cleaner because there was a mess on the floor. That sort of thing happens any time. Probably the cleaner was taking the mop and bucket out the back way.'

'*Io*, that would explain the noise. What time was this?'

'Ah—let me think back. I can't be sure, but probably it was Bima's three o'clock rounds because I know at five o'clock I was downstairs, taking my meal break. So it could have been between three and half-past three. But probably, as it was after she'd finished in Reddy's room, I'd say between ten-past and twenty-past three.' The orderly's face creased into a triumphant smile.

'*Vinaka*, Naca. You've got a logical head on your shoulders. Anything else unusual?'

'No, Josefa.'

Horseman handed him a card. 'Please call me if something else comes to mind. Anything even a little out of the ordinary. I can see you notice everything. It could be important.'

'*Vinaka*, Josefa. I'll try.'

'*Vinaka vakalevu*, Naca. You've been very helpful. Now, where can I find the night supervisor?'

***

'*Bula* Detective Inspector Horseman, I've been expecting you.'

Sister Kesaia Wailoku stood to shake hands. She came up to his shoulder but was as broad as she was tall. Her bright button eyes surveyed him keenly over the top of her round reading glasses. He imagined how the student nurses would cringe beneath her gaze.

'Sit down, Inspector. I've known your mother for a long time. How is she enjoying retirement?'

'She's busier than she expected, but I think she's enjoying it. She's staying with one of my sisters in Lautoka at the moment.'

'I expect she likes straightening out the grandchildren. Well, how can I help you, Inspector?'

Horseman didn't think of his mother as a disciplinarian, but maybe Sister Kesaia's experience was different. Interesting.

'You'll appreciate that now Dev Reddy has died, his assailants of Friday night will now face murder charges. It's even more vital that we track them down. I want to piece together everything that happened to Reddy during this night shift. First, was anyone on duty last night who isn't a regular staff member? Any casual relief staff, for example?'

'I can only speak for the nurses, and the answer is no—no one. Sunday night is always quiet unless there's a major traffic accident, which is rare.'

'Did you notice anyone, not only nurses, who wasn't familiar to you?'

'Again, I have to say no.'

'Any incident, any unusual noise, anything out of the routine?'

'I wish I could help, but it was a typical Sunday night. Even Nurse Bimala alerting me to Mr Reddy's death around five in the morning wasn't unusual. I'm afraid more patients lose hold of life in the early hours than at any other time of day.'

'Could you take me through your actions after the nurse alerted you?'

'*Io*, it was completely routine. Although Mr Reddy was unconscious and his condition was serious, we did not expect him to die. An additional factor was that the patient suffered his injuries during an assault. I knew the coroner had to be notified and a postmortem done. I called the duty doctor, then went straight to Reddy's room with Nurse Bima. I confirmed life was extinct. The doctor arrived and conducted the same tests. We thought if we could speed up the postmortem, the crowds of reporters would be around for a shorter time. The doctor called Dr Young, who kindly came in straight away and brought you along. It's only just seven o'clock now. So, I hope we've succeeded.'

'Let's hope so. You've done everything you could. I have a couple of questions about some things I observed when I was at Mr Reddy's bedside.'

'What were they?'

'His canula and catheter tubes were cut off short.'

'Really? I told Nurse Bima to clamp the tubes. I certainly did not instruct her to cut them off. What was the girl thinking? When the police are notified, we don't touch the patient's body or any equipment.'

'I see. So where are the tubes?'

'I will find out. If Dr Young doesn't have them, I'll locate them. The silly girl probably thought she was tidying things up! Anything else?'

'*Io*, Sister. The nasogastric tube I saw in place yesterday wasn't there.'

Sr Kesaia frowned, pursed her mouth, grabbed a notebook and started a list. Horseman doubted the missing lengths of tubes would prove critical.

'My last query is about the metal frame taped onto Reddy's face and going into his mouth—I don't know what that's called.'

'Jaw support appliance will do.'

'The appliance seemed to be bent out of shape—it looked loose to me, too. Is that significant?'

'Nurse Bima reported the patient tossing his head from side to side. It may have been due to pain. The doctor ordered an increase in the sedative dose, as it's important the jaw is immobile. He may have had a recurrence and his head moved enough to dislodge the appliance.'

'I see. *Vinaka vakalevu,* Sister Kesaia. Here's my card. Please contact me if you think of any extra details about last night that were even a little out of your routine.'

'I will, Josefa. Please give my best wishes to your mother. I know she's very proud of your achievements.'

'*Vinaka* again. I'm proud of her achievements, too.'

22

'Y'know, Horseman, I had trouble hauling myself out of bed this morning. A genuine case of Mondayitis, it was. No wife or kids to bother me in the quiet hotel room, eh? Then the phone rang and you made my day. That bastard Reddy dead—sweet music to my ears. Couldn't wait to get to work and tie off the loose ends.'

Certainly, Acting Superintendent Ratini looked like he'd raced to the station, taking time only to grab a blue tee-shirt and camouflage cargo pants from the floor and pull them on. Horseman refrained from comment on his superior's attitude to Reddy's death. He well knew most of Fiji's population would share it. It was he, Horseman, who was the odd one. He believed justice should be blind.

'Sir, it's going to be quite a job to tie them off. Lots of untangling to do first. While the postmortem is underway, Singh's concentrating on locating Reddy's children. I'm following up the evidence of assault collected from Reddy's farm on Saturday morning.'

Ratini looked affronted. 'Evidence? I suppose his injuries are evidence enough, aren't they?'

'*Io*, sir—evidence of assault, but not evidence that will lead us to his assailants. And if the postmortem concludes he died of his injuries, those assailants are now his murderers.'

'What's the chance of identifying them—sounds like you're assuming there was more than one attacker?'

'I'm trying not to assume anything, sir. *Vinaka* for reminding me of that.'

Ratini glared at Horseman, suspicious. '*Io*, always a danger. Still, what's the chance of catching them?'

'I don't know, sir. Constable Toga took the names of the diehards who wouldn't leave Reddy's place. Took them to Nausori in the paddy wagon. I'm going to follow up with him.'

Ratini sighed heavily and, Horseman reckoned, deliberately.

'*Oi lei*! I can see you've got to go through the motions, but I resent every minute of my officers' time spent on that loony bastard. He doesn't deserve it! I reckon you don't have a chance of bringing charges of murder, anyway.'

'We should know a bit more about that by the end of the day, sir.'

'Keep me informed, Horseman.'

***

'Constable Toga, how did it go with those protesters you arrested at Reddy's farm on Saturday morning?'

'Oh Inspector, I'm pleased you got in touch. There was a bit of confusion when we got back here to the station. Chaos, in fact.'

'Tell me about it, Constable.'

'Ah, please call me Maika, Inspector. I feel I know you.'

Horseman always felt uncomfortable when subordinates expected informality from him. He understood they felt they knew him—the whole rugby-mad country knew him as 'Joe,' because of his success representing Fiji. Loved him for it, too. But he'd slipped up a few times as a sergeant by not insisting on his title. Some subordinates didn't take him seriously as a detective, just assumed it was a sinecure for national reps. These days, he went along with requests for him to address a subordinate familiarly but never reciprocated. Some officers found this standoffish, he knew, but that was too bad. When it came to the crunch, his only authority over them was his official rank, not his rugby status.

'*Vinaka*, Maika. You'd better tell me what happened.'

'*Io* sir. As you know, I was fed up with those troublemakers who wouldn't go away—the damage they'd done should have satisfied them, shouldn't it? We took down their names and addresses there and then loaded them into the van. We only had one set of cuffs each, so we were a set short. When we were processing them at the station, a couple of them started yelling and thumping the wall. It was just a ploy to distract us and it worked, unfortunately. The uncuffed guy darted out—man, he was quick!'

'Go on, Maika.'

'Two of our boys went after him, but you know what it's like here on Saturday morning, Inspector. All the farmers are in town, and we're close to the market, which is in full swing. *Oi lei*, no chance of catching a man who's fast and doesn't want to be caught, eh?'

'Have you followed up his address?'

'Not yet, sir. That's on the list for today.'

'And the others?'

'We put them in the lockup until we could interview them. *Oi lei,* they sparked a commotion in there! Thumping the door, yelling out. Then they started chanting, 'Reddy to die," and the others, maybe five others, joined in. Sergeant ordered me to sort them out quickly, so two of us questioned each in turn. No joy at all. They must have agreed not to say anything. Claimed they were expressing their views, not inciting violence, by chanting "Reddy to die." Swore that when they turned up at the farmhouse, they were surprised by the broken louvres and the graffiti. Had no idea who was responsible. Swore they didn't go in the house and never saw Reddy. We had no evidence.'

'You said they were throwing stones when you arrived at the scene?'

'They were! Flat out denied it, the liars. Swore they were just waving their fists and we were mistaken.'

'The evidence I gave you might prove they were lying, Maika. Has it been processed yet?'

'Not yet, sir. There's not much chance here, with only one forensics officer.'

He'd made a mistake letting the stones and paper out of his hands. He'd let his desire to support a local constable who seemed to do a good job override his knowledge that the evidence processing and analysis in Nausori would not be up to Suva's quality—to put it mildly.

With his hopes sinking, he asked, 'Did you fingerprint them?'

'All three objected. It was getting chaotic, so we put them in the lockup, intending to do it later.'

'And later?'

'After we interviewed them, I briefed Sergeant, sir. He said nothing would stick except trespass. I don't blame him for wanting to clear them out of the station, sir. But we charged them with trespass, disturbance of the peace and damage to property. Sergeant insisted on one hundred dollars bail, to be posted by someone who'd stand surety for them and come in person to the station to take them away. The fingerprinting slipped out of the process somehow, sir.'

'Well, you've verified their details through the bail process, that's something. Can you email me all their details, including those of their relatives who stood surety?'

'*Io,* sir. The same person bailed all of them out. It was the man from the television—Ravai Nata, from the God's Gospel Church.'

'Really? On second thoughts, I'll come and pick up the files myself. Can you make copies for me, please? I'll save you processing the evidence, too. Reddy's death was murder. Suva SOCOs will handle the evidence now.'

23

Much as she wanted to complete tracking down the Reddy family, Singh was happy when Horseman stopped talking on the phone and approached her desk, his satchel over his shoulder. She hoped wherever he was heading, he wanted her to come, too.

'Kau, you can manage on your own for a while, can't you?' he asked the probationer.

Apolosi Kau looked up from Singh's computer screen, his eyes serious behind his glasses. '*Io*, sir. Tracing people overseas is new to me. But once you know the steps and what to do when you draw a blank, it's pretty straightforward. Enjoyable.'

'No one better than Sergeant Singh to teach you procedure, Apo. But I need her now. That's if you can drop everything to interview Ravai Nata?' He stood there smiling at Singh. He knew very well he didn't need to ask. Interviewing was her favourite thing.

'Is it okay for me to keep using your computer, Sergeant?'

'Absolutely.' She looked at Horseman. 'I wouldn't be surprised if he's finished the entire Reddy family tree by the time we get back.'

Kau frowned at the screen but his flushed ears betrayed his pleasure.

***

'Really—Nata stood bail for all three of the Nausori arrests?' Singh asked as the police sedan charged up Edinburgh Drive to Samabula junction. As Horseman drove, she automatically craned her neck to gaze west over Suva's deep jungle-green escarpment to the sea and purpling range of hills beyond. Under today's grey clouds, the slate sea looked sullen, the far hills mysterious. Having paid tribute to her need for order by setting up Reddy's case file, she relished unleashing her creative side to solve a dark crime. If Ravai Nata, founder of HOOK and darling of Fiji's media, could shed some light, she would persuade him to do so.

'Yep, all of them. That suggests they're all members of HOOK, don't you think?'

'Highly likely.'

'We might be in for a runaround. I need to take him by surprise, but I don't know where he is. I'm betting he's at his church.'

'Sounds good. Do you think he was at the attack on the farmhouse earlier?'

'As you just said, highly likely, Susie. As soon as Constable Toga told me about the bail, Nata moved to the top of my list. We must speak to him.'

'Can't wait, sir!'

They had a stroke of luck: Ravai Nata was in the little office at the back of God's Gospel Church. Six colleagues sat with him around the trestle table, on top of which were tea mugs, an open plastic bag of bread rolls, an open tin overflowing with banknotes, several Bibles and a few school exercise books.

Ravai Nata looked up, flabbergasted, and jumped to his feet.

'*Bula*, Mr Nata,' Horseman said genially.

'Um, er, *bula* vin-*vinaka*, Inspector. Oh, um, *bula* Sergeant. How did you, um, why are you here?' His eyes fixed on them.

'We have some questions to ask you.'

'What about?'

'It's about Mr Dev Reddy.'

'I heard he died in hospital.'

'We can drive you to Suva Central station, or we could talk to you here. Your choice.' Horseman sounded helpful.

Nata looked from one to the other, then at the others around the table, most of whom were open-mouthed. 'No, no, I prefer to stay here.'

'As you wish. Before your associates leave the office, we'll take down their contact details.'

Singh smiled around the table. 'You may be able to help us, too. First, I'll give each of you my card. Please call me or come to the station if there's anything you know about Mr Reddy's whereabouts since his release from prison last Friday afternoon—anything at all.'

Continuing to smile cheerfully, she extracted a small lined notepad from her bag, tore off several sheets, and gave one to each of Nata's friends. There were two middle-aged women in calf-length floral dresses and four men of various ages, but all older than Nata. Interesting—it was most unusual in Fiji for the middle-aged to follow younger leaders. What was it about Nata?

'Has everyone got a pen or pencil? If not, I can supply you with one.' All but the oldest man found one. Singh graciously handed him a blue ballpoint. 'Here you are, sir. No need to return it.' She told them the information she wanted, point by point. If she was polite and could keep them busy on minor tasks, they would comply.

When everyone had written what she asked, she said, 'Oh, by the way, before I collect your papers, I'd like one last detail from you, if you would be so kind. Have you seen Mr Dev Reddy since he was released, even in the distance? Please write *yes* or *no*. And if you saw him, please write when and where. Is that clear?'

They all nodded. Three hesitated for some time, but it seemed to her everyone wrote a single word. Horseman smiled politely and ushered them into the church. One woman turned back and took the bag of buns from the table, offering them to Horseman and Singh before exiting. Singh removed all the tea mugs except the one in front of Nata and put them on the narrow counter. She left the cash box where it was.

Nata sat at the head of the table. The two detectives took seats on either side of him.

'Out of interest, when did you hear Reddy had died?' Horseman asked.

'Oh, on the radio news earlier this morning. Nine o'clock, I think.'

'Really? Did the report say how he died?'

'Just that he died in CWM.'

'That's disappointing, isn't it, Sergeant Singh?'

'Indeed, sir. The media usually cooperate with police news embargos. They don't release the names of people who have died before we confirm that the relatives have been told.'

'Have you informed Mr Reddy's next of kin yet, Sergeant?'

'Not yet. It's taking some time to track his children down.'

'Well, you'll have more tedious tracking to check which news outlets broke the rules. I'm sorry. Whoever it was, they'll get an official police reprimand.'

She frowned while she made a note in her book, for Nata's benefit. 'Yes, sir. Which radio station did you hear the news on, Mr Nata?'

He looked from one to the other. 'Look, I'm not sure. My wife put the radio on and she told me the news. I couldn't really hear it.'

'That's okay. Did you already know why Reddy was in hospital?'

'No.'

'Where were you on Friday evening, Mr Nata?'

'Me? Well, I think you know in the afternoon I was outside Suva Prison, waiting for Reddy to be released, protesting against that evil man's release. There were plenty of constables around. When we got word that Reddy had been whisked away secretly, we stayed on. We still wanted to tell the whole of Fiji how wrong that decision was.'

'How did you *get word*, as you say?'

'Oh, I can't remember now. HOOK members were all around the vicinity. Someone recognised him in a vehicle, I suppose, and called me.'

'How did your supporters waiting at the prison gates react to the information?'

'Many felt deceived by the government, as they had been. Tricked. I encouraged them to focus on our core mission to spread Christ's instruction to protect children and especially to condemn those who harm His little ones.'

'Do you know the Reddy family personally? Have you met any of the sons or daughters? Or maybe nieces, nephews, cousins?'

'Not that I know of. His relatives wouldn't be broadcasting their relationship, would they?'

'Why not?

Nata looked at Horseman, incredulous. 'Because of the shame, because everyone hates Reddy.'

'How long did you stay outside the prison gates?'

'Until after dark. Many supporters had to go home before then to look after their children. But some of us stayed on, interpreting Scripture to those who wished to listen. It was a blessed time, despite our disappointment.' A dreamy smile played around his lips.

'Did you make plans?'

'We did. We'd already decided to hold a rally on Saturday morning in Ratu Sukuna Park. There was no reason to change that, but some wanted to keep up our vigil at the prison too, to confront staff going in and out with the enormity of their poor decision. God sent us supporters from all over Suva and even further afield, so there would be no problem holding demonstrations at different locations.'

'What time did you leave?'

Nata was enjoying reliving what he clearly saw as a day of glory. He startled as if from a dream. 'Mm? Oh, I'm not sure—you just get carried along by the Lord's mission, you know? But the evening meeting had finished when we got back to our church.'

'Who's we?'

'Well, the core HOOK members. We've had no time to form a proper committee. You know, I can't believe it was only a week ago God called me to do something about the sin of Reddy's release. This week has seemed like half my life.' His eyes certainly had the intense light of a man on a mission. Singh knew this was a dangerous light.

'Are they the people you've just been meeting with—the core HOOK members?'

'Some of them, not all. We had a lot of decisions to make about Saturday's rallies, more placards to make, signs to write. And most of all, we prayed.'

'What time did you leave the church?'

'Oh, it's hard to say. I suddenly felt tired and knew we would all need our strength for Saturday. It could have been half-past ten or even eleven.'

'Did all of your working party leave together?'

'A few left earlier, but most of us left together and went our separate ways.'

'Was there any talk about going to Reddy's farm?'

'No, we didn't know where it was.'

'Come now, Mr Nata. Tell us what you did for the rest of the night.'

'I went home, ate the meal my wife had prepared, said my prayers and fell asleep.'

'And Saturday morning?'

'My wife woke me at seven o'clock. That's very late for me. I went straight to the church, where we loaded a member's van with everything we'd got ready. Our pastor led us in prayer, and off we went. I was at one or another of our rally sites for the entire day. There would have been scores of witnesses, even hundreds. The media were everywhere—I think I was even on TV quite often.'

'These rally sites you mention. Where exactly were they?'

'The prison, Ratu Sukuna Park for hours, along Victoria Parade, and the government buildings.'

'Nausori airport, perhaps?'

Nata frowned. His puzzlement looked genuine.

'Just a few kilometres from the airport, the Rewa farmlands?'

But now he recognised where Horseman was heading. 'Not at all— what are you talking about?'

'Don't pretend you don't know whose farm I'm referring to, Mr Nata.'

'Well, okay. I know Reddy's farm is somewhere in that area, but I don't know where exactly.'

'You're joking, man! You were there, in the early hours of the morning, rallying your supporters, yelling threats, screaming abuse, chucking rocks. Weren't you?'

Nata reeled back—his body literally pivoted a good ten centimetres in his chair. Horseman's sudden eruption worked every time. He'd shocked Nata, confused him. Singh wouldn't like to be on the receiving end either, but she loved witnessing it.

'No, no—I don't know what you're talking about. Sir.'

Horseman leaned forward, eyes narrowing. 'You're not telling the truth, Mr Nata. You disappoint me—you're a lay preacher in God's Gospel Church! Your overnight rally and invasion of his farmhouse terrorised Mr Reddy, an elderly free citizen. Some of your protestors bashed him up. Your din woke Mr Reddy's neighbour, nearly two hundred metres away! He called the Nausori police, who were still trying to get your supporters to leave at ten o'clock on Saturday morning, when I arrived.'

'No, I wasn't there. Truly, I wasn't. If you think you saw me, it must have been someone else.' Nata swivelled his head to look at Singh, desperate.

'No, I didn't see you there, Mr Nata. The constables told me several demonstrators—whom I call violent vandals—dispersed when asked. Some walked off down the road to wait for the bus on the next corner. I suppose you were among those sensible people. It sounds like some of your troops refused to follow orders.'

Once more, Nata turned to look at Singh with pleading eyes. Soon, her boss, in apparent disgust, would hand Nata over to her and her velvet glove, as he liked to call her method. And Nata would be grateful, relax under her stroking.

'I don't give orders, Inspector. I organise and provide guidance. I wasn't at Reddy's farm. I didn't know people were going there.'

'So you do know the people who went there, then?'

'Well, someone told me on Saturday about a vigil there. But I don't know who the individuals concerned were.'

'You'll know soon enough, Ravai. What's your guess now about the cause of Mr Reddy's death?'

'I don't know. A guilty conscience, I hope.'

'The pathologist is examining his bruised and broken corpse right now. But it's highly likely he died of the injuries inflicted by your thugs in the early hours of Saturday morning. So these people whose names you don't know may face murder charges.'

Had Nata really not seen where Horseman was heading with his questions? But he reeled back again, even shut his eyes. Was he praying? Singh glanced at her boss, who lifted his eyebrows a millimetre. She was ready.

She smiled gently. 'Mr Nata, you may not know Inspector Horseman searched the farmhouse for Mr Reddy and eventually found him unconscious underneath his water tank. He rescued him and drove him to hospital, where he remained until he died. As a religious man, you will surely understand how he feels about his attackers and probable murderers. Am I right?'

'Of course, I understand, Sergeant. But what Reddy's attackers did was nothing compared to what that wretch did to his own son, a tiny child, for years and years. Nothing!'

Singh smiled again, trying to exude sympathy. 'Your passion for protecting children does you credit, Mr Nata. I understand that's your motivation. However, I can't agree that killing a person of any age is nothing. I'm sure you understand my position, too.'

Nata's eyes were still on her face. He nodded, grudging.

'So, I don't quite understand why you won't tell us the truth about what you and others in HOOK did on the weekend.'

'I have. You can check my media appearances, on and off all day on Saturday. In Suva. I didn't control or even know what other HOOK members or supporters did outside Suva.'

'I see. But why should the police, who enforce the law, have to spend countless hours searching through radio and TV archives to check your alibi? It's a waste of our time. We'll do it if we have to, but it would be much better and more Christian of you to help us, wouldn't it?'

Again, a nod, a little less grudging this time.

'Good, I think so, too. We know you weren't in Suva all the time, because you arrived at Nausori Police Station at half-past four and bailed out Joni Kavika, Paula Wairua and Mark Prasad. The sergeant released them on your guarantee they would appear before the magistrate tomorrow. You paid one hundred dollars for each of them. You know them, don't you?'

Nata froze.

Horseman leaned in. 'Tell us what you know. All of it. Now.'

24

'Do you believe Nata?' Dr Young asked.

Horseman looked at Singh. They'd been debating this question on the drive back to the station, where they had to drop the police car, and on the walk through the town centre to Mill Cottage, Dr Young's choice for their lunch meeting.

'His claim that he wasn't at Reddy's farm and knew nothing of the disturbance there is possibly true. We don't know. But he says he didn't know the three men until a HOOK member phoned him and asked for his help. We both doubt that, but why would he lie? It's no crime to know someone who commits a crime.'

'Interesting. Seems like he's back-pedalling from HOOK as fast as he can.'

'Hmm, don't know. You should hear him rant about Reddy. He's still as passionate about his campaign, even though its focus is dead,' Horseman added.

'Anyway, we walked all this way to have lunch with you to hear about the postmortem. Not to repeat what we've been saying to each other for the last half-hour.'

'Fair swap, mate. But let me order first. It's the best authentic Fijian food in Suva but I don't often have time to come here for lunch.'

'The most authentic upmarket food, you mean. This place is a canteen for embassy staff, lawyers and public servants. The market food stalls are even more authentic,' Horseman pointed out.

'Yes, well, I prefer feast food to fish heads—what's wrong with that? I figured it wouldn't be as crowded here as usual, with regulars fearful of more demos around the government buildings. And I was right. What do you want?'

'Goat curry for me,' Horseman said.

'Mm, the baked fish, please, Matt. Cassava chips, too.'

'Goes without saying. Coming up, Detective Sergeant!'

'Matt's looking pleased with himself, isn't he? I hope that means he's got a definite cause of death for us.'

'But you think he'd be bursting to tell us. Why's he holding back?'

'Looking forward to showing us we've been wrong about something all along, I bet. He loves to turn the tables.'

Their meals arrived within five minutes, looking and smelling so appetising that talk subsided to murmurs of praise and pleasure until their dishes were empty.

Horseman couldn't wait any longer. 'Matt, we've gone along with your tasty delaying tactics with good grace. Time to spill the beans. Have we got a cause of death?'

The pathologist's grey eyes twinkled. 'Almost—just waiting for confirmation from Forensics. But that could be a day or two and you two need to know now.'

Singh put both palms firmly on the table. It would be exaggerating to call her gesture a thump, but she displayed more impatience than Horseman had seen in her before. Funny, she was usually so polite to Dr Young.

'Yes, we do, Matt. Put us out of our pain, Doctor!'

'Righto. Well, you might have to downgrade the charges of those three HOOK demonstrators at the farm.'

'What?'

'From murder, I mean. Down to assault causing grievous bodily harm. Because it looks like asphyxia. Classic indicators—petechial hemorrhages in the eyes, et cetera. But the clincher—tiny cotton fibres in his nose and airways and on the skin of his face. You're the detectives, but it looks like murder to me.'

Horseman said, 'Don't want to argue, Matt, but couldn't Reddy have inhaled those from the hospital air? Hospital staff frequently shake out fresh bed linen in the wards.'

'Sure, but there's another piece of evidence that's critical.'

'Matt, tell us,' Singh commanded.

'Yes, ma'am. Two pieces, actually. One, identical cotton fibres under Reddy's fingernails.'

Horseman didn't find this compelling. 'His arms were on top of the sheet when I saw him. But whether they were underneath or on top, his involuntary movements could pick them up easily.'

'You're a good devil's advocate, mate. However, didn't I say two pieces of evidence?'

'You did,' Singh said.

'And I've got your good boss here to thank for it.'

'Really?'

'Yeah, you pulled out a pillow from behind the bedhead and put it back on Mr Reddy's mattress. Made sure it got to my pathology lab. It could well have been missed and ended up on another bed. The fabric of the pillow slip is pretty thin, veering towards threadbare. There are scratches, marginally visible to the naked eye, clear as day under my microscope. The scratches are consistent with those made by adult human fingernails—they've even cut through the fibres in several places.'

All three faces were deadly serious now.

'You mean—someone smothered Reddy with a pillow?' There was fear in Singh's voice.

'I'm ninety-nine per cent sure. Forensics can do precise fibre matching. I'll wait for that before writing my report.'

A waiter came to clear the table. Another brought complimentary banana cake and coffee. Horseman stared at the tablecloth for a long time, imagining an injured old man, roused as he suffocated, tearing at a pillow, his murderer's instrument

25

Just two days before, Albert Park had provided a picnic ground and break-out space for anti-Reddy demonstrators massing at the adjacent government buildings. Despite some remaining litter, the sports ground had returned to normal. Horseman's heart lifted as the Junior Shiners arrived at training in ones and twos, greeting each other with teen exuberance as if they hadn't a care in the world. Yet all were poor; few lived with a parent and those who did had to earn money for the household; none went to school. To them, their lives were normal. From his casual enquiries last Thursday, he estimated half the training squad had no homes—they truly lived on the streets and parks.

They milled around him, happily shouting.

'Joe, Joe, how many you arrest on Saturday?'

'Were you in Ratu Sukuna Park, Joe?'

'No, Victoria Parade—you moved cars off the road! Good job!'

'Not a good idea, Joe! Those protesters think they can boss the police now!'

'Uncle say smash some heads, Joe!'

As the excitement level escalated, Horseman lifted his police whistle to his lips and raised his other hand. Like eager puppies, the boys quietened. Constables Kau and Musudroka arrived together, no doubt wondering why Horseman was early for once.

'*Vinaka* for coming early, boys. I have an important announcement about Mosese. Some of you will know already that he was bashed up on Saturday night underneath our grandstand here. A thug knocked him unconscious and broke his nose. Luckily, a constable heard him groaning and found him, took him to hospital. I visited him there. He's a lot better now and will leave hospital tomorrow. My friend Father Francis will give him a bed in his hostel up at Flagstaff.'

The boys' upturned faces were fearful: wide eyes, mouths open in shock.

'Mosese won't be able to work as a shoe-shine boy for at least a week and he won't be able to train for another two weeks. My clever dog found his shoe-shine box and some of his things on Sunday, but his polish and brushes are gone. The police are checking his box for fingerprints so we might catch the dangerous man who attacked him.'

'Joe, Joe, can we go see Mosese at Flagstaff?

'*Io*, I'm sure Mosese wants to see his friends soon. I told Father Francis some of you will visit, so he's expecting you.'

As the Shiners recovered from their shock, they started talking again, but their volume was lower, their tone more earnest.

Horseman blew the whistle at half-past four precisely. The boys sprang into their usual two lines. Kau and Musudroka moved to the head of each line.

'I'm worried your heads are getting dizzy running around the oval in the same direction, Shiners. So this afternoon, Constable Kau's line will run around clockwise for one lap, then anti-clockwise for the second lap. Constable Musudroka's line will run in the reverse direction. Got it?'

'Apo, clockwise first is fastest, eh?' an eager runner shouted to Kau.

'We'll turn around before you guys are halfway, eh Tani?'

'Take it easy, boys—this is the warm-up, remember?'

Horseman chuckled. Their spirit reminded him of his youth, and, less pleasurably, that he was not getting any younger. He still hoped his sports physician in the States would give him the green light at his review in January, but he was not as hopeful as he had been. Three setbacks—well, injuries in the line of duty, and a broken ankle just two months ago—had rammed it home that his body repaired itself more slowly now.

After driving the boys hard through the skills drill of passing and kicking, he whistled for halftime and the boys sauntered to the taps, quiet now. He joined them.

'A quick law lesson while you're getting your breath back, boys. Three points. One: Fiji is ruled by law, not the police. Our law allows people to gather to protest about something the government has done, like we saw this last week around the prison and government buildings. Two: Fiji law forbids violence by protestors, and indeed anyone. Those people who threw rocks last Saturday, breaking windows and injuring people, were committing crimes. Three: stealing is a crime wherever it happens —from a house, from a shop, anywhere. Those people who stole from the shops with broken windows were also committing crimes. The police will arrest the window breakers and the thieves when we know who they are. Any questions?'

One or two boys hugged their knees and lowered their heads—a sure sign of teenage guilt. Of course, they might have taken part in the looting. He hoped they hadn't. The police had put a quick stop to it.

'Joe, how can you find out who they are?'

'Ah, that's a detective's secret. But I will allow Tanielo and Apolosi, who are detective constables and your trainers, to share their secrets and answer your question.'

The boys started chanting, 'Apo, Tani, Apo, Tani,' until the laughing DCs came forward. Musudroka, who had the more outgoing personality, took the stage.

As he half-listened to Musudroka's comic tale of catching thieves, he wondered what would happen to Reddy's house. Would word spread that the criminal who was beyond forgiveness actually owned land and a house? Reddy had, in the last week, become the focus of the terrors and hatreds of a great many Fijians. Could they tolerate learning the old man had property that would pass to his children? Heaven forbid that angle should occur to anyone in the media. He must look into Reddy's will as a priority. If he'd died intestate, would the usual rules apply?

Musudroka wound up and sent the boys for another drink at the taps before the second half of training. Horseman headed over to organise the teams for the practice match. Pita and Livai, two live wires, intercepted him.

'*Vinaka*, Joe, for helping Mosese. We'll go and see him tomorrow.'

'Great, boys. He'll appreciate seeing his friends. He won't know anyone at the hostel at first.'

'I got a spare black brush, Joe. I'll lend it to Mosese until he can buy another one. Maybe another Shiner has a spare brown one. Could you ask?'

'That's very kind, Livai. You know, I think it's better if you ask the others. It was your idea and you've set an example.'

'I've got another idea. If everyone puts in twenty cents, we can buy Mosese new polish, too,' Pita added.

'No doubt about you boys, you've got good heads on your shoulders. Excellent—you can ask the boys at dinner at the end of the match.'

'They'll do what you say, Joe.'

'These are your good ideas and you can tell the boys. How about I blow the whistle and tell them to listen up? And when you finish, I'll say I support you and I'll keep the money safe for Mosese.'

Pita brightened up but Livai stood, shyly kicking the turf with the toe of his too-tight rugby boots.

'What have you got to say, Livai? I have to start the game right away, you know.'

'Pita and me, we're scared of the grandstand and the market now. Can you ask Father Francis for a bed for us, too? What do you think, Joe?'

'I can ask. I'll do my best. I know Father Francis has a lot of boys in the hostel. He's squeezing in Mosese because he's injured and he'll need looking after.'

What was he saying? They were just kids. They all needed looking after. But they didn't know that. They were reduced to survival mode, except for their precious hours playing rugby. To be safe from attack was all they asked for.

Another thing Pita and Livai didn't know was, they were asking the wrong person. He had yet to find a home for himself.

TUESDAY

26

Horseman's raincoat created a cascade as he climbed the stairs. He draped it awkwardly over a top cupboard in the kitchenette where it could drip into the sink. He pulled a large bulldog clip from papers in his satchel and secured the hood to the cupboard door before entering the CID office.

'*Bula* sir, I think I've done it!' Musudroka called out.

'*Bula*, Tani. What've you done now?'

'Checked all media reports since Sunday night and...' The probationer smiled.

'Out with it, man!' Horseman smiled, too. Musudroka loved a bit of drama and he didn't mind playing along.

'It's disappointing because they've all been good boys and girls. No reports of Reddy's death at all. But that's good, eh?'

'*Io*, Tani. As you've realised, that means Ravai Nata was lying when he said he got the news from the radio.'

'No proof of murder, though.'

'You're right, Tani. My bet is, he's got a relative or supporter working at the hospital. With hundreds on staff, we've little chance of finding out who it is. But now that we're sure he couldn't have heard about Reddy's death on the radio, we can put pressure on Nata and he just might tell us. After all, a media story about their darling lying to the police wouldn't help his cause, would it?'

'Dunno, sir. Some might be impressed.'

'*Io*, but they're criminals, Tani. Remember which side you're on!'

Musudroka gave him an enthusiastic thumbs-up.

Singh piped up. 'Apo's done just as well.'

'Your turn now, Apolosi.'

'Thanks to the Register Office, we've got names and birth dates for all five surviving children of Dev Reddy, apart from Kanan, whose birth was never registered. The hard part was finding where they are now. I confirmed Dr Acharya's information, that four of the five were in New Zealand. They've all moved since the last census and the addresses on their Fiji passports are out of date, too.'

'Sounds like they're doing well for themselves,' Horseman said.

'Or the opposite,' added Singh.

'Whatever, I found three on the New Zealand Electoral Roll and Sergeant Singh has just spoken to Pranjal, one of the sons.'

'Pranjal was a uni student when Kanan was born. Now he's forty-two, an accountant in Auckland with kids in high school. Actually, he's the only Reddy son who's seen his brother, Kanan. He gave me the phone number of the eldest son, Darsh. Officially, I think notifying just one of the surviving children fulfills our duty, but I'm going to call Darsh at least. Pranjal said he knew nothing of his father's will, but his eldest brother might know something.'

'What was Pranjal's attitude?'

'Oh, quite polite, but didn't want to talk much. He displayed no emotion at the news. He said he wasn't in touch with his sisters anymore. The last he heard, the youngest, Ela, was still living with the older sister and her family in Dunedin. He said it's been years since he's heard from them.'

'Not a close family, then.'

'Not at all. Pranjal said the only phone number he had was for Darsh, who's now forty-nine.'

'I suspect Reddy was always a tough father, maybe a tyrant. All his kids wanted to escape.'

'Could be. But after the media furore over the chicken-boy and the trial, their shame could isolate them from each other, too. They might just want to forget their childhood and youth in Fiji.'

Musudroka looked gobsmacked. 'But how could you? Forget your childhood, I mean.'

'For you, boy, that would mean forgetting your entire life! In a new country, establishing new ties, many immigrants want to do just that. How many succeed, I don't know.'

'I'm surprised they haven't changed their names.'

'*Io*, but the married daughter probably did before she left Fiji. Did you get that from the marriage register, Apo?'

'*Io*, sir, I'll email you all their details.'

'*Vinaka*. Singh, please call Darsh. I'll call Taufa Smith in Public Relations and authorise her to release a statement about Reddy's death immediately. She prepared it yesterday. A media beat-up might flush some game out of the undergrowth. Hope so.'

***

Half an hour later, Horseman headed out of the station car park with Singh.

'Did you reach Darsh?' Horseman asked.

Singh grinned. 'Easy, for a change. Darsh works for the government as an agricultural economist. His brother gave me his mobile number and he actually answered!

'Anyway, he's a taciturn type. Pranjal had already broken the news of Reddy's death. When I expressed my condolences, he grunted scathingly and told me not to bother. He was more interested when I mentioned Dev's estate. He said he knew nothing of a will but could give me the name of a solicitor in Nausori that his father used in a boundary dispute he had with a neighbour. It was many years ago, but you never know. We've no other leads on a will. I'll follow up as soon as we've got Nata to confess. How's that for a plan?'

'Sounds promising. I had second thoughts and asked Taufa to delay the release on Reddy's death until one o'clock—just in case we have to hunt Nata down.'

His decision seemed wise when they looked through the open door of God's Gospel Church office. He recognised the woman and the two men sitting at the table with mugs of tea and notebooks. They had all been present at the larger meeting the day before. The same tin money box lay with its lid open, stuffed with notes and coins heaped together.

'*Bula*, everyone. Is Mr Nata around?'

All three smiled warmly. 'Welcome, Josefa Horseman. And Sergeant Singh, too. Please join us in a cup of tea,' the middle-aged woman's invitation was friendly.

'*Vinaka*, you're very kind, but no. Can you tell us where Mr Nata is?'

They glanced at each other. '*Io*, he's gone to the Fiji One studios for an interview.' The woman looked and sounded like a proud and indulgent mother. 'He speaks so well on TV, doesn't he? The news producer told him the camera loves him. Well, I never!' She chuckled and slapped her thighs with both hands.

The older man looked at her, disappointed. 'It's because he's sincere. That comes across.'

'*Vinaka vakalevu*, friends. We'll catch up with him at the studio.'

Singh glanced at Horseman, then said with a smile, 'Excuse me, I'd like to offer some security advice, if I may.'

The middle-aged woman said, 'Of course, my dear.'

'I noticed the cashbox on the table yesterday. Did you bank the money in it yesterday?'

Again, their smiles were friendly. 'Oh, no, but we'll take it today.'

'Has it been sitting open on the table here since yesterday?'

'*Io*, but we lock it when we leave.'

'Anyone could walk in and take it, couldn't they?'

'*Io*, dear, but they wouldn't. This is a church!'

Horseman spoke up. 'Churches are often robbed, madam.'

'No, that is sacrilege, isn't it? Who would steal from God?'

'There are dishonest people about who will steal whenever they spot an opportunity.'

Singh asked, 'Have you counted the money?'

'Oh, no, there's no need. The teller at the bank counts it. We'd probably make a mistake.'

'The teller might make a mistake, too, and you'd never know, would you? People have been generous and given money to HOOK. You owe it to them to count it and keep it safe, don't you agree?'

They nodded.

'Please, we advise you most strongly to lock the box and keep it hidden in a cupboard, not on the table. Count your takings and deposit them in the bank every day.'

They nodded. '*Io*, *vinaka*, *ovisa*.'

***

Ravai Nata sat in a white armchair angled towards Indira Choudhury, the Fiji One presenter. Two cameras obscured their faces, so Horseman and Singh moved around to the side for a better view. Nata's body was tense, but he looked directly into the camera lens when he spoke, just like a professional. For someone with less than a week's experience on television, that was impressive. Maybe he was a natural, as the producer said.

Horseman approached a woman on the outskirts of the action. 'Excuse me, is this interview live?'

'Oh no, there's a police delay on this one. It'll be edited and broadcast on the afternoon news and repeated at five o'clock. Wait, you're Joe Horseman aren't you?' She smiled.

He showed his ID and introduced Singh.

Singh said, 'Thanks for observing the release deadline. I was a bit worried when I saw Ravai Nata in the hot seat. There's only one news item you'll be asking him about.'

'Yes, Reddy's death will be welcome news to most of the nation. For us, though, it'll cut short what could've been a much longer-running story. Still, there are obvious spinoffs and backstories we can chase. Nata is one of them. He's got real presence on TV—charisma. And his HOOK charity is worthy of follow-up, for sure.'

Horseman glanced at Singh, who raised her eyebrows a tiny fraction. 'We want to interview Mr Nata, too. But there's no need to interrupt your recording. How much longer do you think you'll be?'

'I'm not sure. We'll edit it down later, so this take could be longish. You're welcome to wait, though. In here or out in reception. There's a small canteen off to the right if you want to grab a drink or something.'

'*Vinaka*, we're fine here.'

'I can't wait to see my husband's face when I tell him I met Joe Horseman!'

27

'Why are you recording this? Am I arrested for something?' Ravai Nata looked confused. He was still neat in his pale blue business shirt and navy sulu.

'No, Mr Nata. We routinely record interviews here at the station. There can be no dispute then about what was said, can there?' Sergeant Singh said.

'And I'm sure it will be much less stressful than the television interviews you record frequently,' Horseman added. 'There's a discrepancy between what you told us yesterday and facts we've discovered just this morning. When you've set us straight, I'll get you to write a statement and sign it here in the station. Then you'll be free to go on with your day. Any more media appearances planned?'

'Just one radio interview for the Pentecostal Broadcasting Service. I like to be available to whoever wants to hear about HOOK.' His voice was warm and earnest. The microphone would love him just as much as the camera.

'Let's get to the point. Yesterday, you told us you knew Mr Reddy was dead because your wife heard it on the radio. The police placed an embargo on news of Mr Reddy's death until his next of kin could be told about it. Media respect police embargos and the reason for them. We issue an official reprimand when any member of the press breaks an embargo. Do you understand?'

'*Io*, it's a good idea.'

'I'm glad you approve. My officers have spent hours checking every media outlet, including every radio station. They assure me that not one article and not one broadcast has announced the death of Mr Reddy. The embargo will be lifted at two o'clock today. That's why Fiji One was pre-recording your interview, so they can show it later this afternoon.'

Nata continued to look from one to the other detective, attentive.

'So, Mr Nata, you need to think more carefully now. How did you know that Dev Reddy died?' Singh asked.

Nata leaned forward, even more earnest. 'Are you telling me the truth?'

'Yes, we've told you the truth.' Singh replied, then shot a bemused glance at Horseman.

'That means you haven't told the truth, Mr Nata. You're the one who's told us lies,' he said.

Nata closed his eyes and lifted his head back. Was he praying?

He opened his eyes and looked from one detective to the other. 'I thought my wife heard the news on the radio...' He smiled, a radiant smile exposing perfect white teeth.

'How blind I've been. It was God who told me—a direct message from the Lord!'

'Direct, or through your wife?' Horseman asked.

Nata's smile disappeared. He pointed his right index finger at Horseman. 'Do not mock God.'

'I'm not arguing with you, Mr Nata. I never mock God. I asked you a question: did God speak to you direct, or through your wife?'

'My memory is not clear about how the knowledge came into my mind.'

'Really? Does your wife have a job?'

'*Io*, she's the breadwinner, to be honest. I haven't been able to get a salaried job since we came to Suva. But I'm blessed to be a lay preacher, and God will provide. We are staying with her brother and sister-in-law. They are generous, but my wife wants us to have our own home, especially as she is expecting our first child.' His angelic smile returned.

'What is her job?'

'She works in the office at Patel's Hardware. Full-time and salaried, entitled to maternity leave, too.' His face shone with pride.

'That's excellent. And your brother?'

'Brother-in-law. He's my wife's brother. He's a mechanic, specialising in outboard motors.'

'He must be highly skilled.'

'*Io*, they're fortunate. They're good people and share their blessings with us. Even my wife's sister has a full-time job.

'What's your sister-in-law's job?'

'She's also well-qualified. She makes X-rays at CWM hospital. What's that job called?'

'A radiographer, or maybe a technician.'

'Radiographer, that's it. Definitely. She did the full course up at the Fiji School of Medicine. Her family is so proud of her.'

'Is she at work today?'

Nata looked bewildered. 'I expect so.'

Horseman pushed his notebook across the table. 'Please write her name here, Mr Nata. Sergeant Singh will ask you some more questions and help you with your statement.'

***

Akosita Olo smiled as she shook hands. 'I'm pleased to meet you, Inspector Horseman. I can't imagine why you would want to speak to me, though.'

They were in the small side-room, actually more of a closet, where staff retreated while they exposed patients to X-rays.

'Mrs Olo, is there a private space somewhere near where we could sit down for five minutes?'

Mrs Olo smiled cheerfully. Her face creased in the way of faces that smile a lot. She was pleasantly plump.

'Call me Sita, please. Give me a moment to let my colleagues know where I'll be. Fancy me helping the police with their enquiries, eh? Who'd have thought?'

In a few minutes, they were seated on the usual hospital plastic chairs in the Imaging Department's staff tea-room. Like much of the hospital, the room was long overdue for refurbishment. Horseman was grateful for the strong tea Mrs Olo insisted on making for both of them.

'Sita, did you take part in the treatment of Mr Dev Reddy, who was admitted last Saturday around midday?'

'*Io*, I came on duty at three in the afternoon. I don't know why his X-rays were delayed, maybe Emergency was overstretched because of the protests about Reddy himself. Maybe the doctor was hoping he'd recover consciousness and could give him more information about what happened. Anyway, he was my first job on the shift. And a difficult one, because he was unconscious and unable to cooperate.'

'How did he come by his injuries, do you think?'

'Oh, that's up to the doctor to determine, not me, Inspector.'

'Still, you're experienced, you must have formed an opinion.'

'Well, it looked to me like he was beaten up, but as I said...'

'Was that the only occasion you saw Mr Reddy?'

Why did she hesitate? '*Io*, sir.'

'Are you sure you didn't have to go to his ward to deliver a report to the doctor, or for any other reason?'

Mrs Olo shook her head. 'Definitely not.'

'Were you asked by a doctor to take any extra X-rays or other images?'

'No, not at all.' She was sounding stressed. She looked down and drank more of her tea.

'Who did you tell about Mr Reddy's X-rays?'

'The doctor. My colleagues, too. They were really interested, what with the news coverage all last week, not to mention the rallies on Friday and Saturday.'

'Anyone outside the hospital?'

'Well, I mentioned it at home, but not until Sunday morning. I didn't get home until half-past eleven. The others were all in bed. No one told me to keep it a secret. Shouldn't I have told anyone?' She frowned anxiously and hastily gulped more tea.

'That's quite okay, Sita. Did you work on Sunday?'

'*Io*, I always take the weekends if I can—higher pay and my husband and sister can look after the children. On Sunday, I was on the night shift —eleven until seven the next morning.'

'That must be tiring.'

'*Oi lei*, you get used to it. And Imaging isn't busy at night—only new emergency admissions, usually.'

'When did you hear about Mr Reddy's death?'

'I'm not sure. Only a few hours before the end of my shift.'

'Did you see any strangers in the corridors or on the stairs as you were going about your work?'

'No, no one. Just the regular staff. It was very quiet, so I didn't leave the department much at all. I was lucky, actually. I came in here and slept in the armchair in the corner for a while.'

'Who told you about Reddy's death?'

'The technician woke me and told me. Coconut wireless, you know. I bet all the hospital staff found out pretty quickly.'

Horseman smiled. 'I'm sure you're right.'

'Did you make a phone call home to pass on the news?'

Mrs Olo looked surprised. 'No, that's not my style. Of course, everyone was up when I got home—half-past seven on Monday morning. That's when I told them. My husband had already gone to work.'

'Did you speak to Ravai Nata?' Her eyes widened as if she at last realised the point of Horseman's questions. She frowned in concentration.

'No, I'm sure I didn't. I told my sister. Ravai was still asleep. My sister said he was worn out after the Saturday rallies and all the follow-up on Sunday. He got home really late, she said. She didn't even wake up when he came in. He practically lives at that church—when he's not on TV and radio, that is.'

28

The air-conditioning in the old Landcruiser couldn't cope with the afternoon heat. Horseman turned it off and wound down the windows. The rush of air dried his skin but didn't act so quickly on his sweat-soaked collar. He was glad he'd worn a sulu today—so much cooler than trousers.

Gopal Prakash's farmhouse was a few hundred metres along from Reddy's place. A flourishing red hibiscus hedge marked the front boundary. The compulsory mango tree overhanging the corrugated iron roof provided shade and fruit for pickling. The memory of green mango pickles made his mouth water. Like Reddy's house, the central section was elevated on posts, but the lean-to additions were level with the ground. They would flood regularly.

A woman emerged from around the side, carrying a basket of dry washing on her head. Her long plait, threaded with grey, fell to the hem of her faded salwar kameez tunic.

'Hello, are you Mrs Prakash?'

The woman lifted her chin, smiling. Horseman showed her his ID and introduced himself. She offered him her free hand. 'Please come in and have some tea. My sons are working, but my husband's inside—he always does his office work after lunch.'

'Sounds sensible—avoiding the worst of the heat.'

He sat with the farmer at a table capable of accommodating a large family on long benches. Prakash was mellow after his lunch, which for farmers was the main meal of the day. He poured condensed milk into the tea his wife had served.

'The way I look at it is, I'm sorry Dev died, but it was inevitable, wasn't it? I'll never understand why he wanted to come back. He should have realised he was finished here. I mean, at his age, all the children gone to New Zealand...'

'Except Kanan,' Horseman said.

'Yes, except him. I'd almost forgotten about him—not that an albino would be much use on a farm, even if he was able-bodied. Their skin can't take the sun, you know. Just burns up.'

Horseman nodded. 'Perhaps Dev didn't want to die in prison. What was his attitude to the farm?'

Prakash put his tin mug down and steepled his hands together on the table. 'Oh, it was his whole life—he loved it, Inspector. I don't hate him like everyone else. He was a good farmer. He went to all the Agriculture Department field days and read all their materials. He improved the place, tried new crops. I've followed his example. Where he went wrong was with his kids. He was too strict, like their only use was to labour on his beloved farm. He beat them too much, so all they wanted to do was get away. The way I look at it is, every child needs chastising, but in proportion to what they've done wrong. What's the point if your children hate you and never want to see you again?'

'Was Dev a good neighbour?'

Prakash put his elbows on the table and thought for a bit. 'The way I look at it, yes. He wasn't sociable, but he respected the boundaries, kept his animals on his own property and was a fair trader if we bought or sold anything from each other. Our wives were friendly, sharing pickles and chutneys, passing down outgrown children's clothes and so on.' A wistful smile played about his mouth.

'I noticed last Saturday that the farmyard is neglected, but the fields behind it have crops growing. Who looks after the farm now?'

'That would be me and my sons. When he was first arrested, I offered to maintain things for him, temporarily. That was a load off his mind. He was so proud of that land—most of it is freehold, you know. Rare as hen's teeth. He inherited it, but he's bought more. He also applied for land leases whenever any plots for transfer came up. He doubled the size of his farm over time.'

'Freehold, eh? What's the story behind that?'

'It was part of the land bought by Australians from the chief for growing cotton. Long ago, 1870s I think, when the chiefs could sell their land if they wanted. That cotton scheme failed within twenty years—I heard the crops got diseased because of the high rainfall. But the land has always remained freehold, even though it's been subdivided again and again. Dev always had his eye out for more freehold land that he could buy. Me, too. Imagine, if you could bequeath freehold land and a going concern to your children, you could keep them with you in your old age, don't you think?'

'That would certainly be an incentive. But from what I've seen, many young people want to go their own way no matter what. Do you still look after the Reddy farm?'

'Yes, all above board, Inspector. After he was sentenced, I went to see him and asked if I could help. Dev said I could rent the farm on a five-year lease, rolling over for as long as he was in prison. The Nausori solicitor visited him in prison, then prepared the lease papers. I went to his office to sign them.'

'I understand Dev was mentally unstable at that time.'

Prakash steepled his work-worn hands on the table again. 'He was a strange man, but not all bad, Inspector. The way I look at it is, he was out of the real world, out of his mind in many ways. But where the farm and business were concerned, he was sensible, even rather smart, you know. You know, a demon may take over part of you and leave other parts alone.'

Horseman nodded, non-committal. 'I see. Can you give me the solicitor's details, please?'

Prakash frowned.

'He may be able to tell me more about Mr Reddy's legal matters.'

'It's Mr Pandey. Excuse me a minute - I've got a card for him in my desk.'

After Prakash returned and Horseman copied down the details, he asked, 'Did you ever see Kanan?'

Prakash stared at him for a moment or two, his muscular torso rigid. Then he shrugged his shoulders and relaxed. 'Yes, I did, when he was a baby. When Priti, Dev's wife was still alive. My wife and I went to visit first when he was several months old. My wife had been over before but she didn't tell me Kanan was an albino. I got a shock. Priti asked me not to mention the child's condition to anyone. It may be superstitious, but many people believe albinos are bad luck.'

It wasn't his place to question people's beliefs, but he couldn't help it. 'Albinos are the offspring of two parents who both carry a gene that prevents the skin colouring. They are normal in every other way.'

Prakash stiffened again. 'That may be so, but Priti said there weren't any albinos in either her family or Dev's. And look at what's happened. That child has cursed his parents and the entire family. All dead or fled Fiji. What's more, folk around here believe he's cursed the land, too. No one will want to buy land where a demon has flourished.'

'But you don't believe that, do you? You told me what good freehold land it is.'

'Freehold is an advantage, certainly.'

'I noticed Dev has a very nice shrine in his fields. Does the goddess protect the land and crops from evil forces?'

'We hope so, we hope so. That's Durga, the powerful goddess. I'm afraid we've neglected Dev's shrine. It was really Priti and one daughter who were the devotees. They washed the goddess, gave her fresh fruit and so on. Priti taught the little girl to make new clothes for the goddess from scraps. Once she cut a strip from Priti's best silk sari for a sari for the goddess.' He seemed far away in memories. Horseman would not have suspected him of being sentimental, but people could always surprise.

'How has the farm been going lately?'

Prakash focused on Horseman again. 'Not too bad. I've got three sons and a son-in-law working both farms. Dev's idea for a large herb field was brilliant. We export direct to New Zealand, right from Nausori airport here. All the Indians in New Zealand want the tropical herbs that won't grow all year round there.' His eyes lit up.

The rumour that Reddy's land was cursed suited Prakash very well. If it was up for sale, he reckoned Prakash would make an offer.

'Gopal, I've got some photos to show you. Please look carefully. Have you seen any of these men around here recently?'

He laid the mugshots of Reddy's attackers carefully on the table one by one, followed by a photo of Ravai Nata. 'Sorry, but no—oh, except this last one. But I didn't see him around here. I think it was on the TV. Yes, it was. He's a Christian minister, isn't he?'

'Well, a lay preacher actually, but yes. Thanks, Gopal. I'd like to talk to your wife now, as she was close to the Reddy family.'

Prakash glanced at the clock on the wall. 'Oh, you've missed her—she will have left by now. We still have two children at high school. She likes to meet them at the bus stop and walk back with them. They're too big for that now but she enjoys their chat while they walk.'

'No worries. Tell her I'll call in another time soon.'

He would bring Singh along next time.

29

One good thing—Reddy's son and Prakash had named the same solicitor. As Darsh hadn't heard from his father for over ten years, that probably meant Dev Reddy was a longstanding client whom the lawyer knew well. Horseman checked his notebook again. The offices of Navneet Pandey Esq. Bachelor of Laws (University of the South Pacific) were conveniently close to the Nausori police station and magistrate's chambers. It would be a minor detour to drop in on his way back to Suva.

Like most of Nausori, the building housing Pandey & Associates was dusty and in need of repainting. The fine, reddish silt of the Rewa River flats readily broke down under cultivation, to be caught by the breeze and deposited everywhere. School children enjoyed shuffling through it while waiting for the bus, kicking it at each other while walking along the streets. Whether dry, warm and powdery, or wet and gluey, it coated every surface in Nausori, including the open hallway and stairs that led up to the lawyers' offices.

Inside, the ambience was fresh and pleasant. The glass louvres sparkled, the blades of the ceiling fan were free of brown fuzz, the soft mint walls soothed and the deep red curtains added a little drama. Together with the matching timber office furniture, the waiting room might quell the doubts of a new client wondering if he'd made the right choice of legal advisor.

A middle-aged woman in an embroidered salwar kameez greeted him at the reception counter. Her brown almond eyes lit her cheerful round face. 'I am very sorry, Inspector, but Mr Pandey is in the middle of a consultation. I am guessing that he won't be free for another twenty minutes. At least. You are most welcome to wait. I can offer tea.'

'Thank you, but I have another quick errand. I'll come back in twenty minutes if Mr Pandey will be free then. If not, I'll make an appointment for tomorrow.'

'I know he will be making time for you, Detective Inspector.'

His quick errand was to fill his stomach. Because the Indian population was in the majority here, Nausori outdid Suva in the quality and variety of its Indian cuisine. And as a dedicated roti fancier, Horseman knew where to go. Just a hundred metres along the street was a hole-in-the-wall wedged between a pizza café and printery. The spice-infused steam made his mouth water. He was glad it was mid-afternoon and he was the only customer.

Mahen, the proprietor, grinned. 'Nice to see you, Joe! Your usual pumpkin and pea roti, isn't it?'

'Can't resist, man! But I should try something different, too. Your choice.'

'My goodness me, you must be trying goat curry, mango chutney and cucumber, Joe. Come in and be sitting down while you eat.'

He raised the hinged plywood counter and swung back the panel underneath. Horseman stepped through, sidled past the rudimentary kitchen set up in what was just an alley between the shops. Powered by a gas cylinder, everything could be packed up and removed when the council inspectors were about. However, Mahen's rotis were so popular, the council received no complaints and the food inspectors turned a blind eye to his do-it-yourself outlet.

Beyond the few metres of cement floor Mahen himself had put down, a couple of plastic stools stood in the dust. Horseman sat and within a minute Mahen brought him his two warm rotis in a brown paper bag. He bit into the goat curry one. Succulent spiced meat, super-hot chutney and crisp cucumber and yoghurt were a match made in heaven. Why did he always stick to pumpkin-and-pea? And the roti itself was wheaty, soft but strong enough to ensure the contents didn't leak through all over the diner's clothes.

'Compliments to the chef, man. It's going to be hard to beat this recipe!'

Mahen was well-used to praise but he always seemed genuinely grateful. 'Ah, well, wait till you're getting to your pumpkin, Joe. I'm changing it now—less chilli and more of the garam masala I am using for the goat and beef.'

Horseman bit the end off his pumpkin roti and loved the variation in the spice-mix. He continued to take alternate bites until he'd eaten half of each wrap.

'What do your customers think about the attack on Dev Reddy? And his death?'

Mahen wagged his head from side to side. 'My goodness me, everyone's talking about that. Most are thinking he's a very bad man and should still be staying in prison. Some say he was possessed by a demon so what he did is not really his fault, but those who killed him did the right thing. My goodness, what can you do with a demon? Even a few are saying that his son was taken over by demons and that's why Dev couldn't have him in the house. Someone said he went mad when his wife died.' He shrugged helplessly. 'I don't know who is being right, Joe.'

Horseman munched until he could swallow his mouthful. 'I don't know either, Mahen. But I do know beating someone up is wrong and against the law. It's my job to find out who hurt that old man so badly.'

'How's it going?'

'I've some ideas but can't be sure yet. If you hear anything at all, Mahen, I'd be grateful if you let me know.' He fished a card from his pocket and held it out. 'You may have mislaid the last one I gave you.'

***

On his return to Pandey & Associates, the receptionist ushered him into the principal's office, which matched the waiting room in décor. Horseman felt pleasantly relaxed after his late lunch and hoped the rotis hadn't dulled his wits. The lawyer, who greeted him with enthusiasm, looked much too young to have served Dev Reddy for more than fifteen years.

'Mr Pandey, I'm investigating the serious assault on Mr Dev Reddy at his farm last Friday night and his death in hospital on Sunday night. Is it correct that you've acted as his solicitor since before his arrest?'

Mr Pandey chuckled. 'You're right to look so doubtful. I am indeed too young for that to be the case. No, it was my uncle, the late Ramesh Pandey, who helped Mr Reddy with occasional legal matters for many years, and with his trial and afterwards in prison. I worked here as my uncle's associate for only a short time before he passed away three years ago.'

'Has Mr Reddy consulted you at all?'

'Normally, you understand, I would observe client confidentiality one hundred per cent. But I especially want to help the police solve the crimes committed against my unfortunate client. Also, if I can do anything to reduce the scandalous beat-up by the media, I'm happy to do it.'

'Glad to hear it, Mr Pandey. Did Mr Reddy ever consult you?'

'Please call me Navneet, Inspector. Yes, he did. About six months ago, I got a call from Dr Acharya at St Giles, requesting I visit Mr Reddy there. He wanted to change his will, you understand.'

'Was that the only work you did for him?'

'No. Do you know about the lease of the Reddy farm to his neighbour, Mr Prakash?'

'A little. Mr Prakash mentioned it to me earlier this afternoon.'

'Well, the lease was due for renewal around the same time. Dev gave me his instructions on both matters when I visited St Giles, you understand. I drew up the documents and took them back to St Giles. Dr Acharya and that jolly receptionist, Essie, witnessed his signature.'

'Was there any question of Reddy's legal competence, considering his diagnosis and permanent transfer to St Giles?'

'Not by Dr Acharya, who readily agreed to witness the signing. I asked about his opinion, you understand. He said that Dev's delusions were specific and that he was always quite rational about his farm and property, especially so during the past five years when he was taking the right medication.'

'Were there any objections at all?'

'Well, nobody else knew, you understand. Only the doctor and my assistant. Gopal Prakash knew about the lease, naturally. He wasn't too happy about the terms, but he signed.'

'Why wasn't Gopal happy?'

'He'd had two successive five-year leases and he expected another. Dev made it very clear to me he wanted future leases to be for one year only.'

'Was he expecting to be paroled?'

'I don't know—he didn't mention it and I didn't ask him, you understand.'

'Do you expect objections to the will on the grounds of legal incompetence?'

'Expect? I've already had one objection from Darsh, Dev's eldest son in New Zealand. My uncle would be quite bitter about this, you understand. He tried hard to have Dev declared legally incompetent when he was arrested eleven years ago. Dev was clearly deranged, quite unfit to either stand trial or go to prison. But Uncle Ramesh couldn't get two doctors to certify him insane. He believed even the doctors wanted him punished for crimes he committed when suffering delusions. Darsh and the other children gave Uncle no support, you understand. Neither did the magistrate or the judge. Uncle felt they were all scared of the media and the court of public opinion.'

'It must have been a hard time for your uncle.'

'Very. He lost clients because he acted for Dev Reddy. He believed all are entitled to their legal rights no matter what they've done. Uncle would be bitter now. Dev was declared legally competent to stand trial eleven years ago when he was very ill. But Darsh claims his father was incompetent to change his will when he was stable.'

'I take it Darsh doesn't benefit from the changed will.'

'No, he doesn't. Dev was certain that he wanted to leave all his property to Kanan Reddy.'

30

When Horseman got back, he found Singh and Kau updating the whiteboard. He hoped they'd got a lead from their interviews with hospital staff.

Singh looked around. 'Good you're on time, sir. Got a new lead? We didn't get anything much.'

'I was counting on you two!' he joked.

He sat down facing the whiteboard. 'Is Musudroka coming?' he asked.

'He must be still doing the rounds of jewellers.'

'I'll send him a text. We all have to keep up on both cases. If Ratini asks about the jewel thefts, and he will, any of us must be able to fill him in. Get us some tea, please Apo, while I check what you've been doing to the case file.'

When Kau returned with a tray, Horseman said, 'Good work, Apo. Either Sergeant Singh's been brainwashing you, or you're by nature as systematic and tidy as she is.'

Kau kept his eyes on unloading the mugs of tea.

'A bit of both, I think,' Singh said, smiling.

Horseman took a tentative sip at his tea. '*Vinaka*, Apo, good and strong. I'll let it cool for a bit. I have some news you'll be glad about. Fingerprints on Mosese's shoe-shine box scored a match, and the thug's arrested. The man's a pathetic case in his own way—in and out of prison since he was seventeen, crimes escalating gradually in severity until now he's up for violent assault. He admitted the theft, claimed he was drunk and stumbled across the things. He'll likely end up back inside. Maybe that's what he really wants.'

Kau frowned. 'But why, sir? When he can return to his village?'

'We can't know that. Some of our Shiners could end up like him.'

'We've got to stop that, sir,' Kau said, alarmed.

'We can do our best in the time we have, that's all. Hard to accept, I know. But all the Shiners will know the police found Mosese's things and returned them to him.'

Kau brightened. '*Io*, they won't forget that.'

The door banged open and a panting Musudroka appeared.

'*Bula*, Tani, good to see you. Take a seat and we'll begin. First up, you can tell us all about the jewel thieves.'

Musudroka grinned his irrepressible grin. '*Io*, sir. That won't take long. So far, we've found no stranger prints on any surfaces in the houses that were robbed. Ash and the team are doing a thorough job, goes without saying. All jewellers in the whole of Fiji—makers, wholesale, retail, resorts—all of them get emails with descriptions of the stolen items, including photos if they exist. We ring every jeweller every few days, checking if they've seen anything on the list, entire or remade. Me and another two DCs are pounding the Suva pavements, chatting to the jewellers and showing the pictures again, leaving each with a set of high-resolution enlargements. Another DC went to Nausori today. Either no one has seen anything or someone's lying.'

'Of course, it's easy to take a few pieces at a time out of the country by air,' Singh said. 'Even if the airport scanners were working, jewellery in a suitcase wouldn't arouse suspicion.'

'I forgot to mention we send all the details to Customs, too,' Musudroka added.

'When?' Horseman asked.

'Depends when the owners report the theft. It varies. Typically, they're out on Friday or Saturday night and discover the break-in when they get home—could be in the early hours. A few waited until morning to report the theft. One burglary was when the people were away for a few days.'

'At the earliest?'

'If the owners rang the police at two in the morning and they had photos, I reckon the description would be emailed out before midday. I can't really say when.'

'In that case, if the jewellery stolen on Friday night was taken out on a Saturday morning flight, it's gone with no trace.'

Musudroka nodded glumly. 'So unless we can catch them red-handed, this is all a waste.'

'Not a waste, Tani. We've got to follow all these procedures because the thieves will eventually make a mistake, especially after several successes. They get cocky, think they're too clever for us—they've just about reached that stage now, I reckon. But red-handed would be good. Is Inspector Vula considering a trap?'

'*Io*, sir. He hasn't come up with the right plan yet, he says.'

Singh cut in, her eyes bright. 'I'll think about it, sir. In my spare moments.'

'What are you doing with spare moments, Singh? I need you a hundred per cent on the Reddy case!' Horseman winked.

'*Vinaka*, Tani, you're doing well. Looks like it's my turn.'

Horseman valued summarising his actions for the team. So often the process threw up an obvious gap he'd missed, showing him another alley to explore. Or sometimes it was only in the retelling that a deduction occurred to him. So he summarised what he'd done for the last two days, hoping for new insights.

When he told them about Dev Reddy's will, Kau and Musudroka gasped and stared at each other, eyes and mouths wide open. Even Singh raised her eyebrows.

'But how is that possible?' Kau squeaked.

'The solicitor advised Reddy against leaving everything to Kanan for two reasons: first, the other children would be sure to challenge the will, and second, the administration of the property of Kanan, who is legally incompetent, could be more expensive in terms of accountancy and legal fees than the amount of the bequest could justify. However, Reddy insisted, and Mr Pandey drafted a will providing for himself as trustee for Kanan and holding power of attorney to administer the estate on Kanan's behalf.'

'What's your take on the solicitor, sir?'

'I think he's honest, but I've only met him once. His uncle represented Reddy from his arrest onwards, defended his legal rights in spite of losing clients. Navneet's proud of inheriting his values. Darsh has already told him he will contest the will.'

'When did Darsh find out about the will, sir?' Kau asked.

'Yesterday. Pandey told him on the phone then emailed the will to him.'

'You've found out a lot, but we're no closer, really,' said Musudroka.

'You're right, we're not. I've added a suspect, not eliminated any. Gopal Prakash, Reddy's neighbour, definitely has motive. He's ambitious to expand his farmlands. He's worked Reddy's land on five-year leases for ten years, then Reddy switched him to an annual lease this year. Reddy refused his offers to buy the freehold.'

'Reddy sounds kinda business-like,' Musudroka commented.

'I know, it's strange. He was rational about farming and business matters. Reddy probably cut Prakash's lease because he believed his true son Kanan would return soon. Although why he thought he would be paroled so early, I'm not sure.'

'Maybe his lawyer told him he had a good chance,' Kau said.

'*Io*, I'll talk to him some more. Dr Acharya at St Giles, too. But back to Gopal Prakash. He had opportunity and means, as well as motive. He could easily have joined the demonstrators in the early hours of Saturday morning. Great cover for him. He may not have planned to kill Reddy but seized the opportunity the protest provided.'

Singh looked thoughtful as she rotated her empty tea mug back and forth. 'The three men Nata bailed out all maintain they never saw Reddy. They may be telling the truth. Maybe Prakash beat him up before the HOOK lot even arrived. Prakash thinks he's killed Reddy, but Reddy drags himself off to hide under the water tank.'

'And the HOOK protesters arrive later. But Reddy is hiding from Prakash.'

'Wouldn't Prakash know about that hidey-hole?'

'Possibly not. They cooperated as neighbours but weren't friends. The wives were friendly before Mrs Reddy died.'

'Which is when all the trouble seemed to begin.'

'Not if you consider every child emigrated as soon as they could.'

'We've got more to explore. For now, we'll put Gopal Prakash on the board. When he heard Reddy was in hospital, he could have driven to Suva, sneaked into CWM and quickly finished the old man off.'

Singh wrote his name in purple capitals on the board beside Ravai Nata's. 'Kau can get his driver's license photo later.'

'Ravai Nata remains a strong suspect. He's lied to us every time we've spoken with him, only admitted the truth when confronted with unarguable evidence, and he's only admitted as much as the evidence forces him to. He hasn't told us the whole truth. Yet what reason has he to conceal so much if he's innocent?'

'Everyone in his family has a good job but him. Now he's delighted with his media success. He wants to protect that budding career at all costs. He can't be a TV preacher or charity campaigner if there's a whiff of scandal.'

'Unless it's in a higher cause. He comes across as so sincere, he could wiggle his way out of a lot of lies.'

'I can't see him as a murderer, though.'

'I know what you mean, but given the right circumstances, he could kill on impulse. Or he could be protecting a follower who went too far, quite easily. Look at the way he avoided telling us his sister-in-law told him Reddy had died when she got home at seven-thirty yesterday morning. She was the night shift radiographer at CWM! Why didn't he just say she'd told him? Why, in heaven's name? There's some other reason for his lies, one we don't know yet. He remains as a suspect.'

'Agreed.'

'Now it's your turn, Singh. What happened at the hospital? Did you and Kau suss out a mysterious visitor?'

'Not yet, I'm sorry to report. We spoke to all staff who worked on the floor at any time while Reddy was a patient. No one remembered anything out of routine or anyone out of place.'

'It's a case of no stone unturned, then. Expand the interview list to everyone who worked in any department on Sunday, including the night shift. Talk to Bimala again, too. She might remember something more about that stair door slamming shut.'

'I agree, sir.' Singh replied. She glanced at Kau, who looked like he'd rather do anything at all than more hospital interviews. 'Imagine how you'd feel if you uncovered the old man's murderer, Apo.'

'What if the murderer turns out to be a pretty student nurse, eh? Imagine how you'd feel uncovering her!'

Kau glared. 'Shut up, Tani, idiot!'

'Look at the compensations and enjoy your job, man! That's all I'm saying.' He shrugged, laughing at Kau's discomfort.

Horseman cut in, stern. 'Enough, now, Tani. Let's look at what we do next. First, you continue on the jewellery thefts with Inspector Vula. Sergeant Singh, please widen your interview scope at CWM as you've suggested. Kau, continue to report to Sergeant Singh. Remember, I'm relying on you to keep the media clippings file on both Reddy and Nata up to date, too. As for me—'

The door was flung open, banging against the wall.

31

Ratini glared. 'What's this? You're having a case review meeting? I don't believe you'd do this without informing me!'

They automatically sprang to their feet. Kau and Musudroka managed to look guilty. Singh smiled as if delighted to see Ratini.

Horseman did his best to look welcoming. 'I'm glad you dropped in, sir. You're most welcome to join our discussion if you've got the time. It's not a formal case review meeting, of course. We've all just got back and we're sharing what we've done. Right now, I'm allocating tasks for tomorrow.'

Musudroka fetched a chair from a neighbouring desk. They shuffled quickly to give Ratini a clear space. Appropriate for the boss.

'Oh, *vinaka*,' he said in a grudging tone. He didn't take the chair but turned to the whiteboard, shaking his head. 'This Reddy case—sooner you can wrap this one up, the better, eh? Summarise this for me, Horseman. Briefly, mind!'

It suited Horseman to be brief. More than suited him. He identified the two main suspects, outlined their suspicious behaviour.

'Where are you going from here, then? You haven't got enough to arrest either of them.'

'I agree, sir. Tomorrow I'll interview the three HOOK members arrested for vandalising Reddy's house. I'll talk to Mrs Prakash and other Reddy neighbours. Singh and Kau will continue questioning CWM staff and...'

'*Oi lei, oi lei*, you don't understand at all, do you, man!' Ratini threw up his hands and grimaced, shaking his head like the hammiest of ham actors. What a shocking display of lack of control before subordinates.

'No, I don't sir. Please make yourself clear.' Horseman held his body still and spoke through tight lips, lest his own anger get the better of him.

Ratini sighed a melodramatic sigh but managed to calm his voice somewhat. 'Words of one syllable, Horseman. Reddy was a monster. Last week, he turned Suva upside down and provoked riots. The media hate him—they're all glad he's dead. The country thanks his murderer or murderers. No one cares whether they're caught or not. Understand that?'

'Perfectly, sir.'

He noticed Singh frowning at him. She moved her head a tiny millimetre or two to the side, warning him about something. But what? Kau and Musudroka stood with their arms folded, staring down at the desk.

'I'm a fair man, Inspector. The law must be seen to operate without fear or favour and all that. I would have been happy if you'd picked up the monster's murderer in a few days. You failed. When I hear you plan to extend your fishing net wider and wider, what can I do?' He threw up his hands again.

'I must call a halt, that's what. Horseman, you've done your best. Whoever killed Reddy is not going to murder again. The public is in no danger because he hasn't been caught. On the other hand, we have a serial jewel thief, or possibly gang of thieves, who've been on a cocky rampage for months! I must redirect scarce manpower from Reddy to the jewel burglaries. How can you argue against that decision?'

'I don't want to argue with you, sir, but I'm happy to present my case and grateful for the opportunity. Thank God, murders are infrequent in our islands. But when they happen, the police response is always the same, in my experience. As big a team as possible is mustered and they work all hours to find evidence and identify the murderer. That goes on for at least a week and usually the right person is arrested in that time. Inevitably, other crimes will be committed and the initial intensive effort will be diluted after a week or so, but the case is never closed until it is solved. And it may seem like a long time to us, but Reddy was killed less than forty-eight hours ago. If it ends now, the length of this investigation will make a mockery of Fiji's CID.'

Ratini literally took a step back. He rubbed his chin, looked solemn, pretended to consider, but his step had signalled he was, well, stepping back.

'I don't mind admitting you've made a fair case, Horseman. In fact, what with the anti-Reddy protests all the previous week, I almost forgot the devil only died on Sunday night. Seems like Reddy's been the top story in the media a long time now.'

'*Io*, it seems like that to me, too. But the media are unpredictable. One week, they'll be baying for Reddy's blood, the next they could be at the throats of the police for not pursuing a proper investigation.'

'*Io*, they're a bunch of hypocrites, all right.'

'Sir, I've managed my contribution to both cases by allocating Musudroka full-time to the jewel thefts. That's twenty-five per cent of my ongoing team. The three of us left are finding it difficult to cover all leads. Kau is a competent officer, but he has been a probationer detective for only a few months. If we could have Musudroka back on the Reddy case, our progress could be faster.'

Ratini's eyes narrowed. He suspected he was being played and he would not allow that.

'Inspector Vula will argue the same, Horseman. No, DC Musudroka stays on the jewel thefts. But you three, go flat out on Reddy. After all, you've got the SOCOs and Forensics at your service. You can co-opt uniforms, within reason. Case review meeting Friday morning, ten o'clock. If you're worth your salt, you'll accept a challenge!'

'*Vinaka*, sir. We accept.'

WEDNESDAY

32

Horseman felt bad about sending Singh back to the hospital today. But Reddy's hospital ward was the murder scene. It was a staff member, another patient, or intruder who pressed the pillow over the old man's face while he struggled and scratched at the threadbare slip. Singh was more than capable of turning a hospital inside out. And she'd be thrilled if she found the vital clue to the case.

Anyway, he'd seen the three men arrested for trespass and criminal damage at Reddy's farm. Although he didn't know who was who, their charge sheet photos looked familiar, and he hoped he'd recognise the men when he met them face-to-face. He'd brought a fingerprint kit, determined to rectify the mistakes made at Nausori police station. The SOCOs hadn't been able to match the prints they'd found on the evidence gathered at the farm, but it was likely the HOOK protesters had clean police records. One of them could well provide a missing link in the chain of evidence, still in several pieces. And if they didn't, they could be crossed off his list and left to the magistrate's mercy.

But he had another call to make first. If he didn't do it first thing, he'd get side-tracked and the task would remain undone as it had yesterday.

The humble Franciscan Brothers' monastery at the crest of Flagstaff Hill housed a dozen monks and their priest, Father Francis. A long, low building squeezed along one side of the block, replacing the former driveway and car parking. 'Cars don't need homes, but children do,' Father Francis had decreed around five years ago when kids started living on the Suva streets and parks.

Horseman parked in the street and walked through the gap in the hibiscus hedge. The air was still soft and fresh after an early shower. Two boys around thirteen were husking coconuts on a spike driven into a section of tree trunk. They laughed at their own clumsiness.

'*Yadra*, boys. Is Father Francis around?'

'*Yadra*, sir. I'm not sure, but try the last door,' one said.

The other stared at Horseman, trying to place him. He'd been off the field and television screen for two years now—these boys were too young to recognise him. That suited him.

Four doors opened onto a cement verandah roofed with second-hand corrugated iron. They all stood open. The brisk swishing of coconut brooms sounded from within. When he got to the last door, he could see the priest sitting at a small desk, talking on a telephone. Horseman waited. Father Francis spotted him and waved. When he ended the call, he got up, unbending his burly frame to his full height of almost two metres. Father Francis had no discipline problems, although he solemnly maintained this was entirely because of his personality. He adjusted the thick white cord knotted around his brown habit.

The priest's handshake was like an iron clamp. 'Good to see you, Josefa—come to check on Mosese, eh? What a beating that boy took! I was shocked when the ambulance brought him here yesterday. And you know, I'm not easily shocked.'

'How is he?'

'Improved already—nothing like rest and a bit of celebrity, eh? He was anxious about not knowing the other boys, but he's quite the star.'

Horseman lifted the sports bag he'd brought. 'Here are some things for him. I'm pleased to say his attacker is already under arrest. We got prints from Mosese's shoe-shine box that the thug discarded. Sadly, the guy's spent his life in and out of prison. He won't be homeless again for a while.'

Father Francis bowed his head for a few moments then crossed himself. 'The boy will be thrilled to see you. His new friends are at school. Come along.'

'Before I do, I've got another cause to plead, Father. At training on Monday, two boys started a collection to buy Mosese new brushes and polish. Completely their own idea—they have good hearts. Afterwards, they told me how scared they are of their usual camping spots now. They begged me to ask you for a place for them to sleep here. I promised I'd ask. They've been reliable training squad members for nine months, so I can recommend them on that basis.'

The priest looked at him with sad brown eyes. 'I'm always full up here, Joe, you know that. To be fair, we have a rule that only boys who attend school or vocational training in Suva can stay here long-term. I assume your two proteges aren't enrolled anywhere. We have another two communities in rural Viti Levu where we house and train boys such as your Shiners in carpentry and diesel mechanics. Sometimes these street kids have got addicted to the bright lights of the city. Remember

Tevita, last year? You had high hopes for him, but he couldn't take the discipline or rural life.'

Horseman nodded, rueful. 'I think I pushed him into what I thought would be good for him. But recently the police garage has taken him on, washing cars. He boards with the police mechanic apprentices. He's doing really well and he's keen.'

Father Francis chortled with pleasure. '*Oi lei*! Well done, Tevita, keep it up! But for us, you know, Joe, it's hard to decide whether to keep trying again and again with the same boy or give a chance to more boys. It's agonising. Every day, I pray for help with these decisions.'

'Is that a "no" you're building towards?'

Father Francis grinned an enormous grin. 'No doubt about you, Joe. Two boys left last week to begin the carpentry course at our inland monastery. Because they've shown loyalty to you and kindness to their teammate, I could try to get them into a course in Suva somewhere, like I'm doing for Mosese. Do you think they'd stick to training?'

'After Tevita, I can't trust my judgment. You're the one with experience and insight.'

'I'll interview them both, use my judgment and pray for guidance. When will you see them?'

'At training tomorrow afternoon.'

'Tell them to be here at nine o'clock on Friday morning. Now go and see Mosese. You'll do him good, I know. God bless.'

'*Vinaka vakalevu*, Father.'

***

Mosese's gratitude for the bag of decent clothes overwhelmed Horseman.

'The boys here are cool, Joe.' He laughed, then clutched at his ribs. 'I forget I can't laugh. I was scared of such a big gang. But they're happy for me to be here.'

'Why wouldn't they be? You're a nice guy. And they can see how sore you are. Father Francis wants you to stay here and do nothing but rest until you're well enough to help with a few chores. Then he'll talk with you about your future.'

Mosese nodded, serious.

'Have you thought any more about that Sunday night in hospital?'

'*Io*, Joe. It's not clear in my mind. Sorry.'

'No need to be sorry, I know you want to help. But I don't want you to imagine anything—it must be an accurate memory to help me. If something comes back to you, just ask Father Francis to give me a call, okay?'

Horseman felt happy as he drove away. No progress on the case, but progress of equal importance to him. Just another Band-Aid, though.

33

Joni Kavika's home was the closest to Flagstaff so he was first on the list. Horseman took in the grey sea beneath grey clouds as he drove down the hill to Raiwaqa. Whatever the colour, he loved looking at the sea. Perhaps that's what grabbed him about the little tower flat high above Suva.

Like the other two men arrested at the Reddy farm the previous Saturday, Kavika was charged with trespass and property damage offences. Until Matt Young dropped the postmortem bombshell, Horseman believed Kavika and his pals were also guilty of murder, but now? With Gopal Prakash a suspect, the three men were possibly only guilty of the minor offences they'd been charged with.

The blocks of flats were close to degraded wetlands where a creek flowed to Laucala Bay. Kavika's small flat was damp, the mouldy smell inside blending with the ambient swampy air. The tenants had tried to make it cheerful with bright floral fabrics, but the damp won out. Horseman had no clear memory of Kavika from the previous Saturday. He turned out to be about forty, gaining weight around his middle and losing hair from his large head. He was shame-faced but friendly enough. When Horseman refused the tea Mrs Kavika offered, she brought a stool to the table and sat with them, her face enigmatic.

'Are you a member of HOOK, Mr Kavika?'

'*Io*, sir, but call me Joni, please. I've been a member since its foundation. That's a week ago,' Kavika said with a smile. 'Our mission is to protect children by keeping child abusers in prison.'

'Our own four are all at school today,' Mrs Kavika added.

'Do you worship at God's Gospel Church, with Ravai Nata?'

'*Io*, it's a wonderful congregation. Ravai is a truly inspired preacher. When he heard about Reddy's release, God moved him to fight for what's right by starting HOOK. Many at the church meeting that night joined him without question. We felt the same.'

'Joni, tell me how you ended up at the Reddy farmhouse on Friday night.'

Kavika glanced at his wife, who glared at him.

'I joined the rally at the prison gates. When word went around that Reddy had been released up at St Giles, many of us wanted to continue with our mission. To ram our message home, we decided to go to his farmhouse.'

'Very Christian of you.' Horseman was deadpan.

'I'm glad you appreciate that, sir.' Kavika was deadpan, too.

'What time did you arrive?'

'I'm not sure. I came home, ate dinner. Around half-past ten, a friend picked me up here in his taxi. He'd got a radio message, giving directions to the farm. There were six of us in his old taxi but we got there around midnight, after a couple of wrong turns.'

'Then what?'

'We prayed together for guidance. Then more people turned up, walking along the road. They told us they'd walked from the bus stop. Another taxi came along later with another six people. God sent people from all directions. Some neighbouring farmers came along later, too.'

'Which farm were they from?'

Kavika shrugged. 'Sorry, I don't know.'

'Did they tell you their names?'

'Maybe Hari, Sanjeev? I'm not sure.'

'Did you see Ravai Nata there?'

'No.'

'Let's pause here while you write down the names of everyone there that you knew.' Horseman turned to a fresh page in his notebook and passed it over to Kavika.

'When did you start shouting and throwing stones?'

The question earned Kavika another contemptuous look from his wife.

'As more people gathered, someone suggested continuing our chants and waving our placards. Somehow, a few people got agitated. Someone had a spray can of paint, others got hostile because Reddy didn't show himself. A few broke the door in, then some rocks—you saw what they did.'

'Drunk, I'll bet,' Mrs Kavika offered, shaking her head in disgust.

'Who broke the door in?'

Kavika shook his head.

'Who painted the threat on the house?'

'I didn't see the individuals. It was dark. Some of the protesters I hadn't seen before. I didn't enter the house or throw any stones. I'm speaking the truth, sir.'

'We'll soon know. Sergeant Maika at Nausori said you put up such resistance at the station that he couldn't take your fingerprints. I'm here to do that now. We found prints on missiles and other items at the scene. We should get some matches.'

Kavika looked at his wife again. 'Good, God's given you a chance to prove you're innocent of any violence,' she said. Her voice was deadpan, too.

Kavika submitted to the fingerprinting process with good grace.

***

Paula Wairua lived a short distance away in genteel Suva Point, home of successful professionals. It was a surprising address for a rioting thug. However, it turned out Paula lived in a politician's maid's quarters, courtesy of his wife's employment. Paula worked as a gardener a few hundred metres further on, at the University of the South Pacific. Horseman left the police car in the shade of the Suva Point trees and walked. He pushed his way through the soupy air. By the time he found Paula spread out under an old breadfruit tree, his skin was trickling with sweat.

He threw himself down beside Paula and introduced himself. The gardener sat up, apologising. After he recovered from being literally caught napping, he was quite open. Like Joni Kavika, he proudly admitted being a HOOK member and admirer of Ravai Nata, but denied committing any violent acts himself or knowing the identity of anyone who did.

'If all you say is true, Paula, I'm very puzzled by one thing. When the Nausori constables came in broad daylight on Saturday morning and ordered you to disperse, why didn't you? Why did you refuse to leave and keep on shouting until they had to arrest you?'

Paula looked troubled. He picked up a fallen breadfruit flower and twisted it between his hands. 'I don't really know, sir. Looking back, we went a bit crazy. Some protesters were downing beer and they might have had yaqona before they left home, but not me. We were exhausted, too. All the chanting, I don't know. We were just on an automatic track and we couldn't get off.'

'I guess that can happen in a group, all doing the same thing.'

'Io, and there was something weird about that place. A bit of magic, bad magic. Like we were under a spell. I wondered if it was the Hindu god who cast a spell on us.'

'What was that? Tell me what you mean, Paula.'

'Just a weird feeling, like I wasn't in control. I saw this soft light moving away to the middle of a field, suspended above the crop, like it was watching us. Later, it faded and went out. At dawn, I realised the light must have come from the Hindu god. He sits in a glass case on a post in the field. He didn't want us there, so I think he cast a spell and made us crazy.'

'Interesting idea, Paula. The field god is actually a goddess called Durga. She protects the crops. Did you see any people behaving strangely? Apart from you rioters, that is?'

'It was too dark. I wondered when I saw the light moving if it was just someone with a torch. But walking through the crops at night? Unless someone went to pray to the goddess?'

'Maybe. What about after it got light?'

'No, we thought Reddy would come out of his house, but he didn't. Maybe he was never there.'

'Are you positive no one beat up Reddy while you were outside the house?'

'Maybe the guys who went inside bashed him and left him there. I don't know. But I never saw him.'

***

Mark Prasad worked in Carpenters Hardware, over the other side of the peninsula in Walu Bay, near the wharves. It turned out he had a bookkeeping job in the office upstairs. The receptionist smiled when Horseman showed his ID and made a call. She indicated a few armchairs screened off by yellowing potted palms.

'You can talk to Mark there if you like. Up to you.' She smiled and reached for the ringing phone.

A few moments later, a clean-cut young man came out, greeted Horseman and shook hands. His wary eyes sized up Horseman through gold-framed glasses.

'Are you happy to talk in this corner, Mr Prasad?'

'Not really. All my colleagues will find an excuse to walk past and listen in.'

Horseman nodded. 'Okay, we can go to the station if you like.'

Prasad's right hand gripped his left arm as he stood still, considering alternatives. 'I don't want people to see me driven off in a police car either.'

His eyes darted from side to side. 'I can't think of anywhere else more private, actually. So let's sit here. I hope you can make it quick.'

'That's entirely up to you, Mr Prasad.'

They sidled between the palm pots and sat down. The air conditioning was blissful.

'Are you a member of HOOK, Mr Prasad?'

'Yes, indeed. It's a wonderful cause, defending children who can't defend themselves. As Jesus taught us. Don't look surprised, Inspector. I'm a Christian Indian, but not a member of God's Gospel church.'

'Do you know Ravai Nata?'

'Indeed, I do. I met him last Thursday night. He touched my heart when I saw him on TV, so I went along to his church to offer help. They were making placards and signs for the demonstrations on Friday. Ravai welcomed me with open arms.'

'How did you end up outside Reddy's farmhouse on Friday night?'

'I want to say how much I regret that now. I'm not sure what got into us. I thought it was the spirit of God, but now I think we probably just revved each other up.'

'The spirit of the mob is a destructive force, Mr Prasad. Compelling. Now that you've felt it and seen what it can do, run the other way next time.'

Prasad nodded, serious. 'You're right. The prison service tricked us out of seeing Reddy and we wanted to keep fighting for our cause. A few others came with me to the bus stop near the market. We talked for a while, then when my bus came along, I let it go. I told the others I'd get the bus to Nausori and find Reddy's farm and give him an earful. I suddenly felt so angry. The others said they'd come with me. It was well after midnight by the time we found the right farm. We were glad to see others there already.'

'Did you recognise the other protesters?'

'Most of them. It was dark. More came along later. Someone was passing around bottles of beer, which I don't normally drink, but it's thirsty work, yelling.'

'Was Ravai Nata there?'

'No, I'm sure I would've noticed him.'

'Did you enter the farmhouse?'

'No, I was inflamed, but not to that extent. I swear, I did nothing violent. That's not me at all.'

All three had their stories straight, and they were plausible. Still, he must persist.

'Who are the men who broke into the farmhouse?'

'I don't know.'

'Who painted the threats on the wall?'

'Sorry, I don't know.'

'Did you see anyone walking in the farmyard or the fields?'

'No, it was dark.'

'It was light enough before six o'clock. Did you see any strangers then?'

'Some labourers in the distance, perhaps.'

'Why did you refuse to go when the Nausori police asked you to leave?'

Prasad shook his head. 'I don't know—it seems like another life, looking back. I was possibly a bit drunk. The beer kept coming from somewhere.'

'Did you call Ravai Nata from Nausori station?'

'No, I don't know who it was. After hours in the lockup, I've never been so happy to see anyone, though. It was so good of him to come to our aid.'

'Did he bring a solicitor with him to advise you?'

'No. Ravai told all three of us to report to Bailey Chambers on Monday afternoon at five o'clock. I had to say I was sick to leave here early. I could still hardly speak by then, so no one doubted me.'

'Was Ravai there, too?'

'No. We met with Mr Sharma, who told us he would represent us at the magistrate's hearing on Friday, at no cost.'

'What advice did he give you?'

'I'm afraid he told us not to divulge our conversation to anyone else. He said it was strictly confidential.'

'Did he, now? Well, I'm sure he advised cooperating with the police enquiry into Reddy's death. Constable Toga at Nausori didn't get a chance to take your fingerprints for elimination. However, I can rectify that now. This little side table will be ideal.'

Prasad peered furtively through the palm fronds, his face blanching. Horseman pulled the portable kit from his satchel and glanced at his watch. He still had plenty of time.

34

'*Vinaka vakalevu* for your time, sir. You may go now.' Kau said to the orderly. Like all the other staff, the orderly hadn't noticed any strangers on his perambulations through the hospital on the night of Reddy's murder.

Singh didn't like to admit it to herself, and she'd never admit it to anyone else, but she was feeling a little bored. After four hours of questioning hospital staff whose work had not taken them to Reddy's ward, they were no further ahead.

Apo Kau, on the other hand, appeared to be enjoying the process. The repetitive nature of the interviews helped him develop skill and confidence. Witnessing her probationers grow brought her a lot of satisfaction. This had come as a surprise in her early days as a sergeant. Now she appreciated how richly rewarding being a police detective was. She allowed herself a few seconds to imagine what it would be like to be a chief inspector or even superintendent—she would enjoy organising, deputising and directing.

A brief indulgence in these ambitious daydreams was enough. She only needed to find one cleaner, one doctor, one aide, one nurse—anyone who had noticed someone who didn't belong, anyone retreating through an unfamiliar fire door and letting it bang. She might solve the case in the next interview.

But she had somewhere else to be right now.

'Remember, our next interview could crack the case wide open, Apo.'

Kau's eyes brightened at the prospect. He nodded.

'But we need a lunch break now. I've got some errands to run. Let's meet back here in an hour.'

'*Vinaka*, Sarge.'

He didn't realise the rare long lunch was for her own convenience. There were two flats for rent in the same building and she hoped they'd be possibles. They would be open for viewing until half-past twelve.

***

While the rent put the flats in the possible category, their condition ruled them out. They were both on the ground floor of a concrete block building near the bottom of a gully. They were cool, but damp and mouldy. The deep shade would depress her, she knew. She would have to supply her own stove and fridge. Suddenly, the barracks looked like a sensible choice. She ascended the dozens of steep steps up to the street and hailed a passing cab.

Next on her list was a self-contained flat in a family house in Toorak—not far from the police station. She didn't mind that the house had seen better days: it was on the high side of the street and had a verandah shielding the walls from the sun and keeping them dry. The flat was originally the maid's quarters and big enough for her. The Indian landlady was friendly, saying how she treated her lodgers as members of the family. Singh was interested until she twigged that what the landlady meant was that she expected her to babysit the children on demand. Where once a maid had been paid to live in the flat, it seemed the tables had turned and the tenant of the flat had to pay to be a maid.

The cab had waited and whisked her down the hill to a large house on the fringes of Lami. Trimmed hedges enclosed the compound, which had fruit trees and flowers and was well-maintained—just the sort of private environment she would choose. The landlord had recently enclosed the space underneath his elevated house, providing two one-bedroom fully equipped and furnished flats. She liked the place. Given the nearby municipal rubbish dump was due to close in six months, maybe she should grab this flat now before rents rose. The landlord saw her checking the newspaper ad. He cleared his throat.

'Ah—ahem, I'm afraid the newspaper made a mistake. What dopes, putting me in an embarrassing position! The monthly rent is a hundred dollars more than stated in the advertisement, madam. I'm sure you agree that such a beautiful flat is well worth the extra.' He smiled.

'It may well be, but it's beyond my budget. You've wasted my time here.' She turned on her heel, her eyes smarting as her hopes shattered.

'Wait, madam,' he called. She swallowed and turned again. 'Maybe we can compromise. I can see having a tenant who is a police officer could benefit me.'

'How?' Singh wondered if he'd expect her to provide free security services.

'All sorts of ways, I think. You could make sure we get extra patrols here or give me inside tips about criminal activities—I heard there's a jewel thief at large right now. All sorts of benefits.'

'You're mistaken, sir. That wouldn't be possible.' She was aware she tilted her stony face arrogantly but couldn't help it.

'That was quick, ma'am,' the taxi driver said. 'No good, eh? Where to next?'

'That's it. None of them are in the running. But at least I won't be late back to work.'

'*Ovisa*, I know a block of flats open for inspection for the next half-hour. Managed by a proper estate agent—better than these greedy landlords. There are many flats vacant because the Taiwanese aid organisation has closed. Political pressure from mainland China, you know. What a shame. But you might get a bargain.'

'I could never afford a diplomatic rent. I'm a sergeant!'

'You never know. Ten flats, all suddenly free. Prices have dropped. What's the harm in looking?'

'The harm is, I'm always disappointed.' Her eyes stung again. She turned her head to gaze out the window.

'Up to you.' The driver shrugged. 'Close to town, on the edge of Toorak.'

'All right, why not? I've got time.'

When he pulled up, she knew she'd made a mistake, indulging in fantasies that could never be a reality for her.

'You mean here—?' She looked through the window at the eight-storey tower.

'Sure, Sergeant. Seaview Apartments. Go in and meet Kiti.'

'You must be on a commission, driver.' He chuckled but didn't deny it.

She was here now and she'd always been curious about this strange hexagonal building. The Paradise Real Estate sandwich board at the entrance instructed her to press the door buzzer. After a minute, the lift door opened and a smiling young Fijian woman rushed out to welcome Singh. She introduced herself as Kiti Samisoni.

'What an opportunity you have today, Sergeant. How did you hear about ten Seaview apartments all being vacant at once?'

'From the taxi driver, actually,' Singh admitted. 'Look, you should know these will be way beyond my budget. But the driver deposited me here and insisted I take a look. I'm afraid I'm wasting your time.'

Kiti beamed. 'What nonsense. I love helping people find the right homes for them. You know, every property you view teaches you something about the market. And the more knowledgeable you are about the state of the market, the more likely you are to find your perfect place. It's just logical. Are you willing to live in a building with a lift?'

'I think so. I've never thought about it.'

'Good. Here we have a situation where several landlords are competing for tenants at the same time. The supply of tenants is hugely reduced because many Fijians refuse to live in a building with a lift and are suspicious of Seaview because of its unique geometry. So traditional, can you believe it? But that clears the competition for the young and adventurous like you, Sergeant.'

Singh was overwhelmed by Kiti's verbal onslaught. Impressed, though. Also impressed by the cool air conditioning, cream floor tiles, timber and glass.

'There are two identical one-bed flats available on the second floor. Fully furnished. Up we go.'

The same tiles, timber and glass were everywhere and reminded her a bit of the resort *bures* on Paradise Island. Did Kiti have any idea what a detective sergeant earned? Of course, her plans to study for the next inspectors' exam sparked her search for private accommodation. But she mustn't let herself inflate her budget based on her unachieved ambition.

Kiti was curiously silent while Singh inspected the flat, appearing to gaze at the view from the little balcony. Naturally, the views improved from pleasant on the second floor to wonderful on the sixth. But the views were a bonus: it was the harmony, efficiency and privacy she craved.

'Can you see yourself being comfortable here, Sergeant?' Kiti asked.

'Oh yes, but—'

'No buts, just imagine coming home here after a tough day. You need a retreat like this, I can tell.' She handed Singh a card. 'Here are the official monthly rents for the ten flats. Just between you and me, you could drive a substantial additional discount—a third off, maybe. Go home, do your sums and think about it. How would life here be for a stressed-out detective?'

Her smile was empathetic. Singh thought she had promise as a police interviewer. Promise? No, Kiti already had the velvet glove approach nailed.

As she stepped out of the lift, a familiar figure stood chatting to a young woman in the foyer. Horseman! He turned at the clatter of Kiti's high heels on the tiles. Thank goodness, he smiled as if happy to see her, although as surprised as she was.

'Susie!'

'*Oi lei*, you know each other. Stands to reason, I guess. Please consider this carefully, Sergeant. This chance may not come again. Call me—any time, any questions.'

'*Vinaka*, Kiti. I will. Now that the boss has seen me, I'd better get back to work. I'll call you.'

Horseman shook hands with the woman and waited for Singh. They walked out the automatic doors together.

'I can't wait to compare notes, Susie. Have you had lunch?'

'No, but I gave Kau an hour fifty minutes ago. I've got to get back to CWM and resume our interviews.'

'I've got a car. We can go to the hospital canteen.'

What notes in particular did he want to compare? Only case notes, she hoped.

35

Although crammed with tables, the high ceilings and generous windows made the hospital canteen look airy. But an unappetising blend of antiseptic and cooking smells hovered like a mist.

Kau was waiting for them at a corner table with a pot of tea. '*Bula*, sir. Sarge. I've finished my lunch, just been going through my notes.'

'Did anything jump out at you, Apo?' Horseman asked.

'I get that the staff we're talking to now didn't have direct contact with Reddy. But nobody noticed anyone new, anything different. Isn't that odd? I expected patients to arrive without notice, surgeons operating at all hours... not this predictable routine.'

Singh smiled. 'I know what you mean, Apo. I guess if you worked here, emergencies would become routine.'

'I get the impression staff just concentrate on their own jobs and don't notice anything around them much. If they're telling us the truth, that is.'

'You could be right,' Horseman said. 'You're certainly right to remember staff may not want to tell every detail of what they did on a quiet Sunday night. How would you like to continue the afternoon interviews solo while I confer with Sergeant Singh?'

Kau looked at Singh, an anxious frown on his face.

'Yes, you go ahead, I'll join you later.'

'*Vinaka* sir, Sarge.' His eyes shining behind his glasses, he grabbed his neat backpack by one strap and left.

As they carried their trays back to the table, Horseman said, 'I didn't know you were house-hunting. The barracks getting on your nerves?'

'Sometimes. Like now, the plumbing's broken and the whole women's bathroom's a paddling pool. I'd really like my own bathroom.'

He guessed she didn't want to raise the topic of her promotion, so he would. 'When you're an inspector, you'll be thrown out. So it's best to prepare. I didn't—that's how I ended up boarding with Matt. You'll make inspector whenever you apply, so you're doing the right thing scouting around now.'

She relaxed her shoulders. Could she possibly have thought he'd disapprove of her looking for a flat in her lunch break? They both ate their sandwiches.

'Did you see anything you liked?'

'Two horrors, then one I liked at Lami, but the landlord advertised the place at a hundred dollars less than the real rent. Then the taxi driver insisted on taking me to Seaview, which I never would have considered.'

'What did you think?'

She looked at him, considering her reply. Would he hear her true opinion?

'I couldn't believe how I felt. Like I'd come home. I'd move in tomorrow if I could. But I can't. I have to eat as well as pay rent.'

'True, only you can work that out. But I felt the same. I hated the idea of that tower, but when I saw the flat on the fifth floor with the harbour view, I just wanted it. It's a head and heart thing, I suppose.'

Singh's face lit up. 'So you're going to take it, sir?'

'Susie, please don't call me *sir* when subordinates aren't with us. It's Joe. We agreed.'

'Sorry, sir. I mean Joe. It just doesn't come naturally. I don't even know I'm saying it.'

'You'll need to practise, then.'

She shrugged and laughed. It was good to see the tension leave her mouth. 'I haven't decided. It would be a stretch. I'll sleep on it.'

'They may get snapped up.'

'Well, that's what Kiti and her colleague want us to think. And fear.'

'I think they've succeeded with me.'

When they finished their lunch, he said, 'Is Kau right? Nothing's come from this morning?'

She nodded. 'No, but we still need to talk to everyone who was on duty that night.'

'Absolutely, I agree.' He poured them both cups of tea from the pot. 'You drink your tea while I tell you about the three HOOK members our friend Ravai Nata bailed out of the Nausori lockup.'

Singh listened intently. When he finished, she put her cup down. 'It's possible they're telling the truth. Their stories are consistent.'

'It's equally possible they're all following the solicitor's advice. They've agreed on a story that minimises their culpability and they're sticking to it. But we need evidence. It's an outside chance the fingerprints will match anything from Reddy's place, but you never know. I'll take them directly to Ash's lab from here and beg him to prioritise the processing. He's as interested as we are. But it's still Nata who's the mystery.'

'Yes, sir. Sorry—Joe.' She laughed. 'I'm never going to get used to it.'

'Think about this latest round of lies. He told us he didn't know the men arrested at Reddy's farm. Does he just say the first thing that comes into his head? Does he think that's what inspiration means? It's unlucky for Nata that his disciples aren't denying him, isn't it?'

'It's astonishing. According to them, two are founding members of HOOK. And Mark Prasad went to the church to help Nata last Thursday night. If Nata thought for a moment, he'd know they'd be proud of their association with him. There's something I'm not getting with Nata.'

'I'd better get back to Kau.' She grinned.

'After the lab, I'll confront Nata again. I want to see Dr Acharya, too. There's more to understand about the Reddy family situation that could help. I'm convinced of that.'

36

Ash was out at a crime scene when Horseman delivered the fingerprints to the lab. He didn't pick up his phone, so Horseman left him a message, then persuaded a technician to start the processing.

Always a believer in turning up unannounced, Horseman drove to Ravai Nata's church, then his home, only to be disappointed. He had to settle for leaving both voice and text messages on his mobile. But Dr Acharya not only picked up his call, he agreed to meet him at four o'clock at St Giles.

He returned to the station, checked through the case file and added his own actions to the day's running sheet. He followed up on progress in Mosese's attacker's prosecution, which was going ahead with no apparent hitches.

***

Essie, the office assistant, again escorted Horseman from the St Giles reception block to Dr Acharya's office. This afternoon, there was no sea breeze to lift the sodden blanket of hot air. He arrived at the doctor's room feeling all his energy had drained out on his walk across the baking quadrangle.

The sad-faced doctor shook hands and gestured to a chair. Dr Acharya looked at him for a moment, then poured two glasses of water. 'Here, you look like you need a drink, Inspector.'

'*Vinaka.*' He drank.

'If I'd realised that Dev Reddy would be in danger at his home, the poor man would be alive today. And safe here. You predicted that danger.'

'You're in a closed world up here at St Giles,' Horseman said. 'You didn't know the risks.'

Dr Acharya dismissed Horseman's remark with a wave of his hand. 'As a psychiatrist, I should have a better knowledge of human behaviour. There's no excuse for a doctor being so naïve. But enough of that. I won't forget Dev and will try not to repeat my mistake. However, I can see that your health is suffering as you pursue Dev's killers.'

Horseman shrugged. 'It's stressful when you've got little to go on. But statistically, most murders are solved in the first week. So we go all out, trying to crack the case quickly, losing sleep as a result. We can catch up once we've got our culprit.'

'Nevertheless, you need sleep to work at your best. Don't forget that.'

'Well, I went to see Kanan at Sunshine Home as you advised. I didn't know about his albinism. Why didn't you tell me?'

'I didn't want to influence you. What did you think of Kanan?'

'I saw that he was an albino, that he had mobility and coordination problems, and speech and learning problems, too. He played well with the preschoolers and their toys. He was happy and well cared for, as far as I could tell.'

'Well observed, Inspector.'

Horseman was a bit put out. 'Was this a test you set me?' he said with a smile.

The doctor's smile was rueful. 'Maybe a bit. In India, albinos are treated with suspicion and prejudice by others with limited education. Many die of skin cancer before the age of forty or go blind. None of this suffering need happen. Thank goodness medical support and government campaigns are slowly improving their chances in life.

'But in central Africa, where the rate of albinism is higher than in India, the situation is appalling. I worked there for seven years. Superstition about albinos has a stranglehold on the public. They are regarded as supernatural. They are feared and shunned. But to the witch doctors, those jackals, they are a valuable source of ingredients for their vile potions. Albinos simply disappear—kidnapped and killed for their organs, skin, hair and bones.'

Dr Acharya turned and gazed out the window. Horseman struggled to take in what he'd just heard.

The doctor drank some more water and visibly pulled himself together.

'However, this isn't helping you solve Dev's murder.'

Horseman smiled. 'Do you think Kanan's albinism caused his father's mental delusion?'

'I do, at least partly. Dev held superstitions derived from Hindu folk customs. Kanan's whiteness could suggest something supernatural about the child. For someone with a predisposition to schizophrenia, the next step—to belief in possession by a demon—isn't great. But—'

'Oh no, another but,' Horseman smiled.

'I'm afraid so, Inspector. If Kanan was brown-skinned like the rest of us, could any of this have happened? I don't know. Psychiatrists can't deal in the speculative.'

'I agree, Doctor. Neither can detectives. Dev's solicitor told me about the new will he drew up about six months ago. You were a witness. May I ask if Dev discussed his intentions with you?'

'Well, if Mr Pandey saw fit to tell you about it, there's no reason for me to hold back, I guess. Yes, he did. He wanted to make sure Kanan would inherit his property when he died.'

'Which Kanan did he mean? His true son, who went away, or the boy he banished to the chicken shed?'

'I think the law will only recognise the one who is named.'

'We'll have to wait and see. Dev's eldest son has already told Mr Pandey he will challenge the will.'

'I can understand your interest in the question, Inspector. But does this have any relevance to detecting Dev's killers?'

'I don't know, Doctor. That's why I must turn over every stone.'

THURSDAY

37

Horseman's ringtone broke into his sleep. He fumbled on the floor for his phone, managed to lift it up and answer.

'Inspector Horseman, it's Maika from Nausori station.'

'*Io*, Constable? What's happened?'

'Excuse me, sir. The Reddy farmhouse is on fire.'

'What?'

'*Io*, sir. I despatched the fire brigade—they should be there now—maybe too late.'

He sat up, swinging his legs to the floor. '*Vinaka vakalevu*, Constable. Who notified you?'

'Mr Prakash, Reddy's neighbour. It doesn't involve you, sir, but I wanted you to know. Because you're investigating Reddy's murder. Sorry to wake you.'

Horseman yawned. 'Don't apologise, Maika, I'm grateful to you. I'll head out to the farm right away. If I don't see you there, I'll stop by Nausori station afterwards if I can.'

As he pulled on his thickest clothes, he wondered whether he should call Singh. She wanted to expand her experience with an eye on her promotion. Maybe she hadn't worked on any fire investigations. If not, she wouldn't want to miss out, so he called. She said she'd be waiting at the entrance to the women's barracks.

He called the car pool and ordered a Landcruiser to be brought around. While he was waiting, he hurried to make two thermos flasks of tea, grabbed biscuits and bananas, and stuffed them in his emergency backpack, which always held water, wet weather gear and torches. His impatience rose as the minutes ticked by, but there was no point in rushing. He couldn't do anything until the fire officers put out the fire and declared the remains of the farmhouse safe. It must be arson, but the arsonist wouldn't be hanging around now. He'd be hiding, watching his handiwork from a safe distance, gloating.

He heard the vehicle pull up and left quietly so as not to wake Matt. Susie was waiting and swung herself up into the vehicle. She was absurdly bright-eyed and well-groomed, not a hair out of place in her high ponytail.

He told her about his meeting with Dr Acharya. 'He could be keeping what he knows about the family to himself.'

'He could easily justify that—patient confidentiality and all that.'

'As we said yesterday, we need to talk to the Reddy children if we can. Notifying them about this fire could be an ideal way in.'

'*Io*, the house is wooden, neglected. The fire may well destroy it. Probably arson.'

Singh bent down and unzipped Horseman's backpack at her feet. She handed him a bottle of water and pulled out a packet of coconut biscuits. 'Feel like one of these, sir? Sorry, Joe?'

He yawned then downed some water. 'Please, they might help me wake up. I can see either Ravai Nata or Gopal Prakash doing this.'

He crammed a whole biscuit in his mouth and munched.

'What're their motives?' Singh asked.

'Nata's got a fanatic streak, although there's a lot more to understand about the man. He would be destroying the traces of evil from that land, sort of purifying it.'

'Not destroying evidence?'

'You're a cynic, Singh. Worse than me. Nata certainly could've been there that Friday night—we've already shown that.'

Singh swivelled towards him, eager. 'How do you see Prakash, then? The good neighbour or what?'

'He wants the land—most of it's rare freehold. He's ambitious, wants more land to motivate his children to stay and work with him. If the buildings are gone, the price could drop. I need to check by how much. And if he took part in Reddy's attack, he could be destroying the evidence, too.'

'Yep, I agree. Another biscuit?'

They drove in companionable silence. He knew Singh was working through the possibilities just like he was.

'I should travel more often at three in the morning—you make good time!' They crossed the Rewa bridge to Nausori and soon left street lights behind. Horseman drove as fast as safety would permit through the darkness. Colliding with loose livestock could literally stop them dead.

'There it is! Ahead, to the left,' Singh shouted.

At first just a golden glow in the distance, then plumes of sunset orange and red as they approached. When he made the turn into Reddy's road, the raging flames illuminated a cloud of grey smoke billowing to one side. He pulled up well away from the red fire truck.

'Have you got waterproofs?' he asked Singh.

'No, I didn't think. I've got a cotton hoodie. I'll stay clear of the hoses.'

'I should've reminded you.' He pulled on his rain jacket, seized his backpack, and they walked towards the farmhouse. Even at this distance, the smoke assaulted his eyes, nose, mouth and throat. He fumbled in his backpack and handed Singh a mask.

'These aren't proper firefighter masks but they'll help.'

The smoke and flames shot from the right end of the building, but the rotten stairs on the left side and adjacent ground-floor infill boarding were also alight. The white-gold heart of the primary flame plume dazzled him. The mask helped, but every step closer made breathing harder.

Two yellow-helmeted firefighters shouldered the hose trained on the heart of the fire. The centre of the farmhouse must have burned first. A loud crack and rumble startled them both as a rafter collapsed. Other pieces of roof teetered at odd angles before falling against the remains of walls and floors. The mattress on Reddy's small iron bedstead was aflame. Two more firefighters each directed a smaller hose at the periphery of the fire, inching their way inwards.

They watched, mesmerised despite their spluttering and coughing. The central plume of flame steadily reduced while the smoke thickened and billowed further.

'I think our lungs have had enough,' Horseman said. 'Let's talk to the onlookers.' He coughed for a bit, the smoke rasping his throat. They retreated behind the truck. He flashed his ID to an officer using his radio and crossed the road.

'We need some of this tea first,' he croaked, taking a thermos out of the side pocket of his backpack.

'Good idea, sir.' Singh only managed a whisper. Horseman let the 'sir' go. Whether it was the tea or sugar, after two cups he felt better.

'Can you talk? Take names and addresses and so on?'

Singh cleared her throat. 'Sure, I'm much better now.'

'There are eight, so let's take them singly. That way, we'll be quicker. If your voice goes on strike, get them to write their details in your notebook.'

They went up to the group of bystanders corralled behind the fire brigade barricade. Well, well, he already knew two of the bystanders:

Gopal and Maira Prakash. They both stared at the blaze.

'Good morning, Inspector Horseman. We didn't expect we'd be meeting you here.'

'I didn't expect to be here. Listen, I really need to talk to you. Could you wait until Sergeant Singh and I have recorded the others' contact details?'

'Yes, yes. Two of them are our sons. The other four are the Krishna family, the neighbours from the other side.'

'That simplifies things. If you can wait here, I'll be with you in a few minutes.'

He looked across at the house as he waited for Singh to finish with the neighbour she was talking to. The main flame plume had now retreated to roof level. On the left side, the firefighters had extinguished the blaze at ground level while only small flames still licked along the weatherboards and window frames. The shifting light through the windows showed the house interior was still burning, though maybe not for much longer.

It had to be arson—the fire spreading from two distinct sites was a telltale sign. But he was no expert and recognised a fire investigator would observe in much more detail and analyse the physical evidence in a lab. He couldn't wait for that before pushing on. His working hypothesis was arson, and one or more of the eight people behind the barricade could easily have struck the match.

After telling Singh the good news that all the bystanders were Reddy's neighbours, he went back to the fire truck to talk to the boss.

He showed his ID. '*Bula*, officer. I'm Joe Horseman. Thank God for the fire service!'

The khaki-clad officer raised his face shield. 'Fire Officer Peni Naulu. Good to meet you.'

'Any idea when police will have access?'

'*Oi lei*, Inspector, that's not easy. It's coming under control nicely now, but fires are unpredictable, as you know. We're lucky the breeze is light at the moment, but that could change in an instant.'

Horseman coughed. He'd already talked too much. 'If the weather remains calm?'

'A big if. Flare-ups could happen after the sun rises as the day gets hot. Even if the fire's completely extinguished, it's not safe in there. Half the roof and first floor have fallen in, smouldering timbers everywhere, and more are likely to fall. You couldn't get in today. Nothing's safe.'

'You're right. Will you be investigating the cause yourself?'

'I've started already—you have, too. I can see you checking the site from the outside.' He grinned. 'Could be me, but probably the top gun will come in because it's the Reddy house. Nothing gets past our Joni. We've got a great new lab, too, courtesy of Australia. Gas chromatography, all the latest.'

'When d'you reckon it started?'

'I can only guess. But it's a sturdy build, good size structural timbers. This sort of damage doesn't happen in ten minutes, you know. My best guess is ten o'clock, eleven at the latest. Joni the investigator will work that out tomorrow.'

'Have you seen the Nausori police?'

'Not yet. They called us in, but they've not been here.'

'I accept I can't go in, but no one else must go in either. Will the firefighters be mounting a twenty-four-hour guard?'

'We'll tape it off and stick up notices, and there'll be one of us here, but no guarantees. If someone's determined to sneak in, he probably could.'

'*Vinaka* for your honesty. I agree. I'll call Nausori and ask them to send two constables and formally set up a crime scene. In the meantime, are all six of you going to be here for another few hours?'

'*Io*, until daylight and probably longer.'

'Great, I need to talk to Reddy's neighbours—they're gathered over there. I prefer to do that in their houses where they can be comfortable. I don't want to insult you by asking...'

'Don't worry, Inspector. We'll be here. If anyone comes snooping, we'll catch them for you!

38

Gopal Prakash ushered everyone to the table. His wife, Maira, went to fill the kettle and Singh joined her. Horseman pulled out his full tea thermos and held it up.

'While you're waiting for the kettle to boil, please help yourselves to this. I reckon you need something right now after the night you've had.'

The acrid smoke was like sandpaper on his throat. He coughed, poured tea into the thermos cup and drank. Better. The younger son, Sanjeev, brought some cups and Horseman poured.

'I've already added milk and sugar. Hope that suits you. Oh, I've got these, too.' He retrieved his second packet of coconut biscuits from his backpack, tore one end open, and put it on the table.

Prakash seemed embarrassed. 'Thank you, sir, but Maira will make rotis.' He glanced to the kitchen workbench and indeed, Maira was ladling flour into a bowl while Singh was spooning tea leaves into the aluminium pot.

'That's kind but quite unnecessary.'

'She'd be doing it for us in another hour, anyway. My daughter-in-law will wake soon and help. The working day starts early on a farm.'

'Please polish these off first. A drink and small bite will help all of us.'

Gopal took a biscuit and a cup of tea and sat down. The others followed suit.

'A professional fire investigator will take charge of the farmhouse site. I'm taking witness statements. We always begin by assuming a fire was deliberately lit. That means the Reddy farm is a crime scene and no one may enter until the investigator is satisfied that the fire was accidental. Please tell your children and neighbours about that as soon as you can.'

Gopal nodded. 'Go on.'

'I expect you will be the most important witnesses. So let's start at the beginning. Who was the first to notice the fire?'

Gopal, Hari and Sanjeev looked at each other, then Hari spoke.

'I was working very late in my workshop. I don't know the time, but everyone else had been in bed for hours. I decided to call it a night. As I was walking back to the house, I smelt smoke but I couldn't see anything. I came upstairs to the porch but still couldn't see anything. Then I realised the smoke was blowing on the breeze from the direction of the Reddy farm. I ran along the road until I could see an orange glow around the house.'

'Thank goodness you chased the smoke.'

Hari was pleased to be praised. 'You have to. Fires are fatal. I didn't have my phone with me—should have, but I didn't think too clearly. I woke Baba and told him. He handled things from there.'

'I called Nausori police. Constable Maika answered—he's a reliable chap. He told me he'd look after everything. He warned me not to go anywhere near the fire.'

Hari added, 'But once we heard the fire truck sirens, you can imagine. We had to know what was happening so close to us.'

'We knew the firefighters would tell us what to do, so we'd be safe,' Gopal explained.

Maira and Singh brought the tea things to the table, refilled everyone's cups, and returned to roti making. Maira had clearly opened up to Singh—the pair were chatting in rapid Hindi. Singh was the best person to find out what Maira really thought, not only about the fire but about the entire Reddy family history.

First, the fire.

'Who would want to destroy Reddy's property?'

The young men again looked to their father, who shrugged. 'No one. Nobody around here had time for Reddy except us, but he's dead now. Burning down his house can't hurt him. Unless there's one of these mad fire-setters that gets his kicks from staring at the flames they create.'

'Is there anyone around here with that reputation?'

'No, I just saw a movie on TV like that.'

'No self-respecting farmer would risk the fire spreading to crops—his or any neighbours.'

'I heard you'd asked Reddy's solicitor about buying his land.'

Prakash wagged his head in agreement. 'I can't deny it. As I told you last time, acquiring so much land next to my own would be a dream come true. I'm prepared to offer above the going rate to secure it.'

The two sons gazed at the table and drank tea. A sleepy-eyed young woman entered, mumbled a greeting and joined Maira at the kitchen bench. Two doe-eyed schoolgirls in cotton pyjamas followed. They stared curiously at Horseman, then averted their gaze and hurried to the women.

'Do you suppose the destruction of the farmhouse will affect the price of the land?' Horseman asked.

Gopal shrugged. 'That's beyond me. But that house couldn't have been worth much. What do you think, boys?'

Gopal had probably not intended his sons to answer, but Sanjeev, the younger, piped up. 'Outbuildings and equipment can have more value than a farmhouse. Ours sure would have.' He smirked at his brother, surreptitious. His father frowned, dismissing the comment with a flick of his hand.

'I can see you're progressive farmers here—business-like. It's great to see you diversifying. So many farmers don't want to try anything their fathers and grandfathers didn't do.'

'Hari's the one who diversifies, Inspector. He's a craftsman as well as a farmer—a gem-setter and jeweller. His workshop's here on the farm. But our maternal grandfather taught him.' Sanjeev chuckled again. 'So not exactly progressive.'

Gopal glared at Sanjeev. 'Enough, son. The inspector hasn't time for this.'

The warm, nutty aroma of the roti cooking made his mouth water. He avoided accepting hospitality from suspects, but he couldn't refuse to share the family breakfast. They wouldn't cooperate after such an insult.

'Not at all, Mr Prakash. It's getting light now. I'd love a quick tour of your farm, with your permission.'

'I'll show you, sir,' Sanjeev offered.

The younger doe-eyed girl came over and insinuated herself into Hari's lap, leaning into his chest. He kissed the top of her head and relaxed.

Gopal rolled his eyes a bit. 'Okay, I can smell breakfast's only ten minutes away. So make it quick, son.'

'Sure. Have you got a kitchen bucket, Ma? I'll feed the chooks.'

Maira handed him a bucket full of food scraps. Horseman followed him down the steps to the yard. The grey light revealed an ample swept yard surrounded by sheds. Roosters crowed, hens clucked and cattle lowed as the farmyard awoke.

'I'll serve the chooks first—they're furthest away.'

'Fine by me.'

They crossed the yard diagonally to a sturdy wire-fenced run. Sanjeev opened the gate and upended a stream of vegetable scraps along one side. The fowls' shrill squawks prompted a vision of the toddler, Kanan, living in their society. Swiftly collecting eggs from the coop and placing them in the bucket, Sanjeev led him past an open cowshed where a young woman was milking one of three tethered cows. Sanjeev called a cheerful greeting in Hindi to her and went on to a machine shed, his own centre of interest. He pointed out a small dairy, where they produced fresh cheese and butter and a separate shed dedicated to pickling. Attached was a roofed space with racks and trays for drying spices.

On the opposite wing were two large newer-looking sheds, built of sawn timber, closed in on all four sides with weatherboards and corrugated iron. They boasted steel-hinged doors and shutters.

'That's the new packing shed. We export fresh herbs direct to New Zealand now. We pack here, I do the paperwork, then straight to Nausori airport.' Pride rang in the boy's voice.

'Wonderful, I congratulate you.'

Hari was waiting at the open door of the adjacent shed. 'I keep my workshop locked.' He waved a key at them. 'Come in. There's not much to see, just a heap of junk I hope to put together some day, isn't it?'

He switched on bright lights. The scene was chaotic, but there was a system, too. On one wall, pictures from magazines and books were taped. Most were of elaborate Indian jewellery, while others featured simple modern designs. The bench attached to this wall supported piles of magazines and books. Several large free-standing machines stood in front of another wall. The remaining long wall had a full-length workbench with shelves underneath. Half of this seemed to house Hari's components: jars of beads, stones and metal scraps in rainbow colours. Next to these sat a pile of small drawstring bags.

'They're the repair jobs customers have left with me,' Hari said.

'You're in demand, Hari. You must be pretty good.'

'Thank you, Inspector. Usually, I do my current work on the centre bench, here.'

The tools were like toys: tiny vises, clamps, awls and pliers. Grooved velvet-covered boards held necklaces in progress—one had rows of pearls the craftsman was grading from large to small.

'This is such painstaking and skilled work, Hari. I hope your fame spreads far and wide.'

'I'll never be as famous as you, sir. Or nearly as skilled.'

'Nonsense—rugby's rough and crude, compared to this. There is an art to the game, though. Let's go in to your mother's wonderful breakfast now. *Vinaka vakalevu.*'

***

Maira and her daughter-in-law served the fresh rotis with a dry curry of vegetables and a variety of pickles. Singh carried in a tea tray. Horseman caught her eye. She smiled and nodded. Good—he hoped her discoveries were more significant than his. It was daylight now. More kids in school uniforms joined the table and tucked in. Everyone seemed to talk at once, and it was all about the fire.

Horseman addressed the general hubbub. He found children to be observant and in their excited state might let slip things they would normally keep to themselves. He stood up. The family stopped talking and looked at him in surprise.

'I'm truly thankful to Gopal and Maira for their hospitality this morning. Your father did the right thing in reporting the fire to the police. The fire brigade will stay at the Reddy place until it is safe. DS Singh and I have several puzzles to solve about the crimes committed here during the past six days. Some of you have already helped us. Have any of you noticed anyone around the Reddy place or your own farm in the last week? Or on the road? If so, please tell me—even the children. You won't get into trouble and it could be very important.'

Solemn almond-shaped eyes stared at him. A teenage boy raised his hand, glancing at his father with defiant eyes. 'My sister and me, we went to the Reddy house on Tuesday on the way home from school. We found piles of glass where someone had been sweeping up.'

Not to be outdone, the boy's sister spoke up. 'And someone had heaped up the fallen mangoes under the tree.'

The parents exchanged disapproving looks but their children had already spoken. Sibling rivalry would work in the detectives' favour.

'Someone's gone to the field shrine from here—there's a track trodden through the rice,' another child said.

A shrill voice piped up. 'The shrine glass is clean, too. And fresh flowers inside.'

'Fruit, too.'

'Yes, I saw the flies buzzing around.'

'The goddess will be happy and bless us,' said the smallest girl, with a beam.

'There's a track from the Reddy farmyard through the rice to the goddess, too.'

'On several nights, I've seen a light moving in the fields. I can't imagine what anyone would go there for. I don't think it was anyone in our family,' Hari said. He cast a doubtful look at his teenage brother. 'But there are a lot of us. I couldn't say for sure.'

Horseman jumped in to reassure the alarmed-looking parents. 'Don't worry, Gopal and Maira. If you will kindly permit us to walk through your fields, Sergeant Singh and I will check what the children have told us. We won't involve them at all.'

'I want to help the police, be a good citizen. You may walk where you like, without destroying crops of course. But I don't want the children appearing in a law court or their names on police documents.'

'Yes, I understand. Children, many thanks for telling me the truth. You have given Sergeant Singh and me important information.'

'Now, clear the table quick smart and finish getting ready for school. You'll be late!' Maira said sharply.

39

'Susie, what did you wrangle out of Maira?' Horseman asked the moment they were out of the house.

Singh's eyes widened in mock horror. 'Wrangle, sir? Two weary women chatting in the kitchen, making breakfast together? After witnessing a house fire? That's a recipe for sharing. No wrangling necessary.'

'I'm glad to hear it. Let's go and check on the fire.'

They got in the vehicle. 'Spill the beans then, Singh. Please.'

'First, Maira noticed a track trodden through the rice, too. She said none of the family would have done that. Gopal is strict about the kids treading between the rows when they cross the fields.'

'Good point. I wonder why Gopal kept that to himself? He must have noticed, too.'

'Exactly. Second, she said her family aren't very religious—they observe the major festivals, that's about it. But her older friend and neighbour, Priti Reddy, was intensely devout. She loved the complicated Hindu sagas of the gods, which were real and present to her. Dev Reddy built their field shrine to the goddess Durga to Priti's orders—it's more prominent than any others around here. Priti's devoted care for that shrine didn't rub off on her sons so much, but the youngest daughter was a kindred spirit. A shy little girl, years younger than the others and close to her mother. Maira was surprised when she went to New Zealand with her sister and brother-in-law. They sent her for a better education.'

'It's not uncommon. Lucky girl.'

'Sure. Anyway, Maira was surprised—all a bit sudden, she thought. But the main point is that since Priti died, that field shrine has been neglected. Maira's amazed it's still standing and has no idea who has recently taken an interest in it. She supposes it could be someone new in the area—a new bride, or kids who are old enough to follow a mother's interest.'

'Interesting, it fits in with what the children said.'

Horseman pulled up outside the police cordon. Half the Reddy farmhouse had tumbled. The flames had died, but a pall of smoke lingered in the still air like mist. They went up to the official entrance guarded by a firefighter in a yellow helmet and padded khaki suit. After signing in, the guard radioed his superior and directed the detectives to keep outside the barrier surrounding the house.

Fire Officer Peni Naulu came across to the cordon, his breathing apparatus turning him into an alien with a camera slung around his neck. He loosened the straps of his mask and lifted it up over his helmet. His face was running with sweat. '*Bula*, Joe. *Bula*, Sergeant. We've been lucky –the breeze died down and hasn't come back yet. We should get rain later in the day, too. The flames are out for now, but angry embers are smouldering everywhere. The heat's still intense, structural members still falling without notice, so no access for you today, I'm afraid. Nausori police turned up—you'll find Constable Toga near the cordon behind the house.'

'We understand. You and the guys are doing a wonderful job, Peni.'

'*Vinaka*, Inspector. None of us would want a different one. How did you go with the neighbours?'

'Useful—and I'm not just talking about the wonderful breakfast. Over the last few days, the kids have noticed signs of sweeping up here —a few piles of broken glass.'

'*Vinaka*. They're probably dispersed now, but we'll have a look.'

'Paths trodden through the rice, too. We're heading off to look for those.'

'Could be kids telling tales on each other.'

'Could be. Any signs of arson yet?' Horseman coughed.

'I can smell an accelerant—probably kerosene. It's quite strong in a few places. Everything's too hot to take samples yet. I'm recording the scene before more falls. Our top investigator, Joni, is here taking a grid of stills, as much as he can at this stage.' Peni's excitement was palpable. Horseman's was rising, too.

After introducing Singh to Constable Maika, Horseman said, 'Maika, let's get away from this smoke.'

Toga took off his mask and helmet, leaving them at the cordon post. '*Oi lei*, I'm glad to get those off.' He pulled a large handkerchief out of a pocket and wiped down his head and face.

'Put these on instead.' Horseman handed him gloves. 'We'll check all the outbuildings not affected by the fire. Sergeant Singh, can you do a rough sketch, please?'

'Love to, sir. Just a minute.'

She pulled a clipboard from her backpack and quickly marked the positions of the visible outbuildings. Toga watched carefully, impressed.

'Gopal leases the Reddy land and uses one of these sheds for fuel storage. Something else he didn't think to tell me. I spotted it last Saturday when I was searching for Reddy. I can compare what's there now with what I noted then.' They listed and photographed the contents.

They finished the job without incident. Toga looked uncertain. 'Should I go back to the cordon now? Or can I help you some more, sir?'

'What would you prefer?'

'Oh, I'd like to help you. It's pretty tedious standing guard at a fire, suffocating in a hot mask.'

'Come with us, then.'

They stepped over the irrigation channel and into the emerald rice, careful not to trample any. Toga soon spotted the trampled path, which they followed to the shrine, the goddess's home. Four strong posts with diagonal bracing and ladder-like rungs on all sides supported her glass-walled house.

'Wow, I've never seen such a solid-looking field shrine,' Singh remarked. 'It's really a little temple. Look, the roof is like a pagoda, with a lovely carved finial on top. If Dev didn't worship Durga, he must have loved his wife to make this for her.'

'It's famous as the best in all the Rewa farmlands,' Toga said with pride.

The imperious goddess surveyed the rice fields. Her enormous almond eyes, outlined in kohl, were set off by her white skin. A string of marigolds adorned her. Over the years, the fierce sun had faded her tattered garments, which still hinted at their original intense colours. Around her were a candle, a water pot and spoon and pieces of guava crawling with ants.

'I'm not Hindu, but I'll say a *puja* to ask forgiveness for what we're about to do,' Singh said in a soft voice. She clapped once, before chanting her brief prayer. Her two colleagues bowed their heads and waited for her to make a move. She climbed onto a rung, slung her backpack over a corner post and got out her fingerprint kit. Horseman followed suit and handed a spare kit to Maika. By standing on the topmost rung, they could dust the glass and frames without disturbing the resident goddess.

Horseman expected they would get good prints, and they did—full fingerprints and partial handprints. They wiped the black powder off afterwards as well as they could.

'I didn't have the heart to ask the Prakash family for their prints after Maira's kindness. I'll have to send the SOCO team later. It's quite likely one or two of the children have taken to tending the shrine recently, but we'll ignore the small prints. The person we're after is an adult.'

'Do you still consider Gopal Prakash a suspect, sir?' Maika asked.

'*Io*. We haven't been able to eliminate anyone yet, I'm sorry to say, Maika. We're off to talk to the Sharma family, the neighbours on the other side.'

'I think you can rule them out, sir. They came from Ba less than a year ago to take over the lease from distant cousins who died. Their nephew who lives with them is a constable serving with us at Nausori.'

'Good, Maika. We'll talk to them, anyway. You can tell me about them on our way back to the farmhouse.'

40

Although it was scarcely eleven o'clock in the morning, Horseman felt he was at the end of a long day. He dropped Singh at the barracks, ordered her to catch up on some sleep, and picked up Musudroka at the station. Maybe a young person's take on Ravai Nata would be useful.

Horseman believed he got better results from an interview by being friendly, even if he privately despised the person sitting across the table. Sometimes this could be a hard act.

One such was Ravai Nata, founder and leader of HOOK. Horseman couldn't get a handle on this bundle of inspiring preacher and compulsive liar. When presented with evidence of his lies, the man excused himself and then told a different lie. So he would have to try hard to seem friendly yet again.

They ran Nata down in the office at the back of God's Gospel Church. He was alone at the table with his Bible, cashbox and a couple of school notebooks, pen in hand, brow furrowed.

'*Bula*, Inspector Horseman. *Oi lei*, this is a surprise. How can I help you today?'

'*Bula*, Mr Nata. Just a quick chat, a few questions, if you don't mind.'

He introduced Musudroka, who shook hands with Nata.

'I'm pleased to see you following DS Singh's advice.' He nodded at the cashbox. 'It's so important to know what's coming in and going out, especially with charities.'

'True— HOOK started with such a big bang, we were unprepared.' His smile was endearing, with a hint of apology. 'Now, with postal orders and cash still coming in, we're recording everything, issuing receipts, and banking daily. Just as Sergeant Singh advised.'

'She'll be pleased to hear it.'

'But we can't issue receipts when donors don't tell us their details. Many just put cash in an envelope and slip it under the church door.'

'So, Mr Reddy's death hasn't dampened the public's enthusiasm for HOOK?'

He looked confused. 'Not yet, anyway. I've prayed about it and God's telling me that our mission should be loving and positive. I understand some people didn't embrace our cause because they thought we advocated vengeance. Nothing could be further from my intention. We'll make that clear from now on.'

The man should go into politics. His skill at spin and backflip was instinctive.

'That's all to the good. Where were you yesterday evening, Mr Nata?'

Again, the quizzical frown. 'I was here, at choir practice.'

'When did that finish?'

'Around nine o'clock. After that, I worked here for another hour with a colleague, trying to catch up with the HOOK accounts. I got to the stage where I couldn't concentrate, so I went home.'

'Had your family gone to bed by that time?'

'No, my wife was watching television when I got in. She served me food she'd saved, and I ate it in front of the TV. Then I went to lie down and must have dozed off. I woke when my sister-in-law came in from work. That must have been around half-past eleven, as her afternoon shift at the hospital finishes at eleven. I got up, had a shower and went to bed. My wife had a chat with her sister for a bit, then came to bed.'

If all that were true, it wasn't possible for Nata to have lit a fire at a farmhouse in the back blocks of Nausori. He must confirm every step Nata claimed he took last night.

'Who was helping you with the accounts after Bible study, sir?' Musudroka asked.

'Hmm? What? Well, um, it was Mark Prasad.'

'Who is he?' Musudroka asked.

Horseman answered, 'You haven't met him, Detective Constable. He's the bookkeeper from Carpenters who was arrested at Reddy's farmhouse last Saturday. Mr Nata bailed him and hired a solicitor to represent him when he appears before the magistrate tomorrow morning.' He turned to Nata. Am I right to assume the money for that came from HOOK funds?'

Nata gave them his bright, innocent smile again. '*Io*, I'm blessed to have Mark's help with the accounts. And I'm also blessed to help him in return. What is this about, anyway?'

'I'm just checking information we've received,' Horseman said. 'Oh, you might help me with something else, more theological. Is there any religious reason why a Christian could set fire to a place where great sins have been committed?'

'*Io*, but it's Old Testament, rather than Christian. God destroyed places by fire as well as flood. Sodom and Gomorrah, for example. The reason would be to purge the place of the devil's influence, to destroy all traces of evil deeds.'

As Nata spoke, he leaned towards them, his eyes lit by zeal.

'*Vinaka vakalevu*, Mr Nata, you've been a big help to us,' Horseman said.

***

'What d'you reckon, Tani?' Horseman asked Musudroka when they got in the car.

'I was gonna ask you, sir.'

'I've met Ravai Nata several times already. I know I'm prejudiced. I want to know your first impression.'

'I've seen him on TV often enough, so it's not really my first impression.'

'Good enough for me, Tani.'

'He comes across as a friendly guy, sincere, very moral. Somehow, you pay attention to him. As you know, I'm a Catholic. We don't go in for these charismatic preachers, but I reckon he'd be a good one.'

'Do you believe what he says?'

'Hard to say, sir. I know from your briefings that he's lied to you before. But if I didn't know that, I'd probably believe him because he sounds so sincere. I can't pin down why I feel that, though. But I wouldn't assume my impression was correct. I know to double-check his alibi.'

'Interesting, Tani. We'll make a detective of you yet! The problem with chronic liars like Nata is that not everything they say is a lie. It can be a lot of work sifting through the rubbish.'

'*Io*. But he's kinda weird. Like he wanders off to another planet now and then.'

'Hmm. You're right. Wish I knew precisely which planet.'

'Do you think he could have murdered Reddy, sir? And set the fire?'

'He certainly could have, but I don't know yet whether he did. I'm tempted to think one of his misguided followers is more likely, but why? We've got to shake off our prejudice that a preacher couldn't murder and follow the facts. Let's get back to the station. I want you to take me through your stolen jewellery case. I just might have a lead for you.'

***

They pulled into the station yard in hard, driving rain. A foreigner would think it had set in for the day, but the locals knew it would likely stop within twenty minutes. But you would be just as wet after sitting in a hothouse of a car for that length of time as you would after walking through a deluge, and much more uncomfortable. So they got out and hurried indoors, holding their backpacks over their heads. They grabbed towels from their lockers, rubbed themselves down and let the ceiling fans in the office finish the job.

'*Oi lei*, that rain was just what I needed after my night at a fire. So refreshing. I've only skimmed through the file on the jewel thefts. Make us a cup of tea while I check my emails. Then we'll sit down and you can walk me through it.'

When Musudroka had done the honours with the case file, Horseman said, '*Vinaka*, well done, Tani. You're on top of this case. And a good mug of tea, too. Look, by now your team has visited just about every jewellery craftsman and retailer on Viti Levu. Didn't you have suspicions of any of them?'

'*Io*, but we suspected them just because of vague rumours or they acted cagey or uncooperative. DI Vula applied for warrants to search two of them, but they were knocked back for lack of evidence.'

'Okay, the one he applies for this afternoon just might be granted. I visited Reddy's neighbour Prakash this morning. His eldest son showed me his shed where he works as a craftsman jeweller. I noticed three rows of pearls he was grading before re-stringing. I'm no expert, but that long loop of pearls stolen from the Japanese ambassador's house...'

'You recognised them?' Musudroka was super-excited.

'I don't have the expertise to identify pearls. But from the details with the photo, converting that loop into three short necklaces could be feasible. A good way of disguising them. I would have thought enough grounds for suspicion for a search warrant. How about we see DI Vula now?'

***

DI Vula jumped at the new information and chance of a search warrant. Hari Prakash's workshop was unknown to him and their co-opted expert, a Suva jeweller. Musudroka went back to DI Vula's office to help with the warrant applications.

Thinking about the magistrate's warrants reminded him Nata's HOOK disciples would appear before the magistrate tomorrow. He still had nothing from the SOCO office about the fingerprint checks on the pieces of evidence he and the Nausori constables had picked up from inside and around Reddy's farmhouse. With the trio's plausible and consistent denials of doing anything more than standing outside the farm boundary and shouting, even the trespassing charge might fall over. He strongly suspected them of so much more—the callous and brutal bashing of a man in his seventies.

SOCOs hated detectives calling them to check on results, and Horseman sympathised with them. But he lifted the receiver anyway and punched in Ash's direct extension.

'Joe, I was just about to ring you!'

'A likely story! Prove it—what have you got for me on the Reddy house exhibits?'

'Why does no one believe me when I say that? It's true. I just got the fingerprint results from the lab. We've got two matches for you.'

'*Oi lei*! Wonderful! Who?'

Singh walked in, looking fresh and rested, every single hair scraped into a gleaming French twist. He grinned, pointed at the phone and gave her a thumbs-up.

'Sorry, Ash, I didn't catch that.'

'Paula Wairua's prints are on one rock and the paper taped to it, and Mark Prasad's are on the ballpoint pen and another paper message.'

'Really? Fantastic!'

'I'll email everything to you; that's the prints and the technician's report and comparison data.'

'*Vinaka*, Ash. I'll phone the prosecutor now and forward him the email the moment I get it. But I'll come over and pick up the originals from you. A few magistrates are suspicious of digital evidence. I won't be responsible for my actions if this case is thrown out.'

'You're getting paranoid, Joe, but fine. I'll have a cardboard box with fingerprint cards and rocks and stuff waiting for you.' He chuckled.

'Don't joke, Ash—it's happened before!'

Singh joined him when he put the receiver down. She beamed when he told her the news. 'At last, something positive,' she said.

'Care to celebrate with a late lunch? That roti breakfast was a very long time ago. When was it—six?'

'Twenty past, so not so long ago! Thanks, sir, but I won't. I ate something before leaving the barracks and I want to notify the Reddy children about the fire. It's a good pretext to dig a bit more. And I have to go out later if that's okay.'

'Sure, Susie. Anything I need to know about?'

'Of course, I should be working!'

Horseman laughed. 'I'm glad you're not my boss! I trust you if that's allowed.'

'Well, within limits, sir.' She didn't crack a smile.

'The limit is this: it's nearly two o'clock and I need lunch. Your assignment is to come with me and explain your plans for the afternoon while I eat.'

Singh didn't like being beaten, even in jest. Had he gone too far? She saluted, picked up her bag and preceded him out of the office and down the stairs. He looked down at the perfection of her glossy French twist and marvelled.

He didn't feel like more curry. 'How about the food court in the Telecom building? Two minutes' walk and we can choose anything we like.'

'Okay. It'll only be the leftovers now, though. And clashing and clattering as the staff clean up.'

'True. You choose, then.'

'Arabica. That's if the menu's not too limited for you. Further to walk, but it's quiet and I can think there.' At last, she smiled. 'It's your fault, sir, you introduced me to it.'

'Great, let's walk fast then.'

**

Singh swept her spoon across the top of the cappuccino and put it in her mouth. 'That is the best froth—so creamy. I'll come straight out with it. I'm going to see another two flats. They're both open for inspection from four o'clock to five. I'm sorry, you know work comes first with me. But the pond that used to be the women's bathroom floor was alive with mosquito wrigglers when I took a shower this morning. Maintenance said someone would put some kerosene in the water but I'm not especially keen to paddle through kerosene either. It's time I looked after myself instead of relying on the force to do it.'

'Of course you can look at the flats. But Susie, don't be so tough on yourself. The barracks was a sensible choice when you were promoted to Suva and the sergeants' flats are pretty decent. I was happy enough there. If you want to stay until you're kicked out when you make DI, you'll have to harass the manager.'

'It's so frustrating.'

'I know, but harassing a private landlord mightn't be any improvement. Could be worse.'

'I didn't look at it like that.'

'I'm not advising you to stay in the barracks. Not at all. But it's a valid option for you until you're promoted.'

The waiter brought Horseman's sandwiches—thick wholemeal bread with tomato, watercress and cucumber. He took a bite. He'd given Singh all the advice he was prepared to give. And he'd just made a decision of his own he thought he would share with her. Later.

Before he took a bite, he said, 'Now that you've had a break, tell me your thoughts on the Krishna interviews this morning.'

'I don't rate anyone in the family as a suspect, sir. They claim they moved to Rewa from the west less than a year ago. Constable Toga confirms that. They're too young to have known the Reddy family before his wife died—that's nearly twenty years ago. They would've been children themselves then. I believed them when they said they'd never met any of the family. Gopal Prakash said he didn't know them well either. They got together over some fireworks last Diwali and the children got on. The youngest Prakash children go to the same school as the older Krishna kids. But so far, there's not been much socialising.'

'Has Mr Reddy's body been released yet?' she asked.

Horseman waved a hand at his jaw to indicate he was chewing. He swallowed after a few more munches.

'Sometime today. The morgue may already have informed Darsh Reddy in Auckland. I think Navneet Pandey, Reddy's solicitor, will make the arrangements. I plan to call him when I get back.'

'I wonder if the children will bother to come. It's a terribly important duty for the eldest son, even if he hates his father.'

'I suppose the funeral will be tomorrow or Saturday. Could be useful.' He picked up his last sandwich, then put it down again. 'You know, I don't really want this.'

'The waiter will wrap it for you, sir. Just the thing for mid-afternoon. You've got training, haven't you?'

'If I can squeeze it in. But I must go. I've got good news for Pita and Livai—I promised I'd ask Father Francis if he had room for them at his hostel. I asked at the right time and he wants to interview them tomorrow morning. It's up to them now. If they can commit to some vocational training, I think they've got a good chance.'

'That's good.'

He knew she wasn't particularly keen on the Shiners. 'I don't know—maybe it's the fire—seeing what once was a family's home destroyed. Even if it ended up being a perversion of a home. Then going to the Prakash home, then the Krishnas'—nothing's perfect, but they're still homes, where the family should be, where the kids can grow and then branch out if they want. You and I both had that.'

She looked surprised. Maybe he was coming across as too emotional. 'Anyway, as we ran into each other at the Seaview flats, I wanted you to know I've decided to take a lease on one, just for six months. Then I'll evaluate. In the end, what swayed me was that I need a home that's mine, even if I don't own it. That flat on the fifth floor was waiting for me.'

Singh smiled. 'Good for you, sir!'

'I hope you find what you're looking for this afternoon, Susie. I'd better get back. I've got a meeting with the prosecutor about the court case tomorrow.'

Singh stood up. 'Are you appearing?'

'As a witness, yes. Maika Toga from Nausori is the arresting officer. Ash will testify about the fingerprints. I hope it's quick. I don't want to be stuck in court all day.'

'What time's the case review with Ratini?'

'*Oi lei!* I forgot. I'll see him right away.'

41

While Horseman was trying to wind up a call, Singh got ready to leave. She tidied her already tidy desk, snapped the elastic over her notebook, closed down her computer and grabbed her bag. He ended his call before she walked out.

'Sir, I've just sent you an email. Darsh Reddy eventually picked up his phone. He seemed shocked by the news of the fire. Said he wasn't sure if the insurance was up-to-date. But we'll meet him on Saturday because he's officiating at his father's funeral after all. The solicitor is arranging everything. Did you get on to Mr Pandey?'

'I did. He heard about the fire on the coconut wireless breakfast bulletin. He said the property has fire insurance, but somehow I don't think this arsonist's motive was insurance fraud.'

'I agree. The most important info I got out of Darsh was the whereabouts of Reddy's elder daughter, Maha. She's the one who went to New Zealand with her husband and her younger sister.'

'Oh, good. What's the story?'

'Maha, husband Arun and children, together with sister Ela, moved to Australia after a few years in New Zealand. Darsh said he lost touch with them but refused to be drawn about whether there was some sort of dispute. However, I spoke to the other two sons. Pranjal, the closest in age to Ela, told me they had gone to Nambour in Queensland, where Arun got a teaching job. I tracked him down through the education department.'

'Have you spoken to him yet? Or to Maha or Ela?'

'Not yet. The Nambour police spoke to Arun. He wants me to call when he finishes school for the day. Queensland's two hours behind Fiji, so I'll be back from the flat inspection well before then. It may not get us any further ahead, but Reddy's two daughters should know about all this.'

'Absolutely. By the way, Ratini says we'll have the case review whenever I get back from court. Oh, good luck with the flats.'

***

Once again, Horseman was late to Shiners training. Musudroka, Kau and two traffic cops had already put the boys through their warm-up exercises and were herding them together for instruction on illegal tackles. The traffic guys used Musudroka and Kau to demonstrate the dangerous high tackles and spear tackles. Musudroka always played the clown, so the demos had the boys roaring with laughter. The traffic cops joined in with frantic whistle-blowing and exaggerated roars to Musudroka to get off the field. They followed up by showing the legal tackle methods, which didn't captivate the boys nearly as much.

Horseman stepped forward. 'I've got a test for you, Shiners. Groups of five—two on each team and one referee. One instructor for each group. Rotate the referee position so you all get a turn. Which group can make the most legal tackles and the most correct referee decisions? Is that too difficult for you, boys?'

'No!' everyone yelled.

'Instructors, ready to count?'

'*Io*,' the four volunteers roared. They hastily got the boys into groups.

'Ten minutes! Begin now!'

What began as a laugh soon settled into a determination to play fair and win. Each boy's turn as referee was even more instructive than the tackler role. At the end of ten minutes, they clamoured for more time. Horseman gave in.

At halftime, he gave the winning group a bag of oranges to distribute. There weren't enough to go around, so the boys cut them into quarters. Time after time Horseman noticed these street kids, dismissed by many as lawless, could solve such practical day-to-day problems perfectly. Perhaps they were more capable than teens who had parents telling them what to do and how to do it.

He found Pita and Livai and gave them the good news about Mosese and their interview.

'Remember, boys, you must be on time. Wear clean clothes and be polite. Address Father Francis as "Father." He'll only take you if you enrol in a training course, so think of a trade you'd like to do. Speak up, don't be shy to answer his questions.'

He'd better stop behaving like an anxious parent. He blew his whistle. 'Shiners, I saw Mosese yesterday. He's still sore but he's recovering. He wants to tell you *bula*. He hopes you'll visit him and if you can't, he'll see you back here at training in a few weeks.'

They erupted into claps and cheers, which continued until Horseman held up his hand.

'Back on the field now, Shiners.'

Ten minutes later, Dr Pillai pulled up beside the field, and Horseman helped him carry in the boxes of food for the boys' dinner. He resolved to raise the subject that had been on his mind for months—his growing feeling that he must do something to get a home for these boys.

'Doctor, I told you last week how inspired I was by my visit to the Sunshine Home, where Kanan Reddy lives. I thought it would be a sad place, but it wasn't—far from it. More and more, I feel responsible for these kids, especially the ones who don't have any sort of home to go back to. I want to find out how to establish a place like the Franciscan hostel. I have some money saved from my international rugby days for a start. But funding would be needed, ongoing management. I know it would be complicated—more than I could handle. Besi, the Sunshine Home manager, told me the Save the Children Fund office here helped her when she was swamped with unsolicited donations after Kanan's story exploded in the media. They set up a foundation, all legal. Maybe that would be too much for me.'

Dr Pillai stared up at him, open-mouthed. 'Joe, that's a wonderful idea, wonderful. I'm sorry, I never knew you were so troubled by the Shiners' lives. It would give me great satisfaction to do more for them, too. I'd need to think about ways and means, but I like your idea and Save the Children seems an excellent place to start exploring. I'm willing to be a partner if you would have me. So sorry, that's very pushy and presumptuous. Even if you preferred not to have a partner, I would certainly contribute a useful sum of money.'

He couldn't believe this admirable doctor was apologising to him. But humility was Dr Pillai's overriding trait. He thrust out his hand. 'Dr Pillai, I never doubted your generosity, but I'm honoured by your trust. Really? With you as a partner, and maybe others also, I know these boys will have a home one day. Man, you've just lifted a huge load from my shoulders!'

Dr Pillai shook his hand for quite some time, beaming. His hand was small and thin, but his grip was like a steel vise. 'Yes, we can do it, but one cautious step after another on a mapped pathway. Charities can be a minefield.'

Horseman grinned. '*Vinaka vakalevu*, let's go back to your car and bring the bananas and milk.'

FRIDAY

42

Where was Ratini? There'd been no answer when Horseman tapped on his door. The magistrate's hearing was over by half-past ten and here he was, ready for the case review meeting. Well, never mind, there was plenty of paperwork waiting.

When he entered the open-plan CID room, Musudroka and Kau were sitting at Singh's desk, Singh stood at the case whiteboard, coloured marker in hand. In Singh's chair sat Ratini. Horseman had understood the meeting was to start whenever he returned from court. Yet it looked like the meeting was in full swing even though he'd got back a lot earlier than expected. Was this payback for Wednesday, when Ratini had walked in on their team catch-up?

'Pull up a chair, Horseman. All wound up in court, eh?' He didn't sound particularly interested.

'*Io*, sir. Smooth sailing, as I hoped.'

'Well? What was the outcome, man?' Ratini's voice rose.

'All three were convicted of trespassing. The two whose fingerprints matched those on the missiles were also convicted of damaging property and each sentenced to twenty hours of community service.'

'You went to a lot of trouble for that piss-weak result, didn't you?'

Horseman bridled. 'Only the standard enquiry methods, sir.'

'I told you not to bother! And you've been flogging Singh and Kau all week for this? From the beginning, I said the community is against Reddy, happy he's dead and hope we never catch his murderer! Any magistrate is going to be influenced by public opinion, whatever they say.'

'Maybe so, sir. But those bullies were convicted.'

'Let's see what the radio and the afternoon papers have to say, eh. Back to business. Sergeant Singh has been enlightening me about your murder suspects. And arson, now, is it?'

'*Io*, sir. I got a text from the fire investigator just before court started. Ignitable liquid residues in several places. He's asked to take me over the scene this afternoon.'

'Sergeant Singh's been telling us about the neighbour, Prakash. This fire blackens him, eh?'

Horseman wasn't sure if Ratini's pun was intentional, but a smile might help either way.

'He's definitely a suspect, sir. Means and opportunity, no problem. Motive is less strong.'

'You're joking! He wants to buy that freehold land he's now leasing, doesn't he?'

'True, he certainly does.'

'And with no house, the price would drop?'

'Possibly. I spoke to Reddy's solicitor about that yesterday. He's unsure whether the lack of a house would reduce the value much. There are still outbuildings that are dilapidated but usable. In fact, Prakash already uses two of them. Reddy was so notorious, it's possible a buyer would be happy about the destruction of his house.'

Ratini's bushy eyebrows shot up. 'Prakash couldn't know that.'

'True, sir. He's canny, though. And building a new house would be a cost for a rival purchaser.'

'I see. Prakash has already got a house next door—he doesn't need another. *Io*, I reckon he's your man.'

'Possible. Several people reported signs of prowling about the farms at night—trampled crops, moving lights and so on. There could be something in it. Sergeant Singh and I confirmed the Prakash kids' reports of devotions at the Reddy field shrine.'

'Of course Prakash will try to deflect suspicion from himself. Easy to whip up rumours like that. Makes him look more guilty in my book!'

'Could be. Ravai Nata's still in the running too, sir.'

'Sergeant Singh said he had an alibi.'

'Weak, sir. His wife and family again. DC Kau's going to talk to all of them this afternoon. He's thrown so many lies at us, I can't believe he's telling the truth until we can prove it.'

'And his motive?'

'He sees himself as God's avenger, sir. Razing the site of evil and scourging the earth. A purifying fire. A mini-Sodom and Gomorrah.'

Ratini shrugged. 'The world's peopled by lunatics, eh? No, my money's on Prakash. After you meet the fire investigator, bring Prakash in.'

He glanced at Singh. She frowned, moved her head a touch to the right. He ignored her. 'I'll certainly talk to him, either at his house or at

Nausori. Who knows what evidence the investigator will point me to this afternoon? Until I can assess that, I think we should keep our options open.'

Ratini tilted his head back and gazed at the ceiling fan whirring above their heads.

Horseman hastily continued. 'Have you approved DI Vula's proposal for a raid on Hari Prakash's jeweller's workshop tomorrow morning, sir?'

Ratini slowly released the deep breath he'd been holding in and lowered his head.

'*Io*. Warrant applications should be signed off today. DI Vula's planning for dawn on Sunday. I'd prefer to storm in the minute the warrants are signed, but it's his call. Sheer good luck for you, eh?'

Again, Singh moved her head slightly, warning him.

'Partly, sir. Though I did make it my business to inspect every outbuilding on the Prakash farm this morning.'

'Just as well, just as well. Let's pray for a miracle and we wrap the jewel case up on Sunday, eh. Any questions?'

Serious-faced Kau raised his hand, although there were only the four of them.

'*Io*, Detective Constable?'

'Sir, if Gopal Prakash set the fire, does that mean he killed Reddy, too?'

'Until you find some evidence, I don't know that, son. The murder's not my priority. I intended to wind down that case today, you recall. Obviously, we've now got related arson of Reddy's property, so we can't bury the murder yet. You'll have to keep going and try to speed it up, for God's sake!'

'*Io*, sir. Speaking of burying, Reddy's funeral is tomorrow afternoon. At the Nausori crematorium.'

43

The smell bowled him over—more than the sad sight of the farmhouse ruins. The suffocating smoke that scratched his throat and wracked his lungs had gone. What twitched his nose now was acrid to the max, but also held the nauseating odour of rot and something else—antiseptic? Didn't make sense.

Peni, the firefighter he'd spoken to yesterday, waved and beckoned. He came to meet him carrying a yellow helmet and filtration mask.

'*Bula*, Joe. You'd better put these on. The investigator's a stickler for the safety rules. Good reason for them, though. We don't need breathing equipment anymore, but smoke's still in the air.'

'Happy to comply.' As Horseman strapped on the helmet, another man emerged from the ruins, pulling his mask down to hang around his neck. He wore navy blue overalls, yellow gumboots, and a wide grin that took over his lean, narrow face. He held out his hand before he reached Horseman.

'*Bula* Joe—after years of watching you play, I can't call you anything else. Very happy to meet you. I'm Joni Balavu, the investigator. This site's not complicated. Still got all the lab tests to do if it comes to a criminal trial, of course.'

'Happy to meet our legendary fire-buster, Joni. You can tell me about the odd smell here. It's more than smoke, like rot.'

'You've got a good nose. That's sulphur, probably both sulphur dioxide and hydrogen sulphide. They're not the only noxious gases released when materials burn. That's why you need to wear the mask inside the site.'

Peni added, 'It's not just the smoke in the air, we stir up particles when we poke around in the ash and debris.'

'*Io,* and they go straight up our noses and into our lungs. Not good.' Joni nodded with enthusiasm. 'Ready for the tour, Joe?'

'*Io*, I'm in your hands!'

'Let's start at the right end, where there's hardly anything left. Come right in—I've taken all the lab samples already. Over here to what remains of the floor.'

'Here in the back corner. Take off your mask for a moment.' Joni squatted down, pulled his own mask down and sniffed above an area of charred pieces of wood that were once floorboards. Horseman did the same, then stood up. The reek of fuel made him gag. He pulled his mask back on.

'Wow, kerosene?'

Joni nodded. 'It'll smell stronger to you because you've only just arrived. We get desensitised so quick—that's a big problem for us. Just the smell tells us it's an ignitable liquid and my guess is kerosene,. Fire spreads up and out from its origin, so the left side of the house might have been spared if the fire started by accident in this back corner.'

'If an arsonist uses enough fuel, some runs down the joins in the floorboards. Kinda creates a trail for the fire to spread horizontally. Now let's follow that trail—the trail of the most intense destruction.'

They skirted around the fallen joists from the floor above, through more ashes and embers, smouldering despite being soaked by the fire hoses. Around the edges of what had been the room, the floor was still intact. Joni pointed to where a back wall had once stood. 'Here we are at the back again, opposite the front entrance. Look!'

A round area of ash and debris looked identical to the one in the back left corner.

'Sniff if you like, or take my word for it—the arsonist used accelerant here, too, then poured a trail to the front door, where he exited.'

'I'll take your word for it, Joni. So that's why the left half of the house is still standing.'

'*Io*, the arsonist poured the accelerant back right and back centre, then out the door. Without the fluid, the fire still spreads, but much more slowly.'

'Did Peni mention the neighbour uses one of the sheds here as a fuel store?'

'*Io*, he did, and guess what? We have a clever sniffer dog who can identify the most minute traces of seventeen different accelerants. He's a gift from an Australian brigade we helped with their bushfires last summer. We brought him here this morning, and he led us from the front door straight to the shed and to the drums of kerosene. Took a video. Now, we can't prove an arsonist left the trail of drips or spills on Wednesday night. It could have been laid at any time. But I reckon a jury would find that evidence persuasive.'

'*Oi lei*! Reckon I agree, Joni. So can I get to what remains of the first floor by the outside steps? I need to look through what's left.'

Joni shook his head, oozing regret. 'Flames have scorched the stairs and the side wall, even though they're standing. Our hoses almost demolished the stairs. A ladder could get you to the door, but I don't know if the floor could support you.'

'Can you check it out?'

Joni shook his head again. 'Come through here. Peni, you come too.'

Less than half the upper floor still existed, but they each took a long-handled tool and knocked on the scorched underside between the bearers. In a few places, the impact was enough to lift a floorboard loose but as they went further to the left, more boards held firm.

Joni frowned and shook his head again. 'Reckon we could set up two ladders—one outside near the steps and one in here where the upper floor begins. We can run our extending gangway between the two. I'll let you go up if you stay on the gangway. I'd go with you, but extra weight is extra stress. You can use my torch. Best I can do.'

'*Vinaka vakalevu.* I hate to cause you extra work, but I've got a murder as well as arson to solve here.'

'I understand. Let's do it, Peni.'

The experienced firefighters rejected Horseman's offer of help and had the scaffold erected and tested within ten minutes. By the time it was ready, Horseman had downed some water and loaded his pockets with evidence bags of different sizes, gloves and marking pens. Grateful, he took Joni's torch and climbed the ladder, his hopes rising with each step.

He stopped when the upper floor was level with his chest and shone the torch systematically anticlockwise. Dev Reddy's bedroom was gone —its spartan contents burned and tumbled onto the floor below. He gazed into the living room where, just a week ago, he'd sat at the table and urged Reddy to let him find the old man a safer place to stay. The table was still there, and the kitchen worktops and shelves, their contents knocked over and dispersed by powerful hoses. Ironically, the spirit stove was untouched. All was smoke-stained, dripping with water. Everything stank, but the flames hadn't devoured this end of the house.

He expected to see the dresser with the little family shrine, but it was missing. Now, he was further into the living room than he'd thought. The end wall, with the dresser against it, must have crashed down when the floor gave way. He wasn't sure why he felt bereft. Still, he donned gloves and climbed onto the metal gangplank, sitting astride with his feet on the floor. He pushed himself along slowly, looking at every object, all the way to the side door he'd entered by last Friday. Although he bagged a cup, pencil and small, soaked book, he had no real reason for doing so. He just didn't want to return with nothing to show after the effort Peni and Joni had gone to for him. He scooted back again and climbed down the ladder. At least his knee had held up. That wouldn't have been the case two months ago.

'Nothing much of interest,' he said to the fire officers as he showed them his evidence. Would you guys countersign the bags? I've photographed them in situ—you can check on my phone.'

'No problem, Joe.' Joni checked Horseman's phone and signed the bags. Horseman stowed them in his backpack. 'Maybe something useful fell down here. Do you mind if I fossick for a bit?'

'Not at all, Joe. There are rakes and a brush in the corner. We'll take a tea break while you poke about. Take your time.' They pulled their masks down, took off their helmets and headed off to their truck.

He started below where he figured Reddy's bedroom had been, raking gently. Before long, twisted pieces of steel bed frame confirmed his mental floor plan. No doubt the SOCOs could collect and identify hundreds, no, thousands of remnants here, but was it justified? He spotted a lot to provoke sadness, but nothing that made him curious.

He stepped across to the front of the house, below the position of the living room side wall and dresser. He prodded among the burnt bits of wall framing with the handle of the rake, then used the prongs and turned the debris over with care. Something clinked. It was the little brass bell from the shrine. He changed his gloves, picked it up, then found the brass cup. Cheered for no good reason, he squatted down and kept on searching through the debris. There was a photo album, the plastic cover and sleeves melted, the photos beyond recovery. He supposed the dresser and shrine were Priti Reddy's domain. Protected by the bottom cupboard, a crochet tablecloth was ruined but recognisable. Broken pieces of patterned china and glass, dented, deformed metal platters bore witness to Priti's pleasure in serving guests. Since her death twenty years ago, they had never been used.

He stood up to stretch, then started again.

'You're still at it, Joe?' Peni's tall, bulky figure and Joni's short, lean one were a few steps away, grinning.

'Oh, sorry. Look, I've found a few things I want to take away. Can you put in some scene markers? I'll photograph them before I bag them.'

'Sure, we'll wait until you're finished in this area though.'

Two minutes later, his probing produced another satisfying clunk just under the surface. He cleaned off the wet ash with his gloved hands to reveal a metal rectangular box, like one for fancy sweets. It was wet, dirty and dented, but the lid was jammed on tight. He shook it. The contents were light and didn't rattle. There was a chance they'd be dry. He wanted to open the box but he couldn't do it safely here. Best to stop at the SOCO lab on the way back, where he could get the right tools and advice. He photographed, bagged, labelled and asked Joni to countersign.

In another ten minutes, he called an end to his search.

44

Horseman reflected on his boss's order to arrest Gopal Prakash. Everything about Ratini grated on him: he was rude, arrogant, quick to anger and to blame. And inexplicably hostile to Horseman, a hostility conceived long ago. But Ratini was his superior officer. The police force was no less a disciplined service than the army and could not function any other way. Like a rugby team.

But Ratini hadn't thought through the consequences of his order. However likely a suspect, there was no evidence to bring a charge against Gopal Prakash. If arrested, he would only be let go after 24 hours. And he'd told Ratini he would question Gopal, not that he would arrest him. He was likely to divulge more in the security of his own home, where he believed himself the master. With luck, Horseman would take him by surprise.

As he parked outside the Prakash farmhouse, Maira emerged from around the back. Horseman got out and met her at the entrance. After exchanging polite greetings, she said,

'I'm on my way to meet the little ones at the bus stop, Inspector.'

'Is it really that late already? I've been at the fire site all afternoon. I'd like to ask you a few more questions if that's not too inconvenient.'

She smiled. 'Not at all. Gopal has just come in. My daughter will make you a cup of tea.'

'I'm interested in what you have to say, too, Mrs Prakash.'

'My goodness! I'll be back in thirty to forty minutes if you really need me. The kids are such dawdlers.'

'I'll probably be gone by then. It was nice to see you.' He smiled and walked to the front door. Mrs Prakash was evading his questions just as much as her husband. Maybe even more.

An adult daughter introduced herself as Anya and welcomed him, pulling out a chair at the table. 'I'll tell Baba you're here and put the kettle on.' She flicked her lustrous tresses behind her shoulder and smiled at him before she left the room. He felt awkward pursuing this farming family, who always showed him hospitality. And now with the raid on Hari's workshop all set for Sunday morning...well, he was glad DI Vula would lead that. It was a mistake getting cosy with witnesses, but impossible to avoid sometimes. Especially in Fiji.

Anya returned and said, 'Baba would like to talk to you in his office.' She grinned and widened her eyes. 'Lucky you. Very few are invited in there!'

A big, battered desk was wedged into a corner of the office, taking up two-thirds of the little room. Beside it stood a filing cabinet. Open shelves filled the opposite wall and above the desk. A narrow set of louvres looked onto the front yard and road.

'*Bula*, Gopal. I've just been looking at the fire site with the investigator.'

Prakash didn't get up but reached out to shake Horseman's hand. He motioned to a chair beside the desk.

'Thanks for seeing me.'

Prakash nodded, tight-lipped. 'What have they found?'

'Well, there's no reason to keep it secret, I guess. The investigator is certain the fire was deliberately lit. Kerosene was poured on two separate areas and ignited. A trail of kerosene was detected from the front door leading to the shed you currently use to store fuel.'

Was Prakash's look of surprise genuine? 'Those sheds aren't very secure. I'll get that fixed up. But who would think about arson?'

'Did you set fire to the Reddy farmhouse, Gopal?'

Prakash gasped, then thumped his fist on the desk. 'Absolutely not! How could you think such a thing?'

'You had every opportunity. And the means to hand.'

'Why would I?' His voice swelled with anger.

Anya appeared in the doorway with a tea tray. Looking scared, she hastily entered and placed it on the desk. Then, after an eye-roll at Horseman, she scuttled out.

Prakash sighed and seemed to calm down. 'You'll want tea if you've been poking around the fire for hours. Why didn't Anya stay and pour? Lazy girl!'

He sighed again and poured for them both, then passed a milk jug to Horseman, who helped himself. He needed the tea. It was scalding, but he drank it as quickly as he could and nodded when Prakash lifted the teapot, saying 'More?'

They sat drinking tea. Horseman waited. Prakash would break the silence.

'You know, what the children told you yesterday is true. I should have mentioned it earlier, but I couldn't see what it had to do with the demonstrators against Dev. There have been signs of an interloper nosing about the farms. To tell you the truth, I thought it was probably some of our kids or the neighbours' youngsters. Maybe it's this fire-setter who's been hanging around for a few weeks—finally made up his mind when he discovered my fuel store.'

'It's certainly possible,' Horseman agreed.

'I'm sorry, there's nothing more I can tell you.' He stood up.

Horseman stood, too. 'Have you any suspicions about any of the neighbouring youngsters?'

'No, I don't know any of them well. My wife would know them better.'

'*Vinaka* for the tea. I'll go now. But please call me if you think of any incident that, with hindsight, now seems suspicious.'

'I will.'

Anya appeared in the doorway and escorted him out. 'Oh, here's Ma and the littlies.' She waved happily at them from the doorway.

Could she be referring to the two high school kids who dwarfed their mother?

Horseman went down the steps and crossed the yard to meet Maira.

'Did you see Gopal?' she asked.

'Yes, we've just finished talking. Anya made some tea, which I badly needed, so I'm grateful to her.'

'Did you get anything out of Gopal?'

Her tone surprised Horseman. 'Well, he answered my questions.'

She looked at her teens running across the yard to their big sister. 'What's it like at Reddy's?'

'A mess. It smells terrible. And it's very sad.'

She nodded. 'It must be.'

'What I found saddest was the contents of the living room dresser, which had fallen through to the ground. Everything smashed, twisted, melted. But I found bits of patterned china, lace tablecloth, dented metal bowls. It all built a picture of Priti Reddy as a hospitable woman who invited guests to her home.'

Maira nodded. 'She was. She was lovely. Older than me and like a big sister, really. Taught me about farm life—I was a town girl, you know. We were both very busy, but we visited each other, until...'

Horseman waited.

'Until her last pregnancy. Um, it was difficult, she was too old. She didn't have the energy to visit us, she said. After Kanan was born, I hardly saw her. Dev was always unsociable, but then he grew downright peculiar—mad, I guess. I should have helped Priti more, but her youngest daughter, Ela, was there to help. I didn't want to go for fear I'd run into Dev.'

'How did they react to Kanan's albinism?'

Maira looked up, guarded now. She shrugged. 'Shocked. They didn't know of any albinos in their families. I have a distant cousin who's albino, so I could tell them it's nothing to worry about. My cousin's healthy and otherwise normal. She got used to people staring, kids teasing. But she shouldn't have to get used to it, should she? It's so cruel to do that to a little child.'

'Yes, it is. How is she now?'

'Oh, fine. She worked hard at school and now she's a librarian in Labasa. No Indian would let their son marry her, of course. She thinks she's lucky. She went to a library conference in Hawaii last year. So good on her.'

'Indeed, I'm glad to hear it.'

'With Kanan, of course, the cerebral palsy was a much bigger problem. Priti was told it was caused by her overlong labour that deprived the baby of oxygen. So sad. Dev wanted to hide him inside and when poor Priti got cancer and died, well, we know what happened. A tragedy. I shouldn't have allowed them to rebuff me. I should have forced my way in there, but...' Tears welled in her eyes and ran down her cheeks. Her mouth trembled. She wiped them with her scarf.

Horseman spoke softly. 'Did you know Dev kept Kanan in the chicken shed, Maira?'

Maira shook her head. 'No, I swear. But I knew something was wrong. I knew Dev was quite incapable of caring for an infant, that he was mad. For years, I sometimes saw Dev in the distance around the fields, but I never once saw Kanan. I suspected he was dead. After eight years, I went to the police. I couldn't make excuses for my silence anymore.'

'Don't be so hard on yourself. Against all odds, Kanan survived and today he's well and happy. I've visited him twice in the last two weeks. He's well cared for and has lots of playmates.'

'Really? Thank you for that.' She folded her hands and bowed her head briefly.

'Maira, it's possible whoever's been loitering around the farms the last few weeks also set fire to Reddy's farmhouse. You know everyone around here well—mothers always do. Have you any suspicions, however uncertain you may be?'

'No, it could be anyone. Kids often start roaming about at night when they get to high school age. But I've no reason to suspect one more than another. It's possible kids were playing with matches in the empty house and then ran away. But who? I have no idea at all.'

'Whoever it was, they carried kerosene from the Reddy shed to the house, poured it onto the floor and lit it.'

'What? Kids aren't like that around here!'

'Someone did this, Maira. Please call me if you get an idea. Immediately, please. Don't wait years this time.'

45

Singh felt she'd drawn the short straw. She'd much rather go back to the fire scene with Horseman. Having witnessed the blaze, she could learn a lot from inspecting the site the following day, especially from the specialist fire investigator, whom she'd never met before. She'd never worked on an arson investigation and practical experience would be helpful for her inspector's exam.

Still, Ravai Nata's alibi needed checking. It would be progress simply to eliminate him as a suspect. Something definite. He was a peculiar individual, but he didn't strike her as insane. She couldn't see him going out to the farm at night by bus or taxi to set a fire to purge the earth of sin. And as for punishment, the house was empty. Reddy had already been punished, so that motive didn't work.

Horseman was a bit hung up on Nata and HOOK because of the demonstrations and what he saw as hypocrisy. Well, he was right—how could a Christian group come up with such a slogan as "Reddy to Die"? The boss held liars in contempt, and they'd caught Nata lying three times now, always to protect himself. She understood that—Nata was a weak man with the gift of the gab who found himself in the spotlight. His overriding instinct was to protect himself. But the boss, so upright himself, was incensed by his behaviour.

Better get started.

'Apo, we've got four events in Nata's account of what he did last night to check. First, choir until nine o'clock, then doing accounts at the church with Mark Prasad until ten. Next, home alone with his wife until half-past eleven, when his sister-in-law came home from her shift at the hospital.'

Apo's eyes were eager behind his glasses. '*Io*, Sarge.'

'You handle the choir and Mark Prasad. Get in touch with the pastor first and get a few names of choir members from him. Check three of them independently. Close followers of Nata will probably lie if they think it will help him. Then Mark Prasad. Remember he's just been convicted of trespassing and damage to property. I'm not sure whether he'll be angry or relieved it wasn't worse. His details are in the case file.'

'Yes, Sarge.'

'Apo, thoroughness is what counts. Always ask yourself whether what you find will stand up in court. It takes as long as it takes. There's no time pressure on this one.'

'Yes, Sarge.' His grin made his round face rounder. He got up and went to the table he shared with Musudroka.

She would take Mrs Nata and Akosita Olo, her sister. A wife's alibi was not so useful as she couldn't be required to testify against her husband in court. Some wives wanted to do just that, but Singh didn't think Mrs Nata would be one of them. Young and pregnant with their first child? No way. Still, she might learn something useful if she spoke to her face-to-face and was careful to avoid any criticism of her husband.

She'd speak to Akosita first, if she could locate her. When Horseman had interviewed her at CWM, he'd found her straightforward and unconcerned about contradicting her brother-in-law.

She was in luck: Akosita Olo was at home and could see Singh now. She was due to start her shift at the hospital at three o'clock so could spare thirty minutes. Singh took a taxi from outside the station up to Toorak. Akosita's house was an old colonial divided into two. She was lucky to live so close to the hospital, but it was a small place for four adults and two children. Maybe her own expectations of real estate were unrealistic. She climbed the front steps to the verandah and called politely, '*Bula* Mrs Olo. I'm Detective Sergeant Singh.'

A short, plumpish woman came to the door, which she opened wide. '*Bula*, Detective. Come in. Call me Sita, please.'

They went into the living room. A narrow kitchen bench occupied one wall. Sita flicked the switch on an electric kettle.

'Nothing for me, please. I know you're due at work soon.'

Sita smiled a warm, friendly smile. 'Nonsense, I won't get another chance for a few hours, and we can talk while we have tea. Or do you prefer coffee? Only instant.'

'Okay, tea would be nice. I can't get enough now that the weather's so humid. I guess you've heard about the fire at the Reddy farmhouse on Wednesday night?'

'Yes, it's all over CWM, especially as the poor man died there.'

'You're sympathetic to Dev Reddy?' Singh asked.

'To some extent. What he did was terrible, but he was insane and he was incarcerated for eleven years as punishment, only to be murdered during his first night of freedom. The whole thing's tragic.'

'What does Ravai think of your view?'

'He probably thinks the devil's getting to me. But he knows he's only got a roof over his head because his wife's my sister. He knows Laisa contributes less than a quarter of the rent, and he contributes nothing. So he restrains himself from preaching at me. I thank God for that.' Her eyes twinkled as she smiled at Singh.

Just then, the kettle switched itself off. Akosita got up, made the tea and set two mugs on the table. 'To be fair, I don't feel the need to spout my views at home, anyway. Just like at work, it's more pleasant if you keep your opinions to yourself.'

Singh nodded. 'We heard today the fire investigator found evidence of arson. So we're checking the movements of everyone who's been involved in Reddy's case. To be blunt, did you see Ravai yesterday afternoon or evening?'

Akosita's eyebrows shot up. '*Oi lei*! You don't suspect Ravai!'

'No, Sita. It's a routine elimination exercise, but it must be accurate.'

'I see. Like taking a brain scan to eliminate the possibility of a tumour, even though the doctor thinks a tumour's unlikely.'

'Exactly. That's a useful comparison.'

'Well, let me think. He wasn't here when I left for the hospital at half-past two. In fact, he'd already left the house when I got up at ten. My kind husband gets the children up and out in the morning when I'm on the afternoon shift. I didn't see anyone until I got home well after eleven.'

'Did you see Ravai then?'

Akosita paused for a few moments. 'Not really. I assumed he was in bed, but I didn't see him.'

'Where were you in the house?'

'Laisa was watching TV on the sofa there. She made tea and we had a chat for a while until we both turned in.'

'Could you have seen Ravai on his way to the bathroom from the sofa?'

'No, the bathroom's right across the hall from their bedroom door.'

'Did you hear the shower running?'

'No, I wasn't aware of it. But it could have been and I just didn't notice.' Akosita frowned. 'This sounds pretty full-on, Detective.'

'It's routine, Sita. I must be confident enough of the facts to be examined in court, under oath.'

'*Oi lei*! I guess so. I had to appear in court once about X-rays I'd taken. Man, I hope I never do that again.'

'Good, you'll understand. To sum up, you didn't see Ravai Nata all day on Wednesday.'

'I'm a bit surprised, but that's true.'

'You said your husband was up early. He could have seen Ravai before he left. I'd like to check with him, to be thorough.'

'Oh sure. He's got a mobile. Let me write his number down for you.'

'Thanks. Have you got time to write a short statement before you leave for work? If not, you can come to the station whenever you're free.'

'No, let's wrap this up now. Tell me what to write. You'll know the wording better than me.' Sita smiled and the frown left her face.

They dealt with the statement form, finished their tea and left the house together.

***

After dropping off Akosita at the hospital entrance, Singh asked the taxi to wait. She stood in the shade of a nearby rain tree to phone Laisa Nata at Patel's Hardware.

'Good afternoon, Mrs Nata. Detective Sergeant Singh from Suva station. I hope you can help me fill in a few gaps in my file. Could I meet you during your afternoon break for a quick chat? Maybe at the little café opposite Patel's, or anywhere else? Your choice.'

'I'm very busy, Sergeant Singh. I don't have time to take a break this afternoon. I need to complete my own files. I can't imagine how I can help you. But we can talk now.'

Laisa's voice was soft and courteous, but Singh heard steel, too. She wouldn't change her mind.

'All right, I understand. My work gets like that, too. Mrs Nata, can you tell me when you saw your husband yesterday?'

'My husband? What's this about?'

Singh decided she'd need to reveal more than she'd hoped. She abandoned her plan for a friendly getting-to-know-you chat.

'It's about the fire at the Reddy farmhouse. The fire investigator says it was deliberately lit. We're tracing everyone involved in Reddy's case. We need to know where Mr Nata was yesterday.'

'Why don't you ask him?'

'I have, Mrs Nata. Now I'm asking you about the times you were with your husband yesterday.'

Silence for moments. 'I was with him at home until I left for work at eight o'clock. I didn't see him again until he came home after choir practice. I remember clearly because I'd saved his dinner, which he ate when he got in.'

'What time was that?'

'I'm not sure of the time. I'd be guessing. Eight o'clock, or half-past maybe.'

'What was on TV when he got in?'

'I wasn't watching TV. I was doing some sewing.'

'Did he go out again later?'

'No, he was tired and went to bed after he ate. I stayed up until my sister got home.'

'Thank you for your help, Mrs Nata. Goodbye.'

The only help Laisa Nata had given was to show she was a loyal wife. Like most spouses in her situation, she tried to guess what her husband had told the police and support that. Her vagueness about the time, the discrepancy about whether she was watching TV or sewing—all typical and made her account worthless. She'd go back to the station to call Akosita's husband.

***

The temperature shot up when Singh emerged from the shade of the rain tree and headed to the taxi.

'Hello, Susie.'

She looked up at the smiling face of Dr Young, partly disguised by a wide-brimmed straw hat and sunglasses.

'Don't look so surprised, I work here, remember? What are you doing here?'

'I dropped off a witness who works here. I'm heading back to the station now.'

'I'm heading back to work, but it's that time of the afternoon when I need sustenance. How about joining me? The hospital canteen's the only choice, I'm afraid. But it's airy and won't be crowded now.'

'Thanks, I should refuse but I won't. I've just had a disappointing phone call and need to get over it.'

'Hope I can help.'

Singh paid the taxi driver and relaxed. She always felt comfortable with the lanky Aussie pathologist. It was a shame all his patients were dead and couldn't benefit from his cheerful, understanding manner. They strolled to the canteen and chose a table directly under a ceiling fan.

'I'll have lemonade, Matt. Too hot for anything else.'

He returned from the counter with two bottles of lemonade and a plate of iced cup cakes.

'I expect you to help me with these. My eyes are bigger than my stomach.'

'I can do that. My appetite's suddenly perked up.'

Before opening the lemonade, she pressed the cold bottle to her face: both cheeks, forehead and chin. Then she took a swig.

'If you're okay with doing that in public, I will, too. Here, have a cake.'

She took a pink one topped with dried coconut.

'Do you want to talk about it, Susie?'

'Not really, I'd rather move right on to the next disappointment.'

He laughed. 'Whoa, not like you to be cynical.'

Her mood lifted. 'I can be cynical. But actually, this whole Reddy business is depressing. Tragic, really.'

'There's no denying that. But you and Joe will get to the bottom of it. You always do. Have faith!'

'I'm trying!' She smiled and ate some cake.

'Do you know Joe's signed a lease on a flat in Seaview Tower?'

Singh nodded. 'He told me the other day. We ran into each other at the agent's open viewing.'

'Oh? You're moving out of the barracks?'

'Thinking about it. Weighing up the pros and cons but can't reach a decision. Actually, Matt, I'd appreciate your advice.'

'Is this about the inspectors' exam?'

'Yes. If I'm promoted, I'll have to move out. Besides, I'm getting tired of the barracks so I'm tempted to jump the gun. But I'm saving money by staying at the barracks. I had some idea of flat rents in Suva, but I'm shocked by just how bad the flats I can afford are.'

'Now you know that, do you still want to move out?'

'I think I do. But it seems a waste of money. Maybe it's more sensible to wait until I'm promoted. If I *am* promoted, that is.'

Dr Young finished his cake and took another. His grey eyes were serious. 'These head over heart decisions are difficult, especially when money's involved. Your home's part of your happiness. It's fine to sacrifice happiness to save money when you're working towards a goal— more than fine, it's an excellent strategy. But happiness is more important than money in the end.'

She nodded, thinking. 'I rejected all the flats I looked at. Their ads seemed so promising. So I realised I was lucky to have the option of the barracks and resigned to staying there. Then a taxi driver took me to Seaview Tower and I instantly felt at home. I've worked out I could just afford a flat on the first floor although I wouldn't be able to save much, if anything. I was dithering until Joe told me he was signing up for one. Now I feel I can't go ahead. What will he think? That I'm stalking him!'

Dr Young laughed out loud. 'He'd be happy, of course. Why can't you live in the same building as your boss? Aren't there thirty apartments in

Seaview?'

'Twenty-four.' She drank more lemonade, thinking.

'Would you be disappointed or relieved if you didn't go ahead?'

'Disappointed. Definitely.' She looked at him.

'You'll have to decide and as soon as possible. You're troubled, and we can't have that. No one could be more rational than you, Susie. But it's not good to postpone happiness too long. I'd consider going with your heart on this one.'

46

When he parked outside the Franciscan boys' hostel, Horseman couldn't extricate himself from the vehicle without massaging his knee first. Depressing, after only an hour's drive.

He found Father Francis in the kitchen, teaching some boys the right way to cut up a chicken. Father Francis smiled. '*Bula*, Joe. I think I know why you're here,' the priest said. 'You can finish those off, boys. I'm going to the office.' He rinsed his hands, patted them on his brown habit and led the way.

'Don't look so anxious, Joe. Both your Shiners turned up on time this morning. After talking to each of them, I offered them both a place here on the condition that they take up some vocational training. Livai immediately agreed although he doesn't know what he wants to do. He's more desperate to get off the streets than Pita, who wants to keep working as a shoe-shine boy and stay here. I told him he can't do that.'

'I'll talk to them again after training on Monday.'

'They want to please you, but the decision's got to come from them, Joe. Otherwise, they probably won't see it through.'

'If only they could imagine a better, safer future for themselves.'

'You could help them with that.'

'I'll try. Perhaps I've been too pushy.'

'They know you care about them. That's the most important thing. Mosese now, his bashing may have a silver lining. He's really keen to work as a hospital orderly.'

'Is there training for that?'

'*Io*, it's hospital-based. Mosese doesn't have high school qualifications, but I'm satisfied he'll do whatever it takes to become an orderly. I'll get his literacy levels assessed next week and we can go from there.'

'Does that mean he can stay here?'

Father Francis touched the wooden cross hanging around his neck. '*Io*, we can give him a start.'

'*Vinaka vakalevu*, Father.'

Horseman's eyes started stinging—a residual effect of the smoke.

***

When Horseman entered the CID office, Kau looked like he would burst.

'Sir, I've got news! Mark Prasad said he didn't help Nata with the bookkeeping. He agreed to go, but he cancelled because he wanted to prepare for his court hearing this morning.'

'Really? Well done, Apo.'

'There's more! The choir master was sick and practice was cancelled.'

'*Oi lei*! But why should I be surprised at more lies? It's compulsive with him.'

Singh spoke up. 'He's an insecure man, sir. He lies to protect himself when he feels threatened. His sister-in-law pointed out that he's the only one not earning, not contributing to the rent. She thinks that's why he doesn't play the preacher with them at home. He knows he's not top of the tree there.'

'Makes sense. But he's not stupid. How come he thinks we won't discover his lies?'

Singh wrinkled her nose as she considered. 'I think it's an automatic reaction with him, before he has time to think.'

'Hell, what a waste of time that man is!'

'His home alibis are doubtful too. His sister-in-law, Sita, says she didn't see him the entire day. She just assumed he was in bed when she got home at half-past eleven.'

'Well, well!'

'Wait, there's more. Sita's husband said he saw Nata first thing in the morning, but not after he got home. Nata's wife, Laisa, cooked dinner for the family and set aside a plate for Nata, saying he was at choir. Akosita's husband went to bed early at the same time as the children, before either his wife or Nata had arrived home.'

'Aha! And what does Laisa Nata have to say?'

'In my opinion, she didn't know what Nata had told me but was trying to guess. She said he came home about half-past eight from choir and didn't go out again.'

'Which is two hours earlier than Nata claimed.'

'Yes. I wouldn't rely on what Laisa said. She clearly wanted to protect him. Maybe he didn't come home at all.'

Horseman nodded. 'He could have set that fire. But did he? There's not a shred of evidence—won't be for days, even a week. Even then, we may not be able to identify the arsonist.'

'My gut says it wasn't Nata, sir. I understand about purging the site of evil with fire and all that. I just can't see him doing it.'

Kau spoke up. 'He wouldn't have known about the kerosene in the shed, would he, sir?'

'Good point, Apo. If he was at the farmhouse with the baying mob a week ago, he could well have poked around and discovered it then. That's exactly what I did the next morning. I reckon there's a touch of the fanatic about Ravai Nata. His inferior status at home would only add fuel to his fire.'

'Sir, what a terrible pun!'

He grinned. 'My apologies. To sum up: Nata could be the arsonist, but we need evidence. So, he remains a suspect.'

Singh grabbed pens and a duster and started updating the whiteboard.

'Is it sheer respect that stops you two asking me what I've been doing?' Horseman asked.

Kau laughed. 'What have you been doing, sir?'

'I won't bore you with the full account of my searches, which were mostly fruitless. But I recovered a tin box from the rubble. I took it to the SOCO lab, and they pried it open. It was full of old family photos, which might be useful. They're mostly small black-and-white prints, a few in colour. I left them with Photography for processing. They should be ready sometime tomorrow.'

'Could we show them to people at the funeral, sir?'

'No, Apo. It wouldn't be polite. I'd like to show them to Maira Prakash. I dropped in there after I left the fire scene and asked Gopal straight out if he set the fire. He denied it angrily. He thinks whoever's been loitering about the farms at night in recent weeks is the arsonist.'

'I think Gopal's the most likely suspect, sir,' Singh said.

'I agree, but again there's no evidence. I also had a chat with Maira, out of Gopal's earshot. She told me she and Priti Reddy were quite close for years but that all ended after Kanan was born. Well, before the birth actually, as the pregnancy was difficult. Maira stopped visiting but wasn't worried because Priti had her youngest daughter to help her. She's now consumed by guilt for not reporting her fears about Dev's neglect of Kanan. She swears she didn't know the child was kept with the chickens. Dev frightened her. As we know, it was eight years after Priti's death before she eventually reported her concerns to the police.'

All three sat in silence for a while.

Horseman got up. 'We still need critical evidence but we'll persist until we find it. Now we've earned a break. For once, we'll leave paperwork on our desks overnight. We can update that tomorrow, before and after the funeral. *Moce mada*, both of you.'

SATURDAY

SATURDAY

47

Horseman wasn't sure whether to wear his white sulu to the funeral. He didn't have any white trousers, which was what the Indian men would wear. Cream jeans? No, the sulu was more formal. He wanted to show respect. And to be seen to show respect. If he unwittingly offended any of the Reddy family, he could jeopardise the case.

He ironed the sulu and a long-sleeved white shirt, then got dressed. When he opened the door, Tina jumped up from her bed on the verandah, tail wagging, looking expectant. He gave her a rub.

'Matt will take you for a walk later, girl.'

She was miffed but settled her muzzle on her front paws again. He'd miss Tina when he moved to Seaview, which didn't allow residents to have pets. Tina wouldn't be happy confined indoors all day, anyway. He'd still take her for a daily walk, but...

Kau opted to stay in the station, battle the paperwork and chase Photography. Horseman picked up a car and Singh at the station. Singh was perfect in a calf-length white skirt and loose white top.

'We've plenty of time so I'm going the back way. Perhaps the cool hills and forest will let me think better. What do you say, Susie?'

'Fine by me, sir.' He let the *sir* go again. She probably didn't know she said it, as she claimed.

'Nice flowers. I didn't think of that.'

'Visitors aren't expected to bring flowers. But the family will appreciate the gesture.'

'I don't think Dev Reddy's children will be grieving. They haven't seen him for over ten years. I think Darsh will do his duty but as quickly as possible. It will be a simplified ceremony at the new crematorium at Nausori. I'm happy about that. The last Hindu funeral I attended was in pouring rain and the wood wouldn't burn properly. The pyre was at ground level, too. I'm afraid the sandalwood couldn't mask the smell. It was an unpleasant experience for everyone there. Not one I want to repeat.'

Singh nodded, glancing at him in sympathy. 'It's so embarrassing for the family when that happens. One reason why the gas crematoriums are catching on with Hindus, if slowly. Fire liberates the soul, it's not just body disposal.'

'I wonder how perfunctory the ceremony will be.'

'Who arranged the funeral rites?' Singh asked.

'Navneet Pandey, Dev Reddy's solicitor, on the instructions of Darsh, Dev's eldest son. I don't know how many of the other children are coming.'

'Maha, the elder daughter, is coming with her husband Arun. When I spoke to him on the phone yesterday, he sounded anxious about the trip. No wonder, I guess.'

'Is the youngest daughter still living with them?'

'Ela. When I asked, he said "not right now" or something like that. I guess it's not relevant.'

'No, probably not. But Ela's the only one who lived with her parents after Kanan was born. She's the one who can tell us what was really going on at that time.'

'True. I guess someone at the funeral will know where she is.'

***

The crematorium was a neat cream building on the edge of Nausori. A tall industrial steel chimney rose from the back. Liveried staff of Nirvana funerals greeted them and showed them into a white room with some potted palms and a coffin on a wheeled table. Burning incense sticks were set around the table. A priest stood in front beside a man who could be Reddy's eldest son, Darsh. Both men were clad in white.

A few rows of chairs surrounded the coffin on three sides. The numerous Prakash family sat on one side and Reddy's other neighbours, the Sharmas, sat opposite them. There were only a few people Horseman didn't recognise.

Navneet Pandey came over to greet Horseman and Singh. He looked even younger in traditional white Indian tunic and pants.

'Thank you for the flowers, Sergeant Singh. Please place them beside the coffin. Let me introduce you to Darsh. He will be conducting the ceremony with the priest, you understand. Because Darsh is flying back to New Zealand tomorrow, he isn't observing the usual mourning period. Instead, he is providing refreshments in the reception room here immediately afterwards.

Darsh Reddy would be nearing fifty now. He was taller and built bigger than his father, but there was a family resemblance in his prominent nose and firm jaw. He nodded to the detectives over his clasped hands and thanked them for coming. His face was expressionless. Pandey led them to circle the coffin. The top half was open, but Dev Reddy's head was hidden, wrapped in white cloth. Whatever the demands of tradition, even the Hindu priest had deemed his face not fit to be seen a week after his battering and death, Pandey nodded at a bowl of water and spoon beside the coffin. Singh ladled a few drops of water onto Reddy's white-swathed mouth. Horseman followed feeling uncomfortable.

They took seats at the end of the back row facing the door. Soon, the priest began chanting softly. A few minutes later, a 30-something couple came in, paid their respects and sat in the opposite bank of chairs. The woman was familiar.

The male mourners joined the priest in the chant. Then Dr Acharya hurried in, circled the table and placed frangipani blooms at the foot of the coffin. Ah, now he remembered who the young woman was—she looked so different out of uniform.

Darsh and the priest stepped forward to the head of the coffin. The priest sprinkled holy water on the corpse. Darsh poured ghee from a spouted brass pot before arranging dried coconut and pieces of wood on his father's chest. Four other men, Dr Acharya among them, surrounded the table and wheeled it forward to a white curtain in the front wall. An official pulled the curtain aside and slid the exposed steel panel back. Darsh lit the kindling in the coffin. When a small flame appeared, the men rolled the coffin from the table and through the opening. The official shut the panel and drew the curtain closed. The men's song rose as Darsh reached out and pushed a switch on the wall.

Did Darsh think his display of filial duty would add weight to his application for his father's will to be ruled invalid? Or was it possible he regretted not visiting his father for twenty-five years?

The few mourners would not do justice to the finger-food spread in the reception room. The families of the staff of Nirvana funerals would be happy this evening. Horseman rebuked himself for being cynical.

A waiter offered him a steel dish of bara. He accepted—he loved the spicy lentil fritters. Singh took one, too.

'Man, these pack a punch. But we're supposed to be working. Let's split up and circulate. Did you notice Bimala, the nurse from the hospital? Short, thirties, came in with a man, maybe her husband.'

Singh looked around. 'Oh, yes. She looked familiar but I couldn't place her. How kind of her to come all this way to attend a patient's funeral.'

'Hm. What if she's a relative? I'll find out.'

'Okay, I'll talk to Darsh—I've already spoken to him on the phone several times, so it's only polite I introduce myself. I'm keen to meet Arun and Maha, too.'

'Let's get to work then, Susie.'

The waiter offered bara to Bimala and her companion as Horseman approached.

'It's nice to see you again, Bima.' He was about to praise the bara when she looked up. Her long, thin face was anxious and tear-stained. She rubbed her eyes and gave him a sad smile.

Her companion introduced himself as her husband and shook Horseman's hand. 'Bima's especially upset because she nursed Dev,' he said.

'That's understandable.' He smiled at Bimala, who clutched one end of her white scarf. 'And it shows you're a caring nurse, too.'

'She's only a distant cousin of Priti Reddy, you know. A cousin of a cousin—something like that. The women are better at understanding all this family tree stuff, aren't they? Better than me, anyway.' He put a comforting arm around his wife's shoulders, drawing her closer. Bimala looked up at Horseman, a pleading look. She balled more of her scarf into her fist.

'Excuse me, Inspector Horseman. I must talk to Maha. She flew in from Queensland yesterday for the funeral. I haven't seen her since I was a teenager. She was always nice to me.' She paused. 'Not that we met all that often.'

'Go ahead, please. The upside of a funeral is catching up with relatives.'

'I thought Ela might be here—Maha's younger sister. But I can't see her. I must speak to Maha now. Sorry.'

'Bima's rostered on afternoon shift at the hospital today. Unfortunately, this may be her only chance to talk to her cousins,' her kind husband explained.

'That's quite all right, Bima. It was good seeing you again.'

Horseman wandered over to the buffet table and picked up a glass of pineapple juice. He'd always found incense sickly sweet, but today it grated his throat. Probably an after-effect of inhaling smoke at the house fire. The tang of the juice soothed the scratchiness instantly. He took another glass and approached Navneet Pandey, who was standing with his receptionist, surveying the gathering.

He smiled at them both. 'You've done a great job here, Navneet. After all that's happened, it's good to see Mr Reddy get the last Hindu rites.'

The solicitor shook his head. 'My mother here has looked after most of it. Indeed, my practice wouldn't run without her.'

Mrs Pandey, elegant in a white silk sari, smiled. 'You didn't realise when you came to the office, isn't it? Well, that's the way it should be.'

'I'm pleased he has such a trustworthy assistant! My mother's helped me in my work, too. On more than one occasion.'

His expression serious, Pandey continued. 'To be fair to Darsh, he wanted to perform the rituals that were possible, given that there could be no initial ceremony at the family home. And he wanted to play his part as the eldest son. But he insisted on a modern cremation—I guess he's lived in New Zealand a long time now. The second son, Ajit, is also here and took a role. Sergeant Singh is speaking with them now.'

The waiter offered them a tray with bowls of different sweets—all made with condensed milk, all deep-fried, all irresistible. Horseman took a *julab gamun*, hoping it had been soaked in rose syrup. He sniffed before taking a bite. It had.

Mrs Pandey laughed. 'Your favourite?'

Horseman swallowed. 'One of them. Fortunately, they don't come my way often, because I find it hard to say no.'

'Why say no? Look at you, no fat on you at all!'

While he enjoyed Mrs Pandey's motherly attention, he needed to talk to her son. If she was like his own mother, she'd leave at the right time. So he came to the point.

'Do Hindus hold a formal reading of the deceased's will, Navneet?'

'It's not usual, but sometimes they do, especially in business circles. A British custom that rubbed off on the middle classes, I think. As a matter of fact, Darsh did ask me for a formal reading of the will today.'

Mrs Pandey smiled and drifted away.

'Has Darsh consulted you legally? I'm not just being nosey, this whole matter of the contested will could be relevant to our case.'

'I met him yesterday. We went through today's arrangements and the inventory of his father's estate. This could be far from complete—I only know what's in my uncle's files and what Dev told me. Darsh has retained a Suva firm to prepare his claim on his father's estate. But whichever way the case goes, I remain an executor of Dev's estate and Darsh will have to deal extensively with me. It's important we establish an effective working relationship.'

'How did Darsh seem to you?'

'Seem? Well, he was polite, reserved, and clearly under strain.'

'It would be great if you could forward me a copy of both wills and the inventory, Navneet.'

'I'll need to think about that. I do want to help you, though. You already know what's in the latest will.'

'Sure. But I'd like to know what the stakes are for Darsh and the other children. Anyway, please get in touch when you decide. I hope that will be soon.'

'I will indeed. I appreciate your attendance today.'

Horseman smiled. 'In the line of duty, I'm afraid.'

'More than that, I think. You saved Mr Reddy from dying in pain and terror in a hole. I'm grateful.'

'Maybe I just delivered him to his murderer. He might have survived in that hole, Navneet. And who was he hiding from? That's what I've got to find out.'

'I'm on your side, Joe. Please excuse me now, I'd better make sure the Reddy children are clear on the arrangements for this afternoon.'

Horseman joined Singh and headed outside. Small knots of mourners faced the same direction, their faces lifted. He turned. White puffs of smoke ascended from the industrial chimney.

48

'Sir, Sarge, I've got the photos back. Hundred per cent on the originals. Photography emailed them—all max-enhanced. Look at these enlargements!' Kau raised his voice in excitement as his superiors returned.

'*Vinaka*, Apo! Let's sit down and take a look.'

With the flare of a conjuror, Kau fanned the stack of glossy prints in front of them. 'Recognise anyone in this lot?'

'Do you?'

'No, sir. But I've never seen the Reddy family. I bet you will, though!'

'You've challenged me now, Apo! But why are you still here? Isn't there a briefing on for Sunday's raid?'

'*Io*, two o'clock. It's downstairs, so there's no rush. Are you coming?'

'No, Inspector Vula's leading the raid. Sergeant Singh and I need to keep on with the murder. You'll be out at the Rewa farmlands at dawn, so take yourself home after your briefing.'

'*Vinaka*, sir.'

'I know you'll bring credit on us, Apo,' Singh beamed at her protégé.

'I second that. Good luck, Apo. *Moce mada.*'

As Apo checked his backpack and left, his superiors looked at the photos.

'The sharpest is this wedding photo,' Singh said.

'Yes, it's a professional job. So this is what Dev looked like as a young man. You can see the resemblance with his two sons we met today, even though they're middle-aged.'

'Look, the daughter, Maha, is very like her mother. Priti looks so young! Tiny, overwhelmed by her sari.'

'There seems to be a quality studio shot of the family every time there was a new baby.'

Singh was shuffling through the prints. 'Have you seen a baby photo with Kanan?'

'No. Look, this baby must be Ela, the younger daughter. The smallest child looks about six—that's Pranjal. Then there's Maha, who's about ten or eleven. Darsh and Ajit are tall teenagers—young men, really. They're easy to recognise.'

'I'll check through the originals in case Photography didn't process all of them. You never know, some may have been damaged or too poor.' Singh opened the box and laid each small, dog-eared print on top of its processed enlargement. There was a match for each.

'I don't think the Reddys owned a camera. If they did, there'd be a lot more photos,' Horseman said. 'These home snaps were probably taken by relatives when families got together. Are there any larger groups?'

Singh held out a photo. 'Oh, cute—a girls' shot! Look, here's Maira Prakash and Priti with Maha and Ela, who's maybe ten. Look at their enormous eyes—so alike. The other little girls must be Maira's daughters, both much younger than Ela.'

'Here's another of both families, maybe taken on the same day. Gopal isn't in it—he must be behind the camera. Darsh and Ajit aren't there, already in New Zealand, I guess. Hari's the eldest Prakash child—he's maybe fourteen here.'

'I think you're right. Maira can identify everyone for us.'

'If she'll speak to me after the raid on Hari's workshop tomorrow. Are there any people we don't know? Let's put these in two piles first: Prakash family and others.'

They worked in silence, the intensity of their search mounting.

'There! We've done it. Seven with Reddy and Prakash families. Three with Reddys plus unknowns. Three with Reddy, Prakash, plus unknowns.'

'And I'm sure two of our unknown individuals also appear in photos with Prakash family members. Look—this man and this woman.'

'The Prakash family holds the key. They won't cooperate tomorrow. I'll have to see them this afternoon.' It was the last thing he felt like doing.

'I'm sorry, but I won't be able to come with you, sir.'

'That's fine, I don't expect you to. And please, Susie, drop the *sir* when we're alone.'

'Sorry, um, Joe. I meant to tell you this earlier. I'm going to Paradise Real Estate at half-past three to sign a rental agreement.'

'That's great! You've found something! What's that apprehensive look about? Second thoughts?'

'No, I decided yesterday afternoon, and now I'm scared I'll lose it if I don't sign and pay the deposit. I guess I'm a bit nervous because my flat's in Seaview Tower, where you're moving.'

'What? That's wonderful—we'll be neighbours.'

Singh beamed. 'It's such a relief you feel like that. It's a one-bedroom on the first floor but I love it. Kiti reduced the rent even further than the advertised discount, so it seems an offer too good to let go.'

'I haven't had time to move in yet. But I'm paying rent, so I must. It won't be hard—I've got two suitcases to pack, and that's about it. I don't own any furniture—it's a big bonus for me that the flats are fully furnished for the expatriate market.'

'Me, too. The furniture in mine is basic but really decent. I'll enjoy putting my stamp on the place, but I don't need to do a thing before I move in.'

'You'll want more colour, I suspect.'

Singh laughed. It was good to see her so happy about something in her own life, which she never shared unless she had no choice.

***

After another return trip to Rewa, he was beat. He needed to eat. It was dark, a nice breeze stirring the muggy air. He wondered if Matt was eating out tonight.

'You're late, mate,' the cheerful voice called as he opened the front door. Matt sprawled on the sofa, reading a journal.

'Sorry, Mum.'

'I'll ignore that. Been working?'

'Just back from the second trip to Rewa in one day. I can't hack cooking. Are you booked?'

'Nah. I'm buggered, too. I need a quiet dinner. A stroll to the Holiday Inn?'

'I'll be in that.'

Matt groaned. 'No puns, please.'

They chose a table in a dim corner of the dining room, well away from the foyer and the noise from the busy bar.

'Let's order. I'm starving.'

'You're always starving.'

'I had a lot of deep-fried finger food at the funeral reception this morning, so I didn't feel like lunch. Steak and salad for me.' He caught the eye of a waiter, who arrived swiftly.

'How did the funeral go?'

'Smoothly. In the new gas crematorium at Nausori. Three of Dev Reddy's children came. Both sons are returning to New Zealand tomorrow.'

'Did you learn anything helpful?'

'Potentially. Bimala, the nurse on Dev's ward when he died, is a cousin of Dev's wife, Priti.'

Matt's sandy eyebrows just about hit his hairline. 'I don't suppose she thought to mention that when you questioned her.'

'Right. I couldn't say anything at the funeral. She maintained she didn't see Dev's family often, but Singh saw her deep in conversation with the daughter, Maha, for quite a while. Maira Prakash was comforting Bima later. She may have been closer to both families than she told me.'

The waiter served their food and retreated. Another poured Fiji Bitter into frosted beer glasses, placing them on Flying Fijians coasters.

'*Bula*!' they both said, raising their glasses.

'You'd better take the edge off your appetite pronto, mate. I want to hear the rest.'

Ten minutes elapsed.

'*Oi lei*, that steak was perfect.' Horseman piled the remaining salad onto his plate.

'You still want the rest?'

Matt nodded, taking more time over his grilled chicken.

'Kau was waiting for us at the station with the enlargements of the family photos I found in the ashes yesterday. We easily identified the family members we'd just met at Dev's funeral. And some of the Prakash family, too. I knew Maira Prakash could identify some subjects we couldn't, so there was nothing for it but to drive out to Rewa again.' Horseman paused to eat some salad.

'And could she? Put names on your unknowns, I mean?'

'All except two. Mind you, she was bewildered when I turned up at their door.'

'Spill the beans, mate.'

'Man, these beans are staying right in my mouth.' He swallowed.

Matt tried to keep a straight face but broke into quite a loud laugh. Horseman waited until he'd stopped.

'I didn't get the clue that cracks the case, but I feel we're edging a bit closer. Bimala was in two of the photos, as well as her mother and brother. Neither Singh nor I recognised her. Maira said Bimala was a frequent visitor until her family moved to Suva. She was quite close in age and friendship to Ela, the younger Reddy daughter.'

'Bimala strikes a wrong note, speaking as a mere pathologist.'

'She does. I feel like going up to the hospital now and asking her about it. But it's not the right time. I'd rather think it over and talk to her tomorrow.'

'D'you think she could have killed Dev?'

'Easily—top-notch means and opportunity. I'm not so sure about motive. Maybe she hated him, maybe she didn't. But there's more she can tell me, I'm sure.'

'You know best.'

'I hope so. Something else before I forget. I think I'll move into Seaview tomorrow. I've paid the rent, so I should get out of your hair. I wish I could take Tina, but I'll walk her every day.'

'I couldn't do without that mongrel now. I'll run you and your bags to Seaview. I'd like to give the place the once-over myself.'

'*Vinaka vakalevu.* It's been great staying in your house.'

'As I said before, no problem, mate.'

'Oh, Singh signed for a flat on the first floor this afternoon. I was surprised. Pleased, of course. I thought she was too cautious to make a decision like that now.'

'We ran into each other at the hospital yesterday, and she asked my advice. I told her she should make a heart decision for a change.'

Horseman was taken aback. '*Oi lei*, really? But sound advice, Doctor, sound advice.'

SUNDAY

49

The call from Inspector Siale Vula came while Horseman was eating an early breakfast. He planned to arrive at the farm after the raid, to support the family after their shock invasion and explain things to them. But Gopal would see the raid as a personal betrayal and likely reject his support.

'Joe, we found Hari Prakash dead, slumped over his workshop bench. Stabbed in the back. My guess is straight through the heart.'

Horseman froze for a moment, a slice of pawpaw in his hand. 'Have you called Ratini?'

'Not yet. Can you come?'

'Right away. Do his parents know?'

'*Io*, we woke them up, gave them the search warrant, all in order. Two minutes later, I had to tell them their son was murdered. *Oi lei!*' Vula was in shock but had followed correct procedure.

'I guess the SOCOs are organising the scene?'

'*Io*. Thank God they're here on the spot. SOCO says Dr Young doesn't need to come. He's rung the mortuary and the medical examiner on call will attend. Would Dr Young prefer to come in person?'

'I'll ask him. You've done exactly what you should have done, Siale. Keep calm—the team is depending on you. Please call Ratini first, then get right back to me.'

'*Io*, Joe. *Vinaka.*'

Acting Chief Inspector Ratini approved Horseman taking charge of the murder for now, but Vula would continue with the jewel theft side.

When Horseman roused him, Matt Young agreed, yawning, to the SOCO's arrangements. He would examine Hari's body at the hospital morgue.

Horseman pulled up a little beyond the Prakash driveway. Heart thudding, he made his way past the house. He looked up at the lit windows. Small fingers clutched the edges of louvres, shadowy figures of different heights peered out. Hari's parents, wife, children, brothers and sisters would never forget this morning.

It was getting light now, and the familiar barnyard wake-up calls reassured him that life continued, that the world still turned. His thinking about this case needed a reset, though.

The tape stretched from a house post to the nearest outbuilding, blocking entry to the yard behind. A constable greeted him, offered his clipboard to sign in and raised the tape. Six constables in a row fingertip-searched the yard. Kau straightened up and waved. Two SOCOs dusted the windows and doors of Hari's workshop.

Horseman donned blue overalls, bootees and gloves, took a deep breath and went inside. DI Vula stepped forward, hand outstretched as if he was drowning.

'*Vinaka vakalevu*, Joe. I thought we would be searching for stolen jewellery. I'm not over the shock.' He kept holding Horseman's hand with a powerful grip.

'That's normal. You'll get over it soon. We're here to help each other, Siale. Anything happening?'

'No, we're idle, waiting for the medical examiner. At least the photographer came with us. Horseman greeted the dependable Alisi when she turned around.

'*Bula*, sir. Pleased to see you.'

Two more blue-suited individuals emerged from a corner: Sergeant Ash Jayaraman, the SOCO manager, and Musudroka from his own team. Ash and Vula gestured to the body of Hari Prakash, fallen face-down onto his bench against the wall. His light blue shirt was drenched with blood. His face rested on the scrapbook he had shown Horseman only three days ago. He hadn't warmed to Hari but admired his passion for his craft.

'Alisi, are you satisfied you've recorded the murder victim and his surroundings thoroughly?'

'For now, sir. When the examiner arrives and turns him over, there'll be more to do.'

'What about you, Ash?'

'Same for me, sir.'

'Right, then I see no reason why Inspector Vula should wait any longer to start the search he was planning. Musudroka, measure and tape a perimeter of half a metre all around the body, and don't touch anything inside that. The rest of the workshop is yours, Inspector Vula. I take responsibility for that decision. I know you've got expert jewellers waiting and they'll be getting impatient, wishing they'd stayed in bed this Sunday morning. Go ahead, man.'

He looked at Hari again before walking outside. There were times when he wished he smoked and this was one of them. He pulled off the hood of his overalls. At eight in the morning, the heat was still tolerable and a light breeze dried the sweat on his face and head. He stood under the mango tree and kept his eye on the drive. He was no expert, but the appearance of the congealed blood on Hari's shirt suggested he'd died several hours ago. What if Hari was working with the jewel thief or gang? Had they had a tipoff from Vula's team and feared Hari would confess to the police? Possibly, but he hoped not. The enquiry team was small and tight. Surely, it was more likely Hari's murder was connected to his neighbour, Dev Reddy.

It wasn't too long before the medical examiner strolled down the drive, weaving elegantly between the haphazard police vehicles. He'd met Dr Lakshmi Krishna before. Her tight jeans and sleeveless top wouldn't inspire confidence in the traditional Prakash family.

'Good morning, Joe. We've got to stop meeting like this!' She laughed up at him, her gold-rimmed spectacles glinting.

'Good morning, Lucky. Your cheerful smile is just what's needed here. The jewel raiders are reeling with shock.'

'Well, I always expect a corpse, so I'm never shocked. I've got news for you, though.'

They stopped at the tape for her to sign in and suit up. She snapped a band around her long, wavy hair and removed the huge gold hoops from her ears, tucking them in a pocket of her medical bag.

'I lost an earring once when I pulled off a suit and threw it in the bin. Always take them off now.'

He couldn't help grinning. Why did she put them on? Did she always wear thick mascara, or was it out of respect for the corpse she was going to meet?

'Aren't you going to ask me about my news, Joe?'

'Yes, Lucky. What is it?'

'Unofficially, I've got through my pathology finals, and I'm in the running for Dr Young's registrar position!' She brought one scarlet-nailed index finger to her lips and winked. The gold stud in her nose gleamed.

He tried to imagine low-key Matt teaching over-the-top Lucky. He couldn't.

'Unofficial congratulations, then. I hope you get the job.'

He led her to the corpse, introduced her to Vula and Alisi. Dr Krishna's personality changed when she opened her medical bag. She became all focus and method, issuing terse instructions to Horseman and Alisi to assist her in moving Hari's body from one position to another. Maybe she and Matt could work together well, after all.

When she started packing up her bag, she cocked an eyebrow at Horseman. 'You want time of death and you know very well I can't pin it down.'

'But?'

She rolled her huge brown eyes at him. 'Considering the progress of lividity and rigor mortis, I would estimate he died between midnight and three this morning. Cause of death is probably wounding to the heart by a sharp instrument. All subject to postmortem examination findings.'

'*Vinaka*, Lucky.'

'I'll call Dr Young right away. The mortuary guys can take him off your hands now.' She flashed a smile at Vula. 'You jewel experts can get on with your job.'

She kept an eye on the mortuary men as they covered and removed Hari's body. Horseman followed her to the scene entrance. She peeled off her suit, gloves and bootees, released her hair from its band, and replaced her hoops.

'Love you and leave you, Joe!'

'*Vinaka vakalevu*, Lucky.' He found himself grinning again.

When he returned to the workshop, Vula said, 'Is she for real?'

Horseman nodded. 'I think so. Our Dr Lucky Krishna is maybe a bit larger than life. Well, Siale, you're in control here now. I'm going to bite the bullet and knock on the Prakash door.'

50

Anya Prakash opened the door to him again. Her eyes were red-rimmed, her previous flirtatious manner had vanished.

'Come in, Inspector, most of the family are in the kitchen.'

A lamp and incense were burning on the little house shrine. Anya walked ahead of him to the back of the house. The smaller children pressed against the louvres, gazing at the police going about their business below.

He stood before the table and folded his hands together under his bowed head. Gopal turned his head away as if he hadn't seen him. Ingrained politeness forced Maira to return his gesture. She was pale and had aged a decade since yesterday. But she seemed calm, and he was grateful for that. Because he must ask questions of Hari's family without delay.

'Mr and Mrs Prakash, I am sincerely sorry for your loss.' He looked around the table. Only two bent heads looked up at him. He wasn't sure which woman was Hari's widow, or indeed if she was present. 'Everyone, please accept my heartfelt condolences.'

'Thank you, Inspector Horseman,' said Maira. Gopal scraped his chair back and went to the kitchen bench. He kept his back to them, looking out the window.

'You must have known our home was to be raided at dawn! Don't deny it because I won't believe you! And you were here twice yesterday, under the pretext of showing us Reddy family photos! And what's the upshot? Hari is de—' Gopal's voice cracked and he circled his head with his arms.

'Please come and sit down, Gopal. I understand this is a terrible day for you, but please listen to what I have to say.'

Gopal's shoulders shuddered. Maira and Anya went to him and held his arms. He inhaled deeply, pulled himself straight, and allowed the women to lead him back to his seat at the table.

It was best to tell the truth and he would do that. But it would have to be an abridged version.

'Everyone, I ask you to listen. You're right, Gopal. I knew that Inspector Vula's team had magistrate's warrants to search Hari's workshop today. Inspector Vula has been investigating thefts of valuable jewellery over the last several months. He believes the brazen thefts are the work of an organised team with inside knowledge. Everyone involved in the jewellery trade has been checked out. Hari's business, among many others, came to his attention. The search of Hari's premises has no connection to my enquiries into Dev Reddy's murder and the fire.

'Superintendent Ratini has asked me to lead the investigation into Hari's murder, while Inspector Vula will continue to lead the case of the jewel thefts. Believe me, I will do my utmost to discover Hari's murderer. Dr Krishna, a police medical examiner, has just left with Hari for Suva hospital. In her opinion, Hari died from a stab to his heart in the early hours of this morning, hours before the police team arrived here. The officers you see in your yard are searching for the weapon and for any other evidence.'

Anya got up and filled the kettle from the water barrel.

Maira said, 'Thank you for explaining, Inspector. I believe you. In here, it's been nothing but shock and confusion since that first knock at five o'clock.'

Sanjeev, Hari's younger brother, spoke up. 'Yes, what you said makes sense, Inspector.'

A few others nodded. Two girls burst into tears and left the table.

'May I ask you some questions now? The sooner I do that, the sooner I'll track down Hari's murderer.'

Gopal eventually looked Horseman in the eye and nodded.

'Thank you, Gopal. Please, don't hold back. I can decide what's relevant when we know more. First, who was the last person to see Hari last night?'

Gopal spoke without hesitation. 'Probably his wife. She's in her room now.'

'I won't disturb her just yet. What about you, Gopal?'

'I didn't see him at all after dinner. I was watching TV, but he didn't join us.'

'Did anyone here see him after dinner?'

Anya brought a loaded tray to the table. 'I did. I washed my hair, then came in here to sit near the fan to dry it before I went to bed. I think everyone else was in bed already. Hari went out the back door. I said goodnight. I assumed he was going to his workshop as usual, but I don't know.'

'Do you know what time this was?'

'No, but the TV was off and no one was in the living room.'

'Can anyone help?'

'I switched off the TV at nine o'clock and went to bed. A late night for a farmer,' Gopal said.

Anya looked thoughtful. 'I would say the TV had been off for at least an hour when I came in here.'

'I'll say ten o'clock or later, then.' Horseman made a note. 'Next question: did any of you see anything out of the ordinary last night? For instance, the moving lights you told me about before.'

'They looked at each other, then Maira spoke. 'Not last night, no.'

'Did an unusual sound wake anyone up?'

Blank faces stared.

'Did Hari have any enemies?'

'No! He didn't. Everyone got on well with Hari.' Maira raised her voice in protest. Anya poured tea into cups and handed them around the table. 'Ma, someone killed him.'

Sanjeev spoke up again. 'A thief who found out about his jewellery workshop, I bet.'

'Do most people around here know about Hari's sideline?'

'He didn't talk about it much, but all the jewellery shops knew him. He did repairs and remodelling.'

'Did they bring the work to him here?'

'He'd usually collect items from them. Very occasionally, one of his customers would call in. Sometimes he took them to his workshop. Other times, they'd hand over an item and have a brief talk at the door, then leave,' Gopal said.

'Did he ever complain about his jewellery contacts, claim he'd been cheated, for example?'

'No, I never heard him do that. What about all of you?' He looked around the table. No one spoke.

'All right. But there were people in the jewellery trade who knew where Hari's workshop was and visited it. Who were they?'

Again, no one spoke. 'Gopal, you said occasionally Hari had visitors dropping in work or perhaps picking it up, too. Can you remember any of them?'

'I don't think so. I took little notice. I thought he should concentrate more on the farm.'

After some moments, Maira spoke. 'The owner of Golden Dream in Nausori came to see Hari once or twice. I recognised him because I bought some wedding jewellery for my eldest daughter there. Years ago.' Her face softened as she recalled happy times.

'That's very helpful, Maira. Do you recall anyone else?' He drank his tea while he waited. 'Thank you for the tea, Anya. And thanks to you all for your cooperation. I'll now go and check on Inspector Vula's progress in his search. Hari may have kept his order book and records in there. I'll knock on your door before I leave. I hope Hari's widow can answer a few questions then. Perhaps you'll explain how important that will be for my investigation. Is that all right with you?'

'Yes,' Gopal said. The others nodded, their faces blank with shock and grief.

***

It was after nine o'clock now. Singh would probably be up and about. He pictured her methodically packing up her barracks bed-sit. She wouldn't be pleased if he didn't tell her about Hari's murder. He called.

'Horseman, Susie?'

'Good morning, Joe. Are you packing?'

'No, I'm at the Prakash farm.'

'How did the raid go?'

'It was held up because Vula found Hari's dead body in his workshop. Looks like he was stabbed through the heart.'

'I wish you'd told me, sir.'

'It was too early. His body's gone, so the jewel team's in there now. I've just finished the first conversation with the family. Harrowing, but got to be done.'

'I can come out and help you.'

'No need. I'm just going to check on what Vula's found in the workshop. I hope he'll have an order book, receipts, or something that will give us his contacts. Vula will need those documents too, so I'll get them copied. Ratini's given me the murder, the jewel thefts remain with Vula.'

'Call me before you get back. I can come in, any time.'

'*Vinaka*, Susie. I'll keep in touch.'

***

Vula was functioning normally again. His consultants from the trade were working alongside the police officers, categorising and listing the items in Hari's workshop.

'Joe, the search is running properly now. Appreciate your support earlier, man.'

'Don't mention it. We all get thrown off course at times. One reason we have teams. Have you got any leads yet?'

'*Io*, the very pearls that first caught your eye. Our expert's ninety per cent sure they're from the stolen long strand. So well-spotted, man. Then there's a large ruby ring, not yet reset—he's confirmed that. How is the family?'

'Shattered, still shocked. It's a bit strange, though. No one hotly denied that Hari could be involved in receiving stolen goods, or any other shonky jewellery dealings. They said customers rarely came to the farm with items, but one who did was the owner of Golden Dream in Nausori. Is he on your radar?'

'We've been there but got the usual brush-off. "Thanks for the info and pics, we'll be on the lookout and get in touch if anything turns up."'

Horseman chuckled. 'I can imagine. By the way, I admitted I knew about the raid, but I didn't mention that I was the source of your tip-off about this place. Having won back their semi-trust, it'd be good to keep that quiet when you're talking to them.'

'Absolutely. Do you think any of the family could be involved?'

'Hard to say. The parents—I think not. The younger brother Sanjeev is worth probing, though. He likes to air his knowledge, and I sensed a rivalry between Hari and him. I haven't seen Hari's wife yet—I'm going back to see her before I head back to Suva.'

'We've found two safes. I'm going to have to ask the family about keys.'

'No fun, but you don't have any choice, do you?'

'None. Unless we find them hidden somewhere here. There's a ton of stuff to go through.'

'Have you checked their vehicles? Farmers often leave whole bunches of keys in the ignition.'

'I didn't think of that. Musudroka, go and check the farm vehicles for keys.' Musudroka hurried off, looking pleased to get out of the shed.

'What about receipt books, order books, any of that?' Horseman asked.

'Sure, there's that old filing cabinet over there. Locked, but it was easy to open. All the business documents seem to be in the top drawer.'

'Both cases will need some of those. Is it okay if I check through them now? If I find anything of relevance to the murder, I'd like to take it with me. I'll get it copied today and put the originals back on your desk sometime this afternoon.'

'Fine by me. Just make sure they're logged and let me have a quick look before you take them away.'

'Easy, Siale. Definitely.'

'If we have a picture by the time all Hari's stuff is catalogued, I'll fill the family in. If not, I'll ask the usual questions and expect no useful answers.'

'Sounds about right. They'll appreciate you telling them what you can.'

Musudroka came back in, signalling his failure with a thumbs-down.

***

Gulika, Hari's widow, sat on the sofa, her two children huddled into her lap. She was composed but listless, as if someone had arranged her there. Maira sat next to her.

Horseman introduced himself and expressed his condolences again.

'Gulika, can you answer my questions?'

She nodded, her face blank.

'Did Hari go to bed last night?'

She stared at the children cuddling her. 'No. If he did, he didn't wake me.'

'Did he tell you he was going to his workshop?'

'No.'

'Did he often work on his jewellery at night?'

She nodded.

'Did he have quarrels with his customers or suppliers? Did anyone cheat him, for instance?'

'I don't know. He didn't tell me about it.'

'Did he meet customers or suppliers at his workshop?'

'Maybe occasionally. I don't really know. Sometimes I heard voices when I went past.'

Horseman showed her the bundle of Hari's business records he'd found in the filing cabinet. 'This is some of Hari's paperwork. Did you help him with these?'

'No, he did everything by himself.'

'Did he keep any more paperwork in the house? Perhaps in your room?'

'I don't think so.'

'Did he keep any business records in your office, Gopal?'

'No, I only permit farm records to be kept there.'

'What about keys? There are two safes in his workshop. Where did he keep his keys?'

Maira touched Gulika on her arm. 'Where is Hari's bunch of keys, Guli?'

Gulika turned her head and looked at her mother-in-law. 'I don't know. In his trouser pocket?'

'Gulika, Inspector Vula would prefer to open the safes and look at their contents here. That would be better for everybody. But if we can't find Hari's keys, he will have to take them back to the police station and break them open. We don't want to do that. With your permission, a police officer will come and search for the keys in your room. Or if you remember, you can show him where they are.'

Gulika shrugged, listless. 'Yes, all right.'

'Gopal, could Hari's keys be in the farm office?'

'No.'

'I'm sorry, but an officer will need to look in there, too.'

Gulika rose, swept her children aside, and left the room. Maira looked after her, perplexed. The children wailed, clinging now to their comforting grandmother. After a few minutes, Gulika returned, moving like an automaton. She held a bunch of keys out to Horseman, tears rolling down her cheeks.

51

Until Horseman knew about the spoils from Vula's search, there wasn't much he could do except ponder while photocopying Hari's business records. He told Singh there was no need for her to come in to the station.

So, what was she doing strolling into the CID room bearing a large pizza box? And how did she always contrive to look so fresh?

'I bet you haven't had lunch. Neither have I. Take a break and help me with this pizza.'

'*Vinaka*. But you're supposed to be moving.'

Singh deposited the pizza on her desk and rubbed her hands together briskly. 'Done! I'm in! I booked a station wagon taxi. The driver was so helpful; he carried the heavy boxes for me both ends. I've unpacked and had my first shower. The water drained instantly! It was lovely not having to paddle through kerosene-laced water. Not ready to cook my first meal yet, however.'

'You're amazing, Susie. A paragon of efficiency.'

'The pizza's getting cold, sir.' Her tone was disapproving.

No choice but to obey. His appetite perked up as the garlic-and-tomato aroma escaped the box. After two slices each, Singh got up to make tea. As they sat sipping, he filled her in on his challenging morning. Singh quizzed him on every detail while he ate another slice of pizza.

'Were the safe keys on the bunch Gulika handed over?'

'One of them. It contained jewellery items Vula's experts were interested in. No documents. So I left the team to do their job. I promised Vula I'd get the original documents to him this afternoon.'

'How many have you copied?'

'Maybe a quarter.'

'Let's divide the rest between us. I can use the copier downstairs.'

'Good plan. It's impossible to work fast. These cheap bound books split easily. Then the carbon tracings on the receipt and invoice books are uneven and faint. With some of them, I've had to reset the controls three times before I get a legible copy.'

'Can I have a quick look through them?'

'Sure. Like more tea?'

'Yes, please.'

When he returned with their refilled mugs, she was sorting the collection of documents into two filing trays. 'I'm putting all the faint originals into my tray. I'll copy them all on a dark setting, which will be quicker than experimenting with settings for each page. You can do the others, which should be good on normal.'

'Why didn't I think of that?'

'You look exhausted, sir—Joe, I mean.'

'I've had enough of midnight calls and driving to Rewa before sunrise. I want to get to the bottom of this case yesterday.'

'Here's an idea. I noticed Constable Lili Waqa is on duty downstairs. I could ask her to do your tray. She used to be a secretary, so she'd do a good job. How about it?'

'*Oi lei*! I'm shocked, Sergeant Singh!'

She stared at him, mystified.

'I never thought you'd typecast a woman officer for secretarial duties! What prejudice!'

Relieved, Singh smiled. 'Not at all, sir. I know Lili used to be a secretary. I know the other officers downstairs have not had her experience. It's an allocation of duty by individual expertise, not by sex.'

'I'm pleased to hear it, Singh. Okay, give the job to Lili if her supervisor can spare her. I'm going through the Reddy photos again.'

The photos tugged at him. He hadn't scrutinised them since Maira Prakash identified the people he didn't know. First, he looked at the portraits of the dead: Priti, her parents, Dev and his elder brother. And now Hari Prakash was dead, too. He picked out the photos that included Hari. In all of them, taken over ten years, he'd distanced himself from his own siblings and stood among the Reddy children. Horseman smiled to himself, well remembering how he, too, had always wanted to join the ranks of the older boys. He supposed it was innate for children and teenagers to strive for acceptance by their elder peers. Did that impulse lead him to consort with jewel thieves? His involvement was far from proven yet, but it was looking likely. He laid Hari's historic photos flat on his desk and looked them over once more. Possibly there was a different connection...

His strident desk phone jolted him back from his speculations. He snatched up the receiver. 'Horseman, Suva CID.'

'Good afternoon, Inspector. It's Maha, Dev Reddy's daughter. I was talking to Sergeant Singh at the funeral yesterday. Is now a good time to talk to her?'

'Yes, Maha. She's close by. One moment, please.' Singh hurried over. He switched to speakerphone.

'Hello, Maha. Can I help you?'

'I hope so, Sergeant Singh. It was so good to talk to you yesterday. My husband, Arun, agrees we can trust you with our problem.'

'You can trust me to do what I can, Maha. What is it?'

'Remember I told you my younger sister, Ela, had moved away recently. She's been living with us for nearly twenty years, first in New Zealand, then Australia. In fact, she's legally our daughter. Arun and I adopted her to help with the migration approval process. A few months ago, Ela announced it was time she lived independently, that she'd got a job in Melbourne and was leaving us in a few days.'

'Go on, Maha.'

'We were shocked. I mean, Ela is quite withdrawn and shy. She didn't go to high school, you know. After primary, she helped Ma, who wasn't well and lived an isolated life. It does her great credit that she stuck at catch-up classes for migrants at community college and eventually got the child care qualification here in Queensland. However, she was always quite immature and dependent on us—that's why we're so worried. Ela said she'd keep in touch but she hasn't. She could be anywhere. She may even have returned to Fiji for all we know.'

'Is her passport up to date?'

'Yes, we renewed all of them at the same time.'

'I can check whether she's visited Fiji, then. Do you have a copy of the ID page of her passport?'

'Arun has photos of our passports on his phone. Oh, I should have said we're all Australian citizens now, so they're Australian passports. And her surname is Anand—that's Arun's surname.'

'That won't make any difference. Send Ela's page to my mobile number. It's on the card I gave you.'

'Thanks so much! Can I call you Susila?'

'Of course, Maha. Just in case the Internet's not behaving, can you spell out Ela's full name for me now, exactly as it appears on her passport? And also tell me the date of birth on her passport, please. That's really all I need.'

'Oh, you can really do that?'

'Yes, no problem. There may be a delay, though. It's Sunday afternoon and the Immigration Department is closed. I might not be able to get the information until tomorrow.'

'Tomorrow is fine. Really, I thought it would take longer. I'm thankful for your kindness, Susila.'

They looked at each other. 'Wow!' Singh said.

Horseman took in a big breath and clapped his hands. 'This gives us a new angle—could be a breakthrough.'

'Should I contact the Immigration twenty-four-hour desk, Joe?'

'Sure. Say Ela is a missing person, which is true, even if not yet registered officially. You have a friend in Immigration, haven't you?'

'Indeed I have—that nice section head of Passport Control. He should be on deck on Monday morning. But I'll try the twenty-four-hour desk now.'

While Singh called Immigration, Horseman thought some more about the photos in front of him. He sorted through the Reddy family shots once more to select all those including Ela. In the most recent, when she was about twelve or thirteen, the girl looked awkward and unhappy. She leaned into her cousin Bimala, as if for support.

The pleasant background sound of Singh at her most charming ended with an abrupt clatter as she replaced the receiver.

'No go?' he asked.

'Right. "A missing person does not justify the attention of the twenty-four-hour desk unless that person is a child or there is evidence the person is in danger." I bet that so-called civil servant is sitting there with nothing to do, snoozing. I could hear him yawning! Sorry I slammed the phone down.'

'That's all right. It was quite a restrained slam, Susie. I've a hunch we could find out where Ela is without the help of Immigration. Did it strike you as odd yesterday, how upset Bimala was at the funeral of a distant cousin's husband? When I first met her right after Dev Reddy died, she wasn't upset at all. She shed tears later when she got anxious about making a mistake in the post-death protocol.'

'That's understandable. Those matrons—you know.'

Horseman grinned. 'I know they can be dragons. Like my mother. But Bimala said she didn't see the Reddy family often during her childhood. Yet here she is, in family snaps at various ages.'

'No conflict there, necessarily. Extended families often get together once every year or two and record the event. A child wouldn't think that was frequent.'

'True. At this time, Maira Prakash and Priti were great friends. It's no surprise the Prakash family was invited along when relatives were visiting.'

'Exactly. Or the other way around.'

'Bimala told me she was hoping to see Ela at the funeral—that Ela's failure to attend upset her. Yet why would she be so sure Ela would come from Australia if they hadn't been in touch for twenty years? I think Ela could be in Fiji and Bimala has been in touch with her. They may even have met.'

'Why didn't Bimala tell us she was a Reddy relative? If I'd known that before yesterday!' Singh flung her hands up in frustration.

'Exactly—we'd have investigated her more thoroughly. Bimala's husband told me she was on afternoon shift at the hospital yesterday. Nurses are usually rostered on the same shift for a week. I'll call CWM and check if she's at work now.'

Singh was wide-eyed. 'Good heavens! But your theory's possible.'

Horseman made the call. Bimala had commenced duty at three o'clock. He felt his adrenalin rising.

'She's at work. I'm going to see her now. Are you coming, Singh? Bring your velvet glove.'

'Yes, sir! I thought you weren't going to ask. Can you wait two minutes while I put the leftover pizza in the fridge?'

52

'I don't want to waste time booking a car. We'll get a taxi.' Horseman said.

Even on Sunday, a couple of cabs loitered near the station entrance. He hailed the closest.

'Don't you think it's a long shot you're pursuing?'

'*We're* pursuing, Susie. No, I don't. I didn't see grief on Bimala's face yesterday. I saw fear, maybe guilt.'

'She started work an hour ago. She won't be due for a break.'

'No, I'll have to speak to her supervisor.'

***

They waited in the staff break room where Horseman had first met Bimala, just six days before. When Bimala entered, she looked puzzled, but smiled and joined them at the central table.

'Good afternoon, Officers. What do you need me for?'

'To clear up a few puzzles, Bima. I'm glad to see you're recovered from yesterday. You were so upset at the funeral, I didn't want to talk to you there.'

'Yes, thanks for understanding. I'm not sure what came over me.'

'Don't worry. Funerals are emotional occasions. First, I'm puzzled about why you didn't mention your relationship to Mr Reddy when we spoke last Monday.'

'Well, you didn't ask me about that.'

'You told me yesterday that you didn't see the Reddy branch of the family often. I was a bit surprised to see you in these family snaps I saved from the farmhouse fire.'

Singh placed the glossy enlargements one by one in front of Bimala.

'Oh, wow! How come they're so clear?'

'The police photography people are experts.'

She gazed in wonder at the photos. 'These take me back! But it's true, our families only saw each other occasionally. Sometimes there'd be a gap of years. But I loved Priti, whom I called "Aunty," and I always got on with Ela.'

'Yes, I can see that. Here, you're really close, pressing together.'

Bimala looked again. 'Yes, we're at that age—about to leave childhood behind but unsure where we're headed.'

'What a nice way to define adolescence,' Singh said. 'Ela in particular looks worried.'

'Oh, yes! That's because...' Bimala stopped herself.

'Don't you think she's looking worried—even scared, perhaps?'

'Yes, she does, a bit.'

'Why—at a happy get-together?' Singh asked.

'The Prakash boys got on her nerves as they got older. I don't really know.'

'Did you write to each other after Ela went to New Zealand?' Singh asked.

'I wrote a few times, but I never got an answer. I didn't know if Ela got my letters or not. That wouldn't happen now, would it? We'd easily keep in touch with Facebook. But our parents didn't even have landlines then. I didn't even know Ela had moved to Australia years ago.'

'What made you think Ela would be at the funeral?'

'Nothing, really. Darsh told my parents the arrangements, and they told me. Or maybe it was Mr Pandey, the lawyer. I knew some of my cousins would be there. Ela was the only one I was close to, so I really hoped to see her.'

'Of course you did. And you had good reason to expect to see her because you knew she returned to Fiji months ago,' Horseman said.

Bimala gasped. 'What?'

'Yes, Immigration records confirm her arrival in Fiji,' he said.

Singh's brows lifted, but he really couldn't wait until tomorrow. Nothing wrong with a bluff, even if it didn't pay off. He could only be proved mistaken, and that happened every day about one speculation or another.

Bimala shook her head. 'No, it must be someone with the same name. Reddy is such a common name. Maha and Arun said...'

'Yes, what did Maha and Arun say?' Horseman asked.

'When I asked them about Ela yesterday, they said she didn't want to come to the funeral, that she was staying home to keep an eye on their children. I was so disappointed.'

'Really, Bima?' Singh sounded sceptical. 'That *is* strange, because I spoke to Maha just an hour ago. She asked me to help locate Ela, who left them months ago, saying she'd found a new job in Melbourne. They haven't heard from her since then. Maha asked if I could check if she'd returned to Fiji. I put in a call to the Immigration Department.'

Horseman intervened. 'I wonder why Maha never checked if Ela had left the country with the Australian passport control office. My answer is that she never considered it a possibility because Ela was always shy, withdrawn and dependent. But yesterday at the funeral, Maha and Arun learned that Ela was in Fiji. They couldn't believe that she'd done this by herself, so they wanted to check the information. Very sensible of them, too. You told them she was here, didn't you, Bima?'

Bimala stared at Horseman as if hypnotised. In the end, she nodded.

'Why did you tell them, Bima? Didn't you promise Ela to keep her secret?' Singh lowered her voice.

'I've only seen her three times. She hasn't called me for a week now. I was so anxious about her, I just had to tell Maha yesterday, because— because I can't cope. I don't know how to find Ela, but maybe they can.'

'You did the right thing when you told Maha. Definitely. But I'm confused, Bima. Can you tell me when Ela first got in touch with you? Tell me the story from the beginning,' Singh said.

Bimala consulted the nurse's watch pinned to her uniform pocket.

'Take your time. Your supervisor understands our conversation may take a while. You won't be in trouble with her.' Singh spoke gently.

Bimala drew in a deep breath, her long, tense face softening just a bit. Her strongest emotion seemed to be her fear of being blamed, of getting into trouble. What childhood experiences had forged that response? Horseman's anger at her omissions and lies subsided.

'I was so excited when Ela called me here at work—when was it? About a month ago. We swapped mobile numbers, and I called her back during my break. It was as if the last twenty years hadn't happened—we picked up where we left off. We'd always been close—like sisters. We arranged to meet here in the canteen. I invited her home, but she said she'd rather meet me alone. She was always so shy, except with me. We told each other about our lives. How amazing that she's achieved a child-care certificate after all she's been through.'

'What has she been through, Bima?' Horseman asked.

'Oh, um, you know—her father didn't let her go to high school. She had to stay home to work and help her mother. He was crazy.'

'Sorry to interrupt. Please go on.'

'But anyway, when she got to Suva, she got a job in a preschool while she looked around and decided whether or not to stay in Fiji.

'We met here the next week and the one after. I told her how much I wanted her to meet my husband and two children, but she put me off, saying there was plenty of time, that she just wanted to catch up with me first. That was odd, and I was a bit hurt, you know.

'Then, late last Sunday night, she called and asked if she could visit her father—she'd heard he was in hospital. She sounded agitated. I was shocked because she was frightened of her father as a child, and all his kids disowned him after poor Kanan was found and Dev went to prison. But then, I thought maybe after all these years she felt sorry for him. She wanted to come right away, and I couldn't see any harm. I mean, some patients' relatives insist on staying with the patients twenty-four-seven.'

'You knew Mr Reddy had police guards rostered,' Singh said.

'Yes, at first. But they went away. I thought Ela would be like a guard herself. I made her tea, we chatted a bit, then she sat with him. She said she couldn't face being questioned by staff, so could I show her how to get out without going through the main entrance. I showed her the fire stairs.' Bimala's mouth trembled, and she covered her eyes with one hand.

'When did you last see Ela?' Horseman asked.

She took a shuddering breath and looked at them, tears welling once more. 'Wh—when I did my three o'clock checks. Ela had nodded off, but she woke as I took Dev's blood pressure. She thanked me for letting her spend time with her father, said she'd done a lot of thinking and she'd be leaving soon. She promised to call me during the week. I haven't heard from her since. Every time I call her mobile I get the out-of-service message.'

'We need Ela's mobile number. Can I check your phone, please?' Singh asked.

Bima fumbled with her phone, then passed it to Singh. 'Here's her entry. Just the number—that's all she told me.'

'Did Ela murder her father?' Horseman asked.

'I—I don't know. How could I know?' Bimala's voice shook.

'Where is Ela staying?'

'I don't know. She said it was just a cheap room, temporary.'

'Can you tell us anything more?'

'Anything more? I've broken my promise to Ela. What else can I say?'

Horseman wound up. 'Don't hesitate to call either of us if you think of any more details, however trivial.'

'Will I lose my job?' Again she looked afraid.

'I'm not your employer, Bima. I can't answer that. My job is to find Ela.'

53

Horseman and Singh sat in the almost-deserted hospital canteen, sipping awful coffee. At least it was hot. He added a spoonful of sugar—against his personal coffee rules, but this coffee was beyond bitter. Singh had called Ela's mobile number several times with the same result—the out-of-service message.

'It's frustrating to have no idea who the murderer is. It's even worse to have her handed to you on a plate and have no idea where she is.' He rubbed his hands over his head and face.

'Ela was so secretive. She wouldn't tell Bimala where she worked and stayed. That means planning. Do you think she came to Fiji in order to kill her father?' Singh asked.

'No, that's the part that doesn't fit. Dev was a prisoner at St Giles when she arrived here—subject to Immigration confirming her arrival date. Did she imagine she could kill him there?'

'Unlikely, I agree. Maybe she came back to test the waters, see if Fiji could be her home once more, just as Bima told us.'

'*Io*, or maybe she had another purpose.'

'Either way, we can scratch Ravai Nata off our list, don't you think?'

'Yes. I'll be glad not to have to think about his time-wasting lies any longer.'

'And Gopal Prakash?'

'Probably, but there is a connection between Ela and the Prakash family. Maira knew her well as a child. I can't intrude there again today, but I'll call them in the morning. What if the mysterious loiterer around the farms is Ela?'

Singh's cup clattered on its saucer. 'Good heavens! Why yes, that makes perfect sense, now.'

'Maira told me how devoted Ela was to the field shrine. She could have gone to the farms at night, poked around, stirring up memories, peeping into the lives of the Prakash family, twenty years on.'

Singh's eyes shone. 'Yes, she might have wanted to restore the shrine and continue her devotions. But do you think she could have beaten up Dev?'

'I don't know. With the right weapon, maybe. If he didn't resist.'

'We need to ask Bimala about her physical condition. But the psychology of a frenzied beating? I don't know either.'

'*Io*, suffocating an unconscious man with a pillow wouldn't be a physical challenge. I don't doubt she did that.'

Singh was silent for a few moments. 'Unless she let in an accomplice through the fire door when the coast was clear.'

'Possible, but for now let's proceed on the assumption Ela acted alone. We also have to consider the fire. She could have set that, especially if she's been revisiting an unhappy childhood.'

'The sad efforts to sweep up the broken glass and debris. though. If Ela did that, she wouldn't suddenly destroy the house, would she?'

'Why not, if she's reliving past trauma and can't cope.'

'What about Hari? Do you think Ela killed him?'

Horseman sighed. 'I don't know. Was he knifed in a thieves' quarrel? Let's go back to what we know from Bimala. If we're right, Ela's visited the cousin who was close to her, her childhood stamping grounds and her father. People keep saying there are no close Reddy relatives in Fiji anymore. But we've forgotten about her brother.'

'Which brother?'

'Kanan. What if she visited Kanan, too?'

'Of course! How could I have forgotten about him?'

'Everyone does. Until Reddy's new will surfaced, that is. Now he's front and centre in the minds of his brothers and sisters. And vulnerable. I'll call the manager and check if he's had any visitors. I'll warn her not to admit anyone. We'll go there first thing in the morning.'

We're getting quite a list for first thing in the morning, Joe.'

'True. We need to prioritise. Vula took the Prakash family's fingerprints to eliminate them from the prints lifted from Hari's workshop. We need to check them against the ones we got from the shrine.' Horseman said.

Singh's brow furrowed. 'I'll call Vula. I've got to go back to the station to check on Lili's photocopying and pass the originals back to him. If he hasn't got the fingerprints to the lab yet, I'll take them and make sure the technicians are clear about the cross-matching we need.'

'A great plan. I'll move to another table so we can concentrate. This coffee's undrinkable, though. I'll get us a fresh pot of tea.'

MONDAY

54

Horseman picked up Singh outside Seaview Tower. He wondered how long he could keep his own news to himself. It all depended on her providing him with an opening.

'How did you sleep, Susie?'

'Best sleep ever. And do you know why?'

'Why?'

'I'm free from anxiety. Decision's made. What's more, I'm confident —no, I *know* I made the right decision. However tragic this case is, I'm happy.' She beamed at him. 'It's a wonderful feeling, waking up in my own home that I chose myself. I can't believe my luck.'

'That's wonderful. Your anxiety-free mind can solve the case without my help, then.' He laughed. She did, too.

'What's the latest on the fingerprints?' he asked.

'All good. Vula was in the office when I got back. I delivered Hari's business records. The SOCOs had taken the fingerprints direct to the lab, including the adults in the Prakash household. I went to the lab myself, made sure the techs knew which potential cross-matches we were most interested in, and they'll come through today.'

'Excellent. I sense we're closing in now. When I got home yesterday, I spoke to Navneet Pandey, Dev's solicitor. He told me in confidence that Dev's previous will left his farm leases, freehold land and farm business to his three elder sons: Darsh, Ajit and Pranjal. Note that Kanan wasn't mentioned. He left his money, his wife's jewellery and other property to his two daughters, also to be divided equally. Obviously, there's a powerful incentive for the three elder sons to contest the will, which Darsh is doing. Not really the case for the daughters. If Priti's saris and jewellery were still in the house, they're destroyed now, unless the fire officers recovered some jewellery. We should check on that today, too.'

'Get Kau to do that. He can start checking Hari's paperwork, too.'

'Oh—I didn't mention that Vula's keeping both Kau and Musudroka to process the evidence seized from Hari's workshop. There's a mountain of it, apparently. He said they're working partly on the murder because there's such an overlap between the two cases.'

'I guess he's right. Nothing I can do about it from here, anyway. Ratini would support him. So it's you and me, Singh. Let's keep our eyes on today's goal—to find Ela.'

'Let's do it, sir.'

He was tired of picking her up on the *sir*. It seemed petty. She was at work, so the term was automatic.

He turned into the small cul-de-sac and parked outside Sunshine Home. About a dozen kids in school uniform ran down the drive and headed up the street. The younger ones waved eagerly to Horseman and Singh.

Besi stood in the open doorway, smiling a welcome. How fortunate were these kids to have a home here and Besi to mother them—they who had experienced such sad starts in life.

Besi ushered them through to the yeasty-smelling kitchen where Petero poured them tea and served fresh bread and ginger marmalade. 'We're grateful to you for doing so much to protect Kanan and all of us at Sunshine. I'm sure it goes well beyond the call of duty,' Besi said.

'Not at all, Besi. It's our duty to protect the innocent and prevent crime. You told me on the phone Darsh called you yesterday.'

'*Io*, in the morning. What a surprise that was! He said he had to stay for another day in Suva and wanted to visit Kanan today at twelve. I suggested he come either at eleven or one o'clock because we have lunch at twelve and Kanan is so easily distracted, he doesn't eat in front of visitors. I felt I had no reason to deny him.'

'I understand. Please ensure a staff member, preferably yourself or Petero, is with Kanan while Darsh is here.'

'We'll certainly do that, but why?'

'Just a precaution. We know nothing against Darsh. However, someone has been loitering around Dev Reddy's farm and set fire to his farmhouse a few days ago. We also found a neighbour murdered yesterday morning.'

'Well, Darsh told me he only arrived in Fiji on Friday...'

'That's true. We don't suspect Darsh of this. But please, for the next few days can you revert to the security measures you took during the demonstrations? Shut and lock your gates, keep your mini-bus on the street, and all the rest. You know what to do and you've got the padlocks and chains, so it won't be a lot of trouble.'

Besi raised her eyebrows in agreement. 'Of course, we'll do what you say.'

Singh smiled to reassure her. 'We'll catch who we're looking for soon. But they might want to visit Kanan too, and probably won't ring to ask permission like Darsh did.'

Horseman moved the big teapot aside and placed the three large-group Reddy photos on the table in front of Besi. 'These snaps are at least twenty years old, so all the people will be older now, all the kids grown up. Look carefully, Besi. Have any of these people visited Sunshine Home?'

Besi reached for her reading glasses and studied the photos for some minutes. 'I don't recognise anyone.' She sighed. 'That doesn't mean they haven't been here. Petero, can you come and help? You've got sharper eyes than me.'

He sat beside her and they pored over the photos. Petero picked one up, holding it closer to Besi's face. 'Here, isn't this Sachi?'

Besi peered. 'Maybe. This girl would be in her thirties now, I guess.'

Petero picked up another photo. 'Look, here she is again, a different angle. I couldn't swear to it, but I reckon this is Sachi, our children's nurse.'

'*Oi lei! Io*, she could be. Sachi's not rostered to work until Wednesday. She asked for a few days off.'

He turned the photo around and pointed at Ela Reddy, now Ela Anand.

55

Besi, for all her competence at running Sunshine Home, was a rather casual employer. When pressed, she remembered Sachi producing her passport and community college certificates and explaining she hated the name Ela and preferred to be called Sachi. As the woman in front of her clearly matched Ela Reddy's passport photo, Besi addressed her as Sachi and thought no more about the matter. The only address Ela gave was a private box at Suva Post Office. Besi had her mobile phone number but had never called because Ela was so reliable.

Passport Control confirmed Ela Anand, a citizen of Australia, had entered Fiji eleven weeks ago. Horseman issued a detain order and alerted Immigration officials and airport police at both Nadi and Suva.

'However, I don't think Ela will try to leave Fiji, sir. I think she has unfinished business.'

'What's that, then?' Ratini enquired, unimpressed.

'I really wish I knew, sir. Singh and I have checked with her brothers and sister, who have all extended their visit to Fiji by a few days to attend to legal business. They swear she hasn't contacted them. That's likely—if Ela had wanted to see them, she would have gone to her father's funeral.'

'Maybe she intended to, but got cold feet.'

'Quite possible, sir.'

'I agree this Ela is the prime suspect for her father's murder in the hospital. Better get the nurse cousin in here to make a formal statement.'

'Singh and Bimala are doing that as we speak, sir.'

'And about time! D'you think Ela's up for the fire and Hari Prakash, too?'

'I can't be sure, sir. If so, her mind must be quite disturbed. We've got to find her.'

'Exactly. I agree. How do you propose to do that?' Ratini's question was a dare rather than a procedural enquiry.

'I'm not sure, sir. But when I mentioned Ela had unfinished business, it's likely to be near the farm where she grew up. As a child, she was quite close to Maira Prakash. I'd like to talk to Maira again today. Whether she can help or not, I propose to mount a search tonight. If she's going to the farms, she won't go in daylight. We'll need at least a dozen constables in plain clothes—she'll vanish at the sight of a uniform. I propose several conceal themselves near the field shrine, which was a focus of her childhood. We believe she's been worshipping there in recent weeks.'

'Hm. I suppose that's the best you can come up with?'

'Until we get more information, sir.'

'All right. Better than nothing. Go ahead.'

**

Reluctant as he was to intrude once more on a mother's grief for her murdered son, he had no choice.

Anya answered the door and took them to her mother, who sat at the familiar table. Maira looked up, unsmiling. Dark half-moons shadowed her eyes.

'Good afternoon, Maira. How are you?' Horseman said.

Singh brought her hands together under her chin and bowed. 'Maira, I'm so sorry for your loss. Believe me, you're the only one who can help us, otherwise we would not intrude.'

Maira waved her hand wearily. 'I know you're doing your job. But these days are the most terrible of my entire life.'

Horseman sat down at the table and spoke gently. 'Maira, we found out today that Ela Reddy arrived back in Fiji three months ago. Did you know she'd returned?'

Anya brought a tray with cups of water. 'It's all right, it's boiled,' she said. Singh took one, placed it before Maira and sat beside her.

Maira took in a quivery breath, then sipped her water.

'Yes. I thought about her when we noticed the moving lights and the paths trodden through the crops to the goddess Durga's shrine. I remembered happy days. That little girl would visit Durga often, tending to her, talking to her non-stop. She was a quiet little thing with people, but she trusted the goddess. When she was a bit older, her mother taught her mantras and *pujas*. They would chant together, mother and daughter.

'I told myself it couldn't possibly be Ela, that she'd never return after what happened. But one evening she came to see me. Just stepped out of the shadows when I went out with some scraps for the pigs. It took me a few seconds to recognise her. Well, it's been twenty years, isn't it?'

Maira lapsed into silence. Anya had been standing, tray in hand, listening to her mother. Now she placed cups of water beside Horseman and Singh, then sat down with them at the table.

'What did she say to you, Maira?'

'When I got over my shock, I asked about her life. She said she'd never married, enjoyed her work at a preschool in Australia, saved money, but always wondered about Fiji. She wanted to come and see us, particularly Kanan. I thought she was very brave, after all that happened, the shame of her father's evil deeds.'

'I asked if she was tending to the shrine and walking about the farms at night. She admitted it. Retracing her youthful steps eased her troubled mind. She asked if I objected, and I said I did not, but it would be better if we kept her visits between ourselves. Ela agreed. I warned her that people would notice the lights. She said she would be more careful and only use her torch when there was no moonlight.'

'Did she visit Kanan?'

'I don't know. She told me she wanted to.'

'When did you last speak to Ela?'

Maira ran her fingers over her head, pulling more strands of hair from her plait. 'I can't remember exactly.'

Singh moved the water closer to Maira. She picked it up and sipped.

'Have you seen her since her father was released from prison?'

Maira drank some more water. 'No, I'm sure I haven't. Do you think she set fire to the farmhouse?'

'We don't know, Maira. Can you help us?'

'No, I've seen a torchlight a few times since then. I go outside after dark, wondering if she wants to talk to me, but she's never shown herself to me since then.'

Maira suddenly gasped. Her hands clutched her head again. 'Hari! Could she...'

'We don't yet know who killed Hari or why. We have no reason to suspect Ela, except that she's been visiting the farms at night from time to time.'

Maira nodded.

'Why would Ela kill Hari? Is there any reason?' Horseman asked.

It seemed Maira didn't hear. Horseman looked through the photos and placed three in front of Maira.

'I noticed something this morning I'd missed before. See here, Hari is standing next to Ela, but there's quite a gap between them. Ela's shrinking away from him, squeezing behind Bimala. But Hari's grinning at Ela.'

Maira looked at the picture carefully.

'And in this one, there are two rows of people. Hari's in the back and Ela's in the front. Again, Hari's ignoring the camera and looking down at Ela, a broad smile on his face. How old are Hari and Ela in this photo? It seems the most recent.'

Maira looked interested now. 'Yes, this is the most recent. Hari was sixteen or seventeen. Ela was thirteen perhaps.'

'Did Hari have a crush on Ela?'

Maira paused for a while, then sighed. 'I think so, probably.'

'It doesn't look like Ela was interested in him, the way she stands as far away from him as she can.'

'No, she was too young. But anyway, she always avoided Hari and Sanjeev.'

'Do you know why?'

'The boys egged each other on—teased her when they were young. Ela was frightened of them, I think. She was shy and quiet by nature. A busy mother can't know what goes on between children, isn't it? I was looking after a baby at this time.'

Hari looked mature for his years—a young man with raging hormones, flexing his muscles, feeling his power, enjoying bullying a younger girl. But this was sheer speculation.

'Maira, all mothers know things about their children they want to keep secret. You waited years to report your fears about Kanan to the police. You regret that now. I sympathise with you. But please, don't repeat your mistake. Hari is dead, but you still have Sanjeev. If you're afraid for him, please tell us about it.'

Maira burst into tears, her elbows on the table, her head in her hands. Singh put a hand on her shoulder. Anya got up, removed Singh's hand and wrapped both arms around her mother.

56

When the garish orange and purple swirls of sunset faded to grey, the unmarked police mini-bus turned into the Sharma driveway and parked out of sight of the road. Better for the search team to avoid both Reddy and Prakash farms, the focus of Ela's visits. The Sharmas were happy to cooperate. After all, their nephew served as a constable at Nausori. Half the police contingent came from Nausori station. Their local knowledge could only help. While waiting, he tried Ela's mobile again, with the same result—none.

Horseman observed the six men and four women who got out of the bus. Great, they all wore dark clothes, as instructed. He took them through his plan and Constable Maika Toga gave them tips for moving unseen through the flat fields of low crops and supervised testing their radio equipment.

'If you hear or see movement, make sure it's human before alerting me. There'll be cows and goats on the loose, dogs on the prowl, mongoose—you name it. Ela is a short woman. She knows these farms intimately. If you see someone who could be her, alert me by radio. Whisper quietly. I'll take it from there.'

When it was dark, they moved off in three groups, two of which would spread out and head north to surround the field shrine at widely spaced intervals. Each officer would then lie low, watch and listen. Singh and three women officers would be the closest to the shrine. Ela's mental state could be fragile and it would be counterproductive for burly men to tackle her.

He positioned himself between the shrine and the Reddy farm buildings. He and Singh had puzzled about how Ela got here from Suva. Unless she had an accomplice, it could only be by bus or taxi. If she noticed the police, she was likely to escape back to the road. So the third group of police hid near the road at intervals between the Sharma and

Prakash farms. The plan was founded on speculation and few facts, but it was the best they could do. He prayed Ela would show up.

Horseman sat in a small field of tomatoes. He was lucky the bushes were big enough for him to sit up and change his position from time to time. The officers in the rice would have to lie down. More difficult to keep watch.

His eyes adjusted to the dark—he'd be able to detect anyone moving. As for hearing her, he was doubtful. So many sounds came from all directions. The birds seemed slow to settle, perhaps some were nightbirds preparing to hunt. Frogs and insects called each other, a cow mooed from time to time and the inevitable dogs howled and bayed.

The smell of smoke startled him. He raised himself slightly and looked around. He spotted a wisp of smoke twenty metres away among a green herb crop. Furious but relieved at the same time, he realised an officer was smoking. It wasn't worth risking radio communication. He crawled the twenty metres, his knee protesting mightily. Fortunately, the smoker stayed quiet when Horseman surprised him. He gave the man a whispered earful and left, confident he wouldn't light up again.

After an hour, he wondered how many officers were still awake. A few couldn't resist shutting their eyes. He'd have to wear it—even a whispered radio wake-up call was too big a risk.

Another hour passed before a new moon rose high enough to add to the starlight. He reached out and picked a tomato. He bit into it. His mouth puckered—his punishment for stealing a farmer's fruit. But he couldn't waste it now. The sour flavour and fresh juiciness pepped him up.

Just as the birds quietened, his radio came alive. Toga's whisper sounded through his earbuds. He turned the volume down.

'Control, a small person has passed me, coming from the Prakash farm and heading south towards the shrine. Over.'

'*Vinaka* Maika. Keep her in view as long as you can. Did you get that, Singh? Over.'

Singh responded immediately. 'I'm ten metres from the shrine, sir. I can't see her yet. Here's hoping it is Ela. Out.'

A few minutes later, a light illuminated the shrine and Singh's whispered voice came through his earbuds. 'A woman has climbed the ladder, switched on her torch, and placed it on the ledge. She's climbed down now and started whirling around—Durga's devotees' dance. Over.'

He raised his head above the rice crop and could see a small black figure circling the shrine. He radioed again.

'Go in as soon as you can, Singh. Over.'

'Yes, sir. I'm sure it's Ela. She's chanting. I hope she's in a trance. Out.'

A minute later, four officers rose from the rice and closed in on the shrine, step by step. He should have told Singh to leave her radio on but he knew she would handle Ela well.

A woman shrieked, and the figure streaked off, dodging between two officers and into the rice. The others abandoned their gradual approach and gave chase armed with torches.

Horseman ordered the officers in the field to join the chase and those near the road to watch for a person running onto the road from the farmlands.

Half an hour later, officers searched all the farm sheds and irrigation channels and walked the vegetable rows with torches.

Ela had given them the slip. If she was hiding on the farms, the officers would find her. If she'd fled, there was only one place she would go.

He didn't know how Ela would get there, but he'd parked the police Landcruiser at the Sharma farm.

57

As he pulled out of the Sharma farm's driveway, he radioed Singh. 'You're in charge of the search, Singh. If she's hiding out there, you'll find her. I'm going to the Sunshine Home. If she's got away, that's her destination.'

'Okay, sir. Keep in touch.'

'You too, out.'

He called Besi at Sunshine Home, told her what to do and then sped off, only to brake abruptly as a curious black steer sauntered onto the road. Why couldn't farmers mend their fences? A timely reminder to drive cautiously, despite the few vehicles on the road.

What now? He pulled up behind a line of vehicles on the approach to the Rewa bridge. A hold-up at this time of night meant a breakdown or accident. He radioed Nausori police, who told him constables were already on the scene. He got out, jogged onto the bridge and up to the obstruction: a truck's tailgate had sprung open, spilling its load of vegetables across the road, causing an oncoming car to veer and collide with the safety barrier.

Two constables scrambled around the roadway, throwing vegetables back into the truck. Occupants of other cars also helped, or maybe helped themselves to a pumpkin or cassava. 'Not too much damage, sir,' the constable told Horseman. 'The car's still driveable, but he's smashed his left headlight—really can't let him drive it at night.'

'The bridge is well lit. He can safely drive off and park on the verge. You deal with him there. I'm on urgent police business, Constable. Hold the traffic as it is. When I've passed, get that truck moving again.'

'*Io*, sir. *Moce.*'

Horseman went back to the Landcruiser, switched on the flashing lights and siren, pulled out. As the damaged car exited the bridge, he crossed on the wrong side, changing to the left lane once past the truck.

He waved to the constable holding up the traffic for him and accelerated away.

He switched off the siren long before he reached Sunshine Home and extinguished his lights as he entered the street. The home was in darkness except for the brightly lit kitchen at one end and a dim light at the other end—Kanan's room.

Besi opened the door as he came up the path.

'She arrived fifteen minutes ago. Quite calm. Said there was a family emergency and she had to fly back to Australia on the first flight she could get. Asked if she could sit with Kanan for a while and say goodbye. I couldn't see any harm after what you told me.'

'*Io*, you were right not to challenge her. But she may be unpredictable. Where's Petero?'

'He's locked all the gates as you told us. He's hovering near Kanan's door.'

'Good. Leave everything to me now. Deadlock the front door right away. When Dr Acharya arrives, deadlock it again after you let him in. Ela runs like the wind. I'll have a word with Petero before I go in.'

He tapped on the open door, not wanting to surprise her. She sat on Kanan's bed, his head in her lap, his pillow propped up against the bedhead. He breathed heavily as she stroked his hair.

'Hello, Ela. Or do you prefer Sachi?'

'Sachi.'

'I'm Inspector Horseman. I met you here about two weeks ago.'

'I remember.'

'I didn't know Kanan was your brother then. Why didn't you tell Besi who you really were?'

'I wasn't strong enough. I needed to worship at Durga's shrine at the farm to gain the power to do what is right. She's granted me energy and courage to do battle with evil, just like she did. Imagine! She even delivered my evil father from prison into my hands! I never even dreamed that was possible.'

She murmured softly but dropped her voice even lower as Kanan stirred.

'Did you kill your father?'

'Yes. Durga urged me on, gave me strength and will. You know, she killed the demon Mahishasura, who kept changing his shape to deceive her. But she never gave up. In the end, she killed him with her trident and cut his head off. Compared to her feat, pressing a pillow over the face of an unconscious old man is nothing.'

'Why did you worship at Durga's shrine again this evening?'

'She is my inspiration. She blesses her devotees with bravery. When I saw the police waiting, I was tempted to go away but my goddess called me. Durga gave me the heart to complete my task.'

She stroked Kanan's white stubble, touched his hair, which shone gold in the lamplight. 'He's beautiful, isn't he? To my father he was a freak, he had to be hidden away, like me. We both brought shame on the family. Ma cared for him, but she complied with Baba's wish. Then when her baby died...'

'Your mother's baby?'

'Yes, he died and my parents thought they could give me another chance. Maybe even cancel out my shame by pretending Kanan was their son and sending me off to New Zealand with my sister and brother-in-law. Make a new start. I gave birth to Kanan on my fourteenth birthday. I didn't want to be a mother—I was a child myself. But I never forgot my little white baby.'

Something glinted on Kanan's chest. Had the knife always been there? Still stroking his hair with her right hand, she moved the knife to Kanan's throat.

'How could something good come from the rape of a child by a nasty, sadistic bully? Maybe my father was right and my innocent Kanan is possessed by a demon. Look at him—he's albino, spastic and retarded. He's cursed. I'd be doing him a favour, ending his suffering.' A drop of crimson blood oozed onto Kanan's white skin. Shocked, she withdrew it a millimetre or two. Kanan moved, frowning, but didn't wake.

'Kanan is loved and happy, Sachi. He has a home. He's financially independent. It seems to me Kanan is a blessing, not a curse.'

For the first time, Ela looked up at Horseman. 'A blessing?'

He sat on the bed near Kanan's feet. 'Yes. His foundation provides a safe home for twenty children and employment for several adults. People come to visit him from all over the world, inspired by his story. He survived against all the odds. Then he flourished. And hasn't he been a comfort to you these last few months?'

'Yes, it's good to be with him.'

'Sachi, I know you're suffering, but is Kanan? I don't think so. He's happy. You'd better give me the knife. It could slip.'

She looked at the knife in her hand, surprised. Horseman leaned towards her, his hand outstretched.

'I'm too far from Durga's shrine now. My courage is draining. I was close to her when she told me to kill Hari. She strengthened my hand against his wickedness.'

'Kanan isn't wicked. You said yourself he's innocent. Please give me the knife, Sachi. You don't need it.'

He looked away as Dr Acharya tapped on the door and entered.
Ela sighed, lifted the knife and plunged it into her chest.

TUESDAY

58

'I wish I'd been there.' Singh looked reproachful.

'I wish you'd been there, too. Ela was handing over the knife when Dr Acharya walked in. Talk about bad timing.'

'Still, a doctor on hand, and you, Besi and Petero, all with first aid training. It could have been worse.'

'Ela was distracted too—she didn't stab deep. The blade missed her heart, lungs and major blood vessels. She's recovering well.'

Singh looked sympathetic. 'That stab must have shocked you, though.'

'*Io*, I thought she'd come to kill Kanan, not herself.'

'When can Dr Acharya assess her mental state?' Singh asked.

'Later today or tomorrow, probably. He would prefer to admit her to St Giles for secure observation, but he can begin the process at CWM.'

He thought for a bit. 'I still don't know how she got away so fast. It's no big deal, but I'd like to ask her. If we get the chance. In the meantime, we've got to tie up all loose ends, prepare charges and evidence... That'll be enough for today, I think.'

'Enough for the rest of the week! But you could take time to move into your new flat. I don't understand how you can pay rent and delay moving in,' Singh said.

'Oh, I moved in on Sunday night. Matt drove me and my suitcases. Didn't I tell you?'

'No, you did not! Hang on—you picked me up yesterday morning in a police vehicle.'

'*Io*, I walked from Seaview down to the station, got the Landcruiser, then came to pick you up. I wanted to tell you, but you never gave me the chance.'

'Come on!' Singh protested.

'True. I couldn't get a word in edgeways. But half an hour later we found out Ela and Sachi were the same person. That discovery diverted me to more important topics.'

'Fair enough, sir. So, you've had two nights there, just like me. How do you like it?'

'Very much. I'm not sure I can settle there, though. I miss Tina already. Matt's perfectly happy to look after her, but... I'll see how it goes.'

'Have you seen Ratini yet?'

'No, not seen. I called him last night around midnight, once Ela was safe in hospital and the doctor said she'd recover from the wound.'

'Did he blame it all on you?'

'No, funnily enough. He thanked me. He sounded half-asleep. Bound to be a different story today. I'll ring him now. Better report properly.'

'Oh, the lab called before you arrived. Identical unknown adult fingerprints are on the glass at the shrine, the fuel shed door and a kerosene drum. They match those on the knife you gave them this morning. Sounds promising.'

'*Io*. Almost certain. But we have to take Ela's fingerprints. In a case where the culprit's mental state is in question. her confession is too. Physical evidence is even more important. I'll visit her this afternoon with the kit. It's got to be done.'

***

Ela opened her eyes as Horseman and Singh walked into her secure hospital room. Her neck and one shoulder were wrapped in bandages, which extended beneath her hospital gown. She was propped up on a bank of pillows.

'Come in, Detectives. I'm feeling better now. I suppose you want to ask me some more questions.'

'Yes, we'd like to. First, we need your fingerprints, to make sure they match the ones we've found on the knife, Durga's shrine and other places.

'Why? I've told you what I did. Don't you believe me?'

'We need evidence, Ela. People sometimes confess to crimes they didn't commit, often to protect the real culprit.'

Singh produced the portable fingerprint kit. 'We can talk while we're doing this, Ela. And we'd like to record our conversation, too.'

Ela shrugged, then winced. 'That hurt. I have to remember not to move.'

'I'll put the ink pad on your bed-table and wheel it closer to you. Then you won't have to move. May I have your hand, please?'

Ela was very cooperative. Maybe her dreadful retribution had satisfied her.

'I was at Durga's shrine last night, Ela. I wish I could run like you. I can't work out how you got to the Sunshine Home so fast. How did you do it?' Horseman asked.

Ela's lips curved in a slight smile. 'I know every centimetre of our farm, and the neighbours', too. I ran to our boundary, the wide irrigation ditch, across another neighbour's fields and onto their road. That's where I left my car. Every time I visited the farms over the last months, I came that way. For privacy with Durga.'

Why hadn't he thought of that? 'Your car?'

'I bought a second-hand car the first week I arrived—an old Datsun. It runs well and it's been very convenient.'

Perhaps she shared her father's mix of delusion and practical competence. He'd be interested in Dr Acharya's assessment.

Singh deftly wiped the ink off Ela's fingers.

'Ela, your sister is waiting to see you. We'll be back sometime tomorrow.'

ONE WEEK LATER

59

Acting Superintendent Ratini took the floor at the combined CID meeting.

'*Bula*, one and all. I think we can pat ourselves on the back. I was pleased to inform DCS Tawaga that DI Vula has arrested the jewellery thieves who've been leading us on a merry dance for months. Well done! Vula, could you summarise for those officers not on your team?'

'*Io*, sir. The raid on Hari Prakash's workshop cracked the case. Hari kept detailed records. It took us several days to make sense of them but in the end, we identified about half the stolen items as remodelling jobs he'd done for a retail jeweller in Nausori. Presented with that rock-solid identification, the jeweller caved and named his supplier. Predictably, the jeweller claimed he didn't know the items were stolen, but that won't wash when we'd sent him regular updates of stolen items—phoned and visited him, too. When the supplier grasped that the game was up, he gave us the names of his partners in crime, hoping to get marks for cooperation. As for the stolen jewels, we've recovered less than half. I want to thank DI Horseman for the lead to Hari Prakash. If his antennae hadn't twitched at the sight of those unstrung pearls, we'd still be scratching our heads. *Vinaka vakalevu,* Joe.'

DI Vula clapped three times, the Fijian gesture of thanks. Horseman wished he hadn't. Ratini would retaliate, for sure.

'Well, well, we can all get lucky, can't we, Horseman? This Reddy business has been a deplorable mess from the start, but I guess that wasn't entirely your fault. What a fool that Hari must have been to record the details of his crimes!' Ratini sneered.

DI Vula spoke up. 'Sir, Hari's parents maintain he didn't know the items he worked on were stolen. The fact that he kept detailed records supports their claim. I think we should give him the benefit of the doubt, as he can't defend himself.'

Ratini shrugged, unmoved. 'It doesn't matter either way, eh? Just like who beat up that bastard Reddy. Are you sure it wasn't his daughter?'

'Io, sir. Ela hasn't the strength. She says she went into the farmyard that night hoping to catch sight of her father. But she ran away when she heard the HOOK mob yelling and throwing stones. She hasn't kept anything else back, so I believe her. I'm sure some of the HOOK crowd broke in and attacked Reddy. But we've no chance of identifying the culprits now.'

'Just as well, Horseman, we've done all that could be done there. But it's a shame your double murderer has got off.'

'Out of my hands, sir. The magistrate accepted two psychiatrists' assessments that Ela Reddy is unfit to stand trial due to insanity. But because she was charged with murder, she is under a supervision order, which means she'll stay in a secure ward at St Giles for now. I expect her application for transfer to a secure psychiatric hospital in Australia will be approved in time.'

'*Oi lei*, then they'll let her go! What a nest of nutters out in the rice fields! Who'd have thought?' Ratini growled. 'Oh, here's tea.'

On cue, uniformed constables wheeled in a tea trolley. Vula came up to Horseman and shook hands.

'Ratini's a bit of a nutter himself, Joe. Where you're concerned, anyway. I probably shouldn't have thanked you in public.'

Horseman clapped him on the back. 'He'd have seized on another excuse to criticise me. I'm getting used to it, Siale.'

Singh joined them, handing Horseman a mug of tea. '*Vinaka*, Singh. I want to tell you about a phone call I got from Navneet Pandey just before the meeting. Darsh and Maha are staying on here to sort out Ela's legal matters. Forging broken family ties, too. Against all the odds, something good has come out of this horror. They've both been to visit Kanan several times and are deeply impressed by the Sunshine Home. Darsh no longer has the heart to contest his father's will, so Kanan is the sole beneficiary of his grandfather's estate.'

A smile lit Singh's eyes for a moment or two. Then she blinked and looked down. 'Vinaka, sir. You know, Ela told me that you saved Kanan.'

It wasn't like Singh to be sentimental. 'Hardly. Kanan wasn't in any real danger from his mother.'

'Yes, hear me out. You told her that Kanan was a blessing, not a curse, and you explained why. She believed you and turned the knife on herself. But she's even more alone now. Is there any hope for her?'

She looked up at him again, more angry than sad. He couldn't deal with any more emotion. 'More hope for her than for her father and Hari

Prakash. Excuse me, I've got to dash. I don't want to be late for Shiners training.'

Welcome gift for Fiji Fan Club members

I hope you enjoyed this book. Like other *Fiji Islands Mysteries* readers, you may have also enjoyed discovering Fiji. My years in these beautiful islands inspired me to write this series.

When I published *Death on Paradise Island*, I began a blog which has evolved to include Fijian food, customs, history, sport...whatever occurs to me. I was so delighted with readers' responses, I compiled the best into an illustrated volume. *Finding Fiji* is a short, subjective collection of snippets that enrich members' enjoyment of the novels.

Finding Fiji is exclusive to Fiji Fan Club members, so I invite you to join us today. Each month, I'll write to you with a post about Fiji and share the latest crime fiction promos. You'll always be the first to know about my new releases too. As a welcome gift, I'll present you with *Finding Fiji and* my prequel novella, *Death of a Hero: How it all began.*

Join the Fiji Fan Club here: bmallsopp.com

Enjoy this book? You can make a big difference.

As an indie author, I don't have the financial muscle of a major world publisher behind me. However, I do have loyal readers who loved my first book and took the trouble to post reviews online. These reviews brought my book to the attention of other readers.

I would be most grateful if you could spend a few minutes posting a short review on Amazon, Goodreads or your favourite book review site. Just a line or two will encourage potential readers to try a new author..

Fiji Islands Mysteries

DEATH OF A HERO - HOW IT ALL BEGAN:
FIJI ISLANDS MYSTERIES PREQUEL
Meet young Joe Horseman. How much will he risk to save his dead hero's honour?
When Horseman finds his rugby captain's corpse in the changing shed, he vows to help investigate. But the police refuse to pass him the ball.
    Read more... https://books2read.com/u/3Geqnp

DEATH ON PARADISE ISLAND: FIJI ISLANDS MYSTERIES 1
An island paradise. A grisly murder. Can a detective put his rugby days behind him to tackle a killer case?
DI Joe Horseman knows he'll have to up his game when guests at an island resort witness a young maid's corpse wash ashore.
    Read more... https://books2read.com/u/mBP5ok

DEATH BY TRADITION: FIJI ISLANDS MYSTERIES 2
Must DI Joe Horseman sacrifice his chance at love to catch a killer?
Horseman can't wait for his American girlfriend, to join him in Fiji. So he sets a deadline to crack a murder case in the remote highlands, But dangers loom through the mountain mist.
    Read more... https://www.books2read.com/u/4XKwy1

DEATH BEYOND THE LIMIT: FIJI ISLANDS MYSTERIES 3
Can a landlubber detective combat evil on the high seas?
DI Joe Horseman stares into the eyes of a severed head fished out of a shark's gut. Did the tiger shark kill Jona or was he already dead when it clamped its teeth around his neck?
    Read more... https://books2read.com/u/mY7aqY

DEATH SENTENCE: FIJI ISLANDS MYSTERIES 4
A notorious convict is freed. The public wants him dead.
When Dev Reddy is released, the Fiji media whip up an outcry in Suva.
As protest threatens to escalate to riot, DI Joe Horseman fears Reddy's
parole may be a sentence of death.

Read more... https://books2read.com/u/bPQQjx

Glossary and Guide to Fijian Pronunciation

bula – hello
moce – goodbye or goodnight
moce mada – see you later
io – yes
oi lei – wow! /oh no!
ratu - chief
vakalevu – very much
vinaka – thank you
yaqona – kava (the plant, its roots, ground powder and drink)

Acronyms
DI – detective inspector
DS – detective sergeant
DC – detective constable
DCS – detective chief superintendent
SOCO – scene of crime officer

Spelling
The Fijian alphabet is based on English but it is
phonetic, so each sound is always represented by only one letter, unlike
English.

Vowels
a as in father
e as in they
i as in Fiji
o as in or
u as in flu

Consonants

Most consonants are pronounced roughly as in
English, with the following important exceptions.

b = *mb* as in me**mb**er eg. bula = mbu-la

d = *nd* as in te**nd**er eg. dina = ndi-na

g = *ng* as in si**ng**er eg. liga = ling-a

q = *ng* as in stro**ng**er eg. yaqona = yang-gona

c = *th* as in mo**th**er eg. moce = mo-they

About the author

B.M. Allsopp writes the *Fiji Islands Mysteries* series. She lived in the South Pacific islands for fourteen years, including four in Fiji, where she worked at the University of the South Pacific in Suva. She now lives in Sydney with her husband and tabby cat. You're always welcome at her online home: www.bmallsopp.com.

Acknowledgements

During my years in Fiji, the case of Sujit Kumar hit the headlines. Like Kanan in *Death Sentence,* Sujit was cruelly isolated for years in a chicken shed. Also like the fictitious Kanan, Sujit is now a young man who lives in a safe and caring children's home. Beyond these two facts, Kanan's circumstances, history and family are entirely fictitious and my own creation. Sujit does not have albinism nor cerebral palsy and I know nothing at all about his family.

I wish to acknowledge the wonderful work of two inspiring women. Elizabeth Clayton rescued Sujit Kumar and set up Happy Home in Suva to care for him. Dermatologist Dr Margot Whitfield spearheaded education and support services for people with albinism in Fiji and other Pacific islands. Both saw a crying need and did something about it.

I couldn't write about police work in Fiji without the help of Mr Waisea Vakamocea, retired senior officer of the Fiji Police Force, who patiently answered my many questions when I was writing my first *Fiji Islands Mystery*.

Maryna Zhukova of MaryDes once more created a brilliant, moody cover. Copy editor Karen Boston fine-tuned the mechanics. As for the volunteer advance readers of Horseman's Cavalry who pointed out remaining errors and told me how much they enjoyed the story, I can't thank them enough.

Finally, I thank Peter Williamson for his advice through reading draft after draft, his enthusiasm for my writing and constant support.

Made in the USA
Las Vegas, NV
17 December 2021

38334342R00187